Praise for *Life in Miniature*

"In her extraordinary literary debut, Linda Schlossberg has
achieved what few authors dare even attempt:
to tell a sophisticated story of adult psychosis through
the naive voice of a child. *Life in Miniature*
is a stunning double portrait, subtly capturing
a daughter's misconceptions of her mother's delusions—
while simultaneously revealing the consequences for both—
in a compulsively readable and deeply insightful first novel."

—Jonathon Keats, author of *The Book of the Unknown*

"In this poignant and riveting tale, Linda Schlossberg
writes with gritty detail about loyalty, family, and survival.
Responsible for bringing stability to a mother whose
world is falling apart, Adie—a tiny girl with enormous
courage—takes us on a wild ride of compassion and
humor that is a beacon to anyone who has ever been or
known a child who refuses to fall through the cracks.
Life in Miniature is a book of intelligence and
grace that will make you laugh and cry."

—Terry Gamble, author of *Good Family*

LIFE IN
MINIATURE

LINDA SCHLOSSBERG

KENSINGTON BOOKS
www.kensingtonbooks.com

Acknowledgments

This story has taken a long time to tell, and many people have helped along the way. First I must thank my wonderful agent, Carole Bidnick, for her guidance and friendship, and my editor, Mercedes Fernandez, for her insight, patience, and truly invaluable suggestions. Rakia Clark's faith in this project spurred me to keep writing, and Carolyn Stack's intellectual generosity was instrumental in bringing the novel to fruition. My writing group "sisters"—Elissa Alford, Sheri Cooper, Phyllis Florin, Terry Gamble, Suzanne Lewis, Mary Beth McClure Marra, and Alison Sackett—have been a font of humor, compassion, and creativity. For reading earlier versions of the novel, and for their kindness, affection, and support, I will always be grateful to Monya Baker, Michael Bronski, Melissa Fondakowski, Lisa Hamilton, Daniel Itzkovitz, Jonathon Keats, Jeanne Klaiber, Zoey Kroll, Alex Leyton, James Lin, Carla Mazzio, Terri Oliver, Ann Pellegrini, María Sánchez, and Abby Wolf. Much gratitude to Caroline Light, Susan Faludi, and John Plotz for ushering me over the finish line, and to Tom Sanfilippo for holding my hand throughout the writing process. Finally, I must thank my parents, who have always believed in me and who made sure I knew, from a very early age, that no dream is too big.

Prologue

〜

As long as I can remember, people have been telling me how lucky I am to be alive. I was born three months premature. By all rights I should be missing an arm, blind, dead. When I was little I used to be afraid that I was actually incomplete, not fully developed, that one day I'd wake up and find that I was missing something important, an organ or limb I'd never learned to mourn.

I still feel a little unfinished.

My birth made the local papers, even a small article in the *Los Angeles Times*. The articles were full of words like *miracle* and *triumph*. My mother cut them all out and posted them, along with recipes and makeup tips, on the bulletin board above her sewing table.

My birth was also accompanied by a lot of prayers. My mother, who was Jewish and had never been a particularly religious woman, began praying the second she went into labor. Because she didn't have an image in her head of God (her faith forbidding it) she summoned up the only picture she could think of: Jesus, with soulful eyes and hippie-length hair. Jesus, Jesus, Jesus, she prayed, let my child be healthy, safe, beautiful. In the delivery room she saw him, hovering over her, holding, of all things, a pacifier and humming "T'ain't Nobody's Business if I

Do." It was then, she says, that she knew everything would be all right.

The doctors were less sure, not being particularly religious themselves. And they were not very gentle with my mother. People were always imagining that my mother was stronger than she was, and were sometimes too blunt with her, telling her, for instance, that she looked funny in a certain dress or had been too pushy at the grocery store. It was no different at California General. The ob-gyn in charge told my mother there was only a chance I'd survive, and a very small one at that. He said it, she always told me, like he needed the reassurance more than she did. She patted his hand and told him not to worry. It was December 31, 1969, the very last day of the sixties, and people were worried about all kinds of things.

In some versions of the story my mother says that the doctors were hostile and mean, trying to get her to give up hope entirely. She yelled at them from her hospital bed, throwing rolls of gauze tape and pulling the bell for the nurse. In this scenario, she has to be forcibly restrained, even when the labor pains become so intense that any other woman would have been out cold. I am not sure which of these versions I like better. It would be just like my mother to keep pulling that bell, to get her money's worth.

After I was born I was put in one of those special rooms with all the other preemies, where everything's extra clean and neat. My mother was discharged almost immediately, but she came to visit the hospital every day, dragging my sister with her. Together they'd stand and stare at the rows and rows of tiny babies, like they were at the supermarket trying to pick out a box of cereal. According to the newspaper accounts, I did not cry much, though my mother disputes this. Certainly I knew when my own baby cried, she says.

My sister Miriam was already four years old and enjoyed the attention; all the papers were taking pictures of her and my mother, with captions that said things like "Miracle Baby Has Healthy Full Grown Sister," as if she'd won first place in a spelling bee or discovered the cure for cancer. All the same, the reporters were far more interested in my development, monitoring the status of my breathing, my heartbeat, and my weight, which at birth hovered just under a pound. This was my first experience with sibling rivalry.

One pound. Most everything weighs more than that. Pick up a tennis shoe or an old book that's just lying around. That's me you're holding in your hand.

All through elementary school I am the shortest child in the class, by a good five or six inches. Even though the doctors tell my mother not to worry, she becomes obsessed with measuring me—pulling out tape measures when I least expect it, pushing me onto the bathroom scale two or three times a week. I am always seated in the front for school pictures, as if being small is a privilege. Adults are surprised that I can read street signs, usually better than my mother, who refuses to wear her glasses. I feel the world growing larger around me.

My height gives me a special perspective. I know, for instance, when something has rolled under the table, and I tend to notice if shoes are untied. I can squeeze into spaces other children can't—under the fence at the back of the schoolyard, through the tiny window in our basement. I feel a special affinity with small animals, especially cats. I drink lots of milk, which pleases my mother, who is sure it will make my bones grow.

To compete with me, my sister Miriam tries to make herself as tall as possible. She saves her allowance for weeks on end to buy cheap plastic shoes with heels from the neighborhood discount store, shoes she'll have to hide under her bed, since my mother calls them *slut shoes*. Miriam is always breathing deeply, throwing her shoulders back, trying to stand as straight, she tells me, as a tree. She even teases her hair so that it stands a little higher off her head, like a soft crown. Teachers always note that her posture is excellent.

The four-year difference between us is just enough to make Miriam my idol. She treats me like a baby, even though I still catch her looking at my toys when she thinks I'm not watching. ("Someday these will be worth a lot of money," she says, when I find her playing with my model horses.) Miriam is the pioneer, she's allowed to do things first, but she has to fight my mother for them, trying out the smiles and coy looks she'll use later on boys. I watch her closely, picking up tips for future battles.

Four years is also the amount of time Miriam had with my father. He left when my mother was pregnant with me, even before she began to show. Miriam has photographs of him, holding her above his head, at the beach. She keeps them hidden between the pages of the *Encyclopedia Britannica,* changing the location weekly—from *A* to *Q* to *P*—so that I have to pull out the big heavy volumes and search through them all when I want to find the photos. I refuse to fight with her over them, for fear that our mother will take them away entirely. These are the only pictures I have ever seen of him.

My mother is vague about the details of my father's life: he was a plumber, then an electrician. I'm happy when the kitchen sink gets clogged or the TV blows out thinking, *Maybe he'll come back and fix them.* When strange men in overalls come to make repairs, I hover around, getting them drinks or changing the radio station. I watch them work, studying their gestures, their hair color, looking for clues, a resemblance. For a while I think it's normal to know so little about a parent, that having my mother around is a special exception.

So my mother is what some people call a single mother, like Bonnie Franklin on *One Day at a Time.* But we're not poor like the families you see on TV. My mother has money, saved in the bank, from her parents, who died long before I was born. I don't know how much exactly. My mother always just says, "Thank God I have some money tucked away," when she reads an article about social security or inflation.

For school I have to write an essay about my family. It's hard when you have so few people to write about. So I start with: "Some families are large, but not mine. It's a small group of people who live in this house: my mother, my sister Miriam, our dog Maxwell, and me." I show the essay to my mother and point out that they all begin with *M*. That is quite a coincidence. But my mother just frowns. "Your name is Adie," she says. "That doesn't begin with an *M*."

My mother works as an office administrator at a law firm. If I call her when she's at work she answers the phone with, "Dawson, Kessler, Kessler, and Briggs," instead of hello. It's as if she has her own secret language made up of names instead of regular words. When I ask her why Kessler gets to go twice she explains that there are two of them, brothers. I wonder which Kessler comes first, or if they both think they're first.

No one says anything, but I can tell that my mother is different from other mothers. Not at first glance. On the surface, she looks just like the other moms: dark hair tied back from her face, not much makeup but always a gash of dark red lipstick, embarrassingly earnest matching polyester pants sets. If you saw her walking down the grocery aisle, coupons cut in neat squares from the Sunday circulars, or delicately pumping gas at the corner station, you'd never even think anything was wrong.

Still, I'm aware that something's not right. I can sense the ground shifting quietly, right under my feet. I'm not sure how to describe it. All I know is that it reminds me of the earthquake filmstrips we watch in science class. The plates of the earth are moving, slowly. You never know when they're going to bump up against each other and cause something crazy to happen.

Every month or so we have an earthquake drill at school. The bell rings shrilly, three times in a row, then a pause, then another three times; on and on, the loudest bell you've ever heard. We all have to rush under our desks, and everyone shrieks and screams like they're really scared. Usually there's gum stuck under the desk, and it gets tangled in my hair. The only way to get it out is with peanut butter, which is worth it even if it makes your hair smell like a sandwich.

The teacher stands under the doorway, though I've never understood how a doorway is supposed to protect you from anything. "Make sure you always have someplace to run for cover during an earthquake," she tells us.

I'm not scared. All the earthquakes I've ever seen have only lasted a few seconds and don't really do anything. It's like being in the fun house at the fair. When it's over the pictures are hanging a little crooked and maybe something small has fallen, like a vase. Still, you never know.

PART I

1

In Mrs. Hauser's backyard there's a Japanese-style garden with a tiny waterfall and a river. You can tell just by looking that the waterfall and the river are fake. Some of the rocks are plastic, and there's a rubber pump behind a bench, small and pulsing like a little heart, that keeps the water flowing. But the fish are real, and that makes the whole thing worth it, since they are really what my mother would call *the star attraction*. The only fish I've ever had are the tiny goldfish you win at the school fair and carry home in a sealed plastic bag, like a snack.

Mrs. Hauser won't let us throw pennies into the water, even to make a wish; the copper will poison the fish. Anyway, my sister says, it would just be a waste of money. It's not like they can spend it on anything.

"They have everything they need right there," she says, pointing to the waterfall and the rocks. You'd think the fish would start at one end of the river and then turn around and swim back, the way we do in a pool. But instead they mostly hover in one place, keeping still, except for their little mouths making a quick *o o o* at the surface of the water. It looks as if they are trying to speak, especially when they stare at you from the side of their head with that weird glassy fish eye, also an *o*. But Miriam says they're just hungry.

The fish food is all different colors—green, blue, red, yellow—jumbled together like confetti in a clear glass jar. I'm allowed to feed the fish, which sounds fun but is scary in a kind of sneaky way, because if you give them too much food they'll keep eating until they die. And it's hard to tell the difference between a dead fish and a living one. A dead fish drifts around just like a fish that's alive, but then you look more closely and realize something's wrong. One of the bigger fish has already died since I got here, and I lie in bed at night, picturing its little bloated floating body, wondering if I'm the one who killed it.

My mother is in the hospital. When I got home from school last Friday, Mrs. Hauser was waiting outside on the front stoop, fanning herself with a copy of my mother's *Glamour* magazine. She stood with her arms folded tightly across her huge chest, humming quietly to herself, while I packed up my toothbrush and some pajamas and the rainbow-striped sweater my mother gave me a few months ago for my eleventh birthday. "Just for a few days," Mrs. Hauser said. I felt funny having her watch me like that, as if I was stealing things from my own house.

The next day Miriam and I went to Kendall's stationery store and bought my mother a fancy card with raised gold writing and a picture of seagulls flying into the sunset. *Dear Mom, We are having a lot of fun at Mrs. Hauser's. Heidi the cat just had kittens.* More than anything, I want a kitten; Mrs. Hauser has already said it's fine with her; we can even have two of them. I've picked them out: a boy and a girl, the smallest in the litter, both of them mottled in soft patches of white and black. Mrs. Hauser tells me they're called tuxedo kittens, and I imagine how perfect they'd look stretched out on the shiny black-and-white checkerboard floor of our kitchen. But Miriam says no, our mother already has enough on her mind as it is.

"Maybe a kitten would make her feel better," I try to argue. "Or two kittens."

But Miriam just tells me to go away; she's trying to sketch and needs to concentrate, and I'm bothering her. She's using her special artist pencils, the ones that come in a pretty little metal box that I'm not allowed to touch. Even the lid is beautiful, smooth and polished, with a picture of all the pencils, sharpened and lined up in a row, just as they are in the box. She's working on a picture of one of Mrs. Hauser's parrots, the big gray one with the white crown, but he won't keep still—he keeps bobbing his head up and down and swearing in German. *Fahr zur Hölle,* which, Mrs. Hauser tells me, means "go to hell." At night, Mrs. Hauser covers his cage with an old towel so he knows it's time to stop swearing and go to bed; otherwise, she says, he would never sleep and go crazy—sort of like the goldfish who will just keep eating until they die.

The room I'm staying in at Mrs. Hauser's place isn't a real bedroom at all. It's a small attic room with a slanted ceiling; Mrs. Hauser says I am the only person she knows who can stand up in it. There are a few wooden steamer trunks filled with tablecloths and shoes and photographs, but mostly there are round boxes of hats, from when Mr. Hauser owned a store with labels that say, HAUSER'S FINE HATS & NOVELTIES, EST. 1946. Miriam and I have tried them on; they have a deep, damp smell—the kind of smell that makes you think of dead things. Still, I like my little room with the slanted, cobwebbed ceiling, and the tiny lead-glass window with its own lace curtain. The steps, which are kind of like a ladder, are too steep and narrow for Mrs. Hauser to climb. When she kisses me good night her breath, musty and dank, smells as if it's been locked up in a box, just like the hats.

Mr. Hauser spends most of his time pacing the garden, his body hunched over and angry. Sometimes I'll be playing by myself and I'll hear a little coughing noise, just a tiny sound from the corner, and when I look up I realize he's been there for a while, watching me. It's very strange, thinking you're alone, and then noticing someone there—sort of like when you look up from a book and realize an hour has gone by. My mother has told me to be nice to Mr. Hauser; he's a *Holocaust survivor* and has been through a lot, *things we can't even imagine.* He and Mrs. Hauser fight all the time, and when they yell at each other in German it sounds as if they're clearing their throats and getting ready to spit, even if all they are fighting over is what to watch on TV. Miriam just makes her mouth into an empty smile and pretends nothing's happening, but I go outside and sit by the fake river, wishing I could join the fish in the water, where everything is quiet and dark and still.

My mother is sick, but it's not the kind of sickness you get from going out in the cold without a sweater or not washing your hands. "Your mother is very *delicate*," Mrs. Hauser says, and the word makes me think of the tiny glass animal figurines lined up on the wooden shelves in her dining room, dozens of them, horses and cats and birds. I dropped one once—a tiny rabbit curled up in a ball—and it shattered instantly, its smooth little rabbit face disappearing into a thousand shards of glass. But my mother is nothing like that at all. She can lift heavy things and never gets sick—really sick, I mean—the way other people do. The doctors always say that she is in perfect health; she is fond of pointing out that she's never had a cavity and has had only one serious injury, a broken leg from a ski trip when she was sixteen.

"It's not *that* kind of hospital," Miriam says, when I ask her to explain. "It's different."

"Different how?"

"It's for people who need a rest," my sister says, but she looks a little unsure of herself, as if she's memorized the words out of a book.

When I speak to my mother on the phone she sounds the same as always, maybe a little more tired. "It's good for me to be here," she says. "I needed a break." She is finally getting a chance to catch up with all her soap operas; can you believe what's happening with Luke and Laura?

After a few days Mrs. Hauser drives us to the hospital so we can see my mother during *visiting hours,* which are in the afternoon. ("They serve dinner here at five thirty," my mother tells me on the phone. "Have you ever heard of anything so uncivilized?") I am not sure why, but I feel nervous about seeing her—as if she's a stranger I've never met. My sister doesn't say anything to me, just stares out the open window at the afternoon traffic going by. It's cold out, and I poke at her to roll up the window, but she pretends not to notice.

When we go inside I see that the hospital is very white and clean and looks just like a normal building. The lobby has green plaid couches with matching chairs and a few tall plants lined up in a neat, solid row against the wall—the same, really, as anywhere else. It even has the very same poster that's in the entryway of the Jewish Community Center—a dolphin, surfacing from the water, and the words KEEP DREAMING—where I wait for my mother to pick me up after my Saturday swimming lessons.

"Do you think there's a pool?" I whisper to Miriam.

She shakes her head. "I doubt it," she says, her voice a notch lower than usual. She eyes one of the ashtrays, which is filled with cigarette butts.

Mrs. Hauser gives a small grunt and sinks her heavy body into a chair. "You girls go up and I'll wait for you here." I can tell she wishes she were at home, playing solitaire with her old set of Bicycle playing cards, the television tuned loudly to *The Phil Donahue Show,* which my mother won't let us watch. ("All those freaks he has on," she says. "Pedophiles and addicts. It's unhealthy just listening to them talk.")

"We should have brought her something," I say. I'm pretty sure that's what people do when they visit patients in hospitals: they bring chocolates in a little box or flowers. Maybe even a stuffed animal, or balloons, the ones that say GET WELL SOON in shiny silver letters. But Mrs. Hauser shakes her head and tells me not to worry. "Your mother just wants to see you."

I am not so sure about that. I had wanted to come visit the hospital right away, the moment I found out she was sick, but Mrs. Hauser said that my mother was not allowed visitors for a couple of days, that she needed a little quiet time by herself, to *collect her thoughts.* I am not sure exactly what Mrs. Hauser means by that, but I picture my mother stooping over with a dustpan to sweep up her thoughts, which are scattered about on the ground like a spilled bag of popcorn.

Now Miriam and I take the elevator upstairs to the sixth

floor, to room 614—the date of my mother's birth, June 14. Did they do that on purpose, or is it a coincidence? Either way, it's spooky, and I feel a little shiver of excitement run through me. Miriam looks at me, then clears her throat and knocks quickly, three swift violent raps in a row, as if we're in a hurry and have many people to visit at the hospital today.

My mother opens the door slowly, cautiously. Even though I knew she hadn't really hurt herself the way people usually do, hadn't fallen off a bike or tripped on a stair, I still pictured her looking like the patients on *General Hospital*—lying in bed with her leg in a plastic cast, or a tube, filled with blood or something else, snaking into her arm. But she seems the same as always, and her room has nothing special or different about it, nothing that says *I am sick*. No tubes or medical charts, though there is a little table with a tray and the leftovers from a meal: half a sandwich and some orange slices, lying upright in a little row.

My mother catches me looking at the tray. "You girls had lunch today, right?"

"Yes." This is a lie: the only thing I've had to eat today was a few bites of the runny Cream of Wheat Mrs. Hauser makes for us every morning. But I can't imagine swallowing anything right now. My stomach, my whole body, feels as if it's somewhere else, as though I'm seeing everything through a window. I wonder if my mother feels this way too.

"Adie, you know how important it is to get enough nutrients." I am the shortest girl in fifth grade, and even though my mother tells me over and over again that *it's what's inside that counts* and *beauty is only skin deep* I can tell it worries her. The doctors have assured her that there are no special foods that make you tall, but she still believes that one day we'll find the right combination of vitamins that will help me grow. She measures me with her eyes. "Has Mrs. Hauser been feeding you enough?"

I don't say anything, just look around the room. The bed is in the far corner, under a window—a single bed, covered with a dark green comforter. How strange, I think, to lie in a bed where so many other people have slept, people you don't even know. The carpet is one of those brownish-beige colors you never see anywhere except in a carpet—and usually only someplace like a school, where they expect people to spill things or throw up. A wooden dresser stands opposite the bed, and I picture my mother's clothes tucked safely inside, folded carefully (refolded if not done perfectly the first time) just as she folds them at home. I can see the handle of her pretty yellow and white embroidered suitcase, the one she got when she went away to college, peeking out from under the bed.

Miriam sits down without a word and pages through a copy of *Better Homes and Gardens.* "Make yourself comfortable," my mother says. I think she is trying to make a joke. From the window you can see a cement courtyard shaded by palm trees, their leaves green and stretchy and prehistoric looking. Everything is very quiet, the kind of quietness that makes you want to say something—anything—to make it go away. My mother seems glad to see us, but also a little embarrassed, and her eyes are clouded and heavy with sleep.

For some reason the room reminds me of the motel we stayed in when we went to Disneyland last summer. We'd planned to go for three nights; my mother thought it might be nice for us to get away *as a family.* Miriam was grumpy the whole time, she thought Disneyland was for babies, and would rather have stayed home and watched *One Life to Live* and hung out with the boys at the JCC. I was excited about the Mad Hatter's teacups and Space Mountain, but I thought the Disney characters walking around the park were creepy, and I tried to get away every time they came near us. Why was everyone shaking hands with them and pretending they didn't know there were real people inside? There was something frightening about the way they couldn't speak, but just made awkward, shifting movements with their big hands—like the retarded kids I sometimes saw getting on the special bus in the morning. And it was very hot outside, everything seemed coated with a glistening wetness, and I could feel the sweat collecting behind my knees, under my arms, my belly. And then my mother swore she heard the guys next door to us talking in the elevator about smoking pot, and she didn't want us (and especially, God forbid, Miriam, a teenager—Miriam rolled her eyes at that point), to be anywhere near them; they could be *pushers*. The walls of the motel were very thin; I listened closely, but I couldn't hear anything except the television next door, turned to a Spanish soap opera. My mother was nervous all through our fried chicken dinner and the bright exploding fireworks—so much better than any fireworks I'd ever seen on the real Fourth of July—and finally, around nine, she threw our things in the yellow and white embroidered suitcase and told us to get in the car, we were going to drive home tonight, but don't worry, we'd come back another time. It was very hot that night, and our car didn't have air-conditioning. I tried to sleep in the back, but all I could think about were those perfect teacups whirling around in a circle of bright colors. . . .

"Adie? Are you okay?" My mother puts her hand on my face. I want some fresh air, but the window has a little bar in front of the latch so it can't be opened. So it's not a real window: it's just a way of seeing what's outside.

"I'm fine."

My mother's hand is cool and calming. "Maybe you should get something to drink. There's a machine down the hall." She opens her white leather purse, which looks strange here, old-fashioned, out of place, and counts out some quarters. "Anyway, I need a few moments alone with Miriam." Miriam finally looks up from her magazine, her eyes tight and focused.

I hover by the door, not wanting to leave. "Do you want the door open or closed?"

"Closed, pleased." My mother smiles weakly. "Go get your drink, hon."

The door shuts behind me with a soft click. I crouch outside for a moment, trying to hear what my mother is saying to Miriam, but her voice is muffled, a dull echo of her real voice. Everything here seems to have an extra layer of silence around it, like a blanket. On the door there's a tiny bulletin board with a chart and a typed schedule of meals and medications, and I can see that someone has put down my mother's first name as

Melinda—it's her real name, but she hates it, and always tells people to call her Mindy instead. I am mad at the hospital for not even knowing this very basic thing about my mother: how can they make her better if they can't even get her name right?

The sharp smell of burnt coffee drifts down the hall. I look around, wondering if there are other kids here visiting their parents—worried, for a moment, that I might see someone from school, then feeling ashamed of the thought. The walls are lined with pictures of trees and mountains, all in the same black plastic frame. Something about them seems strange, flat, and when I look closely I realize that there is no glass in the frame, just the picture itself.

I find myself in front of a wooden door with a handwritten sign that says: LOUNGE: NO SMOKING, PLEASE, propped open with the same kind of metal folding chair we use for school assemblies. Inside, a few women sit around a table, a giant bowl of pretzels between them. At first I think they are having a conversation or playing a board game, but then I notice that they are not really talking, just staring into space. They are all gazing in their own private direction. A couple of them look like they're scanning the air for something in particular to arrive, but the others just seem to be resting their eyes quietly in that nowhere place between looking and daydreaming. Overhead, the fluorescent lights buzz gently. Every single light is on, even though the day is sunny and bright.

I buy a Tab from the drink machine and press the cool shiny pink can against my cheeks. A dull pain travels my chest. I wonder if my mother is really happy to see us, or if she's just pretending, just being polite. Sometimes at home she'll lie on the couch with an ice pack on her head and say that she *needs a little time to herself, can we please be quiet.* When that happens, Miriam tries to get my mother's attention by turning up the stereo, or walking through the house with heavy, booted steps, but I make myself as invisible as possible, knowing that after a nap my mother will be herself again, sweeping through the house in her terrycloth bathrobe, checking on the plants. Sometimes I curl up on the floor outside the living room and listen to her fast-asleep breathing, hoping my own breath won't wake her.

When I get back to the room my mother is perched on the edge of the bed, filing her nails with one of those extra tiny emery boards. I am not sure what to do so I look through the stack of old *Reader's Digests* piled on the dresser. Half of them are missing the cover, and they all look shrunken and wrinkled the way my books get when I've been reading them in the bathtub. "This is all they have to read here," my mother says. "It's pathetic." Miriam stares out the window, not saying anything.

"I could get you some books from the library." If my mother's going to stay in this room with the old blankets and a fake window that doesn't really open, she should at least have something good to read. Some mysteries maybe—those are her favorites. "I could go first thing tomorrow."

"You have school, sweetie." My mother unwraps a stick of gum and hands it to me. "Anyway, I'll only be here for another day or so."

"How much longer 'til you're better?"

My mother smooths out the gum wrapper and folds it over and over until it is a tiny silver square. "How much longer," she says, her voice a deep sigh. "That is a very good question."

Then she says that sometimes she feels as if she's wearing a cloak—a dark, majestic cloak like you'd see in a fairy tale. On most days it keeps her warm and protects her, but other times it just feels hot and stifling, like when you're wearing a wool sweater on a warm day. "So sometimes I take it off and that feels good, but then later I want it back again." She rubs my hand. "Does that make sense?"

I don't know what to say. I know she's not talking about a real cloak, but I picture her wearing one anyway, thick and black. I wonder if it itches. "I guess."

She looks at me for a second and throws the wrapper in the trash. "It's a stupid explanation anyway."

When my mother comes back from the hospital, exactly one week, six hours, and thirty-seven minutes later (I kept track, in the *Charlie's Angels* notebook I use for secrets), it's as if nothing has changed. For some reason I thought you'd be able to see a difference: maybe my mother would start wearing brighter colors, like orange or yellow, or maybe her voice would be different—higher pitched, shrill. But really she's just the same, and I can't tell if that's good or bad. She wears the same clothes as always, and she's relieved to get home to her pink plastic curlers, which she wears to bed every night even though they hurt her head. "I was so sick of straight hair," she tells me.

"Do you miss the hospital?"

"Some of the nurses were nice," my mother says. "But I sure don't miss it."

My mother even goes back to work the next day. The only thing she's annoyed about is that she had to use some of her vacation days for the hospital.

"Does that mean we don't get to see the giant redwoods?" My mother has promised us a driving trip up north. Just the words *up north* sound cold to me, chilly and mysterious, as if the sidewalks might be made of ice. We're going first to San Francisco, where they have the *crookedest street in the world,* and then to Muir Woods, with the thousand-year-old redwoods, so big you can drive a car through them. When my mother first showed me the photos, I thought they were of a tiny toy car and a regular tree, but no, it's the tree that's extra big, like a haunted, hulking tree out of a ghost story.

"I'm not sure." My mother flips through the calendar on our refrigerator, the one we got from the insurance company, with pictures of *Waterfalls of America.* "We'll figure out some kind of trip this summer, don't worry."

"Why don't you just tell them you were sick?"

My mother frowns. "It's a little complicated."

She doesn't seem worried, and neither does Miriam, who's as sulky and distant as ever. But now I am scared: it turns out you can go to the hospital even if you're not really sick. What if I'm supposed to be in the hospital and don't even know it? I measure my pulse and even take my own temperature with the old thermometer in the medicine cabinet, but everything seems the same as always.

All I know is I can't get that one song from my mother's The Guess Who record out of my head: *She's come undone. . . . She didn't know what she was headed for. . . .* I hear it everywhere: under my bed with the dust mice; in my closet, hiding among my clothes. It floats in the air when I'm trying to sleep at night, the opposite of a lullaby.

2

My mother has always been one of those people who *enjoys her own company and keeps to herself.* "It's important to be comfortable in your own skin," she likes to say—an expression that always makes me think of the *National Geographic* special we saw in school, of a snake shedding the scaly outer layers of its skin. But for the last few months, ever since coming back from the hospital, she's pretty much stopped seeing her friends altogether. Over the summer she is invited to fireworks and cookouts and even a party to celebrate Charles and Princess Diana getting married, but my mother says no to all of them. "I just don't feel like *talking* to anyone," she says when I ask her why she rarely answers the phone or bothers to check the messages. "Anyway, I'd rather spend more time with my beautiful girls." She clutches me in a tight hug.

The only person she ever talks to on the phone is Mrs. Hauser, and that's because Mrs. Hauser calls almost every day—*just to check,* she says. We've only been to her house once since my mother was in the hospital, for an end-of-the-summer Labor Day picnic. Everything was just the same, except that the kittens were almost full cat size. Sometimes I miss my little room there, the swearing parrot and the dead-still goldfish.

In the past, my mother kept the house spotless, and she'd get mad if we left out dirty dishes or didn't fold the laundry properly. ("You can tell a lot about a person by their housework," she'd say.) But now our plates and glasses pile up in the sink and the garbage disposal clogs. Every once in a while, my mother will suddenly notice the mess and will bark at us to clean up, and the house will look normal again. But most of the time the dishes are piled up in the sink, the empty water glasses lined up on the counter, a recording of the last few days.

One morning I open the refrigerator and realize that it's starting to smell a little; a funny bitter smell that makes the corner of your mouth move. I'm not sure what it's from: there are a few packages, wrapped in tinfoil, that we haven't touched in weeks, and I'm scared to open the plastic drawer where we keep the fruit.

I turn to my mother, who's watching the little black-and-white TV we keep perched on a stool in the corner. "The milk's gone bad again."

"Shhh, hold on. The First Lady is speaking." Nancy Reagan is on one of the morning talk shows, which my mother likes to watch while sipping her coffee. Miriam ignores her, flipping through the paper for her daily horoscope.

I look around the kitchen for something to eat. I'm never hungry early in the morning, but my mother, who grew up eating big breakfasts of eggs and toast and bacon, thinks it's important to start the day with *something in your stomach*. I finally decide just to have dry cereal in the chipped bright-red Pyrex bowl my mother picked up at a yard sale. Miriam, who is trying to lose weight, always has exactly the same thing: plain, fat-free yogurt, which she spoons as slowly as possible, savoring the calories.

"You know she used to be a movie star," my mother says, putting a little more sugar into her coffee. "She was quite beautiful."

Miriam looks up from her yogurt. "I thought President Reagan was the movie star."

"They both were," my mother says. "Now, shhh, listen."

She turns up the sound. Nancy Reagan is talking about *our country's drug problem* and peer pressure and what parents can do about it. Her voice is calm but serious.

My mother nods appreciatively at the TV. "I want you girls to know that you can talk to me about anything. It's important for us to have open lines of communication." She clears her throat. "Miriam, I want you to be very careful when you walk Maxwell at night."

My mother has decided that at fifteen and a half, Miriam is now old enough to take the dog on his after-dinner walks. It's an important job, his last walk of the day, and she gets to go all by herself, even though it is dark. I'm stuck with the mornings before school, when I'm barely awake and there's still frost on the grass and Maxwell doesn't seem so happy to go out anyway. I want the evenings, which in the spring are warm and laced with twilight.

I stare at the fluorescent light in the center of the ceiling. Maybe it will burn up, explode. "But I'm in sixth grade now," I say for the hundredth time, as if my mother might have forgotten. "I want to walk him at night."

My mother shakes her head. She refuses to discuss it with me anymore. She turns to Miriam. "If anyone offers you drugs—marijuana, anything—you just walk away," she says, pouring out the last of her coffee. "And you tell me about it."

Miriam nods, her face bright and tense with excitement. The evening walk means she can take Maxwell to the grassy area near the 7-Eleven, where the older kids hang out, smoking and holding hands. She can tie his leash to a parking meter and get a Slurpee and flirt with the boys. It will be like a date every night. Maxwell just sits in the corner, licking his privates eagerly, unaware of the decisions being made in his name.

My mother stacks the breakfast dishes in the sink. "I really need to get that dishwasher fixed," she sighs. Miriam combs her hair, even though we're not supposed to do that at the table, and looks through the ads for the JCPenney's one-day sale. She needs new bras, her chest has already gone from an A to a B cup, and my mother has promised to take her shopping. "They're two for one," she says. My mother nods absently and turns on the radio, begins humming along with a commercial for laundry detergent.

"I need new underwear," I say. But no one pays any attention to me. I lock myself in the bathroom and practice my anger in front of the mirror.

Mrs. Hauser drops by the house one evening and starts crying when she sees us, even though my mother smiles brightly and tells her she feels like *a million bucks.*

"I picked up something for you in Chinatown," Mrs. Hauser says, handing my mother a tortoiseshell barrette in a little satin bag. "Just to cheer you up."

"I feel fine," my mother says with a cough. "I don't need cheering up." She gives Mrs. Hauser one of those grown-up looks that means *not in front of the kids* and sends me and my sister into the other room to watch TV. Later, after Mrs. Hauser leaves, she tells me that she thinks the barrette is *a little on the tacky side.* "I guess it's the thought that counts," she says, tucking the barrette away in the wooden jewelry box she keeps in her bathroom. My mother's bathroom is filled with all sorts of interesting things: curling rods and lipsticks, and her sanitary napkins, which Miriam and I used to cut up when we were younger, to make cushioned beds for our dolls.

On the top shelf of my mother's bathroom cabinet, behind the old-fashioned mirror with the gold frame, I've found a neat line of plastic bottles. The bottles are filled with pills, very pretty, like sugared jewels. Sometimes I like to pretend that my mother collects them for fun, the way I collect clear green marbles and small smooth, stones from the beach, but I know that's not right.

The names on the bottle are long and confusing, as if whoever invented them was trying to squeeze in as many letters as possible. I want to tell my mother, *That would be a good Scrabble word,* which is what she always says when we come across a word with a lot of consonants, but then she'd know I was looking at her pills. And in that way you know something without being sure how you know it—like that in a few minutes it's going to rain, or that there's a fly buzzing around the lamp across the room—I know that my mother doesn't want to talk about those pills with me, good Scrabble word or not.

Miriam warns me to stay away from my mother's cabinet. "You'll get in trouble if she catches you looking in there again," she says. Anyway, Miriam does not care about my mother's medicine chest. She is more interested in the drawers next to her bed, where she keeps her makeup. My mother has exactly twenty-three lipsticks in the drawer—I've counted them. They are all nearly the same shade of dull brick red, which my mother says is her favorite, so why change? "Sometimes buying new makeup just makes a gal feel better," she tells me, and the lipsticks do look nicest when they're brand new. But there's something wrong with having so many lipsticks of the same shade. It would be like having a box of Magic Markers all in the same color; every picture would look the same.

My mother has read about burglaries in our neighborhood, and she's started making sure that all the windows are locked before we go to bed at night. This would be fine except she checks not just once, but twice—sometimes even three times. She calls this *making the rounds*. She starts with the big, curtained windows in the living room (which we never even open), and then the kitchen, then the bathroom, which only has a tiny window much too small even for me to climb through, then her bedroom, then Miriam's (which Miriam hates; she is always telling our mother to *please respect her privacy*). My room, tucked away at the very end of the hall, is last.

Every night, my mother and I have the same conversation.

"Adie, how many times do I have to tell you?" my mother will say, looking almost pleased. "You need to lock your window."

And my response: "Sorry. I was really hot." But the truth is, I unlock it every night, right after I brush my teeth. That way my mother won't think she's been checking the windows for nothing.

In school Mrs. Tennelli assigns us a story about a little boy who carries his grandfather's pocketknife with him everywhere for good luck, the way some people carry around a rabbit's foot or a lucky penny. "It's called a talisman," Mrs. Tennelli said, writing it on the chalkboard in her shaky cursive script, "and it will be on your vocabulary test this week." *Talisman:* even the word sounds safe, proud, powerful, and I wish I had one. But my mother's never going to let me play with a knife, and my grandparents, who I never even met, are dead anyway. So I start taking things.

I discover that it's very easy to slip things into my pocket. The salesclerks at Third Avenue Drugs & Novelty always watch Miriam and her friends carefully, knowing they might shoplift something, that's what teenagers do, but they barely seem to notice me. Sometimes I'll steal bubble gum, or a Mars bar—my mother rarely has sweets around the house; *You'll rot your teeth, and once you get a cavity, that's it*—but what I'm really after are the tiny coin purses, jeweled combs, pocket mirrors, anything shiny and bright. If I'm about to get caught I just open my eyes wide and dumb, and smile in that half-demented way adults seem to like. Sometimes they'll say, "Aren't you a cute thing?" and pat me on the head, even though, truthfully, I'm not that cute at all.

It's even more interesting to steal things around the house. My mother is so confused about where she leaves things that it's easy to fool her. She'll rummage though her green and blue plaid canvas bag, looking for the hairbrush with the real mother-of-pearl handle, or the silver monogrammed pen she was given at work, the one that says THANK YOU FOR YOUR DEDICATED SERVICE. I don't steal these things for real, of course. I always put them back, the reverse of stealing. And I leave them someplace my mother will be sure to find them, like a kitchen drawer, or the bathroom shelf.

"That's so weird," my mother will say, sounding spooked. "It was here all this time."

It's not fair, I know. It's like playing hide-and-seek with someone who doesn't know all the rules. But for some reason I can't stop myself from taking things: my mother's powdered blush; her new pair of nail scissors, still in their package. Even though my mother is worried about burglars breaking in from the outside, she doesn't seem to notice that I'm taking things, and I feel as if I'm half daring her to catch me. One morning, without really thinking about it, I steal the tortoiseshell barrette Mrs. Hauser gave her—not to wear, just to keep in my pocket. It's not really made of shell, but it's still pretty, different shades of brown, which you'd think wouldn't be pretty at all. My barrettes and headbands are all bright pink or red—solid girl colors that don't mean anything. But this, with its swirling, spotted pattern of muddy browns, looks like the ocelot's coat in my *Big Book of Wild Cats*.

My mother hasn't really given it to me, of course, but I pretend she has, that she's presented me with a family heirloom that's been around for generations. I imagine her saying: *Here, my dear, I want you to have this. It was my grandmother's—she got it from her grandmother. I wanted you to have it instead of Miriam, because even though she's older you're more mature.* Alone in my bedroom I hold the barrette tightly, trying to summon up its magical, protective powers. If I carry this barrette with me everywhere, I decide, my mother won't have to go back to the hospital, no matter how *delicate* she is. It's my talisman, and I feel a small rush of excitement realizing that I am the only one who knows about it. From then on I keep the barrette with me at all times, in my book bag, or the pocket of my jeans, and when I'm lonely I take it out and study the pattern.

One night, lying in bed, I squeeze the barrette too hard, and it breaks in half. I hold the pieces in my hand, not sure what to do. Fear clutches my stomach: Mrs. Hauser gave it to my mother to make her feel better, and now I've broken it. Does this mean my mother will get sick again, even worse than before? No, I think to myself, imagining what Miriam would say. *That's just stupid. Don't be a baby.* I throw the broken pieces into the bathroom garbage can, hiding them under a big pile of wadded-up tissue paper so my mother won't see. From then on I stop taking things from around the house.

3

It's three o'clock; the school day is almost over. Mrs. Tennelli walks around the classroom with slow, quiet steps, handing out the November issue of the Scholastic Book Club newsletter, which is printed on the same kind of thin gray paper newspapers use. Order three books and you get a poster, your choice: a basket of kittens or a puppy playing in a shoe, always a cute baby animal with enormous eyes.

When Mrs. Tennelli is in the back of the room Christie McPherson leans over and pinches my arm. "Hey, midget." She's wearing an over-sized *Star Wars* shirt with an iron-on picture of R2-D2 that has almost peeled off. "My mom says your mom was in the loony bin. Just like John Hinckley Jr."

My face is burning. I shift in my seat and try to concentrate on the dull *tick tick* of the classroom clock. It's been a long time since I've seen Mrs. McPherson, a large woman with lots of red hair and big, swinging breasts—a grown-up version of Christie. Mrs. McPherson and my mother used to walk around the track at the high school every evening, to *get a little fresh air and exercise,* which my mother thought would be good for her nerves. Christie and I would hang out at her house and play video games on the computer and sneak chocolate bars from the shoe box where Mrs. McPherson keeps them hidden in her bedroom closet. But then one night my mother came home looking upset and told me that she wouldn't be walking around the track with Mrs. McPherson anymore—that they had been having a conversation about drugs, and that Mrs. McPherson thought marijuana should be made legal. ("For *medical* reasons," my mother had said, frowning. "Does she think sick people can't get addicted?")

Now Christie leans in closer to me, her eyes tight and focused. "You're a crazy psycho." She draws the words out slowly, as if she's taking the string off a spool of thread. "A freak. Just like your mom."

I pretend not to hear her. I try to remember the relaxation exercises my mother learned in yoga class: breathe in through the nose, exhale through the mouth. I breathe, slowly and loud, trying to picture the oxygen filling my body, my lungs swelling and big with air. Steven Passer, who everyone calls Steven Passes Gas, turns around and hisses that I should shut the fuck up.

"You shut up," I whisper, crossing my legs tightly. I really have to pee, and I try not to think about Mark Steinberg, the boy who used to wet his pants, almost on schedule, every day after lunch. He left our school in the middle of the year—to go to a *special school,* people said—and I always imagined him in a classroom of pants-wetters, everyone soaking but happy. Now there is a picture of Mark floating around in my head, saying, *Don't pee, Adie, or they'll send you to the special school. . . . Don't pee. . . .* I can will myself not to pee, I think. Like those men on TV who walk on hot coals. They don't even feel the fire.

Finally the afternoon bell rings—a sharp, electric *bzzz-bzzz* that isn't really a ring at all. Everyone shuffles out of their seats, in groups of two or three, talking and laughing. "Don't forget your homework," Mrs. Tennelli says, rolling her eyes the way she always does. I grab my books and jacket and run to the bathroom at the back of the building, the one with the big wooden door with the word GIRL spelled out in brass letters. The S has been missing forever.

I wipe the tears from my face with a piece of toilet paper. *I'm not a psycho, I'm not a psycho,* I repeat to myself, *and neither is my mother.* I think about my mother's soft voice, how pretty she is. Total strangers stop at the grocery store to comment on her beautiful hair. Last week the teller at the bank said she had never seen such gorgeous eyes. "Your mother is what the kids used to call a knockout," Mrs. Hauser once told me, and I thought the word was strange, as if my mother was going to punch someone in the face. I stare at my reflection in the cracked mirror above the sink. I have my mother's same heavy-lidded eyes and dark hair, but I am definitely not a knockout. I splash my neck with cool water and go outside.

Only a few minutes since the bell, and the schoolyard has already emptied out—everyone has gone home. Under the jungle gym there's a plastic key chain in the shape of a dog. I wipe it off and put it in my pocket. The school looks completely different without any kids or teachers, and smaller, like a toy school.

Above me the clouds are a pinkish gray; it's going to rain, just like my mother said it would. I head over to the back fence at the far side of the yard. A few months ago, a man had stood on the other side of the fence and pulled down his pants in front of three of the eighth-grade girls. They weren't scared, just stood there and watched until one of the teachers came to get them. After that, we had a special assembly and were warned to keep away from the back fence if we saw anyone lingering about. The whole thing had seemed strange to me. During recess, the boys were always threatening to pull down the girls' pants: if your pants were down, you were the one being picked on. The distribution of power was clear.

On the other side of the fence is the woodsy area, dark and shaded, that my sister and I have been forbidden to play in. The stoners from Jefferson High hang out there, and once, a long time ago, a girl was raped, though no one's really sure if that is true or not. The fence is rusted and bent and there's a little gap where it's broken, just enough space for me to crawl through. I squeeze close to the ground and squirm under.

I pick at a piece of gum that's stuck to my shoes. For some reason things feel different on this side of the fence, as if I've just traveled a long distance. Everything seems very still, framed by silence. All around me is the smell of eucalyptus, heavy and damp. I take a deep breath, inhaling the musty air. I think about how upset my mother would be if she knew I was here by my-self—*I would prefer for you not to go there alone,* she would say, in that measured, careful way that means it's serious.

I feel a little chill, realizing that I've broken the school's rules and my mother's rules all at once, but now I'm not sure what to do next. The woods seem to go on forever, muted and cool. In front of me is a fallen log, stretched out over a small ditch. I scramble on top of it and close my eyes, trying to keep my balance even without seeing.

"Hey," a voice says, startling me. I lose my balance and fall over, right into the ditch.

I look up. For a second I think it's a boy, but then I realize it's a girl; this fat girl who sits in the back of the classroom and looks like a boy and even has a boy's name: Sidney. The other kids call her *lesbo*—she always wears faded jeans with holes in the knees and a baseball cap—and the only place she has friends is in gym class, where she's chosen first for kickball and softball. I know she sits by herself at lunch too; I've seen her hunched and silent in the corner, picking the lettuce out of her sand-wiches.

"Are you okay?" She shifts her weight from one foot to the other, looking at me curiously but keeping a careful distance, like I'm a dead bird she's found in the woods.

"Yeah." I sit up and wipe the dirt and pine needles from my shirt. There's a strange pain shooting through my leg. It's like a burn, but on the inside.

We just stare at each other for a minute. The trees are quiet all around us. Finally, she says, "Wanna see my puppy?"

I get up and follow her, limping slightly, through the damp shaded woods. Sidney walks much faster than me, and every once in a while she stops and waits for me to catch up. "Sorry," she says. "I guess my legs are much longer than yours."

"I guess so." She really is so much taller than me; it's as if we're different species.

"Is your foot okay?"

"Yeah." It still hurts, but I don't want her to think I'm a

wimp—she is the strongest girl in sixth grade—so I don't say anything. After about fifteen minutes the trees start to become fewer, and more light seeps in, and then we come to a clearing and I realize we are behind a house: the secret back part of a house that you can never see from the road. Sidney whistles sharply and the puppy comes running over, a tiny wagging bundle of white-blond fur. "He's a golden retriever," Sidney says, scooping up the dog. "A purebred. He even has papers."

I don't know what that means, but I nod anyway. "Cool," I say, trying not to stare as she leads me around the side of the house, which has big leaded windows and a long driveway. There's a huge green lawn, as neat and clean-looking as a carpet, and a pool with a little humming hot tub. I have never been anywhere like this, and already I am imagining Sidney having me over for sleepovers and pool parties—parties that Christie McPherson will not be invited to.

Sidney takes a key from around her neck and opens the door. I follow her inside and sit down carefully on a couch, my leg still throbbing and warm. The room is bathed in soft light, and it's full of things that seem as if they should be in a museum: old paintings in real wood frames and vases that look like they'd break if you touch them. But the strangest thing of all is what's just sitting in the corner, a whole suit of armor, on display like a giant doll.

Sidney catches me staring at it. "It's real. You can touch it." I trace its cool surface with trembling hands, wondering who had worn it in the past, what battles it had seen. Now it's beautifully still: a shining, polished, violent thing.

Sidney goes into the kitchen and comes back a minute later with a bag of potato chips. "Want something to eat?"

"Yeah, okay." I watch as she opens a jar of onion dip and spoons it into a bowl. She hands me a bottle of A&W root beer, cold and wet from the fridge, and sits down on the floor in front of me, setting everything up like a picnic.

I drink my soda slowly, licking the foam off the top, trying to act casual. But inside I am doing somersaults. It's basically fate that Sidney and I have met, that we're going to be friends. We're both different from the other kids at school: she's fat and looks like a boy; I'm small and wear glasses and my mother was in the loony bin. I don't say any of this out loud, of course. It's the sort of thing you just understand.

My mother is furious when she finds out that I went into the woods and then home with a stranger. "You could have been *killed*," she says. "Or drugged. Don't you know what's going on in the world these days?" But the next night we drive past Sidney's house, so she can look at it, and she changes her mind. "I guess it can't hurt to have a friend from such a good family," she says, staring at the pool, which is glowing and still and lit up by outdoor lamps. I duck down in my seat, hoping Sidney won't see us.

Sidney and I start hanging out together at lunch and after school. To my surprise, my mother doesn't say anything about her appearance, except to point out that her friends had always been tomboys too. This confuses me: I had always pictured my mother, as a child, playing with delicate glass figurines or china dolls, with friends who looked like china dolls themselves.

"You should try growing your hair out," I tell Sidney. We spend hours studying the pictures in *Teen* magazine, picking out the styles that would look best on her. I shoplift a lip gloss that smells like bubble gum and some Goody hair clips, the ones with the plastic flowers, and give them to her. I'm pretty sure she can look like a girl if she just tries a little harder and *puts her nose to the grindstone,* as my mother likes to say.

Sidney's father is a surgeon, and my sister thinks he's *a total fox.* "Dreamy," she says, her voice a low purr. "Like the doctors on *General Hospital.*" But Sidney tells me it's no fun having a dad who's a doctor—you never get to stay home sick from school. I guess she's right; all Miriam and I have to do is cough a little bit and our mother rushes us to bed with lemon drops and magazines, but the only time Sidney was ever allowed to stay home was when she had mono.

On weekend afternoons, if it's really hot, my sister comes with me to Sidney's house. We stretch out by the pool, and

Miriam slathers on baby oil, carefully timing things so both sides of her body get equally dark. "I really need to work on my tan," she says, though I don't see how that's work at all.

"What's new with Sidney's dad?" my mother asks one night, rinsing off some carrots.

I look up from my homework. My mother's face is thinner than usual. She's started a new diet from a book at the library— a special diet that will help *regulate her blood sugar* and *keep her on an even keel.* ("I think I'll feel a little less jumpy if I get more protein and vegetables," she told us. "Not so many carbohydrates.") She has been watching *The Richard Simmons Show* and telling us what an inspiration he is, even with all those crazy outfits, and over the last week she's been bringing home all kinds of vegetables I've never heard of before, like *kale* and *rhubarb,* and mixing them in the blender. She even ordered a special Japanese knife from the TV so she could cut them up extra fast: *chop chop chop chop chop.*

I watch nervously as she uses the knife, hoping God will spare her fingers. "I don't know."

My mother chews on a piece of carrot peel. Vitamin A. "How's he doing?"

"Okay, I guess." I open my workbook, *The World of Mathematics,* and stare at the mess of numbers jumbled all over the page. "He's usually not home."

"I was thinking, since you spend so much time over there, that it might be nice to have him over for dinner." My mother scoops up the rest of the peels and throws them in the trash, which is overflowing. "With Sidney too, of course."

I look around the kitchen. There are old newspapers piled up in every corner and a couple of bags of empty soda cans we keep meaning to bring to the recycling center. In the sink, a stack of this week's dishes, caked with food and grease, threatens to topple over, and by the refrigerator there's a hamper of dirty laundry, socks spilling out onto the floor. Miriam's left her nail polish and remover on the table, along with a few scattered nail clippings: tiny half-moons. I picture Sidney's kitchen, with its gleaming surfaces and light green tile. "I think he's kind of a fussy eater."

My mother rinses the special knife in the sink. "I'm sure I can come up with something he's willing to eat."

I don't doubt it. When she tries, my mother is the kind of person who can throw together all sorts of things without even consulting a recipe. Anyway, as she points out, when someone invites you for dinner, you don't show up for the food. You come for the company.

It's all set: Sidney and her father are coming over to our house for dinner. I'm not sure what to wear, so I put on my orange corduroy pants with the matching orange vest and a green shirt. "You look like a pumpkin," Miriam says, stuffing extra cotton into her bra. She and her friends are going to see *Raiders of the Lost Ark,* even though she's already seen it twice. "Give Sidney's dad a big sloppy kiss for me. With tongue."

"You're gross," I tell her, but she looks pretty, especially with the fake boobs.

My mother looks nice too: for the first time in a while she has put on a dress—a light blue dress with a neck that dips to a sharp V—and her Star of David necklace, which she dug out of her old jewelry box and cleaned with silver polish. For dinner she's made chicken, along with a salad, and has even put the dressing in its own little glass server, instead of just leaving it in the bottle the way we usually do. "That's called a carafe," she tells me. I smooth out a wrinkle in the tablecloth. There's a stain in the middle, but we've covered it with a vase of daisies.

Earlier in the day we drove to the Dee-Luxe liquor store, a grown-up place I'd never been. "You get to pick the wine," my mother said, squeezing my hand tightly. "After all, Sidney's *your* friend." I wasn't sure what to do, and I kept worrying that I was going bump into something and knock down the gleaming glass bottles. Finally I just chose a bottle with a picture I liked: a gold-winged bird taking flight. It was pretty, and the writing on the label was in French, which pleased my mother. "You can never go wrong with French things," she said. "They're classy."

Now everyone's arrived and the bottle is sitting right in the middle of the table. Sidney's father gives a little cry when he sees the label. "That wine is fantastic," he says. I can feel the admiration warming his voice. "Not many people know about it."

I'm about to say something, but my mother shoots me a look to keep still. "It's one of my favorites," she says. She puts one of her Neil Diamond records on the stereo, and Sidney's father smiles to himself. You would think we had people over every night of the week. I think about the hospital, the food and the little milk carton served on a sad plastic tray.

I listen carefully, but all they talk about are grown-up things I don't understand, like mortgage rates and tax cuts and Reaganomics. For a moment things go still and I'm looking at a picture of a family: a father struggling with a corkscrew and a bottle of wine, a mother taking dinner out of the oven, two girls washing their hands at the sink. We sit down to eat, and I realize that one of the girls in the picture is me.

4

The next week in science class we study genetics. Our first assignment is to map out a family tree, so that we can trace our family's hair and eye color. Mrs. Tennelli hands out Magic Markers and large pieces of butcher-block paper.

Christie McPherson leans over and whispers, "Don't forget to put your loony-bin mom in." Her words come out with a trace of spit. "Put her right at the top."

I pretend not to hear her and raise my hand. "Are you allowed to put pets in?" I ask, thinking about Maxwell, who sleeps curled up at the end of my bed every night.

Mrs. Tennelli looks at me and frowns. "No. It's a *family* tree."

I stare at the paper. Family tree. What a strange idea, I think, picturing all the trees I know: the ones that are good for climbing, tall, thick, supportive, with lots of little branches to guide the way; the ones by the side of the road on the highway, lonely and mysterious; the ones chopped down behind the mall, in preparation for the new parking lot, sacrificed to make room for bigger and better things.

When I ask my mother what's going on with her and Sidney's dad, she just laughs. "We're *friends*," she says. "You girls are so suspicious about everything." But she always puts on some perfume when she drives me to Sidney's house, from her special *L'Air du Temps* bottle with the birds on top.

We go to the ladies' wear section at the Emporium-Capwell department store, which my mother always says is *a step up* from other places, so that she can buy herself some new clothes. "Something a little nicer than the usual rags I wear," she sighs, riffling through a pile of half-price underwear. Miriam just stands there with her head down and her arms folded. "I'll kill myself if we run into anyone I know," she whispers, as if my mother is committing a crime and not just trying on some bras.

Sidney and I are not even sure if they've kissed yet. But they keep finding ways for us all to get together: an afternoon at the Lanes and Games bowling alley, a visit to the Museum of Locomotive History, where Sidney's father buys us little chocolate trains wrapped in shiny foil. One night, in the parking lot at Chuck E. Cheese, he hands Sidney a twenty-dollar bill and tells us to have fun. "We're going down the street for Japanese," he says, helping my mother out of the car. My mother has a special look on her face, something quiet and gentle, that I have not seen for a very long time.

In the past, my mother always had to hustle me and my sister out of Chuck E. Cheese. We'd play Pac-Man and Asteroids for as long as possible, until she got desperate and finally grabbed the joystick out of our hands, forcing us to end our games right in the middle. But tonight Sidney and I are allowed to play for as long as we want. Out of quarters, we cross the street to the sushi place and find our parents still deep in conversation. I never knew my mother could talk like that.

My mother polishes her nails a deep red and walks around the house playing her old Bee Gees records and humming along, a secret smile playing around her face. She cleans everything, and the house smells different, somewhere between sour and sweet from all the vinegar and lemon. My job is to vacuum. *Everywhere,* my mother says, and she tries to look strict about it, but the truth is, I like vacuuming, the way the loud *rrrrrrr* hushes the rest of the world. The vacuum roars over the carpet, and I imagine it sucking up the dirt and dust from the past, leaving everything smooth and clean in its place.

Sidney's hair has finally gotten longer; it's sort of a cross between Dorothy Hamill and the Prince Valiant cartoons. *A pageboy,* she calls it. She's been wearing Bonne Bell scented lip gloss, the kind that promises to make your lips *kissibly soft,* and spraying Sun-In in her hair at lunch and recess. Now her hair is a golden-blond Farrah Fawcett color, shiny and thick, just like a golden retriever's.

She is also trying to lose weight and get rid of what she calls her *baby fat.* In the back pages of her Trapper Keeper notebook she's written down calorie counts for all kinds of foods, and she's only allowing herself eight hundred calories a day. She shows me the chart: a can of tomato juice has thirty calories. A small apple, sixty. I tell her she'll end up looking like Karen Carpenter if she doesn't watch out. "I *wish,*" she says, chewing on a piece of celery.

Her father is proud. "Sidney's really growing up," he says. For her birthday he gets her three of the polo shirts everyone wants, the ones with the tiny alligator, in different pastel colors: soft pink, baby blue, and pale yellow. "It's called *butter yellow,*" Sidney says, fingering the collar carefully. It's her favorite, and I think she likes it best because of the name, since she doesn't eat butter anymore.

When Sidney first started trying to lose weight the other kids at school made fun of her, shouting, "Good luck, blimpie," and writing the words *Fat Dyke* on her locker. But then one day Christie McPherson shuffles over to our table in the back of the lunchroom and hands Sidney a note folded up in a special way, like the paper designs in my sister's *Easy Origami* book.

I lean over my meat loaf, trying to get a look. "What's that?"

"Nothing," Sidney says, carefully tucking it in her pocket. She looks at her tray and sighs. "Do you want my cookies?"

That afternoon, during science class, Christie pulls Sidney aside and invites her to a birthday party at the Skate Palace

Roller Rink. "Everyone's coming," she says. "Including the boys." She does not even say hi to me.

Sidney gives me a quick look that says *sorry,* but I know she's not, really.

For school we have to make a shoe box diorama of a Miwok village. You peep through a little hole and inside there are three tiny tepees and an Indian squaw holding a baby. I even drew a fire, wearing down my orange marker to make the flames look just right, and put in some sticks for logs. This is the second year in a row we're studying the Indians. I am a little sick of them.

Mrs. Tennelli always gives us drawing assignments on Fridays so she can sit at her desk and read the paper, and today she has us draw a picture of the animal we'd choose for a totem. I pick a cheetah, which I draw running, in mid-motion. The legs are the hardest part.

I look over at Sidney, who's already done with her picture. There's something funny on her arm. "What's that?"

She takes it off and hands it to me without saying anything. It's the friendship bracelet Christie gave her, with white plastic beads that have both of their initials. "They look like teeth," I tell her. Sidney just shrugs and rubs her wrist. The bracelet has left a little mark on her skin, like a tiny wound. I turn away and pretend to adjust my shoelaces, and I realize with a sinking feeling that she's becoming popular, and she's not taking me with her, even though it would be so easy. All she'd have to do is say, "Let's ask Adie to sit with us," or "Let's make sure we invite Adie to the movies too." A slow burn slices through my body.

Mrs. Tennelli walks slowly around the room, looking at our work. When she gets to my desk she leans in close to me, her long hair almost brushing my face. "You can't have a cheetah," she whispers, as if she's telling me a secret. I can smell her breath, hot and dull.

"Why not?" I've always loved cheetahs, with their long limbs and beautiful sleek fur, their ability, my *Encyclopedia Britannica* says, *to reach speeds of up to eighty miles an hour.*

Mrs. Tennelli sighs. "There aren't any cheetahs in California, Adie. Just Africa." She takes the piece of paper and stares at it as if I've drawn a Martian. "Why don't you do a fox instead? They're pretty, and they move fast."

I slide the picture between the pages of our workbook, *California: Our Beautiful State,* and turn back to Sidney. "What'd you draw?" I whisper. She hands me her paper and sneaks some Life Savers out of her bag, which she likes to suck on to keep herself from getting hungry. She's drawn a giraffe, the skinniest animal she could find.

In the past, Sidney would have said, *Mrs. Tennelli, she's so smelly.* But Sidney and I aren't really friends anymore. I see her and Christie at lunch, talking about which boys are the cutest and trading stickers. Sometimes I sit at the corner of their table, but mostly they act like I'm not even there, making the cafeteria seem even louder and more crowded than ever. The room is filled with people—kids banging their plastic trays and having food fights—but I am all alone. Christie ignores me completely unless I give her my cookies or potato chips, which she eats in quick, greedy bites without even saying *thank you, Adie, that was really nice of you*; and Sidney barely talks to me unless she wants to copy my homework. I stare at their friendship bracelets with the little teethlike beads and drink my milk and think about the Indians, how some tribes treat people who are bigger or smaller than usual like they're extra special, and wish I could live inside the Miwok shoe box.

A few nights later, my mother takes me to Sidney's house. She has spent the last half hour styling her hair and it sits in perfect dark hair-sprayed waves, even prettier than Lynda Carter's hair in *Wonder Woman.* It's still warm out, and she and Sidney's father go out on the porch, under the shaded plastic canopy. I can hear the clink of the ice tray, and their laughter—the special low laughter grown-ups only have with other grown-ups.

Sidney and I stay in the rec room with the air-conditioning on full blast. We're hunched on the big green beanbags, which make a funny pebbly sound when you move, watching *For the Love of Benji* on TV. "This movie's so babyish," Sidney says with a frown.

"I like it."

"It's not very *realistic.*"

Sidney polishes her nails a pale, silvery pink, making sure each coat dries before doing the next one, just like the magazines say. When the phone rings she jumps up to answer it. "Hey, Christie!" she says, trying to keep her nails from touching the phone. She turns away from me. "I can't really talk," I hear her say. Even her voice sounds girlier, squeaky almost. I play with the puppy, which is a lot bigger now.

Suddenly my mother flies into the room. "Adie, get your things." Her voice has a tone I've never heard before. "We're leaving."

I look up at her. "What's going on?"

"Just Get Your Things." It's as if each word is capitalized. She doesn't even say anything to Sidney, who sits on the floor with her nails in the air, looking pretty and confused.

Sidney's father follows us outside and grabs my mother's arm and says, "Hold on a sec, Mindy; just calm down." He looks at her. "I didn't mean to make you uncomfortable."

"Get away from me!" she shouts, pushing me into the car, and suddenly I realize that she is not just angry, but also frightened. "And get away from my child. Don't ever come near us again." He stares at her, a strange look creasing his tanned, handsome face.

In the car my mother clutches the steering wheel tightly. I have never seen her drive like this—so fast. For a few minutes she doesn't say anything. Finally, at the stoplight, she turns to me. "Listen to me carefully, Adie. We're never going over there again. And you are not to talk to Sidney at school."

"What happened?"

"He had pot. *Marijuana.*" She says the word slowly, carefully: MAR-UH-WANNA. "I can't believe I let the two of you go over there alone."

I'm not sure what to say. My mother is always warning us

about *teenagers who like to party and who might try to get you high,* but she never said anything about grown-ups—especially not grown-ups who are actual parents, like Sidney's dad. Outside, a woman struggles to push a shopping cart over the curb.

My mother's voice is rough, persistent, like the scratch on a record. "He never offered anything to you or Miriam, did he?"

"No, of course not."

"Are you sure?" Suddenly her face is suspicious, hard. Behind us a car honks fiercely; the light has turned green. My mother steps on the accelerator, too fast, and we lurch forward. "Stupid asshole," she says, and then puts her hand over her mouth. I think she's shocked herself.

As we pull into the driveway at home I steal a glance at her, and I realize that her face is that of another woman, not my mother. At the same time, she is my mother. It's as if I can just catch a glimpse of her, on her way somewhere else.

The phone rings all weekend long, but my mother refuses to pick it up. "I really thought this was a safe neighborhood," she tells me, curling a strand of hair around her finger. She squeezes her eyes tight, as if trying to erase something shaky and dark from her vision. "What is the world coming to, when even respectable people—*professionals*—are doing drugs? A doctor, for God's sake."

She won't let me and Miriam answer the phone either, and my sister makes some comments about how *her friends won't be able to reach her and our mother is ruining her life* and then locks herself in her room like a mole burrowing itself in a hole. A bouquet of flowers from Sidney's father arrives at the door, but my mother just throws it in the trash. I try to concentrate on reading a mystery, but I keep losing my place and all the characters have jumbled together.

Finally my mother picks up the phone. I hear some shouting, some crying, my mother's accusations. Then she slams down the phone.

Four days later my mother announces that she has found us a new place to live, about forty-five minutes away. We will be in a new school district. The really good news is that Miriam's school has an accelerated arts program, which means she can do advanced painting and photography. They even have a photographer on staff and a darkroom. The movers will be here by the weekend; they'll pack up all the plates and glasses and delicate things, but Miriam and I should take care of our own clothes. Let's see how much stuff we can get rid of and give to Goodwill; there's no point dragging it to a new place where it'll just sit in the closet like it does here. As for books, just put them in boxes and make sure the bindings face out; that way the spines won't get crushed. Throw out all the perishables, and don't tell anyone our new address or phone number. We can always contact people when we get there.

Our new suburb is called Las Palmas. The Palms. I picture huge hands cradling me, stroking my hair as I drift into dreams, until my mother ruins it by telling me it just means trees.

5

Our move is over before I know it.

The drive to Las Palmas, short as it is, takes us away from everything I've ever known, the bits and pieces of things that make up my world. From an adult's perspective, like my mother's, moving thirty or forty miles away might seem close. But to me it's a lifetime away. What's important to me is what's close up: the neighborhood park with the hot dog stand and the broken swing. The ice-cream shop with the misspelled sign in the window (FRIDAYS ONLEY—TWO SCOOPS FOR A DOLLAR), the dog next door, three-legged and hobbling. A swallow's nest on the roof of the drugstore. A smooth surface at the grocery store parking lot, just right for roller-skating.

What matters to adults is much larger.

Our new place is not a house, but an apartment, a giant brown building of look-alike doors and windows. "The truth is we really didn't need all that space," my mother says. "Anyway, having less room means less to vacuum, right, Maxie? You won't have so many places to shed." The dog gives a small tail wag and barks as if he's trying to sound happy, but I think he's confused: this new place is nothing like our old house, where we have always lived; it is not home at all.

The apartment is on the edge of the part of town where the rich people live, and it shows. Everything is manicured and neat.

It even has its own name: Westlake Terrace, even though, Miriam points out, there is no lake and no terrace.

"It would be better if there was a lake," I tell her. "Then we could go swimming."

Miriam sighs and scratches her arm, which is covered with mosquito bites. "Lots of things could be better."

In the lobby of the building there are a few potted plants and a double stacked row of metal mailboxes. My mother is pleased when she sees how clean the place is. There are no hidden corners, no crevices for dust, everything is shiny and bright. The mailboxes don't have the names of the tenants on them, just numbers, so we can't scan it for Jewish names, the way my mother likes to do, as a game, she says, though I think she takes it more seriously than that. There is no way to know who lives in the different apartments—forty-two apartments in all.

It is a little scary.

Miriam takes the move as an opportunity to reinvent herself. She is already experimenting with new hairstyles, tying her hair back with plastic clips and elastic bands. My mother has promised her a perm, the kind you do at home, out of a box. But it is still a perm.

"Wait 'til you see," says Miriam. "I'm going to look like a whole new person."

I'm just glad she's talking to us again. At first when our mother said we were moving, my sister shouted that our mother was crazy and overreacting and that Sidney's father had never tried to get us high, and that if she had to switch schools her life would be destroyed: she would be a *social pariah,* a word I had to look up. Then, for the next few days, she didn't say anything to either of us—not even *thank you* or *please pass the salt* at dinner—just went about the house quietly, neatly packing her clothes into boxes, sorting them by color and season. I was impressed by how easy it was for her to put all her things in order. My mother too was able to weed through her shoes and purses and get rid of the ones she no longer liked, shoving them into a big plastic garbage bag as if they'd never been hers in the first

place. I was not sure what to leave behind, so I just took everything, even the things I didn't want anymore.

To start us out at our new schools, my mother brings home a
pile of supplies: brand-new backpacks, Pee Chee folders, multicolored pens, and, for me, a three-ring binder with pictures of
stars and unicorns. ("No, thanks," sniffs Miriam, when she sees
the glittering unicorns, preferring her own plain black binder
with the AC/DC sticker in the corner.) My mother also gets me
a pair of Gloria Vanderbilt jeans, with the little gold swan. "It's
about time you had some real clothes," my mother says, hemming the jeans so they're not too long. I study myself in the mirror, hoping that the new pants, with their gold stitching down
the side, will make me look taller.

But the thing I really need is a haircut. For a long time now
my hair has concealed a terrible secret: a huge rat's nest. Just
under the smooth surface are snarls and snarls of hair in a thick,
dark ball, about the size of a small apple. It refuses to come un-
tangled, so I've allowed it to stay, brushing the rest of my hair
over it. Even Miriam, whose newly permed hair is a perfect
shiny mass of curls, feels sorry for me. "Maybe you should try a
different conditioner," she says, trying to work through the
knots with her fingers.

Finally it is too much. The plastic brush keeps getting stuck in
my hair; one day, it breaks in half. My mother gives in and decides it's time for me to get a haircut, a real haircut, instead of
the trim she usually gives me over the toilet. We drive to the
place at the mall, Hair Apparent, where you can get a wash and
cut for only seven dollars.

At the salon, the hairdresser just stands there, touching my
head in disgust. "I cannot *do* anything with that," he tells my
mother, who frowns at my hair as if she's never seen it before.
"It's a mess." I feel incredibly humiliated, the source of so much
controversy sitting right there on top of my head, and I try not
to meet his eyes in the mirror.

But I can tell from something hanging around the edge of his
voice that he's not really mad at me. Instead, he seems upset

with my mother. The look on his face says, *How did you let this happen?* Finally my mother sighs and says, "Cut it off." My hair falls slowly in angry swirls, stark and black against the white linoleum floor. My mother pretends not to watch, hiding her face behind a magazine.

On my first day at the new school I am taken to the infirmary, where I am given a tetanus shot and a "Just Say No" spiral notepad with a picture of Nancy Reagan on the cover. I look at Nancy's soft, kind eyes, the red dress she always seems to wear, and decide to give the notepad to my mother. ("Even though I'm a lifelong Democrat and always will be," my mother likes to say, "that woman is doing more to help the war on drugs than anyone. *She* should be president.")

The nurse weighs me, and then measures my height, in centimeters instead of inches. "You're very small for your age," she says, sounding a little annoyed, as if I am not trying hard enough. She consults her chart, which puts me in the twelfth percentile. I feel like a slab of beef.

Here in Las Palmas I have what my mother calls a *fresh start*. My haircut is smooth and neat and my bangs are no longer flopping over the top of my glasses. This morning I put on my new jeans and a striped, button-down shirt, which I'm wearing untucked. Miriam told me to undo the top couple of buttons, even though, of course, I don't have cleavage the way she does. "It'll make you look older," she said, frowning at me.

Because the school is so big, and I don't know my way around, the homeroom teacher sends a student to meet me outside the principal's office. I've only been waiting a few seconds when she shows up. As she walks down the hall toward me I try to meet her smile with confidence, thinking about the little framed sign that sits above my mother's desk at work: YOU NEVER HAVE A SECOND CHANCE TO MAKE A FIRST IMPRESSION.

The girl is wearing a red tank top with a matching red headband and the plastic wedge high-heel sandals that everyone has, the ones my mother won't let me get because they are not practical. According to her, they will squeeze my toes together and permanently damage my feet, crippling me for life. "Look at those poor Chinese women in *National Geographic*," she says. "Their feet will never be the same."

The girl stares at my shirt. Now I wish I had tucked it in. "Are you Adie?"

"Yeah, hi." I try to look cool. She smiles at me, but I can see she's already summed me up and placed me on a chart inside her head.

She takes me down some stairs, past banners advertising the Annual Ice-Cream Social and Costume Contest. "A girl got in trouble last year for dressing as a French maid," she says, and now all the costumes have to be approved by the principal. She tells me that her name is Caitlin, that she is vice president of the sixth grade, and that I should avoid the meat loaf in the lunchroom. "Someone barfs every time they serve it," she says, lingering over the word *barf*. Her hair is perfect.

When we get to the classroom the homeroom teacher, Mrs. Pernice, takes my hand and whispers, "It'll be okay, dear," as if she's trying to warn me about something. She gives me a little smile and introduces me to the class. Someone whispers, "She's so short," and I feel a sea of eyes wash over me. I try to stand firm under its force.

Mrs. Pernice asks me to tell the class where I'm from, if I have any brothers or sisters, what my parents do. I clear my throat and tell the class that I have an older sister, Miriam, who is in high school, and that my mother is an office administrator.

My father, I tell them, is a doctor.

In geography class the seats are alphabetized by last name. I am next to a girl named Lainey, whose curly dark hair brushes the back of her seat. When the teacher hands out a stack of mimeographed United States maps for us to fill in with states and capitals, she pencils hers in with lightning speed.

She sees me struggling over the map and whispers, "That one's North Carolina. The capital is Raleigh." When the teacher looks over she just smiles.

At recess, she tells me that her best friend has just moved

away to Long Island, New York, as part of a divorce. "Divorce is a social epidemic," she says somberly. I nod, not sure how to respond to this.

Lainey and her best friend are writing letters to each other every day, at least three pages each time, which takes a lot of stamps. She shows me her stationery: lined, lavender writing paper with the words *From the Desk of Lainey Aronowitz* printed on the top in cursive purple script. She's trying to find as many different kinds of stamps as possible, and she shows me the ones she has in her bag: tiny, repeating pictures of flowers and boats.

"You can get all different kinds of stamps at the post office," she says. I know this already, but I act like I'm interested. The stamps really are kind of cute.

There's no field, but kids are playing four-square and kickball anyway, running around over the hot cement. I just want to sit down. It's only ten thirty in the morning, but it's warm out, and I can already feel the sweat collecting between my legs. Miriam insisted on wearing a tight black turtleneck for her first day of school, wanting to show off her breasts, and I wonder if she's sweating as much as I am. I cross the schoolyard to get a drink from the water faucet and am surprised to find that Lainey is tagging along after me.

We huddle in a tiny patch of shade by the side of the building. "I wish we could have ice cream for recess," she says, staring at the cluster of popular girls, who are giggling loudly, deliberately, over something in a magazine. "Or a milk shake."

I look at her, curious. She's almost pretty, with all that curly dark hair, and I can't figure out why the other girls are ignoring her. But then she tells me that she and her best friend, the one who's in New York, had their own private club, the Very Best Friends Club, with secret codes and handshakes and even some secret dance moves they had learned from *Solid Gold*. No one else was allowed in, no matter how much they begged. Now that her best friend is gone, the other girls are taking their revenge. "It's as if I don't even exist," she says, her voice suddenly small and wounded.

I pick up on the gap that's been left behind and find a place to insert myself.

"31 Flavors is only a block from where I live," I tell her. "We could go after school."

"Yeah, okay." Lainey tells me she's sick of writing letters, that she's looking for a new best friend. She says this as if she's shopping for a new sweater or pair of shoes. "Mint chocolate chip is my favorite flavor," she says. "Second best is pralines and cream."

I decide that I will do whatever it takes to become her best friend.

It's hard to fall asleep in our new apartment. There are too many strange noises: doors opening and closing, cars starting, the flushing of toilets. At our old place I'd sometimes hear crickets, or a dog barking. My mother always said that it was so quiet in the evenings that it was like being in the middle of the country. But here it is all people.

Late at night I can hear the upstairs neighbors walking around, the muffled sounds of their conversation. Every once in a while I can make out a few words, or even a whole sentence, like, "They're coming over tomorrow at seven," or "Don't forget to pick up the dry cleaning." I fill in the rest of the conversations myself.

Miriam has become popular. At her old school, she was always on the cusp of it, hovering on the outer circle of the most favored girls. She was nicer than most of them, but maybe not as pretty, so she never really made it in. But she had learned a lot from watching the girls at her old school.

On her first day at Benjamin Franklin High School, she strode into her first period classroom, breasts jutting out under the black turtleneck, and the boys stared. Those boobs could have counted against her, but she knew better than to blush or look away. Instead she met the boys' stares straight on, daring them to find her attractive. "That's the only way to deal with guys," she told me later. "Let them know who's boss."

She also knew how to handle the girls. Instead of using the boys for points, she dismissed them as silly and immature. "Rejects," she called them. She told me she complimented the girls on their hair and clothes, made sure to ask about dances and parties, as if she already knew she'd be invited. They fell for it.

As for me, I'm just happy to have Lainey on my side. We work together on art projects and sit together in the lunchroom, right under the American flag and the U.S.D.A. poster of the four basic food groups. She makes me a lanyard key chain with a complicated green and yellow swirling pattern. My apartment key hangs from it and I carry it everywhere.

I have landed safely.

After we've known each other for a few weeks, Lainey tells me a secret: she believes in God. I've never known anyone who believes in God, at least not for real, but I try to play it cool. "Me too," I say, wondering what God likes to eat, and if he keeps kosher.

Lainey isn't religious in a weird way, like the Jews for Jesus, who hang out in front of Albertsons grocery store, always dressed in black suits, no matter how warm it is. Most of the time she just prays to get something, like extra tater tots at lunch or a good grade on a test. One morning at school I think she's whispering to me, but then I realize she's praying: "*Baruch atah adonai, eloheinu melech ha'olam.* Please grant me the strength necessary to get an A on my Cultures of the American Indians test, eleven o'clock sharp, February 3, 1982, room 302, Laurel Grove Middle School, California. Thank you very much for your time. Amen."

Besides believing in God, Lainey has other secrets she is eager to share with me: a locked diary filled with dirty words and drawings of naked people; an old *Playboy*, hidden under her mattress. On the inside of her closet door she keeps a private, handwritten list of all the kids in our year, alphabetized by first name. Kids who partner with her in science class get a gold star;

those who don't pick her for a team get an F, in ugly green ink. "It's good to know where you stand," she says.

Ranking things, putting them in their place, becomes our favorite kind of game. We're too old for dolls, but we still like to line up her little sister's Barbies for beauty contests, pitting them against one another. "And now the judges will decide," Lainey intones, making her high-pitched voice as deep as possible, imitating the pageant hosts on Miss America. The same Barbie wins every time; there's no way she can't, with that long yellow hair and blue satin jumpsuit. Midge, with her dark hair and pretty-idiot smile, usually comes in second.

One afternoon Lainey sits me down in her bedroom with the door locked and gives me a serious look. "We're Very Best Friends now," she declares, "which means we have to tell each other *everything*." She takes a deep breath and tells me about the time she let the old guy who works in the stock room at Randolph's Sporting Goods touch her between the legs, in exchange for a Nike sun visor and a pair of imitation Ray-Ban sunglasses. "It was just through my jeans," she says, sounding nervous but also a little proud. "It wasn't like he really touched me." She watches me carefully, waiting for my reply.

I don't have any secrets like that, but I can tell this is a kind of test. So I tell her about shoplifting from the drugstore with Miriam and her friends. "We even stole some rubbers," I say, which isn't true at all; they're kept behind the counter.

Lainey nods admiringly. "That's a *real* crime," she says, studying me with new respect. "You've actually broken the law." I just smile, trying to look casual, as if this is only the very beginning of my life of crime and I will break all sorts of more important laws in the future.

There are other secrets I could tell her, of course: things much bigger than stealing a few mirrors and headbands, or even rubbers, from a drugstore. But somehow I know that even if we're best friends, I'm not supposed to tell her anything about the time my mother went to the hospital, or about what happened with Sidney's father or why we moved to Las Palmas in the middle of the school year. It all seems too complicated—the kind of thing you'd need a map and a guidebook and maybe some charts to explain. It's as if my mother and sister and I have our own Very Best Friends Club, our own secrets—things that are so secret that we don't even talk about them with each other. The three of us have made a pact not to say anything, but the strange thing is that we've never even talked about the pact itself. My mother never sat us down at dinner and said, *Don't talk about this* or *If someone brings that up, just change the subject.* It's just a vapor, gentle and odorless, that we've breathed in from the air around us. After a while, you don't even notice it.

6

One of the things that makes our new apartment building at Westlake Terrace kind of fancy is that it has a covered garage with a gate that opens with an electric door opener. My mother always hands me the door opener when we pull into the driveway. I love pushing the large plastic button and watching the door rise, slowly, in response to my touch. It's like magic.

But my mother worries about it. She's afraid that someone, a very sneaky criminal someone who has been waiting for such an opportunity, could get into the garage during the few brief seconds that the door is open. "They could be hiding in the bushes," she says. And it's true, there are giant rhododendron bushes lining the drive, where it would be very easy for someone to hide.

Miriam assures my mother that this won't happen. "They'd have to be a marathon runner," she says. But one afternoon when my mother has put on her leotard and leg warmers and gone to her Feel the Burn Over Forty aerobics class we decide to test her theory. We wait outside the apartment for a car to come through, and when it does, we dash under the door. There is plenty of time to get through, even if you don't run very fast.

I am not sure what to think. Does this mean my mother is right? Yes, a person *could* run in, could just make it without being hit by the automatic door. But then what? Is this something worth being scared of, like lightning and bees?

My mother also says she feels a little nervous about the strip mall downtown, the one with the pizza place and the Everything-a-Dollar store where Miriam and her friends buy their eyeliner and lipstick. The *Las Palmas Weekly Bulletin* had an article on "The Secret Drug Trade in Your Neighborhood" and there are always strange men there, she says, middle-aged guys, sitting alone in their cars. Idling. What are they doing, just sitting there like that, in the middle of the day? A lot of teenagers hang out there, getting pizza, and it would be a good place for drug dealers. Wouldn't it?

My mother returns to the subject of these men again and again. "You can just tell people like that are up to no good," she says one night when we're watching a *Laverne & Shirley* rerun on TV. Miriam shifts in her seat by the window and tries to ignore her. She's hemming a pair of jeans, a very tight, black denim pair, with purple flowers stitched over the seat. I realize that I want a pair of black jeans too. The dog snuffles at something on the carpet.

My mother turns down the sound on the TV. "Listen," she says. "I don't want you girls getting pizza there anymore." Her voice is light, but behind it I can hear something else.

I try to reason with her. After all, sometimes *we* sit in the car for a few moments after we've gone shopping. Counting our change. Adjusting the seat belt. Opening a can of soda. Sometimes the motor is running, even though we know it's a waste of gas. And you can't say we're up to no good. We're normal people—aren't we?

"But we're not just sitting there alone," my mother says, as if it's a crime in itself to be alone. "We're not by ourselves." I think about how often I sit by myself in class, with none of the other kids talking to me, and all of the time I spend in my room, reading.

"Maybe they're retired." I try to come up with a reason. "Or they don't have any friends, so they go out alone." On the TV, Laverne bumps into Squiggy, knocking over a pile of dishes.

My mother stirs her tea, the herbal kind with the funny name that sounds like camel meal: chamomile. (She's been feeling *nervy* lately, she tells us, and is trying to cut back on caffeine and sugar.) "It just makes me a little uncomfortable." She takes a sip of her tea and puts it back down quickly; I can tell that she doesn't really like herbal tea.

Miriam, who hasn't said anything yet, finally looks up from her sewing. "You're right, Mom. They're probably jerking off."

We both stare at her. I hold my breath, waiting for her to apologize. My mother will forgive a dirty joke if we say sorry quickly enough.

But then I realize that Miriam's not trying to be funny. She's angry, and her voice comes out hard and sharp, each word glinting like a little knife. "Or maybe they're snorting coke."

"Miriam." My mother's eyes have filled, instantly, with tears.

"Or maybe they're going to rob the grocery store and shoot everyone. Let's be scared of *that*." Miriam throws the jeans on the couch and bolts out the door, grabbing her keys on the way.

This is so unlike Miriam, to just get up and leave, that both my mother and I are taken by surprise. My mother jumps up after her.

"Miriam! Get back here!" She opens the door and runs out to the hall, Maxwell trailing behind her, but Miriam has already disappeared down the stairwell. My mother throws on her jacket and looks for her own keys, but can't find them. Her confusion buys me the time I need.

"It's okay, Mom." I try to make my voice calm, the way you talk to a puppy when it's shaking and scared.

"But where's she going?"

"She'll be back in time for *Fantasy Island*. And she only hemmed one of the legs."

My mother sits back down on the couch, still wearing her jacket, the pain in her eyes fresh and real. "Your sister thinks she knows everything," she says.

I turn back to the TV. *Laverne & Shirley is filmed before a live studio audience,* I recite to myself over and over, turning the words over in my head. I try to concentrate on the *L* on Laverne's chest, wondering what the kids at school would say if I sewed an *A* on all of my clothes.

My mother has started watching me from her bedroom window whenever I leave the apartment. Sometimes I stop for a moment at the end of the driveway to tie my shoe or adjust my socks, just to give her something to look at and think about. But even then I pretend I don't know she's watching. If I were to turn around and wave, even in a friendly way, I might hurt her feelings, which is the last thing I want to do. Still, I can sense her eyes on me as I walk down the street.

My mother likes to say that Lainey's family lives in *a good part of town,* as if all the other parts are bad, rotten like an old piece of fruit that's sat on the shelf too long and started to smell. Still, she says, *"You never know, things are so crazy these days,"* and she always calls Lainey's mother to make sure I've arrived safely.

"Yes, she got here just fine," I hear Mrs. Aronowitz say to my mother one afternoon, sounding a little insulted. "It's really quite safe around here, you know." She spreads some sugar-free jam on a slice of bread and licks her finger. When she hangs up the phone she looks at me quietly for a moment and then says, "Adie, your mom seems a little edgy lately. Is something the matter?"

"Everything's fine." I can't tell her the truth, which is that just this morning my mother quizzed me about Lainey's older brother, who goes to high school with Miriam, asking me what his friends are like—*are they partiers?* I told my mother the truth, which is that Lainey's brother takes violin lessons and goes to Sacramento for chess tournaments and doesn't get invited to parties at all, at least not the kind of party my mother is worried about.

Mrs. Aronowitz puts the jam back in the refrigerator. "She seems to think I let you girls run wild."

I pretend to study the giant calendar on the wall, which says FAMILY ORGANIZER and has all of the kids' doctor's appointments and sports practices and music lessons written in Magic Marker.

Everyone has their own special color: Lainey is purple, her little sister is pink, and her older brother is dark green, and I want to ask if I can have a color too, red maybe, just for when I come over. Looking at the chart, I see that Lainey's job for the week is to "set the table, clear the dishes, and empty the dishwasher." We don't even set the table ahead of time at our place, just grab forks and spoons out of the mixed-up utensils in the drawer and hand them around, hoping that some of them match. I think about how when I was younger my mother used to keep everything *neat as a pin,* how she taught me the right way to fold the bottom sheet, saying it was important to do it correctly even if nobody knows, and wonder what happened.

I look at Mrs. Aronowitz, who is frowning at a fork; it has a stain. "I have no idea how that got there," she mutters, pulling a little jar of silver polish out from under the sink. She's wearing the kind of matching top and sweater my mother calls a twin set and an Add-a-Bead gold necklace with big fake white-yellow pearls that perfectly match her bracelet and earrings. Everything is just so. Sometimes when I go to Lainey's house I imagine what it would be like if Mrs. Aronowitz adopted me, if I could move in with Lainey and live in their always-tidy house with as much matching silverware as you need: lamps that never have the lightbulb burned out, full sets of towels with special little towels just for your hands and washcloths. But I know this is impossible. Mrs. Aronowitz likes me and thinks I'm a good influence on Lainey, but you aren't allowed to adopt someone just because you'd like to. It doesn't work that way because of the law, and otherwise everybody would just go around adopting and being adopted by other people. Instead you are sort of stuck with what you get. But often it seems as if things would be less muddled and confusing if I lived in the kind of house that had a family organizer posted on the wall. . . .

Lainey's house is always tidy and neat and clean. It is in a neighborhood with a lot of houses for sale. Everywhere you look up and down their block there is another FOR SALE sign stuck on a lawn or peeking out from a window. My mother says that this has to do with the state of the economy, that people are losing money in the stock market and can't afford their homes anymore. Lainey says no; her block is cursed.

"Someone put a hex on it," she tells me. "An evil curse."

As evidence she shows me the empty building next door, a large, shuttered house hedged with rosebushes dying in the sun. On the overgrown lawn there's a wooden sign stuck politely in the grass, with the words CALIFORNIA REALTY: IT'S TIME TO COME HOME! printed in faded red letters. The sign has been there for over a year, Lainey says, and even though people come to look at the house almost every weekend—young couples with kids or a baby—no one ever buys it.

"Don't you think that's freaky?" She opens her green-gray eyes as wide as possible, trying to be scary. It just looks like a house to me.

The empty house is supposed to be locked, but the back door has a broken hinge, and if you wiggle the door just right you can sneak in. It's spring, but even with the sunshine coming through the windows there is something dark, eerie, about the empty house. Sometimes Lainey and I pretend it's a haunted house, jumping out at each other from bedroom closets, daring each other to go into the basement alone, which is filled with cobwebs and dust and a few old cardboard boxes we're still too scared to open. I steal Miriam's Ouija board from under her bed, and we huddle in the middle of the bare living room, our legs getting sore from the hard floor, trying to summon the spirits that Lainey says must be haunting the place. For fun we throw rocks and sticks in the toilet, trying to get it to overflow, and write dirty messages on the California Realty notepad that's been left in the kitchen: *Your mother sucks cock. Fuck you bitch.*

We even let Maxwell pee in the empty house, in the large, wood-beamed room that would probably be the dining room if there was any furniture. Maxwell is housebroken, and never pees indoors, but the house, so bare and quiet, seems to make him nervous. Lainey takes that as a further sign that it is cursed. "Animals know these things," she tells me. "Instinctively." It's true that Maxwell looks spooked and always wants to go back outside.

Lainey says she fantasizes about what happens in the "for sale" house at night. Murders, ritual killings. Dead babies. "Maybe a serial killer hides out here," she says. "Like Ted Bundy."

"Isn't he in jail?" I study a stain on the floor; it does sort of look like blood.

"I said, *like* Ted Bundy. Not Ted Bundy for real," Lainey says. She hates being wrong about things.

We decide that we have to leave our mark on the house somehow, so that if it ever sells we'll still be a part of it, just like the ghosts. In the back of one of the bedroom closets, near the floor, we write our initials in red Magic Marker. Not our real initials, since we're scared of getting caught, but our secret initials. Lainey is S.C., for Sexy Chick. I am F.G., for Foxy Girl.

Everyone at school is reading *Flowers in the Attic,* the story about the evil mother who secretly locks up her children in a little room. Lainey lends me her copy, and we read it aloud in hushed voices, sitting in the empty rooms of the "for sale" house, imagining what it would be like if our mothers locked us away for years and years.

The gap between me and Miriam widens. All she wants to do is light patchouli-scented candles and lie on her bed and listen to the David Bowie tape she stole from the Wrong Side of the Tracks record store. Usually she locks the door and if I knock she just ignores me and turns the sound up louder. But every once in a while she lets me come in, and we lie there together in the drawn-curtained darkness, listening to his weird English voice: *Ground control to Major Tom. . . .*

She plays the song over and over, until finally my mother shouts, "Miriam! Put on something else, for Christ's sake!"

My sister sniffs and turns on the light. "Mom just doesn't *understand* Bowie."

My mother is just as fed up. "Your sister," she says, "is at *that age.*"

That is not all. Miriam and her friends have started smoking. Not a lot. They use the cigarettes the way they might use a key chain or a purse, as something to hold on to and fiddle with, something to keep their hands busy. Watching them play with the cigarettes, I think about one of my mother's favorite sayings: *Idle hands make idle minds.*

Miriam never brings the cigarettes home, since our mother has started going through her purse and backpack every day after school, searching for pot. She has read in the paper that *over 60 percent of American teenagers have experimented with drugs.* ("You know this is for your own good," she tells my sister, who stands there with her arms folded over her chest, refusing to say anything.) Instead she hides the cigarette boxes under the rhododendron bushes bordering the driveway. Sometimes she just throws them away altogether. "It's a waste of money," my sister tells me. "But what am I supposed to do if Mom's going to treat me like a baby?"

You'd think it would be difficult for a teenage girl, even a mature-looking girl like Miriam, to buy cigarettes; but it's not hard at all, especially when the boy working at the corner 7-Eleven has a crush on her. And there are always cigarette machines, the different colored boxes displayed like candy. The sign taped to the glass says: NOT TO BE PURCHASED BY ANYONE UNDER 18, but, as Miriam points out, how can a machine stop you?

At first it seems like Miriam is becoming a bad girl—the kind of girl my mother would call *fast,* as if breaking the rules was a matter of speed and not courage. But at home Miriam is still Miriam. On school nights, if I am quiet enough, she will let me sit on the edge of her bed and watch while she experiments with makeup and hairstyles.

"Don't bug me," she always says, but after a few minutes she gives in and lets me fool around with her makeup. Sometimes she even lets me try on her clothes, rolling up the sleeves and the pants legs so they'll fit me. I squint at my image in the mirror, blurring it on purpose, trying to catch a glimpse of myself as a teenager.

7

The school year drifts by slowly, each month folding into the next like a paper fan. Every night before bed I peel off a page from my 1982 Word-a-Day Vocabulary Builder calendar. *Petrology*, a word that should be about pets, really means "the study of rocks in relation to their mineral content and structure." I fall asleep saying the words aloud to Maxwell, trying to work them into sentences, hoping they'll seep into my dreams and make me smarter. The back of the calendar promises that "an improved vocabulary enhances social skills and interpersonal communication," and I picture myself at the popular kids' parties—the kind with loud music and beer disguised as cola—impressing them with my ability to use long words.

One day in world history class we watch a filmstrip called *Nostradamus: The Great Seer.* Usually Mrs. Braude shows filmstrips so she can take a nap in the back of the room, but this time she seems excited. "Nostradamus was blessed with a second sight," she tells us, her thick eyebrows knotting together. "He even predicted John Lennon's assassination, may he rest in peace." She crosses herself quickly. I think about one of the words on my vocabulary calendar: *thaumaturge*, "a person who can perform magic." All day long I can't get the sentence *Nostradamus was a thaumaturge* out of my head.

That night, when we're in the kitchen trying to figure out

what to do about dinner, I ask my mother if she believes in Nostradamus and ESP. "Do you think it's real?"

My mother frowns at a pan caked with tomato sauce. "There are some people who say they can predict the future." She hands me a couple of glasses to rinse out—they're half filled with rotten milk, and the smell is heavy and overwhelming. "But most people don't believe in those things."

My mother hasn't gone to the grocery store for a few weeks—*it just keeps slipping her mind,* she told us—so for the last few nights we've been putting together meals based on whatever we can find in the cabinets and the back of the refrigerator. *Jumble sale meals,* my mother likes to call them. Last night we had tuna fish, with instant onion soup stirred in for flavor. The night before we had canned beans and ketchup, along with some olives. "For a vegetable," my mother said, making a joke. The counter is lined with empty cans of tomato soup.

I quickly pour out the milk glasses—holding my breath so I don't choke from the smell—and run hot water over the pan, which is brown and crusted around the edges. "It sounds spooky," I say, thinking of the haunted "for sale" house, and the time the Ouija board predicted that Lainey's father would bring home pizza for dinner, and he did.

My mother shakes her head. "All of that stuff is just fake."

"Some of it's real," Miriam says, opening the refrigerator door. "Like palm reading." She closes the door quickly. "The fridge is really starting to smell."

"So clean it," my mother says, her voice suddenly knotted with anger. "It's about time you girls took some responsibility for the way things are around here." She clatters the plates on the counter and storms out.

For a moment Miriam doesn't say anything, just stares at the stains on the floor like they might magically turn into something to eat. Then she takes a box of saltine crackers down from the cabinet I can never reach and arranges them on a plate. "We'll have this for dinner," she says, handing me a package of American cheese, the kind that's sliced ahead of time, each piece in its own private wrapper. "And cereal if we're still hungry."

She sits down in my mother's chair and pours some water into a paper cup. "C'mon, Adie, sit down."

I fiddle with the can opener, which has gotten stuck again. "I don't want anything."

"Sit down anyway," Miriam says, pretending not to notice that I'm crying. "And give me your hand. I don't care what Mom says. I know how to read palms."

She takes my hand and cradles it awkwardly in her own. "Let's see, let's see," she says, her voice low and serious. "You've had a very complicated childhood." She squints and runs her fingertip over the surface of my palm. "See this here?"

I nod. A slight shiver travels down my back, something between fear and excitement.

"This is your love line. You're going to marry a very handsome man." For some reason I feel shy with her, as if my hand, limp and exposed, might tell her something I don't even know. She bites her lip. "A very *sexy* man." I stare at the marks creasing my palm. I never thought before about how all those lines might mean something. I just thought they were wrinkles. But now I realize they've been there the whole time, just waiting for me to notice them, a secret code right there on my skin.

Suddenly, from the other room, we hear my mother shout, "Girls! Could you come here for a second?"

Miriam clenches my hand tightly and gives me a look that says *oh, no*. When my mother calls us like that, it means something is about to happen. We're never sure exactly what. But there's a tone to her voice that's as clear to us as a warning bell.

My mother is standing in the bathroom without her shirt on. She's just wearing her pants and a bra. One of the straps is twisted.

She pulls the small lace curtains aside carefully, so no one can see inside, and says, "Do you think this looks funny?"

"What do you mean?" my sister asks.

"This." At first I don't see anything, but then I realize she's talking about a faint, dull mark running the length of the window. "It looks like someone's been fiddling with the window. Like they've been trying to break in." My mother's voice is sharp, strangely high-pitched.

"I don't think so, Mom," Miriam says smoothly. "That's just where the screen scratches the wood." She even unlatches the screen, showing my mother how it rubs up against the edge of the frame, leaving a little mark.

"Oh, I see." My mother smiles weakly. "Thanks, sweetie." She grabs a tissue and a jar of Pond's cold cream and begins wiping off her makeup. "Let me just put on my bathrobe and we'll have some ice cream, okay?"

A few minutes later we're back at the kitchen table, silently spooning the ice cream into the little yellow bowls my mother likes to use for dessert. Everything seems calm again, and the ice cream is sweet and cool. But later that night, after Miriam has gone to bed, I find my mother huddled in the bathroom, running her fingers over the window latch, staring at something only she can see—her own version of second sight.

My mother spends most nights just lying on her bed, staring at the wall. Not in it—on top of it, the bed still neatly made. If I come in and ask her what she's doing, she just smiles and says, "Nothing. What are you doing?" When I tell her nothing, wanting to match her reply, she asks if I want something to eat, some cereal maybe? I say yes, but only to get her off the bed. We sit quietly at the table, the only sound the clank of the spoon against the bowl.

Sometimes she watches the news, always turning up the sound and making us watch when there's a story about drugs. Every week it seems as if some celebrity whose movie we've seen has died of an overdose. My mother watches all the reports on John Belushi's death. "He seemed like such a nice person," she says, shaking her head ruefully. "I would never have taken you to see *The Blues Brothers* if I'd known he was such an addict." She also lies around reading a lot of romance novels, which she passes on to Miriam when she's done. I'm not interested. I've been making my way through her old paperback collection of Agatha Christie mysteries, even though I'm sometimes scared to be alone while reading them. I slip into her stories of small English villages, with their poisonings and stabbings, trying to figure out the end, even though I never can. I'm always stumped. I force myself to stay awake, eyes hurting, to finish them, the resolution as satisfying as a sigh of relief.

On the day before spring break begins my mother sits me and Miriam down on the couch. She clears her throat, the way people do before they give an oral report at school, and gives us her "serious topic" look. "I'm worried about something," she says, clutching a sofa cushion tight against her chest. Maxwell, his brown-gray hair trimmed short for the hot weather, is curled up at her feet, chewing the ears of a stuffed toy rabbit.

Miriam shifts slightly. I'm sure she thinks my mother has found the diet pills she keeps hidden in an old Tupperware container under her mattress. But that's not it at all. My mother's seen *suspicious characters* lurking outside our apartment building, right near the wooden sign at the entrance that says Westlake Terrace.

"They could be casing the place," she says, biting her fingernail.

Casing: I've heard that word before, on cop shows and old black-and-white movies, when someone's about to rob a store or hold up a bank. The only people I've ever seen hanging around out front are a group of older boys, with long hair and skateboards—Miriam knows them from school—blaring AC / DC's *Back in Black* and jumping off the edge of the curb.

My mother tells us that if we look closely, very closely, at the front door we will see that there are some funny scratches around the lock, as if someone has been trying to break it open. "Take a look if you don't believe me," she says, sounding a little defensive.

Miriam and I go downstairs to see what she's talking about. There *are* a few scratches on the door. But my sister shakes her head. "That's from people scratching the door with their key." I think Miriam's right. It's a little tricky, fitting that key into the lock.

But my mother says no. She's already made up her mind; it's not safe here. We're going to move again. "It's really for the best," she says. "I don't like all those teenagers making noise outside. And I overheard one of them say something about getting stoned." She swallows hard. "At a party."

Miriam folds her arms across her chest. "Mom, those kids are *freshmen*. They're total losers. They wouldn't even know where to get pot."

My mother stares, her eyes wide with fear. "What's that supposed to mean? Do *you* know where to get it? Are you buying drugs?"

"Jesus, Mom, no." Miriam is trying to be tough, but I can hear the funny, wavering sound a person's voice makes right before they start crying, like something about to fall off a shelf. We all go quiet. I get the dog brush and start combing Maxwell's fur as fast as I can, so hard he gives a little whine of protest. Outside, I can hear the steady warning sound of the garbage truck as it makes its way down the street.

"I'm sorry, sweetie. The world is just such a scary place." My mother sinks back down on the couch. Something in her face looks sad, defeated, as if she's lost a game or failed a test. "It's not like when I was a girl."

"It's not *that* scary." Miriam grabs her jacket—the green and white Esprit jacket my mother finally bought her after much begging—and runs out of the apartment. The door slams behind her: definite, final.

I wish I could go with her, but I know, somehow, that it's my job to stay at home, to keep my mother company so she won't be scared. I get some apple juice and a can of mixed nuts from the kitchen, which I put in a pewter bowl decorated with flowers; my mother's favorite—the bowl she always saves for special occasions. I pour the apple juice into the short, beveled green glasses my mother found at an antique shop in Los Angeles—exactly the ones, she says, that she had growing up. With everything sitting on the coffee table it looks almost as if we're about to have some friends over, to hang out or watch TV—a small party maybe.

My mother starts munching the nuts absently, not bothering to pick out the cashews, which she usually puts aside for Miriam, since they're the only nuts she likes. I fiddle with the knob on the radio to find KCLA, the classical music station.

My mother always says she finds classical music soothing. To me it is just sleepy. But that's okay, because really what I want to do now is take a nap, tucked quietly in my bed, or even on the couch. As my mother would say, *The world is such a scary place*.

Our new place is much closer to Lainey's house, and we won't have to switch schools again, but I am still upset. We have not even unpacked everything from the last move; the wall hangings and my mother's good china are still in their cardboard boxes. Some of my clothes never made it out of the storage area in the garage. I am not even sure if they will still fit.

When I point this out, my mother laughs. "It'll just make our job easier. Less to pack." But it seems wrong, against the order of things, to move our belongings in the same boxes again. We have barely made a mark on this apartment at all. We should at least have different boxes.

My mother opens the yellow and white embroidered suitcase and sighs. "Hello, my old friend," she says to it. "I'm certainly getting my money's worth out of you."

Miriam is not happy about packing. She leaves it to the very last minute, ignoring my mother's pleas to *hurry it up; get going*. She sits and stares stonefaced at the TV, eating Oreo after Oreo, not even bothering to open them up and eat the cream filling first. When I ask her for some she just hands the bag to me, not saying anything.

The night before the move I find Miriam in her bedroom, looking at the empty closets. She is staring at her different colored plastic hangers, which she picked out so carefully and coded by clothing—yellow for tops; blue for pants; green for skirts. They seem a little spooky, hanging alone like that. I think about our new apartment, which my mother says will give us more space.

"It's not that bad," I say to Miriam. "It's not like we have to change schools again." I look up at the marks on the ceiling, those strange marks that always show up, even though you have no idea how they got there.

She's quiet, and for a minute I think she's just going to tell me to shut up and leave her alone, the way she usually does. Then suddenly, her eyes fill with tears.

"Come over here," she says, opening her arms.

I crawl onto the bed, and she strokes my hair, dividing it into sections like a doll's. I realize that she's going to French braid my hair, something I've been begging her do for a long time. "Hold *still*," she commands. I sink into Miriam's touch, trying to translate the marks on the ceiling into words.

8

Usually at school the teachers want us to read as much as possible, but every once in a while they remove a book from the library, like *Forever* and *Wifey,* saying, *The subject matter is not appropriate for children our age,* and that is what has happened with a book everyone is reading called *Go Ask Alice,* about a girl who is just a regular girl and then gets into drugs. The copy I'm reading has been passed around by all the girls at school. Usually the books that get passed around have sex in them, but this one only has a little sex. It is a *true story,* written by a girl too scared to use her real name, so the front cover just says "By Anonymous," which makes it seems even more exciting and sort of bad and dangerous. The cover is creased and torn in the top corner, and some of the girls have written dirty words in the margins. On the last, blank page of the book, everyone writes their name and grade in school and how long it took them to read the book. Lainey wrote her name in purple ink and said she read the whole thing in one night, but I am not sure that's really true; Lainey is a fast reader, but not that fast.

"You know that book isn't real," Miriam says to me one Saturday morning. We're sitting in her bedroom; it is one of those lucky mornings when she is allowing me to keep her company while she gets dressed and does her hair and makeup.

I watch as my sister unbraids the tangled strands of her hair.

"But it says it's real right on the cover. That's why it's anonymous."

Miriam shakes her head at me. "It's supposed to scare us," she says, squinting at a pimple in the mirror. "So we won't try drugs."

"But it *is* scary." All kinds of bad things happen to the girl in the book. It is like an ABC after-school special movie, but true. It must be true; the book says so.

Miriam looks bored with explaining it to me, and when the phone rings she turns away and picks it up quickly. "Hey," she says, shooting me a look to leave her room, *this is private*, but I pretend not to understand. From the tone in her voice I can tell it's her friend Shauna, the one with the cigarettes that come in the red and white box and the mother *who will kill her if she finds out she's been smoking*. I pretend not to listen, but I'm trying to hear their conversation, trying to pick up on some of the details of my sister's life, which is becoming more and more secret. Miriam has lowered her voice, but I can still tell through her mumbling that she is saying something about meeting a couple of older guys from Randall Junior College at *The Rocky Horror Picture Show,* which plays every Saturday at midnight at the Playhouse Movie Theater next to Tyler's Novelties and Cigars downtown. Miriam has figured out a whole lie ahead of time and has already told our mother that she's going to a slumber party at Shauna's house, and even packed up a duffel bag with her pajamas and toothpaste and a few fashion magazines. I will have to remember this, I think to myself, for when I am older and sneak out to meet college boys at midnight, but somehow that seems like a long time from now.

Miriam fishes a razor out of her drawer and runs it over her calves, even though they are completely dry. "That's gonna sting later," I tell her, but she's not paying any attention to me, and I watch as she moves the razor up and over her bare legs. I look again at the creased cover of *Go Ask Alice,* the girl's face hidden in shadows—a haunted, half face—and wonder how Miriam knows it's not a real story. This is only one example of the things my sister knows that I don't, and lately it seems like that list is getting longer and longer: boys, sex, cigarettes, drugs, parties. It used to be that she knew more than I did about history, and math, and animals, and music, and finally I started catching up, but now the list is completely different, full of things I hadn't even thought of.

I can hear my mother making a pot of coffee—she gave up on her decaffeinated herbal teas with the funny names long ago, saying that *they just didn't do the trick*—and the sweet, stark smell of coffee fills our little apartment. I look at the clock radio my sister keeps plugged in on the other side of the room so she's forced to get out of bed in the morning to turn it off; it is almost eleven a.m. Lately my mother has been sleeping in, later and later, even though she used to be the kind of person who believed in *early to bed, early to rise; the early bird gets the worm,* and other sayings like that. In the past, she would sometimes sneak to my bed early in the morning and quietly wake me up, before it was even light out. She would make me a special cup of hot cocoa—real cocoa with milk—and we would sit by the window and watch the sunrise: a haze of dull color crossing the sky. ("This really is the best time of day," my mother would sigh, cradling her coffee cup. "Everything is still ahead of you.") All of that seems gone now.

I finger Miriam's shiny green glass earrings, the ones my mother gave her last Hanukkah. I think they're beautiful, like pools of still green water frozen in time, but my sister never wears them, I think because our mother gave them to her.

My sister hangs up the phone and starts combing out her hair, which has become long and shiny like a horse's mane from the deep conditioning Mane 'n Tail treatments she uses every Sunday night. The last time Shauna came over my mother asked her all kinds of questions about the kids at school, if any of them were *using,* if she was experiencing a lot of *peer pressure* to try pot or cocaine or anything else. Shauna tried to answer her questions, but she seemed really confused, and Miriam was embarrassed and angry. "Jesus, Mom," she said. "No one uses the word *peer pressure* except grown-ups." After Shauna went home my sister locked herself in her room for the rest of the day and when she finally came out she did not talk to our mother or me, even though I had nothing to do with it, for two whole days. It is at moments like this that I start to realize what it would be like if my sister was not around: it would be very quiet, but not in a good, calm, looking at the ocean way—more like in a dead way.

Now my mother pads her way into Miriam's room in her fake velvet slippers; the heel is coming off on one of them. She tugs at my shirt to say hello and then turns to my sister. "What time do you need me to bring you to Shauna's house?"

For a brief second, because she is my sister and I know how to see these things, I can sense the quick flash of panic stirring my sister's body, but she covers it by bending down to retie a shoelace that's already tied. "You don't need to drive me," she says, her voice as smooth and polished as glass. "We're just going to meet after aerobics."

"I didn't know you were doing aerobics," my mother says, frowning. "I thought you said it was gay."

Miriam turns away and brushes some nail clippings off the end table. "At the Y. I haven't gone yet. This is the first class." Outside, one of the gray squirrels from the lot next door makes that strange chirping noise they make when they are being circled by a hawk: a cry to warn the other squirrels.

My mother watches Miriam carefully, her face a puzzle of confusion, and I can tell she is trying to figure out if this is something she should be worried about. There are a lot of older teenage guys hanging out at the YMCA, and they are not the *nice Jewish boys* she would prefer Miriam to date. The funny part is that Miriam isn't going to the Y at all, but instead to *The Rocky Horror Picture Show*, where there will definitely be kids getting high, though maybe not my sister. The dull light of late morning sweeps the apartment, burnishing it with a still softness.

Miriam sucks in her stomach and looks at her reflection in the mirror. "I'll need a new leotard. My old one is getting a little tight." She turns to our mother. "Maybe we can go to the mall this week, just the two of us?"

My mother catches the offer eagerly. "That would be great," she says, but then she stops and looks at me. "You wouldn't mind, sweetie, would you? Your sister and I get so little time together these days."

"Of course not," I say, because this means I am part of the lie with Miriam; it is because of me that she is going to be able to get away with meeting boys at *The Rocky Horror Picture Show* tonight and smoking cigarettes. Just lying like this makes me feel older, as if I am one of Miriam's tough friends like Shauna, and I peer at my fingernails carefully, the way Miriam is always looking at hers, though I'm never really sure what she's looking for.

"Actually, could I have some money for tonight?" my sister asks. "We're going for pizza after."

My mother gets her purse and hands some money to my sister. Then she notices the copy of *Go Ask Alice*. She looks at the description on the back. "My God, Adie, you shouldn't be reading this stuff!"

"But it's good. *Everyone's* reading it."

My mother starts flipping through the pages. "Jesus, Adie, this is all about drugs!" She looks at me. "Do you have any idea how many young kids these days, kids your age, are on drugs?"

"Not really."

"Well, a lot of them are." She sounds very definite about this. "Where did you get this? I didn't buy it for you."

"All the girls are passing it around. They won't let us read it at school."

"Well, I can see why," my mother says. "My God, it's a true story."

Miriam finally speaks up. "It's not saying doing drugs is a good thing," she says. "The girl dies in the end."

I can't believe Miriam has just given away the end of the book, but even worse, my mother says, "Adie, there's no way I'm letting you read this."

"But it's not even mine. I have to give it back."

My mother shakes her head. "Your friends shouldn't be reading it either. It could be a very bad influence." She leaves the room, taking the book with her.

Miriam and I look at each other. "Oh, man," my sister says.

"What am I going to do?" I sink down on my sister's bed. "It doesn't belong to me. I have to give it back."

Miriam opens her purse. "Here," she says, handing me the money our mother just gave her. "Just buy another copy." She peers at a tube of mascara. "I was going to use that money for the movie, but oh, well. I'll just get someone else to buy me a ticket."

"Who?"

"One of the guys." A quick smile of satisfaction crosses her face. I put the money in my pocket, wondering when I will be old enough to get boys to buy me things. "Have fun tonight," she says.

"Yeah, right."

That night, when Miriam is out at her pretend slumber party, my mother and I sit down together to watch *The Wizard of Oz* on TV. We're sharing a bowl of popcorn, having finally figured out how to get the electric popcorn popper to work right, without smoking up the whole kitchen.

My mother looks at me. "Are those the earrings I gave Miriam?"

"Yeah."

"They look very nice on you." She hands me the bowl and the saltshaker shaped like a tiny boot with the word TEXAS on the side. The other boot, the pepper shaker, got lost in the move. "It must be kicking around somewhere," my mother likes to joke, but seeing just the one little lonely boot makes me sad.

"I'm sorry I got so upset earlier," she says. "I just don't want you and your sister to end up in any kind of trouble. You know, like the girl in the book." She sighs. "I wish you didn't have to grow up during such a difficult time." She picks a kernel from her tooth and peers at it. "We didn't have to worry about cocaine and marijuana and all those terrible things when I was your age."

I stare at the screen; the Munchkins are showing Dorothy the yellow-brick road. "Did they even *have* drugs back then?"

"Of course they did," my mother says, sounding slightly insulted. "Some of these things have been around for centuries." She pauses. "Like Oscar Wilde. He did lots of opium. And Sherlock Holmes was addicted to cocaine, though I guess he wasn't a real person."

This is one of those times when I'm really not sure what my mother is talking about. I pick up the little Texas boot to add more salt to the popcorn, but the top comes loose and salt spills everywhere, dusting our black sateen couch cushions with tiny white specks.

My mother scoops up a bit of the salt and practically forces it into my hand. "Quick, throw it over your left shoulder. Quick, quick."

I do as she says, wondering if any of it has gone down the back of my shirt. "Is it good luck?"

"Not exactly." My mother frowns and sweeps up the salt with an expired catalog from the Columbia Record & Tape Club. (It had seemed like such a good idea at the time—*Eight Cassette Tapes for Just $2.99 Shipping and Handling, Plus 4 BONUS ALBUMS!*—but my mother always forgets to send the card back, and now we have a pile of country-western tapes no one wants to listen to.)

"What then?"

"It wards off bad luck."

I'm still confused. "I didn't know we had bad luck in the first place."

"Well, we don't," my mother says, sounding impatient. "That's why you do it."

"Oh, okay." I still don't get it, but I figure this is one of those things, like checking the windows a couple of times at night, and triple-checking that the door is locked, that makes my mother feel just a little bit safer. Or maybe it is not that different from the way Lainey believes in God—as something you don't have to think about every single day but is worth keeping in mind just in case, sort of like the way you might pick up a lucky penny on the off chance that it could really help you. There are many things like that, that you are not quite certain about but have to watch out for anyway, because as my mother likes to say, *You never know. The world works in mysterious ways.* We make another bowl of popcorn and settle in to watch the rest of the movie, singing along with Dorothy as she finds her way home.

9

In science class we have to dissect a frog. I am partners with Stephanie Samuels, a retarded girl who is always trying to be my friend. "Can I cut it?" she asks, holding the miniature knife our teacher has given us. I nod, already dizzy with the smell of formaldehyde.

Stephanie has a steady hand and slices open the frog's stomach in a single line. The skin opens easily, like an envelope. Inside, the tiny organs are neat and clean, every piece sitting exactly where it should be, just like in the mimeographed chart Mr. Michaels gave us. The tiny heart is not heart-shaped at all. Stephanie pokes at it with her knife.

The boys start taking out the hearts and bringing them to the girls, trying to disgust them and flirt at the same time. Jonathan Newmeyer picks up his frog's heart and holds it out to me, waving it under my nose. "Hey, Adie," he says. "I left my heart in San Francisco!" Stephanie giggles, her laughter, like everything else about her, not sounding quite right. A strange feeling roils my stomach, but I can't tell if it's from Jonathan's words or the stink of the heart.

Lainey and I have started biking to the park every weekend. We always head for the same shaded spot at the edge of the baseball field, right near the big metal sign that says ANGEL

GROVE MEMORIAL PARK AND RECREATION AREA in rusted capital letters. We've discovered that some of the boys from Washington High hang out there, eating snacks from the small wooden trailer that sells microwave nachos with yellow cheese, out of a tube, for a dollar. The boys trade cigarettes and talk about girls, which ones are *easy* and will *put out*. Sometimes they pass a dirty magazine back and forth, their voices full of something harsh and wistful. We watch without saying anything as they graffiti their names with a big black marker on the back of the trailer: *Marcel Rules. J. P. was here.*

Lainey says it's good for us to be outside. "You should spend more time in the sun," she says. "The vitamin C goes right through your skin to your bones." She squints at me. "Maybe it'll make you grow taller."

I'm not sure about that. I've had what my mother calls a *growth spurt,* but really it's only a couple of inches, and I'm still the shortest girl in our class. Already, Lainey is almost a foot taller than me. She shows me her best designer jeans, the ones with tricolored rainbows embroidered on the back pockets. "Look how short they are," she says proudly. It's true: she got them at the beginning of the school year, and now she needs to take the hem out. Just in the last couple of months she's grown a whole inch. Everyone always thinks she's older.

Lainey and I stretch out on the grass, which is dry and patchy. She has a new plan for us: a hundred sit-ups a day, so we'll be ready for summer and *bikini season.* Her brother has taught her the best kind: lie on the ground with your arms folded over your chest and lift yourself up, as slowly as possible. Breathe out. I can only do a few at a time, and they make my stomach hurt—a tense, low pain.

Lainey tells me that's okay, just to get through as many as I can. I watch as she does hers in quick sets of ten: *updownup-downupdown.* "You'll see, it'll get easier," she says, her voice coming out in little spurts. "And we're going to look totally *hot.*" On the other side of the lawn a man lies down on a blue plastic mat. I think he's doing yoga, or maybe even meditating, but I'm not sure, maybe he's just taking a nap right there in the middle of the park. I stare at my legs, thinking how they look especially naked against the grass.

The day is warm, easy. People walk by pushing baby strollers and eating ice cream, the cones dripping in the heat. Every once in a while a dog, damp and smelly from the duck pond, runs up to snuffle at our feet. A bird lands on the grass near us, searching for scattered crumbs.

Suddenly I notice something—a blue car with a slight dent in the front, that looks just like my mother's. Right by the entrance to the park.

I stand up for a better look. It *is* my mother. Just sitting in the car, like it's no big deal. Watching us. She waves, but I turn away, pretending I don't see her, and pull at my shoelaces, which are tangled again.

Lainey notices something's wrong. "What's the matter?" she asks, her body raised halfway off the ground.

"Nothing." I lie facedown on the grass. "I thought I saw someone I know."

My stomach doubles into a low ache. I know why my mother's here. Just this morning at breakfast, she told me to be very careful, that she saw something on the ten o'clock news about gangs hanging out at Angel Grove. "There are always kids there looking to score," she said, pouring out her muesli, and I could tell she was trying out the word *score*—testing it to see how it felt. Sometimes I come here after school to sneak a candy bar, and I wonder with a sudden pang if she's followed me all those times as well.

Lainey finishes her sit-ups, counting out the last ones slowly. Then she pulls up her shirt so her stomach can get tan. For a while we just lie there, pointing out the shapes in the clouds. They float by slowly, taking their time across the sky. One of them looks like a horse's head, another, a balloon. The sun suddenly breaks through, and the cloud is illuminated, as if from within.

"I wonder if that's what God looks like," Lainey says. She is always asking questions like that—questions you can't really answer. "Want a Tootsie Roll?" she says, taking a little package out of her bag. "After all those sit-ups we deserve something." She unwraps a piece and offers it to me. I pop the little brown roll into my mouth gratefully, chewing so quickly I almost choke.

When I get home later that afternoon I find my mother in Miriam's bedroom, riffling through her desk drawer. She doesn't look up when I come in.

I put my bag down on the desk. "Mom, what's going on?"

"I'm just trying to find a pen that actually works," she says, sounding annoyed, as if the pens have banded together and are not working on purpose. "All of mine seem to be out of ink."

"That's not what I mean," I say, trying to keep my voice steady. My heart taps out a fast little beat, and I take a deep breath to steady myself. I am reminded of how it feels when you're on the balance beam in gym—when you don't want to lean over too much on one side or the other or you'll fall right off. "What were you doing at the park?"

She straightens up and looks at me, her eyes bright and hard. "Is there a law against going to the park?" she asks, sounding a little like my sister when she doesn't get what she wants.

"You were watching us." My voice breaks in half. "We weren't doing anything; we were hanging out."

"Look, sweetie, I just started to get a little nervous about you and Lainey being at the park by yourselves. I thought it couldn't hurt for me to drive over, take a look."

"Mom. There were tons of people around." I think about all the baby carriages, the kids fighting over Popsicles in the hot sun. "There were *babies* there. With ice cream." But my mother isn't paying attention to me anymore. The look on her face has gone rigid, and she is holding a little box that she found in the drawer: Miriam's cigarettes.

"Miriam! Get in here right now!"

Miriam comes running in. Then she sees the cigarettes and stops. "What were you doing going through my desk?"

"That's not the important thing." She turns and shows me the little box. "Adie, it seems that your sister has been smoking, despite the fact that she has promised me—has sworn to me—

that she would never smoke." Something about the tone of my mother's voice, the way she is holding the box for me to see, makes it seem as if they are both on stage—actors in a scene from a play. Miriam rolls her eyes. The room feels hot and close.

Miriam tosses her hair in that way that reminds me of a horse trying to shake itself free and sinks down on her bed. "It's no big deal," she says. "Some girls at school were just fooling around."

"Fooling around smoking?"

"We were just pretending to smoke, to look cool."

"Well, why do you have them then?"

"They're Jennifer's," my sister says quickly, but I can tell the minute she says Jennifer's name she knows it's a mistake. Jennifer Samuels is the coolest girl in Miriam's group of friends, even though our mother has said many times that she doesn't think Jennifer is an *ideal companion* for Miriam, because she does not wear appropriate clothing and has a *smart mouth,* which I found out after being confused for a while does not really mean smart at all but is a way of saying *smart-ass* without actually saying the word *ass.*

Now Miriam just stares at the floor. Her voice is empty, hollow. "She gave them to me to hold on to. Her mother wouldn't understand."

"Well, your mother doesn't understand either!" my mother practically shouts. She is shaking, but she also looks strangely proud of herself: all these months of searching through Miriam's drawers and purses and underneath the bed with all its dust bunnies, and she has finally found something, something real: *proof.* "Don't you know that kids who smoke are more likely to drink, and then to turn to drugs?"

"Mom, seriously, no one at school does drugs."

"Don't change the subject! As if smoking isn't bad enough." All three of us stare at each other. From the other side of the room, Maxwell gives a low whine.

"Maxwell, be quiet," my mother snaps.

"I think he needs to go out," I say, always ready to defend the dog, and looking for any excuse to get away from my mother and sister when they are having a fight.

"That can wait." My mother's face is a tight ball of worry. "Adie, you tell me the truth," she says. "Did you know about this?"

"No." I can see my sister's shoulders relax slightly, a small letting go. "Miriam doesn't smoke. She tells me all the time how gross it is." Miriam shoots me a grateful look.

My mother sinks down on the bed, her face filled with pain. "I can't believe this is happening." She starts crying, her sobs as quiet as the clouds drifting overhead.

My sister crouches down next to her, suddenly soft. "Mom, nothing is happening. Nothing has happened." Miriam sounds determined now to fix everything, make it better. As if we could just erase the last few minutes and start over, wipe it away, like when the teacher erases the chalkboard, but there are still ghost-white traces of what was written before. Everyone pretends it's completely gone, but all you have to do is look and you can still make it out. That's what this is like. Miriam is whispering, "It's okay, it's okay, nothing happened," and my mother is holding my sister's hand tight, the way you hold tight to an umbrella in a windstorm that might blow away. Right now it looks as if Miriam is the mother, calm, comforting, and my mother, a little girl crying over a lost toy or a skinned knee. There is nothing for me to do but stand and watch, and I feel outside of everything, as if I am watching a movie of my mother and sister, a movie I've seen many times before. I'm not really in the same room with them at all, or even in the same house—not even on the same planet maybe. All I have to do is keep watching and the movie will keep playing, and if I don't say anything, I think to myself, no one will notice me and I won't have to be part of the movie at all.

Maxwell whines again, this time a little more sadly, and my mother finally looks up. "Sweetie, maybe you should take him out now," she says, and all of a sudden I'm jealous, because she and my sister have something between them—something built out of fighting and making up—that I do not have. I unwind Maxwell's leash from the metal hook by the door and he comes bounding over. My mother and sister are clutched together like those cloth monkey dolls with the long arms that hook around each other's bodies. With their long dark hair and black wool sweaters they are almost like twins.

I hurry out the door with Maxwell, relieved to lose myself in the boring, reassuring everydayness of things you see outside. The hard cement sidewalk underfoot, the muted blue of the sky. All the houses are lined up just the way they always are; even the telephone pole on the corner looks solid and sure. Maxwell stops to nose a dead squirrel that's been run over by a car and I pull him away. "Leave that alone, Maxie," I tell him. "Don't disturb the dead." I try not to look at the smashed little body— just an approximation of a squirrel—and wonder if the run-over squirrel's ghost is watching from the tree above, and then, if animals have ghosts at all, or if their ghosts are like our ghosts.

I wonder if my sister really is doing drugs. I think about the boys Miriam sneaks out to see, the jewelry she shoplifts from the mall (real silver teardrop earrings, not the plastic bangles Lainey stole from the ninety-nine-cent store), the way she locks herself in her bedroom at night, doing—as my mother would say—*who knows what*. My mother has a triangle glass prism paperweight she keeps on the coffee table, and when you look through it everything is multiplied and spinning, and lately, that is how I feel about Miriam. Lately everything my sister does is just a little different and strange—a surprise, as if one day I knew her really well, and then something shifted, and now she is someone I only sort of know from school who just happens to live in the same house as me.

At the empty lot I let Maxwell off the leash. A heap of trash and garbage fills one corner of the lot: packing crates, part of a sink, an old bicycle tire. I turn to look at the sky. The trees are crowded together, bowed over by the wind, as if they are in conversation. I'm startled when a woman pokes her head out of the building next door. "Young lady, please don't walk your dog here." Her head is covered with light-pink curlers, the old-fashioned kind even my mother doesn't use anymore. "This is private property."

Maxwell is digging hard at something in the dirt, another

dead squirrel maybe? I snap the leash hard. "Maxwell, get over here," I say in my sternest voice, and he bounds over to the heap of trash. The pages of an old magazine rustle in the wind. When I get back to the house everything is calm again, and my mother and Miriam are sorting through her closet, something she's been meaning to get to for a long time. But something in me is peeling away. I feel a part of me coming apart, as if something is falling off. I think of the frog we dissected in class, its little brown heart being sliced into tiny pieces. It's not so hard to pull out a heart, I think to myself, not so hard at all.

10

It is summer, and my sister has started spending most days hanging out with her friends, not coming home until right before dinner, where she barely says anything to us, just picks at her food quietly and then goes into her room to talk on the phone. She refuses to let Lainey and me tag along, but sometimes in the afternoons we run into her at the 7-Eleven or at McDonald's, surrounded by a flock of bored-looking boys. "She thinks she's so great," I say to Lainey, pretending I don't care. But even when Miriam ignores me I get points for having such a cool sister. "When are you going to get boobs like Miriam?" Jonathan Newmeyer asks.

If my sister has nothing else to do on the weekends she'll take me to the Playtime Pinball and Video Arcade at the Fashion Island shopping mall. It's right next to the food court, so sometimes we sit in the plastic chairs and share a drink from Orange Julius while Miriam pretends she doesn't notice the guys looking at her.

Miriam's really good at the driving games, especially the ones with race cars. She sits back in the fake driver's seat, zipping around the on-screen corners like a pro. The boys gather around the machine to track her progress and look down her shirt. Privately, Miriam tells me that there's nothing to it. It's just a game, so why not take chances?

Still, the race car games make me nervous. They seem almost too realistic, as if I might really crash into a building and hurt myself, and I actually feel a little carsick when I sit behind the plastic wheel. But I am a genius at the games that involve killing aliens and monsters, proudly typing in *ADI* when I beat the high score. I drop quarter after quarter into the blinking machines, losing myself in the comforting darkness of the game parlor, which smells like sweat and junk food.

My mother usually picks us up from the mall. She says she might as well, because it's a lot quicker than taking the bus, and she has to go out to do some errands anyway. "Plus, it'll save you the fifty-cent fare," she points out. But Miriam and I know she's worried about the dropouts who hang out at the arcade, the ones who might be *a bad influence,* and are known for having *substance abuse problems.* "She thinks people are shooting up right here in the middle of the mall," Miriam says, rolling her eyes. It is true that the mall has signs at the entrance that say THIS IS A DRUG-FREE ZONE.

We always meet her in the same place, by the Salvation Army stand outside the mall entrance. If we are even a minute or two late, my mother becomes anxious. Once she told us that she almost called the police, thinking that we might have gone home with someone else. "I can't tell you how worried I was," she said, her voice breaking. After that Miriam and I made sure to get to the Salvation Army stand a few minutes early, just so our mother wouldn't have to feel scared.

But today it's our mother who's late. We wait outside in a patch of shade. I finish the last few sips of a chocolate milk shake. Miriam pulls at her hair, trying to untangle a stubborn strand. A guy from her school comes over and talks to her for a minute, his voice low and suggestive, but then his friends yell something at him, and he walks off. "He's such an asshole," Miriam says.

Suddenly there's a honk. "Hey, girls!"

I look around for our car, but don't see it anywhere.

"Over here!" It's our mother, but she isn't driving our car, the blue station wagon we've had for as long as I can remember. This car is completely different, a small brown car with a thin white stripe down the side. My mother smiles, but she looks a little nervous, as if she's just brought us a gift we might not like. "Get in, girls."

Miriam just stares. "What's going on?"

My mother reaches across the seat and opens the passenger side door. "I decided it was time for a change," she says, trying to look cheerful. I notice that she's given herself a manicure. Her nails are a bright pink, almost purple color, a color I recognize from Miriam's stash of makeup.

I climb in the front, since Miriam's still standing there. "Where's our car?"

"I traded it in." My mother fiddles with the controls. "This car's much better. Look, it has a tape player." A car behind us beeps for us to get out of the way. My mother is blocking the exit. Miriam finally gets in the back, shoving her bags across the seat.

As my mother drives slowly out of the parking lot, I realize that this car isn't nearly as nice as the blue station wagon. It's a little clunky, and it's making strange noises. And it doesn't have air-conditioning. The upholstery on my side of the seat has a small tear, just big enough for me to stick my thumb in.

"Take your finger out of there," my mother says. "You'll just make it worse."

We stop at the red light on the corner of Third and Delray. Across the street I can see a couple of boys from history class sitting at the bus stop, passing a bag of potato chips back and forth. In school they act like they hate each other, so it is strange to see them together, eating out of the same bag.

No one says anything as we drive home. Twice, my mother steps on the brakes a little too hard, and we lurch forward. "Put on your seat belt," she tells me, even though I already have it on.

When we get back home my mother pulls into our parking spot and kills the engine with a small sigh of relief. We sit for a moment in silence, waiting for my mother to say something, but she just plays with the controls on the dashboard. Finally Miriam speaks up. "Why'd you get a new car?"

My mother looks back at her in the rearview mirror. "I liked it." She starts to rummage around in her purse.

"Mom." I can feel Miriam shifting around in the backseat. Her voice sounds funny, as if it's on the edge of something. Like a tear about to fall.

My mother sighs deeply. She looks around the parking lot to see if anyone's there. It is completely empty.

Then she speaks.

"I didn't want to tell you girls any of this. But some very bad things have happened to me lately. I think I'm in real danger."

She tells us about the men she's seen hanging out in the parking lot across from her office building. How she thinks they are drug dealers. Mafia maybe. And that she saw something she wasn't supposed to see. That she was a witness, and now she's afraid they'll want to get her.

I don't get it. "What do you mean?"

My mother seems confused too. "I don't know. . . . I just saw them, talking to some guy in the parking lot. I think it was maybe a drug deal. Cocaine, or heroin." She sounds like a character on TV. I think about *Matlock*.

Miriam takes a deep breath. My mother fishes a ChapStick out of her purse. "All I know is that they're out there all the time. And they've been following me home."

Miriam rolls her eyes. "That doesn't make any sense."

"I've seen them." My mother's voice is insistent, sure.

"So where are they now, if they know where you live?"

My mother speaks slowly and carefully, as if Miriam is a very stupid person. "I got lucky. They were never able to follow me all the way home. And they won't be able to find me, now that I've got a new car."

So far I haven't said anything. I am just trying to absorb all the information, put it in an order that makes sense. But now something occurs to me, a hitch in my mother's plans. "What happens when you go to work tomorrow?"

My mother shakes her head. "I'm not going back."

Miriam is angry. "This is fucking insane." She gets out of the car and slams the door shut. I can feel it rattle. Miriam runs up the stairwell to our apartment. She doesn't even remember to take her bags.

My mother sighs again. Then she leans in close to me and whispers, "Adie, I want you to know something."

"What?" I try not to look at her.

"I might have to go away for a while."

There is no real response to this, at least not one I can think of, so I just sit there, studying my cuticles, which Miriam has warned me to take better care of.

"If that happens, don't call the police." She stops for a moment, coughing. "Don't tell anyone. Just take good care of your sister." For some reason, I feel embarrassed.

I sense that this conversation is a turning point, something I will remember all my life. I know this is unusual, that things don't usually announce themselves this way. After all, life is not usually full of dramatic moments, blinking lights and signs that say LOOK OVER HERE or REMEMBER THIS. Usually life just passes, and you don't see the crucial moments until they're over. But this one I recognize right away.

My mother gets out of the car and stretches. "Help me carry the groceries in."

My mother quits her job, just like she said she would. "I'll have to find something else," she says, "where they won't be able to find me." She doesn't mention the parking lot men again, but I can tell she's worried. Every once in a while she stops in the middle of whatever she's doing and looks out the window. Now that she's not working, she says, she has time to do all the little things she's been meaning to do, like put her recipes in order or organize her scrapbook. But she can't seem to concentrate. I notice that sudden sounds startle her. She jumps when the phone rings.

Then one afternoon, a few weeks before the summer ends, she tells us that we're moving again. She's found a house to rent on the other side of town, closer to the shopping mall and Miriam's school. The ad in the newspaper calls it a "cottage," which makes it sound like it should be cute, but really it's not. The paint is chipped, and when we move in we find a dead mouse behind the refrigerator. It does at least have a yard.

"You'll get to start the school year in a new place," my mother says, packing her sweaters carefully in the yellow and white embroidered suitcase, which is starting to get discolored around the edges.

Miriam and I have become used to living out of boxes. We don't even bother to unpack most of our books. "It's not like we're going to read them again," my sister says. She has not even unpacked her beloved Dolls of the World collection ("Twelve Beautiful Ladies from Around the World in Authentic Costume" the package says). When she was younger, she saved her allowance for weeks on end to buy them; the flamenco dancer, the geisha girl. They have always presided over her things, looking out at the world through their weird glass eyes. Now they're wrapped in tissue paper and shoved in a cardboard box, along with my old model horses and *Charlie's Angels* cards.

Lainey doesn't understand why we move so much. She thinks it's because we're behind on our rent. "Are you guys in debt?" she asks one day. We are sitting in her room, drinking hot chocolate, even though it's still warm out.

I shake my head. "My mother's just fussy." One place, I tell her, was too close to the airport and you could hear the planes landing; the other had a weird smell, mildew or mold.

"I always thought that place smelled funny," Lainey says, just as I know she would, since she always wants to be right. And she's envious: "You get a new room all the time." Her own room has yellow walls and a green rug, and she hates it. She's lived in the same house her whole life.

My sister becomes even more distant. She locks herself in her room and doesn't answer when I knock—doesn't even bother telling me to *leave her alone,* just silence, nothing. About the only thing that makes her a little happy is being in the car: she's started taking driving lessons. One night, after everyone's off the road, my mother and I go with her on a practice drive. I watch carefully, thinking that maybe if I spend more time in the car I'll become a good driver too.

Miriam circles around the grocery store's empty parking lot, pulling in and out of parking spots, practicing her three-point turns. She drives with confidence, as if she's been doing it all her life. "All of those hours spent playing video games have paid off," my mother says, laughing.

Miriam smiles, biting her lip as she concentrates on her parallel parking. For the first time in a while, it seems as if she and my mother are having fun. "How do I turn on the brights?" she asks. My mother shows her the knob, which is trickier than it looks.

My mother is impressed with Miriam, but still cautious. After all, not everyone can drive as well as Miriam. "Treat every driver as if they're dumber than you," my mother says, as we sit parked in a tight spot, relishing Miriam's success. "As if they might crash into you at any second."

Miriam turns to look at me. Her eyes have become hard again, and the expression on her face is impossible to read, like a Doll of the World.

11

Our new house at 43 Parrott Drive has a tiny downstairs room, next to the washer and dryer, which we call *the den,* filled with dust and junk. Miriam hates it down there. "It smells terrible," she says, which is true. "And there are spiders everywhere." The carpet, an orange-green pattern, is moldy and strangely damp.

But Lainey and I have discovered its coolness. Even the word *den* is cool: what is a den, really? To us it feels like a clubhouse. There's a small bathroom attached to it, just a toilet and a sink, and an old, beat-up desk that was already there when we moved in. A slightly cracked mirror hangs on the wall opposite the desk, old, wood-framed, and if I look at it really quickly, before turning on the light, I can spook myself. I've put my tape player down there, along with my favorite tapes, and I have a secret stash of candy bars in one of the desk drawers. To combat the bad smell, I've bought some incense from the man who has a table set up outside the bus terminal downtown. The label on the package says JASMINE DREAM in long, silver letters, and the smell is dusty, exotic: from someplace mysterious and far away. My mother hates the incense, thinks it's tacky—and if I want a nice smell I should use the peach-scented candles, six to a box, that she picked up at the Hallmark store. "Inhaling all that smoke can't be good for you," she says. "Think of what it's doing to your lungs." I promise to burn only half a stick at a time.

One night, just after the school year has started, Lainey comes over so we can do our homework together. Math class is much harder than last year, and we're trying to develop a system so that we each only have to do half the problems. "There's no point in learning math now that calculators have been invented," Lainey points out. After a while we give up and start practicing some of the dance moves we've seen on *Solid Gold*.

Lainey isn't supposed to wear makeup, but she's shoplifted some eyeliner from the ninety-nine-cent store. I watch as she puts a thin line of purple on her inner eyelid, wondering why she didn't steal it from someplace better. "Let me use it," I say, and she hands it to me, her eyes watering. I have some of Miriam's old lipsticks, and we use those too, trying to make our lips look *plump and full,* just like the magazines say. When we're done we pose and coo in front of the mirror, singing the words to the Enjoli commercial, which is about bringing home the bacon and frying it in a pan.

"That's actually a real song," Lainey brags. "Not just a commercial." She's starting to annoy me. I stare at my reflection, sticking my chest out as far as it will go. It's still not very big.

Then I hear my mother's voice, shrill and sharp. "Adie? What are you girls doing?"

I look at Lainey. "I'll be back in a sec." She nods, still staring at herself in the mirror.

My mother is standing at the top of the stairs. I notice she's wearing the quilted bathrobe Miriam and I gave her for her last birthday. It's pink and green, the edge of one sleeve frayed from where Maxwell has chewed it.

My mother's face is somewhere between crying and smiling. "I don't want you girls playing down there."

I take a deep breath. From downstairs, I can hear Michael Jackson singing *Billie Jean is not my lover* . . . Lainey is still in the den. I'm sure she's wondering what's going on. Mrs. Aronowitz loses her temper all the time, screams at us for something small, like having the TV on too loud, or forgetting to close the screen door, and then comes up to Lainey's room a half hour later with homemade brownies or a bottle of soda. She even apologizes, telling us that she needs to watch her blood pressure, *the doctor has warned her a million times*. But my mother, with her soft voice and quiet smile, is not known as a yeller.

My heart sinks, with embarrassment and shame. "It's okay, Mom." I look into her eyes. "We're not doing anything." I keep my voice low. I don't want Lainey to hear any of this.

My mother tries to laugh it off. "I know." She avoids my eyes. "I just thought you'd be more comfortable upstairs."

"We're fine down there." I want to tell her: *We're not doing drugs, we wouldn't even know how to do them, or where to get them. We don't even smoke cigarettes, even when the kids at school dare us to try them. We're good kids, really.* But instead I just say, "Are there any cookies left?"

"I think so." Usually my mother is so confident, so sure of her convictions, but this time she gives in, as if confused by her own ideas. Suddenly she grabs me, gives me an enormous hug. "I love you, honey." The familiar smell of her shampoo overwhelms me.

"We'll be up soon," I promise, wiggling out of her grasp.

When I return to the den, Lainey is lying on the floor, her eyes a mess of purple. I lie down next to her, and we stare up at the ceiling, which is cracked and stained from an upstairs leak. "Do you want some cookies?"

"What's up with your mom?" Lainey asks.

"She's just in a weird mood."

"What kind of weird mood?"

"I think she's menopausal," I say, using a word we just learned in science class. The whole thing had seemed creepy: the opposite of getting your period. But I know my mother isn't going through menopause at all.

Lainey makes a face. "Gross." I can tell she's not satisfied, but she lets it drop. I feel myself separating from her, quietly— the slow drift when one cloud breaks away from another. There is a big gap where I can't tell her things.

The next day, when we're in the car, my mother says to me, "Adie, what are those marks on your arm?"

We're on our way to Cliff's Variety Store to purchase a new shower curtain. The one we have, she has told me and Miriam, is too old, too moldy. She's been reading about mold, the way it gets in people's lungs and makes them die. She showed me a newspaper article, "Mold: The Secret Killer in Your House," to prove her point. I think the curtain looks fine, and I like its blue and green pattern: pictures of dolphins, whales, and seals playing in the water. But my mother said, *There are plenty of things to worry about in this world without also being scared of your own bathroom,* and that she'd been thinking it might be time to change the colors anyway—maybe get a set of bright new towels in orange and yellow.

Now my mother clears her throat. "I asked you a question, Adie."

"What marks?" I scan my forearms, which seem like they're getting hairier. My legs get a lot of hair too, but right now they're silky smooth, from endless applications of Nair. For the past couple of weeks, Lainey and I have spent our afternoons after school lying by the pool at the Las Palmas Community Recreation Center, playing gin rummy with Lainey's special set of waterproof cards. Lainey's mother wants us to hang out at the JCC ("I guess I'm just spending all that money for nothing," she grumbles, "since my daughter apparently does not even care about her heritage"), but the boys there are ugly, Lainey insists. "Everyone knows that Jewish males don't get handsome until they grow up," she points out, as if she learned this fact in science class, and I just nod, wondering how she knows this.

My mother keeps her eyes on the road. "Those marks on your wrist."

I look again. She's right: there are some scratches on my left wrist. Where did they come from? "They must be from when Lainey and I were climbing the fence." I touch the scratches gently, thinking about how strange it is that things like that can just show up on your body, without you even noticing them.

"What fence?" my mother says, her voice light but suspicious.

"The one behind her house." The fence separates Mrs. Aronowitz's neat little flower garden from a woodsy area with wild apple trees. Most of the apples are gnarled and yellow, covered with spots, but sometimes Lainey and I take a few bites out of them anyway, which makes me feel like I'm in a Tom Sawyer book. I think about the apples and picture myself wearing an old-fashioned dress, something with petticoats and a ruffle skirt, flirting with Huck Finn, who I like better than Tom anyway.

My mother pulls over and parks the car, right in front of a fire hydrant with a rusted base. We are far from our house, on a long, narrow street lined with big houses, someplace where I've never been.

I look around. A squirrel darts across the lawn, nervous and quick. For a moment I wonder if we're going to visit someone, if she has a surprise for me.

"Adie, I want you to tell me the truth." She grabs my wrist, hard. "Are you doing drugs?"

I try to twist out of her grasp, but she's not letting go—for such a small woman, she's surprisingly strong. Her fingernails dig deeper into my arm.

"Are you shooting up?"

"No!"

My mother's eyes are fierce. I think about an after-school special I'd seen about a girl who was addicted to all kinds of drugs. The girl, who looked a little like Lainey, reminded me of me: the sort of girl who is kind to animals and likes to read. But then she went to a party, and her friend's brother gave her some cocaine, and that was that. The girl ran away to New York and became a hooker with fishnet stockings and black leather boots (the kind Miriam wants, but my mother says, *Absolutely not*), and then she had a baby. Almost everything I'd seen in health class or on TV made it seem like once you started taking drugs you got pregnant.

My mother's anger has diminished to fear. "You wouldn't lie to me—would you?" Her voice is barely a whisper.

"Of course not." This itself is a lie: I'd lied to my mother many times, about all sorts of things, from the time I'd actually gone to bed at night to whether or not I'd brushed my teeth. But I know that's not what she means. I fiddle with the knob on the glove compartment, which is always getting stuck.

Now my mother looks more closely at the scratches on my wrist, tracing them curiously with her finger, just as I had a minute before. "Does it hurt? Maybe we should put some iodine on them."

"It's okay," I say, rolling down the window. A gentle breeze has settled on the day. "We should go. We're in front of a hydrant."

My mother turns on the ignition. "You don't want it to get infected." She pulls away from the curb, too quickly, and a driver coming down the street behind us honks. "Screw you!" my mother shouts, giving him the middle finger. Then she ducks down, shocked by herself. "I shouldn't do that. You never know what kind of people are on the road."

"I know." Miriam told me about this when she was taking driver's ed, that you should never antagonize another driver. They could have a gun, or they might just ram into your car.

Still, I can tell my mother is pleased with herself. For a moment, it is fun to see her flout the rules. She is not typically a rule-breaker. But now I realize there is something new flashing in her eyes, a light unlike anything I've seen before.

12

In developmental arts class, Mrs. McIntyre assigns us a project—a *collage,* a word that sounds like *college,* but isn't. We're supposed to put together photographs of ourselves from different ages, along with images and words that *represent us,* and arrange them all on a piece of construction paper. "It's a visual representation of your life story," says Mrs. McIntyre, looking flushed and excited. The title of the project is "My Life's Journey."

Miriam scoffs at it. "That's not art," she points out. "It's just gluing things together." Still she agrees to help me, even letting me use the pens from her special collection, the ones she keeps hidden in a shoe box in the back of her closet.

Lainey's collage is perfect. She's arranged all the pictures clockwise, so you look at them in a circle. It makes me a little dizzy, but Lainey says it shows the passage of time. In the center is her school picture from this year, her gaze at the camera poised and angry. Her hair is pulled back and a few loose curls brush her shoulder, like the old-fashioned ladies in the *Masterpieces of World Art* book we have on our coffee table. My mother always says it's good to have books like that lying around, even if you don't really read them. They show you are cultured.

I'm having a hard time finishing my collage. For one thing, I can't find very many pictures to use. Even though we've been in this apartment for almost four months, a lot of our things are still packed up in the blue plastic bins my mother bought at Kmart, sealed shut with shiny silver duct tape. My mother's bedroom is full of large plastic garbage bags filled with clothes and shoes and purses. The old Chinese prints of birds and flowers are stacked outside the bathroom, the walls of the apartment are bare—except for one little corner of the living room where we've tacked a picture torn from a magazine; an image of the Canadian Rockies, cold and white. To me the walls look blank and empty, but my mother just says, "I can't seem to find the hammer. Anyway, the walls are so nicely painted, it seems a shame to stick a nail in them."

The only photos I've managed to find are blurry or have the top of my head cut off. Last year Sidney and I took some pictures by her pool—I remember my shoulders were covered with a terrible, painful sunburn and my hair was wet and plastered over my face—but they were with her camera, and we never got them developed anyway. There's a Polaroid of me and Maxwell on the refrigerator, but I'm petting him, not even facing the camera.

"I think all the photo albums must still be downstairs," my mother says, when I tell her about the project. "In the basement."

She's hunched over at the kitchen table, reading yesterday's newspaper. Except to take us places, she's mostly been staying indoors, and her skin, usually a soft olive brown, has gone pale. She looks thinner too, and I realize suddenly that she hasn't been eating very much. ("You might as well finish this up," she'll say, pushing her plate to me. "After all, you need the vitamins.") Sometimes at night I hear her pacing the apartment, humming a tune from one of the old musicals she likes so much, *Show Boat* or *Porgy and Bess,* but it doesn't sound like a happy humming—it's more like something to fill the space.

My sister looks at me. "I'll help you find them," she says, putting on her sandals. I think she feels sorry for me.

We go downstairs to the basement. A few weeks ago I went

down there to get my roller skates, and for some reason the exposed pipes and dank quiet scared me. But with Miriam there I'm not spooked at all.

The basement is damp and covered with dust and peeling paint. My sister flips on the light switch and surveys the boxes. "God, what a fucking mess." For a moment her whole body seems limp, exhausted, and I worry that she's just going to tell me to forget it, that she's going to meet up with her friends at the mall. But then she pushes aside an old brass lamp without a shade and a deflated bicycle tire and gives me a weak smile. "Here, take this," she says, handing me a box marked PER-SONAL, MISC. in my mother's shaky handwriting. "It's not too heavy."

We lug everything upstairs and open the box. It's packed tight with paper—unopened bills, dry-cleaning receipts, old report cards, sheet music. A crumpled sketch of a dog and cat, curled up together in a tight ball, that won Miriam the prize of "Most Creative" in ninth grade. ("What a piece of shit," she says, smoothing it out carefully.) There are other things too, that must have been tossed in during the rush of moving: a pair of heart-shaped sunglasses with a broken frame, boxes of paper clips, a wooden spoon. Thumbtacks in a small green envelope. Strands of plastic beads from a Mardi Gras party last year. Our school vaccination records. A Phillips-head screwdriver.

Underneath everything, at the very bottom of the box, I find the photo albums. We have not looked at these, I realize, in a very long time.

"Let me see," Miriam says, scooting next to me.

The pages of the album are stuck together. In one of them I find sheet after sheet of my school photo from last year. The same image of me, lazy eye squinting a wink, stares out from the pages, over and over again. Other than the school picture, the only photos I can find of me are from many years ago. The last few years have disappeared. The only other pictures are of scenery—places, woodsy and dark, that my mother has been without me.

"They've got to be somewhere," my mother says, digging

through the box. "Hey, here's my old hair dryer. I was wondering where that went."

"But I've looked *everywhere.*"

"So let's just take some pictures now." My mother struggles with the hair dryer cord, which is tangled in knots and coils. "I'll get them developed tomorrow."

"But it's *due* tomorrow."

"Jesus, Adie." My mother pushes the box into the corner. "If you didn't leave everything to the last minute we wouldn't have this problem." But then she sees the look on my face and her voice softens. "Maybe there's something we can use in here," she says, ripping open a large manila envelope that's been taped shut. Inside are some old black-and-white photos.

I pick one up and study it. "Who's that?" The edges of the picture are frayed, and the picture is off center, but the image itself is clean and sharp: a woman wearing a polka-dot dress and laughing, shading her eyes from the sun. It's daytime, but something about the picture seems dark, haunted.

My mother shakes her head and sits down on the floor beside me. "Sweetie, you've seen this picture a million times. That's Grandma."

My grandmother died before I was born, when my mother was only twenty-two, and I know I've never seen a picture of her, no matter what my mother says. Something hard catches in my throat when I think of Lainey's house, the front hallway lined with photos of her family: grandparents, aunts, uncles, cousins. ("None of them *understand* me," she likes to say dramatically, but at least she has pictures to look at, unlike our walls, which are just big empty spaces.)

Miriam takes the photo and studies it. "What's she laughing at?"

"I don't know." My mother frowns. "She wasn't a person who laughed a lot, that's for sure."

"What do you mean?"

"If I had a date or wanted to go out with friends, she'd get very nervous. She was always thinking something bad would happen to me. Everything startled her." My mother leans back against the sofa. "We had a beautiful old tree outside our house, a flowering tree with long branches, and on windy days, when the branches scratched the window she'd think someone was trying to break in." She looks suddenly tired. "She had this lifelong fear that people were following her."

Maxwell whines softly, his tail beating a gentle thump on the carpet. My sister and I look at each other. We don't have to say anything; there's a sudden understanding between us. My mother picks at a loose thread on the couch cushion.

Miriam leans forward. Her voice is careful and gentle, as if she's trying to catch a butterfly. "Do you think that's why *you* get so scared about things?"

My mother answers, her eyes dreamy and distant. "I'm not sure. Maybe."

A hush clears the room. I feel a tickle run up my spine, the beginning of something forbidden.

My mother stands up and grabs her purse. "The difference is that people really have been following me." The moment is broken, gone. "I'll be back soon," she says, pulling on the red and white flannel jacket with the missing buttons. She leaves, locking the door behind her.

Outside, rain hits the window, a sharp, almost metallic sound. Miriam doesn't say anything, just starts pulling the dead leaves off the spider plant we always forget to water. I put all the papers and photos back into the box. Our vaccination records go in a small pile, sorted by year. One of my report cards is torn at the edge, stained with coffee. The newspaper clippings are yellowing. I'm not sure what to do with them, so I lay them carefully on top of everything else.

"I'll tell you what," Miriam says after a few minutes. "I'll draw your picture." She pulls me up from the floor and almost pushes me onto the chair by the window, where the light, she says, will be better.

"Now stop crying," she says. "You'll be the only one in class with an actual *hand-drawn* portrait. Drawn by a *real* artist. And it'll be right up to the minute." She gets out her best sketchbook and a brand-new box of pencils and perches on the couch across from me. "Hold still."

I steal a glance at her. She's biting her lip and has one eye squeezed shut, the way she always does when she's concentrating. I listen to the rain, feeling myself come into focus as she draws me. If I try really hard, I can almost feel the pencil mapping my flesh.

By the time my mother returns, a couple of hours later, Miriam and I have already returned the box to the basement, sealing it shut to protect it against the dampness.

13

~

Having the right clothes and shoes and bag is much more important in seventh grade. If you don't have the right things, even if it was an honest mistake, the other kids will say you are a *total loser,* or *gay,* or *retarded.* If you get unlucky and happen to wear the wrong jeans or wrong shoes, you can suddenly be stuck with no friends at all, for the entire rest of the year, because who wants to be seen with you? "My God, you can't wear that," my sister sometimes says, right before I'm about to leave for school. "You look completely retarded." I feel lucky to have her looking out for me.

Right now the most important fashion trend of all is barrettes with long leather strings hanging down to your shoulders, and feathers dangling at the end. The barrettes are called "roach clips," though nobody seems to know why. Everywhere you look the girls have feathers flowing along with their hair, as if they are some sort of strange animal, a mix of girl and bird. If your hair is too short or you don't want something in your hair that day, you can just attach them to a purse or backpack; Lainey and I have matching ones that we've attached to our LeSportsac bags as well as our hair.

Usually none of the teachers say anything about our clothes, except for Mrs. Bensen-Allen, who always frowns at our skirts and says they are too short and boys *might get the wrong idea.*

But then one morning Mr. Healy walks into our second-period science class with Principal Sheen by his side. He clears his throat and says, "Before we start, Principal Sheen and I have something to tell you." I've never seen Principal Sheen close up, just at morning assemblies and school rallies. From here I can see that he is really not as tall as he looks from far away, and his arms are extremely hairy. He looks very serious, standing right under the solar system chart with the moons of Jupiter over his head. He says, "Starting next week, you are no longer allowed to wear the barrettes with the feathers to school."

Everyone looks at each other, and a small murmur of complaint travels the room. Lainey raises her hand and says, "Why not?" without even waiting for either Mr. Healy or Principal Sheen to call on her. "They're just barrettes." Lainey has started talking back to adults and has told me that it is important to *question authority,* just like the bumper sticker on her older brother's skateboard says. ("Otherwise we'll all just be indoctrinated, like the people in *1984,*" she tells me. "Like the commies. Or the Jamestown people who drank the Kool-Aid.") It is driving her mother crazy.

Mr. Healy leans back against his desk and steals a glance out the window. He seems uncomfortable, and for a moment I think that maybe being a teacher is harder than it looks. Principal Sheen steps in and says, "The PTA has learned that these barrettes are sometimes used for smoking marijuana."

I pluck the barrette out of my hair and look around the classroom. A few of the boys snicker loudly, but most of us just look confused. I know there is something about the barrettes that is cool and slightly forbidden, but I don't understand how it can have anything to do with drugs. I try to remember if my mother has warned me against wearing headbands or barrettes or anything like that, but all she has ever said about our hair is that Miriam and I are going to end up dead from toxic fumes if we keep using so much Aqua Net hair spray every morning.

Mr. Healy says, "I have a form for your parents to sign. Just turn it in on Monday." He turns back to the chalkboard. "Okay, how many of you are ready to diagram a cell?" Everyone groans.

Later that night I unfold the mimeographed letter that Mr. Healy gave us and show it to Miriam. We read it together:

> *November 20, 1982*
> *Dear Parents:*
>   *Here at Laurel Grove Junior High we are, of course, deeply concerned about drug use among the student population and wish to assure parents that there is a zero-tolerance policy for drug possession of any kind. In light of this, students will no longer be allowed to wear the hair accessories colloquially referred to as "roach clips" to school. In addition, any student found to be in possession of marijuana ["pot"], cocaine, heroine ["smack"], acid / LSD, amphetamines, or any other illicit substance(s) will be immediately suspended and will face expulsion. We consider your child's health and safety paramount and appreciate your cooperation.*
> *Sincerely,*
> *Principal Michael Sheen*
> *Task Force on Drug Use / Laurel Grove Junior High*
> *"Just Say No" Campaign*

"They spelled heroin wrong," Miriam points out.

"What's a roach clip?" I ask.

"It means you're smoking pot and the joint gets all the way down to the end and you need to hold it with the clip so you don't burn your fingers," my sister explains, sounding very grown up and bored. "Anyway, you're gonna need Mom to sign that."

I reread the note and a deep weight sinks in my chest. "You know how she is about drugs. She'll freak out."

"Here. I'll do it." Miriam takes a pen from her pencil case and scrawls our mother's signature on a piece of paper for practice, and then signs the note itself. "How's that?" she asks.

"Okay, I guess." I'm not sure what to think. "What if they can tell it's fake?"

My sister rolls her eyes. "It's fine."

Just then our mother walks in. Miriam glares at her. "Mom, I've told you a million times to knock first," she says, but our mother doesn't even reply, because the first thing she sees is the note, which she reads, and then she sees Miriam's fake signature—her signature—at the bottom. She looks back and forth at both of us and then she says, "Why didn't you show this to me, Adie?"

Miriam starts fiddling with her pencil case. "Mom, it's no big deal. Adie doesn't even know what these things are for. The whole thing is just stupid."

"It's not stupid at all!" my mother says, her eyes darker than usual. "I've heard about this kind of thing. You think all you're doing is wearing a pretty barrette, and next thing you know you're addicted to marijuana!"

My sister and I look at each other. My mother continues: "You see all these kids walking around downtown wearing those Grateful Dead T-shirts and their parents think it's just a fashion trend and they just want to impress their friends, but really it's a way of signaling to other kids that they are into drugs." She looks at the note again. "It's a way of letting other kids know they want to party."

Miriam shakes her head. "No one listens to the Grateful Dead anymore."

"I really thought this was supposed to be a good school district," my mother says, her voice wavering. "It's supposed to be one of the best in California. I didn't think the school would have such an *active drug culture*."

"It *doesn't*."

My mother looks a little ill and she puts the piece of paper down and then opens the window. She leans her head out, as if she's trying to suck down as much fresh air as possible. "Why didn't you tell me about the note right away?"

"Because." I'm not sure what to say. Outside the stars are bright, full of possibility.

"Adie, I want you to be completely honest with me. Are you doing drugs? With Lainey, or anyone else?"

I am not sure what to say. I study the circle pattern on the hallway rug, which repeats over and over, noticing for the first time that it sort of looks like little faces, one after another.

My sister steps in. "Adie just didn't want you to feel bad."

My mother looks confused. "What are you talking about?"

Miriam sits next to my mother and takes her hand. "She knows how much you worry about things like this—kids doing drugs and stuff—and she just didn't want you to be even more worried." She steals a glance my way. "She was just trying to be considerate."

My mother swallows hard and turns to me. "Is that true, Adie?"

I nod dumbly. Miriam tosses her hair, seeming pleased with herself, as if she has just found the last piece of a jigsaw puzzle.

My mother is quiet for a minute. Then she says, "Adie, if anybody wearing these barrettes tries to be friends with you, just walk away. Don't even talk to them." She shudders and holds up the barrette carefully, as if it might bite her with its little metal clip. "I still can't believe how pretty I thought these barrettes were. They're so feminine. I had no idea they were a sign of drug abuse."

"I guess I'll just wear them on the weekends."

My mother shakes her head. "You're not going to wear them at all. We're throwing them in the trash right now."

"But Lainey gave them to me."

"Well, I'm sure Lainey's mother doesn't approve of roach clips either."

Miriam looks like she wants to laugh, but she keeps her voice even. "Mom, trust me. Adie and her friends aren't getting high."

"Well, that's the point, isn't it?"

"Can't I just keep them in my jewelry box?" I ask. "I promise not to wear them."

"Absolutely not." My mother leaves the room, holding the barrettes slightly away from her body. The room feels suddenly still, quiet. My sister gets up and puts Pat Benatar's *Crimes of Passion* in her tape player. I watch as she tries on her new beret, the one she got to match her leg warmers. "Man, Adie, you would be helpless without me."

It's true. If Miriam weren't around, who would show me which were the right clothes to wear—who would keep me from looking like a *total loser?* Who would show me how to feather and hair spray my hair so it comes out the right way? And who would be there if my mother gets sick again, if she has to go back to the hospital? I realize that I have no idea who I would call if that happened: Lainey's mother maybe? But even Lainey doesn't know about my mother, and I don't want to tell her. On the tape, Pat Benatar growls *Hit me with your best shot. . . .*

A small shaking fear trembles my body. "Promise me you'll never leave," I say to Miriam.

My sister runs her fingers through her hair. "Do you think if I cut my hair real short I'd look like Pat Benatar?" The beret, which flattens out her hair, makes her look older, distant, foreign, as if she is not actually American at all but instead French. A French sister—what would that be like? She turns back to the plastic heart-shaped mirror hinged at an angle over her desk and peers at herself, then draws a thick line of eyeliner on the inside of her lids.

"Seriously, I mean it, don't go away. Don't go anywhere." I'm babbling, and I sit down on the edge of her bed, pretending to smooth out a wrinkle in the flowered bedspread so she won't see that I'm about to start crying.

"Where would I go?" Miriam says. "I'm always going to be here." She drops the can of hair spray on the floor and picks it up. "Well, until I go to college, I guess." She frowns at herself in the mirror. "*If* I go."

"What do you mean, *if?*" My sister has always been so smart, had almost straight As until last semester, when some of the teachers gave her Cs on her report card and wrote that she had *stopped applying herself* and *was not performing to the best of her ability.*

"Jesus, Adie, there's more to life than school." She jumps up. "Hey, let's go. *The Love Boat* is gonna start."

"Okay." I pretend I'm going to follow her, but then I hang

back a minute, looking at all the things in her room. Without Miriam, they're just things, shapes taking up space on the table and the bed and the floor. Her stuffed panda, the one Maxwell chewed, stares at me with one plastic blue eye, the missing eye a deep, dark hole in its face. Because of the missing eye, the panda always looks a little sad and confused, even with its big felt sewn-on smile. Somehow that doesn't seem fair. "You poor thing," I say aloud, petting its soft head, the fake fur worn down and dirty with age. "You poor, poor thing."

"Adie, come on," my sister's voice trips up the stairs. "Mom made some Jiffy Pop."

I prop the stuffed panda against Miriam's pillow and make my way to the living room. The TV show has already started. My mother is wearing my sister's old Garfield T-shirt that has a hole under the arm and says YOU ARE PURRFECT, except the letter *P* has worn off, so now it just says URRFECT. For a long time Miriam and I used to run around saying, "That's urrfect!" whenever we liked something, and if we really liked something, we'd say, "That's totally urrfective," but we haven't done that in a while, and thinking about it, I'm not sure why. My mother also has a purple towel wrapped around her head, and her face and neck are coated with a brownish-gray goop: an oatmeal facial that's not real oatmeal at all, but a strange, smelly mix that reminds me of Elmer's glue, out of a plastic container from the drugstore. She's not allowed to talk or smile when she's in the middle of a facial—or the wrinkles will freeze in place—but she gestures for me sit next to her on the couch.

"I'm okay over here," I say, sitting down on the floor next to Maxwell, who thumps his tail in response. My mother looks at me, but the oatmeal facial has covered everything in a lumpy sheet of brown, and her expression is missing: a mystery. My sister, leaning back in the old rocking chair with the missing arm, stays silent, staring at the TV. Every few moments she reaches out without looking and takes a piece of popcorn from the bowl, which she chews slowly, carefully. The smell of the oatmeal-glue facial and the fake buttered popcorn covers the room, a sweet-salty smell that makes me feel a little dizzy and

sick. I rest my head on Maxwell's strong back, soft and muscu-
lar at the same time, and pretend to watch the show, though
really I am looking at my mother and sister. My sister still has
the beret on, though now it's falling off slightly, and next to my
mother with the towel wrapped around her head they both look
strange, as if something has grown out of their heads. My
mother studies her nails and toenails, and I realize that she's polished them a gleaming apple red, and so can't move at all until
they dry. Looking at my mother's frozen face and fingers
splayed carefully apart I think of a word from last week's vocabulary test: *immobile,* which has nothing to do with the mo-
biles we made in art class, bits of shiny colored glass hanging
prettily from old wire coat hangers, but just the opposite: unable to move, still, *inert*—another vocabulary word. My mother
is immobile, and watching her, that's how I feel too—stuck here,
in place, like something glued to a shelf. Maxwell shifts slightly
under me; I can hear his stomach rumble. For a moment I wonder what it would be like to run away, to be one of those missing girls you hear about on the TV news—*She went to school
one morning and then disappeared, never to be seen again.* Each
day is so long, how will I ever be old enough to leave? Then I realize there are not that many places to go. It is too much to
think about. I settle back against Maxwell and lose myself in the
dull glow of the television screen.

14

*

Every third Sunday of the month Lainey and her mother have what Mrs. Aronowitz calls a *ladies' day out*. Mrs. Aronowitz goes to the La Bella Femme day spa and gets her hair colored a deep russet red, while Lainey gets a pedicure and reads old copies of *Cosmopolitan* and *Mademoiselle* and picks all the red candies from a shiny glass bowl. After the hair is finished and Lainey's toes are dry, the two of them go out for a special lunch at a restaurant called the Forest. When Lainey first told me about the Forest, I pictured something like the house in *Little House on the Prairie,* an old-fashioned wooden cabin by a stream with lots of redwood trees around: a deer or maybe a rabbit. But really the Forest is just a diner on a busy street downtown with all the usual things like hamburgers and grilled cheese sandwiches you'd eat at any old restaurant with a normal name that didn't sound like it was in the middle of the woods.

Whenever I go over to Lainey's house Mrs. Aronowitz asks how my mother is doing, not in a casual way, but really *how is she doing?* in a way that makes it clear there is a deeper meaning behind the question. I am never really sure how to reply, so usually I just say that *she's fine*. I guess that Mrs. Aronowitz decided to find out for herself because last week she called my mother and asked if we'd like to come along for the next *ladies' day out.*

"I think it will be fun," my mother had said. "Like a mother-daughter double date."

We arrange to meet my mother at the diner at noon, after we've gone shopping, and I am secretly excited because even though I sometimes don't answer right away when my mother asks me a question and act like I don't care what she thinks, I have been very jealous of Lainey and Mrs. Aronowitz and their days out together. My mother says she will even *do her hair special* for the occasion, in a little bun. "Like Audrey Hepburn," she says.

"Who's that?"

My mother sighs. "A very famous actress. Anyway, I'll see you at the restaurant." She gives me a kiss and says it will be nice to have a chance to catch up with Mrs. Aronowitz. But when we get to the Forest later that afternoon my mother isn't there.

"I don't know where she is," I say to Mrs. Aronowitz. "She's supposed to be here."

"I'm sure she'll show up any sec," Mrs. Aronowitz says. "Let's just sit down." We follow the waitress to a booth at the back of the diner. I look around: the walls are painted with pictures of trees and mountains as if we're really in the woods, and the place mats are covered with illustrations of forest animals, and there is a Styrofoam cup of crayons for little kids to color with. In the corner is a papier-mâché deer. Lainey and I order iced teas with lemon, and Mrs. Aronowitz gets coffee, asking the waiter to please bring her skim milk, not cream, as she is trying to watch her cholesterol, and then sits back in the booth.

She looks at me. "Are you sure your mother knows where to go?" she asks. "There are a lot of diners around here."

"I think so. We've driven past it a million times." I stare at the place mat picture of the forest, tracing the outline of the trees with my finger.

"Well, maybe she's just having a hard time with parking. It can be heck at this time of day."

"*Hell*," says Lainey, playing with the glass beaded bracelet she bought in Chinatown; it is supposed to bring her *good health and riches.* "You mean it's *hell* at this time of day."

"Lainey, stop it." Mrs. Aronowitz's whole face looks worn out, as if she's bored with telling Lainey not to swear and doesn't really care anymore. I think about how strange it must be to be a parent, to have days where you don't really care if your children are swearing, or eating with their fingers, or burping at the table, but have to pretend you do, because that's what parents are supposed to do: care. I look at the little cup of crayons, wishing for a moment that Lainey and I weren't too old to color. All the good colors are gone; the only ones left are brown and gray and black.

"Your hair looks very pretty, Adie," Mrs. Aronowitz says. "Like that actress. The one who was in *Taxi Driver?* Jodie Foster."

"Thanks." I'm not sure where my mother is, and something in my stomach sinks deep, a bitter pang of regret and fear. I wish we hadn't planned this *ladies' day out,* that Mrs. Aronowitz had just said good-bye and put me on the number 76 bus home, which circles through downtown and then out to our neighborhood, past Miriam's high school and the city recycling center where they give you five cents a can. I glance at the clock. It's already fifteen past—then the minute hand ticks over, and it's sixteen past. Sixteen minutes late; and my mother is never late. *Punctuality is your secret weapon,* she likes to say. No matter how crazy everything gets, you can always be on time. I stare at the plaster deer in the corner, one of the antlers has come off, and now there is just a strange hole in its head.

The waitress is starting to look impatient with us. She's been to our table three times and all we've ordered is our iced tea and Mrs. Aronowitz's coffee, which has already been refilled twice. I think about how when I stay the night at Lainey's house Mrs. Aronowitz makes everyone go around the house picking up newspapers and magazines and toys, putting dirty dishes in the dishwasher, arranging the throw pillows on the couch so they look fancy and neat. "I think of it as putting the house to bed," Mrs. Aronowitz told me, and I thought it was amazing, to have everything tidy and in its place for the next day, as if the house, like everybody who lived there, needed to get a little sleep too. Then in the morning when you wake up, the house is rested and ready too, all set to start its day fresh and new. This is basically the opposite of how things are at our house, where everything seems to be asleep, never fully woken up. A fly crawls quietly on the outside of the window, a small black spot against the glass.

Twenty past twelve. "Well, let's just order," Mrs. Aronowitz finally says, signaling at the waitress. "We can get something for your mother when she shows up."

I look out the window, thinking how perfect it would be if my mother came running down the street now, clutching her shopping bags, her long hair drawn out behind her, laughing and apologizing for being late. *I'm so sorry,* she'd say. *I just got distracted by the beautiful day, and look, Adie, I got this for you, from the woman who sells jewelry on the street corner,* and she'd hand me a beautiful bracelet with different colored beads and stones—even prettier than Lainey's, and even more full of good luck. But my mother is not there at all.

I order macaroni and cheese and Mrs. Aronowitz nods. "That seems like a great choice," she says, as if she is trying to be extra nice to me because my mother is not there, but the whole thing feels stupid and fake, because complimenting someone on what they're eating is not a real compliment at all. "Do you want the usual, Lainey?"

Lainey makes a face. "I'm going to get the diet plate." Today Lainey was mad because she couldn't fit into her favorite jeans. The diet plate is just tuna fish on romaine lettuce with a sliced egg on the side.

Mrs. Aronowitz frowns at her. "Sweetheart, you're thin enough as it is. I'm the one who needs to watch my weight," she says, patting her stomach. She looks up at the waitress. "At my age you can't be too careful." The waitress just gives us a half smile; I'm sure she's heard this same conversation a million times.

Mrs. Aronowitz finishes ordering and when the waitress leaves she turns to me. "I hope everything is okay," she says, fiddling with a sugar packet. "It's not like your mother to stand us up this way."

"What does *stand up* mean?"

A funny look crosses her face. "Leave us hanging." I'm not sure what that means either, but I picture a tire swing hanging from a tree, alone and still. Mrs. Aronowitz has a funny fixed look on her face and keeps stealing glances at the clock. I imagine her driving home to call someone on the phone and saying, *You won't believe it, my friend stood me up for lunch today. She left me hanging.*

For some reason, even though I'm sitting right there, and I'm not late at all, I feel as if I should apologize. "I'm so sorry," I say, trying not to catch Mrs. Aronowitz's eye, who is looking at me the way you look at a dog with three legs. "I don't know where she is." My voice is a funny little whine of complaint; it is the only way I can think to keep myself from crying.

"Maybe you should try calling her. I think there's a pay phone over by the ladies' room."

"I don't have any change," I say, staring at the floor. First my mother is late and now I don't even have money for the phone. Mrs. Aronowitz leans over awkwardly and fishes through the side pocket of the handwoven wallet she got in Mexico and hands me money for the pay phone. I can't even say thank you, so I just nod dumbly and scoot out of the little booth, almost knocking over Lainey's iced tea.

The phone is next to an old black-and-white photo of a lake, and for a few moments I stare at it before dropping in the coins. I take my time, dialing the number as slowly as possible, because I know that any second now my mother is going to show up and I won't have to feel as if she and Lainey are looking at me like I'm one of those poisonous bugs you see pictures of in *National Geographic*. I am so tired of feeling different—of always feeling as if everyone else has a normal life, and mine is the broken one, like the broken toys at Marshall's Toys and Games that are sold for half price at the back of the store under the sad handwritten sign that says AS IS—NO REFUNDS. ALL SALES FINAL. Staring at the numbers on the phone, I realize that's how I feel right now—as if everything looks normal and safe on the outside, but really, inside, where no one can see, something invisible is broken.

At last I dial the number, but the phone just rings and rings, until finally the answering machine comes on. I don't really want to leave a message, so I just hang up, even though my mother always says that's rude. ("Just think how frustrating it is for the other person," she says.) When I get back to the table the food is already there.

"Maybe she just forgot," Lainey says. I push the macaroni and cheese around on my plate. I have that horrible hot feeling that comes right before you're about to throw up, and I know better than to try to eat anything. I focus on the bright orange smear of lipstick staining the rim of Mrs. Aronowitz's coffee cup.

"Adie, you're not eating anything," Mrs. Aronowitz says.

The heat travels up my arms and covers my neck. "I guess I'm really not that hungry."

"Well, I wish you'd thought of that before you ordered," she says. But then she sees the look on my face. "Never mind, it's no big deal. You can take it home and put it in the microwave for later." Across the room, the busboy wipes off a table in slow circles.

"My mom can pay you back later."

"No, hon, that's okay. My treat. Let's just get you home after this." Everyone is quiet. The macaroni and cheese grows cold on my plate. I watch the street outside; a bus goes by, the people inside framed by the windows.

On the drive back I scan the streets, thinking maybe we'll see my mother coming from the other direction, hurrying her way to the restaurant. Lainey is tired and cranky from the day out and does not say anything to her mother when she reminds her for the second time to put on her seat belt and lock the door. "I locked my door already," I say. Lainey gives me a look and slumps down in her seat.

Mrs. Aronowitz drives me home, and just as she is parking her car in front of my house my mother pulls up behind us.

"Hey, there's your mom," Lainey says.

My mother gets out of the car and gives us a little wave. "I'm so sorry," she says, looking at Mrs. Aronowitz. "I wasn't able to make it to the restaurant." Her hair is falling down from its careful bun, which I realize must be the Audrey Hepburn bun, and she looks very red.

"Mindy, I don't understand." Mrs. Aronowitz frowns at my mother, but I can tell from the look on her face that she is more worried than angry. "We waited for you for over an hour." She doesn't say anything about the bill, or the money she gave me for the phone, and that makes everything even worse. The same tense heat I felt in the restaurant flushes my neck.

"I'm really sorry," my mother says, her voice a little shaky and over-bright. "Something came up. Trust me, if you knew why—" Then she stops, gazes at the sidewalk as if searching for something, a key or a coin, she dropped there. I pretend to be busy getting my things out of the car, but really I am trying to do anything to keep Mrs. Aronowitz from catching my eye, and especially not Lainey—why does Lainey have to be here?

Mrs. Aronowitz looks at my mother strangely. "What are you talking about?"

My mother places her hand firmly on my arm, as if I might try to run away, which truthfully, is what I feel like doing. "Nothing." Lainey gives me a hard stare of confusion and something else I can't quite make out.

"Seriously, I'm worried about you," Mrs. Aronowitz says. "You seem very jumpy lately."

My mother tries a smile—a smile anyone could tell isn't real at all, just a slow movement of her mouth. "I'm fine, really." From inside the house I can hear Maxwell's high-pitched bark, and even that sounds slightly off. My mother looks through her bag for her house keys. "Let's go inside, Adie. You must be starving by now."

"We already had lunch." Mrs. Aronowitz has the funniest look on her face, as if she's just on the verge of figuring out the answer to a crossword puzzle, but can't quite think of the right word. "Remember? You were supposed to meet us."

"Right." My mother fake-smiles again. "Of course." She steals another glance behind her; what is she looking for? "We'll just have to do it another time," she says, jangling the keys. I wonder if Mrs. Aronowitz will ever invite us again to a *ladies' day out*, or if that was it, our one chance, and next time she will invite somebody else, who has a daughter who will become best friends with Lainey. I wish I was anywhere other than here, that I could circle up in the sky with one of the birds.

I turn to Lainey. "I'll see you tomorrow," I say, trying to act as if everything is just the same as always.

Lainey looks at me doubtfully. "Yeah, okay," she says, playing with the glass beads of the Chinatown bracelet. The four of us stand silent for a moment, listening to the small *clink-clink* of the beads. The dog barks again and we say good-bye and watch as Mrs. Aronowitz and Lainey drive away. My mother takes a swift glance around and then lets us in the house, pushing me in before her, not even bothering to wipe her feet first, the way she always does. She locks the door and sinks down on the couch.

Maxwell gives a low growl. I pull him by the collar so he is as close to me as possible. "Mom, what happened?"

My mother pulls off her shoes, and I notice how rough and calloused the bottoms of her feet are. She leans back against the cushions and runs her fingers through her hair. "Oh, sweetie, it was so scary." She tells me how she had given herself plenty of time to get to the restaurant, and how she even remembered to put some extra quarters in her bag for the parking meter (at this point I think again about the coins Mrs. Aronowitz gave me for the pay phone), and had made it all the way down Prentice Street, past the service garage where she gets her oil changed, when she looked in her rearview mirror to quickly check her hair and (as she says this I know, even before the words come out, what's coming next) there was a car. A white car, and all of a sudden she realized it had been following her for blocks, maybe all the way from our apartment. It wasn't the kind of car most people would ever really notice—just a plain, normal-looking white car—but she, thank goodness, had noticed it. "It was *them*," she says, her voice small and quiet; a little girl with a secret.

"Mom." I try not to look at her. "There are a thousand white cars."

"No. It was them," my mother insists. She drove around for over an hour, circling the streets downtown, and only when she was sure she lost them for real—*for good*—did she make her way to the Forest. By then we were gone. "You can imagine how terrified I was when you weren't there," she says. "I almost panicked and called the police. But then I realized you had probably just left."

"I really need some water," I say. I lock myself in the bathroom and clutch my stomach. I imagine the wonderful *ladies' day out* we all had, in which my mother sat next to me in the small booth with her Audrey Hepburn hair and laughed at adult things with Mrs. Aronowitz, and Lainey and I played gin rummy for jelly bean stakes across the table. And then, when the bill came, my mother fought with Mrs. Aronowitz over it, insisted on paying for the whole meal, saying, *Oh, no, let me get it. It's the least I can do, you were so sweet to ask us to join you* . . . A small ring of sadness chokes my heart.

Later that night, when I am already in bed reading a book about Helen Keller for social studies class, I hear my mother knocking softly on my door. "Sweetie, are you still awake?" She peeks in. "I just thought of something."

I turn over and clutch the Snoopy pillow I've had since I was a little girl close against my chest. Maybe she's going to tell me that she was just imagining things, that the white car was just that, a car, and the people in it were just normal people out for the day—for all we know, a mother and daughter on their way to meet their friends for lunch at a diner just like the Forest. That she has what my teachers refer to as an *overactive imagination,* and really she's just tired and confused from not getting enough sleep these days and not eating right—not balancing the four basic food groups like we learned in health class. That everything today was obviously a misunderstanding—a silly mistake—and nothing like it will ever happen again.

My mother hovers in the door, halfway in and halfway out. I think about a word from my vocabulary calendar: *threshold.* "I never gave you any money for lunch," she says, her voice sounding a little shy. "I'll leave you some cash to give to Lainey next time you see her."

"Oh. Okay." I lean back against the wooden headboard. It feels solid and stiff against my spine: something grounded and real.

My mother says, "I'm sorry about today, but there was no way I was going to put myself in danger. Or you." I pretend not to hear her. "Well, good night, Adie."

I open the book again, but I can't seem to pay attention, and the words just circle slowly on a track inside my head. I know it is a sin to think this, but in some ways it seems like it would be easier if I couldn't hear anything at all, if I was completely deaf and blind like Helen Keller. I wouldn't have to hear the fear in my mother's voice when she rushes home to tell us about the men she saw outside Douglass Hardware & Novelties, men who looked for all the world as normal as can be, with their plaid flannel work shirts and jeans, but there was something about them—*something she couldn't quite put her finger on*— and when she looked at their faces and saw their vacant, red-rimmed eyes, she knew, just knew, that they were *on something*. I could just sit in the corner and breathe deeply when she and my sister fought over the party Miriam was invited to. I wouldn't have to see the look on my mother's face or notice the slight tremor when she said, *I don't know about that. . . . What kinds of people will be there?* and Miriam, finally fed up, said, *Probably lots of coke addicts,* to which my mother started crying, *That's not funny, Miriam, not funny at all.* I wouldn't have to hear or see any of it and could just curl up tight, in a small quiet place inside my head. But the funny thing about life is, you don't get a choice: I am not Helen Keller, and I can see and hear. And somehow I know that I'm not going to be able to shut my eyes to my mother's fears or block out the sound of her crying. You have to see and hear the things that are right in front of you.

15

The next week in writing class Mrs. Ramirez tells us to write an essay about something special we've done with our family. It would be preferable, she says, if we used it as an *opportunity to explore our feelings* and *get to know ourselves better.* Mrs. Ramirez often gives us homework assignments that she calls "personal writing," asking us to write poems about our dreams, or a time when we were embarrassed. Once she even asked us to imagine ourselves as a body part. I picked the big toe.

Mrs. Ramirez has said that we should think of her as a friend. "Like a big sister," she told us, playing with one of her big plastic beaded necklaces. She has long, thick lashes and blue eye makeup and high heels and truthfully looks nothing at all like anyone's big sister. The boys think she's *fine* and are always fighting over who gets to help her set up the projector when we watch filmstrips.

Mrs. Ramirez also teaches Spanish, where she is Señora Ramirez. Along the back wall of the classroom she has tacked up photographs of Julio Iglesias, along with A-plus essays and group projects. Julio peeks out from between construction-paper maps of Mexico and our reports on the Spanish Civil War, his smile sexy and kind.

Lainey says she's going to write about the time her mother

took her to see the movie *Grease,* just the two of them. "I can't wait to write my essay," she brags. "What are you going to write about?"

"I'm not sure yet." Usually I am okay with writing, but something hard and wooden settles in my stomach when I think about this assignment.

A few days later Mrs. Ramirez hands back the essays. "Very nice work," she says to the kids who have done well. For the kids who didn't do such a good job she just places the paper on their desks and gives them a disappointed look, as if they have hurt her feelings. She is what my mother would call *a very sensitive person.* She stops for a moment in front of Lainey's desk. "I love John Travolta too!" she says. "He's such a cutie." Then she taps me lightly on the shoulder. "Please see me after class, Adie." She crosses the room with a sharp *click-click* of her high heels. Lainey gives me a funny look.

When the bell finally rings I sit still at my desk, pretending to look through my bag for something important. The other kids gather their books and papers and rush out the door as quickly as possible; it's lunchtime. Mrs. Ramirez waits until everyone has left the room, and then she looks at me. "Come over here, Adie." She rummages around in her desk. "Do you want a piece of gum?"

I am too nervous to chew, so I just say, *"Muchas gracias, no."*

Mrs. Ramirez winces at my accent. "English is fine," she says, unwrapping the gum. It's sugarless. "Adie, I'm concerned. How come you didn't turn in an essay? That's not like you."

I am not sure what to say. I stare at the giant map of Mexico that hangs behind her desk, trying to sound out the words in my head. *Acapulco. Mazatlán.* For a moment my mind drifts into a little place of its own, and I think about what it would be like if Mrs. Ramirez was my mother. How she would take me and Miriam to dance parties and to all the R-rated movies our mother won't let us see, like *The Blue Lagoon* and *Little Darlings,* and let me borrow her sparkly tops and makeup, and how all the boys at school would think I was fine too.

"Adie, I asked you a question."

"I don't know." Everything is quiet except for the sound of Mrs. Ramirez chewing her gum and tapping her foot softly against the desk. "I didn't feel like writing about my family."

"Why not?"

"I just didn't."

"But that was the assignment." I don't say anything. There are some moments that go by quickly, when you don't notice what's happening at all, and then there are others where you are stuck, unable to move. This is one of those times. All of a sudden I am crying, the kind of crying that just comes and you cannot stop it.

"What's going on, Adie? Do you want to tell me what's happening?"

I shake my head no and keep my eyes on the floor. A small part of the linoleum floor is missing in the corner, like the missing piece in a jigsaw puzzle, making the whole room look strange, unfinished.

Mrs. Ramirez waits a few moments and then she pats my hand gently. "Adie, I'm going to excuse you from class tomorrow so you can go to Dr. Chu's office, okay?" Dr. Chu is the school guidance counselor. I am not the sort of person who usually goes to the guidance counselor's office or the principal's office or any school office at all. She gets up to erase something from the board. "I'll let him know that he should expect to see you."

The next morning all through homeroom and first and second period I pretend I don't care but really my body feels as if it is tied in a thousand little knots, each tighter than the next. When it is time to go to Dr. Chu's office I make my way down the hall and wait outside and then take a deep breath and knock on his door.

"Adie, there you are. Have a seat." He gives me a smile—one of those awful grown-up smiles that says *let's pretend we're friends.* I make a move to sit down, but then stop. There are two chairs to choose from: one is a plain metal chair like the folding chairs in the auditorium, and the other is exactly the opposite, a big, blue and white comfy chair like the kind you would have at home; it even has a matching blue cushion with white fringe. I wait by the door, wondering which chair he wants me to sit in: it feels like a trick.

Dr. Chu looks at me. "Are you okay, Adie?"

"I'm fine." The second bell rings shrilly, and the sound of kids shouting and rushing to class echoes down the hall. I sit down in the metal chair, hoping it's the right choice, and stare at his smooth gleaming desk, which is the yellow-gold wood color I once heard my mother call *blond wood*. Dr. Chu gets up and takes a file from the large filing cabinet in the corner, and when he puts it down I see that it has my name on it. He opens it up and writes something at the top of the page. I can't see what it is since it's upside down, but even from here I can tell that he has beautiful handwriting, almost like a girl's, the kind of handwriting teachers always give extra credit for.

I have never been in Dr. Chu's office, have never really even talked to him, but just a few weeks ago he gave everyone in the seventh grade an aptitude predictor test that was supposed to help us figure out the answer to the question adults always seem to ask: *What do you want to be when you grow up?* The directions said that the test was *scientifically designed to help us identify our interests and abilities,* and that there were *no right answers,* which I found confusing—did that mean all the answers were wrong? I filled in all of the little oval bubbles with my number two pencil as fast as possible, but the answers didn't come out the way I thought they would. I wanted the test to say that when I grow up I should get a job with animals: a vet, or one of those people who feeds the elephants at the zoo, or maybe even a circus performer: a lion tamer! Instead it said I should be an artist—which just proves the test is broken, since every time I try to paint anything the colors drift all over the place and make a big wet blob—or a teacher. Now Dr. Chu leans forward and looks at me steadily. "Adie, Mrs. Ramirez said that you started crying after class yesterday, after she asked you about your family. She thought you might be having some issues at home?"

I try to speak, but nothing comes out, even though I know exactly what Dr. Chu wants to hear. He wants me to tell him everything, to tell him all about those *issues I'm having at home* so he can write them down in the file with his fancy pen in his A plus handwriting and tuck it away in the little folder. He looks so eager, so excited to hear what I have to say, as if he's one of those contestants on *The Price Is Right* and I might just hand him *the keys to a brand-new car!* "I think she likes to be called Señora Ramirez. At least, that's what she makes us call her."

"Okay, Señora Ramirez." Dr. Chu clears his throat. "Adie, sometimes when kids don't want to talk about their families, it means something difficult is happening at home." He pauses. "Sometimes when kids cry, it means their parents are being mean to them."

I don't say anything.

Dr. Chu looks at me funny, as if I'm an especially tricky knot he has to untie. "Or sometimes it means they're drinking?"

"My mother doesn't drink. She's worried about drugs."

"What do you mean, worried?"

"She thinks there are drug people everywhere." I swallow hard; my spit tastes sour. "She thinks everyone around us is trying to give us drugs. Everywhere we go." Outside, a moth struggles against the window screen, its little paper-brown wings fluttering madly. "She worries about it all the time."

Dr. Chu nods. "Well, Adie, there are a lot of things for parents to be worried about these days. It's not like when I was a kid. Did you know, when I was your age, we used to just leave all our doors unlocked all the time?" He sighs. "And no one even thought about locking up a bike. We just left them outside."

I pick at a splinter that's been stuck in my finger for a long time, maybe from one of the wooden benches in the playground. There is nothing to say to this, it's the kind of thing grown-ups say when they've already forgotten you're there and are just thinking about when they were kids. Dr. Chu gets up to shut the window. "Look, Adie, I want you to feel like you can stop by and talk to me if you need to." Dr. Chu tries another version of a smile. "I'm here every day until five."

I keep my eyes on at the small American flag in the corner, gray and drooping with age. "I'm sort of busy after school," I say, thinking about my sister, who has been staying out later and later. I make an excuse and shuffle out, and as I leave I see Dr. Chu write something else down in his little file.

The next day when I see Mrs. Ramirez she smiles at me and says, "Did you have a nice visit with Dr. Chu?"

"Yes."

She smiles. "Sometimes it's just helpful to talk to someone else, you know? It makes you realize how your problems are just like everybody else's."

Just like everybody else's. I think about the sign that I saw in Dr. Chu's office that said RESPECT OUR DIFFERENCES: BEAUTIFUL PEOPLE COME IN ALL COLORS, SHAPES, AND SIZES, but the thing I've noticed is that in real life, which is not like a school poster at all, no one thinks that's true.

When I tell my sister what happened with Dr. Chu and Mrs. Ramirez and the writing assignment, she just sighs. "Adie, you shouldn't tell people about that stuff."

"Why not?"

"You just shouldn't," Miriam says. She reaches for something in her purse, and I notice a little square wrapper that looks like a piece of candy. "What's that?" I ask, picking it up.

"Jesus, Adie."

"What is it?"

"It's a condom." Her voice is a whisper. "A rubber. Don't tell Mom, okay?"

I nod dumbly. That I understand. But how come Miriam is suddenly so much older, and I'm still a kid? A wave of tiredness floods my body, and I put the condom back in my sister's purse. It's at times like this that I realize that even though it seems as if Miriam is right next to me, solid and real, the truth is that she is on the other side of a window I am just looking through. I just hope she can still see me.

16

A few months ago, when we first moved into the house on Parrott Drive, our new next-door neighbor, Mrs. Demarco, greeted us with a giant glass jar of homemade pesto sauce made with the herbs from her garden. She was the sort of person you can tell is just looking for a new friend. Every few days she'd stop by to say hello and bring us some more sauce. "I really can't go through all of this myself," she'd say, patting her stomach. "I have to watch my figure." My mother just smiled; and it was impossible not to compare the two of them, my mother so slim and put together, Mrs. Demarco's fleshy arms spilling out over her dress.

Mrs. Demarco even came over for coffee a couple of times, to sit and chat with my mother, and I began to think that maybe, just maybe, my mother would start to have friends again: that she might go out and not just lie on the bed or watch TV or jot down notes in her journal. But lately my mother has been keeping the shades tightly closed, even during the day, and not answering the phone. I've seen Mrs. Demarco stop on the steps in front of our house a couple of times, pretending to look at our flowerpots, her head tilted to one side like Maxwell when he's confused.

One day I see her at the Emporium-Capwell department store, bent over a bin of half-price handbags. I wave quickly and try to avoid her, but she follows me into the cosmetics department, where everything is brightly lit and mirrored. Everywhere I look I see a reflection of me, small and contained.

Mrs. Demarco's brown knee-high stockings have rolled down around her ankles, and she's sweating. "How's your mother doing?" she asks, patting her face with a handkerchief.

"She's fine," I say automatically. I know this is the correct response, even though it isn't true at all. What I'd like to say is, my mother—who used to get up every morning at precisely six thirty a.m. without the help of an alarm clock—did not get out of bed today. She went to sleep right after dinner, in the clothes she wore from the day before, and when it was time for bed I had to sneak in quietly and click off her bedside lamp. This morning when I left for school she was curled on her side, her body forming a sinewy *S*.

"Will you tell her, please, that I'd love to see her? Maybe have lunch or something?" She picks up a perfume bottle shaped like a swan and puts it down again quickly.

I nod without saying anything. My mother has told me and my sister to stay away from Mrs. Demarco and her garden. The herbs she's growing have a *funny look to them*. In fact, they look just like marijuana plants, something my mother knows from looking in the *Encyclopedia of World Plants* at the library. "Here's the thing," my mother tells us. "Even the most normal-seeming people are getting stoned and high. Even people like Mrs. Demarco."

A few weeks ago, Mrs. Demarco had taken me around her garden, pointing out all the seedlings that would soon become food. *Oregano. Basil. Rosemary.* I remember how proud she looked, her hair covered with an old-fashioned red-checkered handkerchief, dirty hands toying with the thin little leaves. She gave me a plastic container to take home, full of homemade tomato sauce—*her grandmother's secret recipe*—but my mother just shook her head and poured it all down the drain. ("I would hate for you and Miriam to get inadvertently high," she said, rinsing out the container. "Do you know what the word *inadvertent* means?")

Now Mrs. Demarco is studying me carefully. I try to think of something I can say, something that will make sense of why my mother hasn't returned her phone calls, or answered the rich hum of the doorbell. I'm too embarrassed to tell her the truth— *my mother thinks you're growing pot in your back garden, next to the thyme*—so I just stand there dumbly, looking at myself in the reflection of a makeup mirror.

"Are you okay, Adie? You look a little flushed."

"I'm fine." I don't know what to say to Mrs. Demarco, and I feel ashamed somehow, as if I've done something wrong; something very terrible, which must be kept secret.

I'm relieved when the saleswoman, tall and thin, comes over. "Can I help you?" she asks Mrs. Demarco, looking bored. She's smooth-skinned like the girls in *Seventeen,* with straw-colored hair pulled back in a tight blond bun. "Maybe your daughter would like to try some eyeshadow?"

"I'm not her daughter," I say quickly. It comes out meaner than I intended, and a quick blush spreads over Mrs. Demarco's fat apple cheeks, as if she's been caught stealing something.

The saleswoman coughs slightly. "You can still try it." Close up you can see that her skin isn't perfect after all; it's just mapped over with makeup—a mask on top of a face. I think about my mother's dark, casual prettiness, how she only wears that one shade of lipstick and a little mascara, and feel a rush of pride, even though her beauty, of course, has nothing to do with me.

I turn away and brush the gleaming eyeshadow on my lids. In the package, it looks bright, almost glaring, but on my skin it's nearly invisible.

Mrs. Demarco hands me a tissue. "Is your mother sick again?"

For a panicked moment I think that Mrs. Demarco is talking about the time my mother had to go to the hospital. . . . How she's *delicate* and was in *the loony bin.* . . . And suddenly it seems as if *everyone* must know: the bored saleswoman, the little boy across the aisle tugging at his mother's hand, the teenagers with the frozen yogurt. . . . But then I realize that she's just talking about the flu my mother had last month—she'd stayed in bed for almost two weeks, reading magazines and blowing her nose.

"She's just busy," I say, wiping the shadow off my eyes. I'm not sure where to put the dirty tissue when I'm done, so I just bunch it up and stuff it in my pocket. Suddenly I feel very tired, like a curtain has fallen.

When I get home that afternoon, my mother is sitting cross-legged on the floor, surrounded by a circle of bills and receipts. For a moment she doesn't notice me, and I watch her silently, listening to her count quietly under her breath. Sitting there, in the middle of the circle, she looks almost like a child playing Duck, Duck, Goose.

Then she looks up. "Hey, sweetie." The expression on her face is easy and calm, a trace of my mother the way she used to be. "This place is such a mess, I figured the least I could do is organize the bills."

I take off my jacket and sit down next to her. Seated like this, on the floor, we are almost the same height. I pick up a book of stamps. *American Presidents.* I remember the first day I met Lainey, her little collection of flower stamps, and a funny pang crosses my chest. . . . It all seems like a very long time ago. "Mom, are you sick?"

She looks at me. "Of course not," she laughs, shoving a pile of credit-card receipts into a small plastic envelope. "I'm perfectly healthy." And she does, at that moment, seem perfect: her long legs tucked neatly under her, her hair a shining dark mass. How is it that my mother always looks so neat, so pretty?

"Here," she says, handing me a copy of *People* magazine. "I picked this up for you." I move closer to her and we page through it together, stopping at the pictures of the celebrities, making fun of their clothes and hair. At times like this, my mother's stay at the hospital seems like something that didn't really happen—a schoolyard game I must have played with my friends when I was much younger. It seems impossible that this is the same mother who checks Miriam's arms every few days for track marks, who looks fearfully at any trace of redness in my eyes and asks if I know what heroin is, who reminds us, every morning when we're packing our lunches for school, to *just say no*. Right now, laughing, she seems like everyone else. And knowing this—knowing the way she comes and goes—all I can do is settle in next to her and force myself to remember every detail of this moment. Because soon, I know, it will be gone.

17

~~

When we come back to school after winter break there's a thick blue booklet on each of our desks: *Understanding Your Body: The Adolescent Years.* Our class is starting a special six-week unit on health and reproduction, and everyone is jumpy and excited, as if we're going on a trip.

Mrs. Pallari, usually so self-assured, seems nervous, and her voice is unnaturally high. "For the first few days on smoking, alcohol, and drugs, we'll all be working together in this room," she says, clutching one of the booklets tightly. "After that the boys will go to the gym, and the girls will stay and do a special project with me." There is murmuring all over the classroom, and I hear someone whisper the word *abortion.* Mrs. Pallari looks like she needs something to hold on to.

Lainey leans over the aisle and passes me a note. I wait until Mrs. Pallari, chalk in hand, turns back to the blackboard, and then quietly unfold it in my lap. It's in Lainey's usual purple ink. *Mrs. Pallari is totally freaking out! Let's go to 7-Eleven after school. xxxooo forever, L.* Her writing looks different, and it takes me a minute to figure out why. She has stopped dotting her *I*'s with little circles. I nod at her, but she ignores me; she wants me to write a note back. I rip a piece of paper from my notebook.

Mrs. Pallari passes out a mimeographed handout, still damp

from the machine, and dims the lights. She has set up a film-strip, which she struggles with for a few minutes until one of the boys gets up to help her. I look at the handout, which has a picture of a cigarette and the words "A Young Person's Guide to the Dangers of Smoking." There is a subheading that says "Signs of Addiction." I glance down at the list. None of them apply to me.

The film begins. It opens with a young woman who can barely talk. Her voice is scratchy, abrasive. "I always thought smoking looked cool, like something that would make me seem grown up. But then I found out that you don't have to smoke to be cool. I found out the hard way." I tune her out. Jeremy Bernstein is sitting next to me, his hand down the front of his corduroy pants.

Lainey is looking in her pocket mirror, trying to get her hair to stay behind her ears. She takes out a small pot of lip gloss and dips her finger in it, then slowly brushes it over her lips, as if she's performing a delicate operation, one that requires special girl skills. I can smell it. Strawberry, or maybe cherry.

I turn back to the film. Now there is a big picture of a diseased lung on the screen, and everyone is making noises like they have to throw up. "Quiet down now," Mrs. Pallari says. I think the lung looks kind of interesting, more like a map than an organ.

All of the seventh-graders had to get special permission for this part of the class, a signature from a parent. Some kids aren't allowed to watch the films. They have to go to the library instead, to help the librarian or do homework, and everyone makes fun of them. "If you don't watch the reproduction films you'll never get your period," we tell Kristin O'Leary, even though that isn't true, she already has it.

Miriam forged our mother's signature for me. She's gotten much better at it since she's been doing it a lot lately, to cut class or get out of gym. Her signature looks just like our mother's: big, dramatic letters, proud and upright. My signature never seems to come out the same way twice.

Miriam had to forge the note for me because our mother didn't come home yesterday. Usually she is home by six at the latest. But last night, Miriam and I sat waiting and waiting for her, wondering if maybe she had gone to pick up something for dinner, until finally we thought to check the answering machine. She had left a message for us, saying she would be back tomorrow, or the next day at the latest, and not to worry. And to walk Maxwell and to remember to bring plastic bags to pick up his poop.

I tell Miriam what my mother had said to me that time in the car, about *having to go away sometime.* A look of doubt crosses her face. "I guess it's okay," she says slowly. "She'll probably call us later anyway." Then she smiles. "Just think, we can eat whatever we want." Miriam opens the plastic bag of chocolate chips my mother insists on saving for baking cookies, even though she hasn't baked anything for months. But the little chips are stale, with a strange chalky taste, and we just end up throwing them out.

The house suddenly looks different, full of possibilities, though really, it's just the same place as always. Miriam sneaks some sherry from an open bottle in the back of the kitchen cabinets, and plays her new Foreigner album as loudly as possible, dancing around the living room in her bra (now size 36 C) and underwear. I riffle through the drawers in my mother's old-fashioned roll-top desk, not really sure what I'm searching for. All I find are a bunch of unopened bills and some parking tickets, along with some articles cut out from the paper, about local gangs and drug abuse, arranged in a neat pile with a plastic blue paper clip.

That night my sister and I stay up until one in the morning, surrounded by bags of potato chips, watching reruns of *Mary Hartman, Mary Hartman* and *Welcome Back, Kotter*—shows my mother always insists are *a little on the crude side.* When the "Star-Spangled Banner" plays, we know it's time to put on our pajamas and go to bed.

No one wants to admit it, but with our mother gone, bedtime is scary. I coax Maxwell upstairs, wanting his furry warmth nearby, and climb into Miriam's bed, tucking myself under the bright green fringed bedspread my mother bought for her last year. I'm afraid to turn off the lights, so Miriam leaves them on. "I don't want you to have trouble falling asleep," she says, but I know she wants the light too, and even though the whole house is lit up like a party, we get under the covers, and only then do we talk about where our mother is and what she might be doing.

"Do you think she's by herself?" I ask Miriam, not wanting my mother to be lonely, but also not wanting her to be with anyone but me.

"She's probably with that guy from the supermarket." Miriam pulls the covers over to her side. "I bet they're doing it right now." She means the man who works at Register 8: Ten Items or Less—the one who always tells my mother she's *a dead ringer for Rita Hayworth* (an actress from old movies, my mother tells me, secretly pleased) and how seeing her *makes his whole day.* My mother always smiles kindly and says thank you, and tells me that some men are just born flirts, while Miriam and I like to joke that she should marry him, because then we could sneak more than ten items into the line. But I know Miriam is just trying to make me feel better, that my mother is not with the guy from the supermarket at all.

I flip my pillow over so the cool side is next to my face, but I still can't get comfortable.

"Miriam," I whimper. "Can I get closer to you?"

She makes a clucking noise, like a hen, and scoots nearer to me. "Sure." She smells like lemons, from the special soap she's been using.

I get as close to her as possible, my head nestled in the crook of her arm. Crook of the arm, I think as I fall asleep. A comforting spot with a dangerous-sounding name.

The next morning Miriam and I wake up and pour ourselves some juice and for a few minutes don't say anything. Then my sister stretches slowly and tells me not to worry. "I'm sure Mom will come back later today," she says, opening the freezer.

"Here, let's have ice cream for breakfast." But there is only an old freezer-burned spoonful left at the bottom of the carton.

I finish my juice and then go into my mother's bedroom and open her closet door, feeling like a thief, and having some strange half hope that maybe she'll be hiding inside, playing a trick on us, a game. I imagine her saying, *I'm sorry I scared you, sweetie, but I just wanted to see how the two of you would get along without me for a night, and look, you were so brave. I am so proud of my beautiful girls.* But the closet is just the same as always, except that her old yellow and white embroidered suitcase is not in the corner where it usually sits with shoe boxes piled on top of it. Now there is just an empty space and the shoe boxes are tumbled out on the floor, one of them opened to reveal a pair of fancy dress shoes—black satin heels with a little rhinestone over the toe—that I'm sure my mother has not worn for years. I look through the closet, and then in my mother's drawers, hoping to find a piece of clothing I can wear or take with me to school—right now I want something of my mother's with me, close against my body—but everything is much too big. Finally I put on her favorite orange-striped sweater, even though the sleeves hang over my hands and I have to roll them up several times. *My brave, beautiful girls,* I imagine her saying. *How proud I am of you.*

That afternoon, my sister and I come home from school to find the answering machine blinking bright red, like a warning. It's another message from our mother—much shorter than the first—and her voice is barely there, just a soft, quiet whisper: *Hi, girls, it's me—Mom. I don't want to stay on the phone very long, but I just wanted you to know that I'm safe, and I'll be away for a few more days. Miriam, make sure you lock all the doors and windows at night, and, Adie, drink your milk, remember what the doctor said about your bones. I love you, and I'll see you soon, sweeties. . . . Oh, and remember to give Maxwell his medicine, okay?*

"Fuck, I forgot about the meds," my sister says, staring at Maxwell, who just stares back at her with that empty look dogs sometimes have. Last week he went rustling around the bushes behind the Jewish Community Center and ate something funny—a rotten piece of meat, probably, or something dead—and threw up three or four times, for some reason always in the same spot, right on top of my mother's favorite Afghan blanket. When we took him to the animal clinic, the veterinarian shook his head and told us not to worry and gave us some medicine, a pale pink thick liquid that looks just like Pepto-Bismol, which we have to force down Maxwell's throat.

I open the kitchen cabinet where we keep Maxwell's things—an extra flea collar, dog biscuits, a rubber chew toy shaped like a hamburger—and unscrew the lid, sticky and pink, from the medicine bottle. It was nice of our mother to remember that Maxwell's sick, but why did she call us during the middle of the day (*exactly* at twelve thirty, according to the machine), when she knew we'd be at school and unable to answer the phone?

"Maybe she didn't really want to talk to us," Miriam says, pressing the erase message button before I can stop her. "Message deleted," the machine tells us, its electronic voice strangely cheerful.

"Miriam?"

"What?"

"Do you think we should tell someone?"

My sister looks at me and shakes her head. "She said she'd be back soon, right?"

"I guess so."

"Anyway, if we tell someone we might end up in foster care or something."

"What's that?"

"You know. . . . It's the people who get paid to take care of kids no one else wants."

"They get paid?"

"Yeah, and they take all the money for themselves and barely feed the kids anything real to eat."

"How much do they get paid?"

"Jesus, Adie, I don't know." My sister pours some dry dog

food into Maxwell's bowl and stirs in a little of the canned food he likes.

Even though our mother is not around, I do everything the same as always. I leave for school at seven forty-five, which gives me just enough time to get to my first period English class before the morning bell rings. After school I come straight home to give Maxwell a dog biscuit snack and take him for a quick walk around the block. Then I settle in front of the TV to play Space Invaders on the Atari set my mother brought home for Hanukkah—crouching in front of the screen for so long that my legs cramp with muddled pain. At night I brush my teeth for three whole minutes, trying not to cheat, counting out the seconds slowly, the way the dentist told me to.

But Miriam changes everything around: she smokes her cigarettes right in the living room, using one of my mother's hand-painted teacups for an ashtray, and puts her feet up on the couch—shoes and all. She calls the registrar's office at school and, without even practicing, impersonates our mother: *I'm afraid my daughter Miriam has picked up a terrible case of strep throat and won't be in school for the rest of the week.*

"If Mom can take a break, so can I," she tells me, lighting a cigarette with the skull and crossbones Zippo lighter her new boyfriend gave her. She hands me the lighter, but I have a hard time making it work.

She's been keeping the boyfriend a secret from our mother. His name is Julien, which sounds like a girl's name, but really he's just French-Canadian. He's older, a student at USC, Miriam likes to brag, even though he has dropped out. Just for a semester, she says. He spends half of his time living at his parents' house near the beach, and the other half living out of his van, the windows shrouded with batik curtains, so he doesn't always smell that good. On the back of the van there's a bumper sticker that says GAS, GRASS, OR ASS: NO ONE RIDES FOR FREE. "What does that mean?" I ask.

Miriam looks away. "Never mind."

Julien has a guitar and always seems to be playing the same

song, which he tells me is called "American Pie," stumbling over the chords and getting them wrong and swearing at himself. But he's nice to me. "Let Adie choose," he says, when we're trying to decide what to watch on TV. He brings me big bags of licorice candies and helps me with my algebra homework, which has become harder than ever, a jumble of numbers tossed loose on a page. Even Maxwell likes him, but I think that's just because of the way he smells.

After our mother has been gone for a few more days, Miriam lets him sleep over. It's getting colder, and there's no reason for him to sleep all by himself in the van, which has a window that doesn't shut all the way. "It's nice to have a man around the house," Miriam tells me (sounding for a brief moment, just like our mother), even though Julien is really only nineteen. Of course, this means I have to go back to sleeping alone in my room. I make Maxwell stay with me, even though he whines and scratches all night at the door to be let out. Lying alone in the darkness I listen to the sounds coming from Miriam's bedroom: Julien strumming his guitar, and Miriam's soft laughter, and then some other sounds that I realize must be sex.

For the next couple of nights we eat in the dining room, television off, just like a real family. Julien sits at the head at the table, joking about his beautiful wife and kid. Maxwell huddles near us, begging for scraps. Everything we eat is fast food, paid for with the giant jar of change my mother keeps in the broom closet, or out of a can, which Miriam lets me open with the electric can opener. But even with the canned soup and the buckets of fried chicken, it feels more like a family than anything I've ever seen.

18

The next weekend Julien says he wants to have a few people over: just a couple, he promises Miriam. Some of the guys he knows from his old summer job at the gas station, a few others from school. Some beer and pizza, no big deal. Why not? He balances the guitar on his hip and looks at my sister.

Miriam doesn't say anything. I can see her mapping it out in her head. It's been a long time since we've had anyone visit the house at all. Miriam stopped inviting her friends over when my mother kept asking them if they knew anyone who smoked pot, if they were aware of any sort of *drug problem* at their school. (*Have some more ziti,* she'd say. *Did you hear about those kids at Crescent Valley High who were picked up on drug charges?*)

"Just a few people," Julien says, resting his hand on her back, a gesture that makes me think of petting a dog.

Miriam gives in. He is very persuasive, especially when he offers to pay for everything and clean up after. Julien calls a nearby liquor store to see if they deliver kegs. He gets in touch with his friends from his old job and tells them to bring their girlfriends. I can invite Lainey because she looks older (she gets stopped on the street by men, real men, more often than you'd think), but that's it, no more kids allowed.

"Can I stay up for the whole thing?" I ask Miriam.

"Of course," she says, looking surprised. She ruffles my hair, something she's never done before. "You don't have to ask my permission."

That evening, I try on four or five different outfits, trying to get just the right combination. Finally I settle on a pair of jeans with different colored stars embroidered on the butt and a light blue tank top borrowed from Lainey. It almost makes me look as if I have breasts. "You'll need a real bra soon," Miriam says, studying my chest.

Miriam herself is blooming like a bride. Once she gave in to the idea of the party she got excited. She made a list, in purple pen on a yellow-lined piece of notepaper, of what we need: chips, dips, soda, beer. She is asking people to bring certain things: ice, for instance, or a bong. Some people don't have a car and can't get here by bus without switching several times, so she's assigned others to pick them up. My mother always says that Miriam has good organizational skills.

Normally, Miriam is a little possessive of her beauty products. "Those are fucking *expensive*," she says whenever she catches me pawing through them. But for the party she gives me a *head-to-toe makeover,* just like in the fashion magazines. First she helps me feather my hair. When she's done I brush it out and mist it with hair spray, keeping my eyes closed as instructed. Then she unwraps a brand-new eyeshadow, the kind with three different colors, and gently brushes my lids. My eyes look like peacock feathers when she's finished. They are so shimmery and soft-looking that I want to touch them, but Miriam tells me not to.

Julien knocks on the bedroom door, coming in before we can stop him. He laughs when he sees us, half dressed but all made up. "You look great," he tells me, winking at Miriam. I can feel myself blushing under the makeup.

My sister steps back and looks at her handiwork. "She does look good." I can tell that she's genuinely pleased, and for a moment I catch a glimpse of Miriam the way she used to be—when she looked especially proud of one of her watercolors or sketches. In a small way, I'm a work of art.

Julien grabs my hand and forces me into an awkward, shuffling dance, even though there's no music on. "Adie's going to be the prettiest girl there," he says, shifting me around the room, humming "Stairway to Heaven" in a tuneless whine. Miriam watches us with a quiet half smile; something in her eyes is clouded, older than usual. Standing in the doorway, her long hair wet from the shower, she is a shadow version of my mother. For a moment I imagine it really is my mother standing there, proudly watching me get ready for my first real party, thinking how nice I look, how grown up I've become. The music gets louder, and I become more graceful, my hair swinging to the beat. Then Miriam says, "Fuck, they'll be here soon," the music stops, Julien lets me go, and everything is back to normal.

A few months ago Lainey and I snuck in to see *Fast Times at Ridgemont High,* a movie my mother didn't want me to see because it has marijuana in it, and that is what the party reminds me of: teenagers and beer and dancing. At first everything was quiet, and then all of sudden dozens of people showed up, some of them people my sister has never seen before. Girls in clingy Ocean Pacific shorts; boys pretending not to look, but studying them carefully. There are beer cans everywhere. Someone has already thrown up on the lawn. I watch the crowds that have suddenly turned our house, usually so quiet and still, into a living, breathing thing.

Lainey is impressed, and for once I feel cooler than her, more confident. "This is totally fucking rad!" she keeps saying, over and over again, even though she absolutely has to be home by midnight, or her parents will *pitch a shit fit.* (This is how Lainey talks now; every other sentence has to have a swear word in it.) No one speaks to us, but I've seen some of the boys staring at Lainey's purple tube top and tight black pants. She plays with her long curly hair, flipping it first this way, then that, pretending not to notice, sipping daintily at a plastic cup filled with beer. The music gets louder, and I remember how my mother is always telling us to *turn down the music, you'll make yourself deaf.* A small hot shiver of fear shimmies down my back as I think about where she might be. . . .

"I can't believe how lucky Miriam is," Lainey shouts over the music. "Julien is so fine." She leans closer to me. "Where did she meet him?"

"I don't know." I try not to think about how all the beer cans are leaving rings on my mother's old oak furniture, how some of the kids are throwing the couch cushions back and forth, much too close to the glass centerpiece in the middle of the coffee table. "At the mall, I think."

"Hey, wouldn't it be weird if he turned out to be a murderer or something? Like the Zodiac Killer?"

I ignore her and try to stand up straighter. My hair, tamed by Miriam, is still behaving itself. I like the brittle, metallic taste of the glitter lipstick she let me borrow, the heavy weight of my lashes, coated with mascara. There is something about the loud music, the clear night sky, the noisy energy of it all that makes me feel older.

Or maybe it's just the beer. Before the party, Julien took me aside and warned me not to have too much. "You're so tiny, it'll go right to your head," he said, and he was right. For the first time in my life, I'm a little drunk. The alcohol has taken over my body quietly, a gentle, soothing warmth. I float on its edge. As I weave my way through the crowded rooms, clutching at the furniture to steady myself, I realize: this is what it means to be an adult.

Miriam sees me holding on to the back of a chair. "Go lie down for a bit," she says, handing me a glass of water. Her voice has a funny lilt; I think she might be a little drunk too. "And whatever you do, try not to throw up." She looks around. "We'll have enough to clean up as it is."

The room swims prettily before me. I make my way down the hall to my mother's room, thinking I'll curl up under the thin cotton blanket she has draped over her bed. But there are already a couple of people there: a tall guy with long hair and bad skin and one of the senior girls from Miriam's school, making out on the bed. The girl squeals when she sees me and the guy looks up and laughs. "Is this your room?" I back out slowly and wander around the house, trying to find Lainey, but I don't see her anywhere. It's almost midnight, and I wonder if she's already left.

Someone turns the music up even louder, and I can feel the bass reverberate in my chest. Our stereo, a giant set of black boxes stacked on top of one another, is expensive and new; my mother bought it after the last move. (*A welcome home gift*, she had called it.) "Don't touch that," I say, even though everything in the house has been touched by now.

And then we hear the sirens.

A police car pulls up in front of the house, its flashing lights sending rays of color through the night. I can hear the buzz of the radio, an authoritative *brrzzz brrzzz*. Everyone starts shouting.

"Oh, fuck," says Miriam. I look out the window. Two officers get out of the car and walk across the lawn.

Everyone scatters and runs, pulling on jackets and shoes, chugging down the last of their beer. A swell of car motors start up noisily, all at once, and the cars take off down the street. Outside, one of the officers looks at the other and shrugs his shoulders.

The doorbell rings, even though the door is open.

Miriam looks scared. She turns to Julien for help. He puts his arm around her and quickly sweeps some empty beer cans into a garbage bag. "Relax," he says. "Everyone here was twenty-one, okay?"

Miriam nods and looks at me. "You've got that, Adie?"

"Sure." I watch as Miriam smooths down her shirt and tucks her hair behind her ears. Then she goes to the door.

The officers tell her that they've received complaints from the neighbors about the noise from the party, which is obvious, and where are her parents?

"My mother's away for the weekend." Miriam says this with as much confidence as she can muster, but her voice is shaking. The officers ask her to step aside, and they begin looking around, taking in the beer cans and keg, but not the bong, which somehow made it out with the shuffle of kids.

The older officer looks at Miriam's friend Bev DeAngelo,

who is sprawled out on our living room couch. "Is she okay?" It turns out that Bev has passed out. The officer is about to call an ambulance, but then Bev sort of shakes herself awake and vomits all over the couch. The officer pats Bev on the hand. "Okay," he says. "I'm going to send for someone to drive you home." He turns to my sister. "It looks like things got a little out of hand here."

Miriam doesn't say anything. She looks very quiet and small, not like my sister at all. Maxwell comes over to nuzzle her, but she pushes him away and he slinks back into the corner.

The younger officer turns to me. "Do you have anything to drink? Water, I mean."

He follows me into the kitchen, which is a mess of junk food bags and beer cases. He opens up the cabinet himself and pours a glass of water from the tap.

"We have bottled," I offer.

"That's okay." The officer drinks the whole glass at once and rinses it out in the sink, which I would have done for him. Then he sits down at the kitchen table, next to the telephone.

"So where's your mom? We're going to have to call her."

I tell him I don't know.

He raises an eyebrow at me. "You don't know?"

I try to fix it. "My sister knows."

We go back into the living room, where the other officer is already asking Miriam some questions. My sister is crying, the snot running down her face like a little girl. The officer pulls a tissue out his pocket and hands it to her quietly. "Hush now," he says, his voice surprisingly soft. "Everything's going to be okay."

Everyone seems to be speaking very slowly. I listen to the conversation, but barely hear it.

It is Julien, finally, who tells them that Miriam and I don't know where our mother is—that she's been away for a week and has only left a couple of messages on the answering machine. As for the party, it was his idea, and he will take responsibility for what's happened. "The whole thing's my fault," he says, taking out his driver's license to show the officers, as if he's been pulled over for a speeding ticket.

The officers wave it aside. It turns out that they are not that interested in hearing about the party or the noise or even the alcohol. They are much more interested in figuring out where my mother is. "When did you say she left?" the older one asks my sister.

"Monday," my sister sniffles. "In the afternoon, I think."

Some phone calls are made. The senior officer tells us that we will receive a call in the morning from Children's Services—not too early in the morning, because it's the weekend and none of us are infants, but sometime around ten or eleven, and we'd better be there to answer it. We should not avoid the phone call; if we do he will have to come back with a court order and place us in some kind of custody. If they can't find our mother within forty-eight hours there will be a lot of paper work to fill out, let me tell you, and nobody likes that, right?

I nod dumbly as his words pass over me. I don't usually stay up this late, and it's getting harder for me to make sense of what's happening. They throw questions at us, one after another.

"If you had to guess, where do you think she'd go?"

"Is there any place she's talked about—a favorite town?"

"Did she ever mention wanting to visit someone in another city?"

Miriam and I stumble over the questions. I suddenly realize how little I know about my mother. Where has she traveled in the past? She spoke once about visiting London, when she was in her twenties, but she obviously didn't go there. Does she have any relatives, even second or third cousins, that she might have decided to visit? Miriam and I look at each other. We're really not sure. I feel ashamed: aren't these things we're supposed to know?

The younger officer clears his throat. "I have to ask you something difficult." He looks at the other officer, as if for permission. "Does your mother ever talk about hurting herself?"

At first, I think he just means falling down or burning a hand on the stove. But then Miriam answers. "She would never do anything like that," she says firmly. "She would never kill herself." The officers exchange glances, and one of them writes something down on his small pad.

I don't know whether to believe my sister. How can she be so certain? Now that the police are asking me questions, I realize that I don't even know what year my mother was born, when her life began—how would I know if she was thinking about ending it?

After they leave Julien just looks at us. "Do you want me to stay?" he asks my sister. Then he catches the look in her eyes and says, "Tell you what. I'll just camp out here in the living room."

By the time Miriam and I get to bed it's already past three in the morning. I can't sleep, but it feels better just to curl up someplace dark and warm. I lie awake, clutching my pillow, eyes open. Studying the shadows on the wall, wondering what else I don't know about my mother.

By the next morning, the police have tracked her down. It was easy enough to find her; all they had to do was follow the trail of credit card receipts.

When the hotel manager knocked on the door and told her she had a phone call, she panicked. Was this some kind of trick? But when she found out it was the police, calling about her children, she took the call.

What she had done, we are told, wasn't illegal. There's no law against going on a trip and leaving a child, who at the age of thirteen is really an adolescent, in the care of an older teenager. If both kids are in good health and continue to attend school, what you are doing may look weird or seem like you're a bad parent, but it's not against the law. You do, however, have to tell people where you're going. The police officer explains all of this to us, sounding a little bored, as if he's had to explain it many times before.

Immediately after she hears from the police, my mother calls us and tells us she's coming right home. That it will take her about five hours to make the drive, assuming she doesn't hit too much traffic. We should think about what we want for dinner. She hasn't had pizza for a while and would like to order one, the kind with the thin crust, not the thick one, which is really too thick as far as she's concerned. Have we been taking good care of Maxwell?

"It'll be good to come home," she says. "I've missed you, Adie." Her voice, on the telephone line, comes through clearly, no static at all. It's as if, as they say, she's right next door.

19

It's almost noon. My mother should be back in just a couple of hours, and I'm excited to see her. And nervous. And scared. And angry. A whole jumble of emotions that add up to a sad, muddled kind of relief. But Miriam has taken her bags out of the closet and started to pack.

It's time for her to leave, she tells me. She's old enough to be on her own, and Julien wants her to go north with him. He has a friend who runs an organic farm in Oregon, near Ashland, where they have the Shakespeare festivals. They can get jobs there, he promises, picking apples and shoveling manure. The weather there is much colder, but it's supposed to be beautiful, and there's a freshwater lake where everyone goes swimming. Nude, she says.

"What's manure?" I ask.

"Horse shit."

Miriam's going to fit as much stuff as she can in Julien's van, though she doesn't want to weigh it down too much, since it has trouble getting up hills as it is. Julien keeps bringing it into the shop, but they still can't figure out what the problem is. Probably just age.

I sit on the edge of Miriam's bed, watching as she goes through her things. She pulls a blouse from a hanger, a brown one with small yellow and pink flowers. It's 50 percent polyester, won't wrinkle. She puts it in her duffel bag and throws a box of cigarettes in after it, then changes her mind and takes one out and lights up.

Miriam has always been logical and unsentimental—a *cold girl*, a friend of my mother's once said. But I can tell this is difficult even for her.

I make my final plea. "Take me with you."

"I can't. You know that." She takes a drag on her cigarette, in the detached way she's picked up from Julien, but I can tell how scared she is, and her eyes beg me for forgiveness. Never has Miriam looked as beautiful as she does now, frozen in the moment of leaving me.

I can feel the tears streaming down my face. I've learned how to cry quietly, without making a sound.

Miriam throws her favorite jeans and shirts, makeup and shampoo into an old green gym bag. She hesitates over her perfume collection, the tiny glass bottles of Promise and Elixir, mostly shoplifted from the drugstore counter, and decides that they're too much trouble.

I try to stay calm, though all I want to do is grab her and keep her from leaving. "What am I going to do?"

Miriam stubs out the cigarette and zips her bag. "Live through it."

After Miriam leaves I wander slowly through the house, picking up dirty glasses and emptying ashtrays. There's a lot to clean up. I decide to start with the refrigerator, which is filled with half-eaten pizza slices and Chinese takeout. The smell of sour milk and rotting vegetables almost makes me sick. There's a huge pile of plates in the sink, and I leave them for last. The dishwasher has been broken for a long time, and I never understood why my mother didn't seem interested in fixing it. Now, as I wash the enormous pile of sticky dishes one by one, I see how comforting the hand bath of hot water and soap can be.

I run the vacuum cleaner, humming along with its steady drone, and change the sheets on both my bed and Miriam's, since she'll have to come back after a few days. She can't live in a rusty old van with Julien, not the Miriam I know, who is so attached to her favorite television shows, her nightly hot bath with scented salts, her record collection.

I clean all morning and afternoon, stopping only to take a quick shower and walk Maxwell around the block. After everything my mother's been through, I don't think she should have to come home to a messy house. Also, I want her to see that we did just fine without her, that we're not babies, that *we can take care of ourselves.*

I think about a litter of feral kittens I once saw, big eyed and shy. Calico cats, with fur that was all different colors. For a few weeks they lived in the bushes near the school parking lot, cute and fierce all at once. Some of the teachers brought them food. Then, one day, they were simply gone.

When my mother finally walks in the door I'm so relieved to see her that at first I don't ask where she's been. I'm satisfied just to see her sitting on the couch, legs tucked under her, sipping her favorite drink: seltzer water with cranberry juice and a slice of lime. I make it for her and serve it in a tall chilled glass, just as she's taught me.

"Thank you, sweetie," she says to me. "This really hits the spot." Her eyes are puffy with tiredness, but she looks just as pretty as ever, her hair ponytailed with a rubber band.

I haven't told her yet that Miriam has left with Julien, that by now they're probably almost all the way to Sacramento. That Miriam really isn't ready for this, that most of her sweaters are cotton, not wool—how will she stay warm in the damp weather?

Instead I lie and say that Miriam is staying over at Bev DeAngelo's house for the night. "She was a little upset that you went away like that," I say carefully. "Without telling us where you were going."

My mother makes a face, but says she understands. Miriam has been so temperamental lately. "It's something all adolescents go through," my mother sighs. "Hormones and all that."

My mother putters around the room, looking at the mail

piled up by the door, checking the coupons in the weekly circular. Finally I get her to tell me what happened.

She was at the grocery store, trying to decide between the different kinds of lima beans, when she heard someone coughing behind her. "A very strange coughing," she says to me, gesturing with her hands, as if they might produce the sound of the cough.

When she turned around, she saw them. You know, *them*.

"Who?" I ask.

"The guys from the parking lot." My mother suddenly gets nervous. She gets up to check that the windows are locked and the curtains completely drawn. "The ones with the white car, the Continental."

Somehow they had found her. For almost a half hour she had been in the grocery store, trying to figure out what to make for dinner, and it wasn't until that moment that she realized she was being followed!

My mother was so frightened that she didn't even bother to pay for her groceries. Instead she left the shopping cart right where it was, in the middle of Aisle 4: Canned Goods, and ran out of the store. She drove home as fast as she could, breaking her own driving rules and running the lights, and threw some clothes and toiletries, just random things, into the yellow and white embroidered suitcase. She was glad, to tell the truth, that Miriam and I were at school when it happened. It would have been difficult to explain everything, especially to Miriam, who was always so full of questions, and she had to move quickly.

The men from the parking lot hadn't followed her from the store, hadn't, thank God, seen where we lived. "That would have been the end," my mother says. But if they were as crafty as she suspected it was only a *matter of time* before they tracked her down again.

She drove as fast and far as she could. It wasn't until the tank started to dip low, the little red light burning its warning, that she pulled over at a gas station. There, unable to eat, she bought a diet soda and a local map. It was getting late and she had no idea where to stay for the night, wasn't even sure if there were any motels nearby.

I try to imagine what I would do in her situation, alone and lost in a strange town. "Why didn't you ask someone at the gas station?"

"I was being followed." My mother frowns at me as if I've broken a rule. "I wasn't about to have a conversation with someone about where to stay."

Fortunately, the next exit, on a quiet stretch of road, had two motels. She took a chance and picked the one on the right side, which turned out to be a good decision. She considered asking for a room facing the front, so she could look out the window and see who pulled into the parking lot, but decided that it would look too suspicious. "Most people want a room in the back, where it's quieter," my mother says, finishing the last of her seltzer and cranberry juice. "And I didn't want to call attention to myself."

"Right," I say automatically. I imagine my mother checking in for the night, glancing nervously at the door to make sure no one had followed her. Would a clerk remember her face or voice? It seems impossible that they wouldn't. My mother is so pretty, the kind of woman people always notice.

She stayed at the motel for a couple of days and nights, mostly watching TV, only leaving the room for quick trips to the snack machine, which was well stocked with peanuts and potato chips. But she soon realized that for safety's sake she'd better keep moving. Anyway, she was getting tired of eating out of the machine. "You can't live on that kind of food," she says. "It's disgusting."

For the next couple of days, she followed random roads and highways. One night she stayed at a small family-owned motel; the next at a bed and breakfast. A few times she thought she saw the men in the white Continental, but she wasn't sure. "I wasn't taking any chances," she tells me. She would purposely circle around and keep her route as confusing and illogical as possible, to throw them off the scent.

"The good thing is that I got to see a lot of places I'd never been," she says. "California really is a beautiful state."

I open the bag of pistachios my mother bought from a roadside stand. "I wish you'd told us where you were," I say, as carefully as possible. I'm worried that if I say the wrong thing she'll run away again, leaving me alone, this time without my sister. I begin shelling the pistachios one at a time, a little shakily.

"I couldn't take that chance, sweetie. They might have been able to track me down." She picks up a pistachio and runs her finger over its smooth shell. "These are the kind without the salt." She pops one in her mouth, cracking the shell loudly with her teeth, and sighs. "Anyway, enough about all that. What's been going on around here?"

I rush through everything I can think of, telling her about my classes at school; how Mr. Markowitz, the history teacher, was fired for looking funny at the eighth-grade girls, and how some people are saying it's anti-Semitism, but it really isn't because he does look at them funny; how Lainey's oldest cousin was in a car accident on Potrello Road but is fine now. My mother asks lots of questions, wanting all the details, eager to catch up on everything she's missed. Maxwell sits at the floor by her feet, occasionally wagging his tail for no reason at all, refusing to leave her side. "What a good boy you are," my mother coos, stroking his ears. She's the only person he lets touch his ears at all.

I can hear myself speaking, laughing even, taking part in what sounds like a conversation. The thought of asking my mother what happens next is too scary, even though she seems calm now, at once rested and alert, as if she took a trip to one of those mineral spas with the bubbling, healing waters, instead of hiding out in strange motel rooms like a runaway. I sweep the pistachio shells into a little pile, my fingers sticky and pink, and look around. I help my mother bring her things in from the car, being careful not to let the yellow and white embroidered suitcase touch the ground, hoping with everything inside me that Miriam will come home soon.

Early the next morning I am getting ready for school when my mother comes rushing into my room, crying and clutching a piece of paper. It's a note from Miriam, written on the yellow Garfield stationery I gave her for her last birthday. The paper comes with a matching set of yellow envelopes, with a picture of Garfield's face and a place to write the address, but Miriam did not use one of the envelopes. She just left the folded note by itself on top of my mother's dresser, next to her jewelry box.

My mother sits on the edge of my bed and chews nervously at her fingernails, something she is always warning me and my sister not to do. "Read it," she says.

I can tell my sister wrote the note in a rush—the writing is a scrawled mess across the page, not her usual neat handwriting at all. Even the letters themselves look as if they are in a hurry and trying to get away. It says: *Mom, I know you're coming home soon, and I'm sorry about this and don't freak out, but I really need to get out of here for a while. I'm going away with a friend. I don't know how long I'll be away for, but I'll get in touch soon. Please don't try to find me. I just need to find myself and be free. Peace & Love, Miriam.* She's drawn a peace sign and a heart next to the words *peace* and *love*. I think she did this to try to make my mother feel a little better, but of course nothing can make her feel better about finding out that Miriam has run away, definitely not a stupid heart and peace sign drawn on a piece of Garfield stationery.

A cool chill of fear and anger coats my stomach as I look at the note. I think part of me still believed that Miriam hadn't *really* left, that I would wake up this morning and she would be there, hogging the bathroom and complaining that we were out of her citrus-scented body lotion, the kind I always think smells like lemonade. I figured she and Julien might have driven for an hour or two in the rusty old bumpy van, at first holding hands and singing rock songs from the radio, but then it would have gotten darker and she would have realized how silly, how wrong, the whole plan was. She would have asked Julien to pull over by the side of the road (making sure he put his blinkers on; my sister is always very safe about things like that), and then she'd turn to him with that fixed look she always gets when she *really means business,* and she would say, *I think this craziness needs to stop right now.* She would tell him to turn the van around and drive her back to Las Palmas, *thank you very much.*

She was only a few months away from graduation, and it didn't make sense for her to go to Oregon now, they could always go later, during the summer, when it was more convenient. . . .

My mother takes the note from me and stares at it again, as if there is a secret code buried deep in Miriam's handwriting that she might be able to figure out. Her face is wet with tears. "I don't understand, Adie. You told me she went to her friend Bev's house."

At first I was going to defend Miriam, was going to tell my mother that Miriam was fed up with how crazy things were around here and had to run away, but now I am so angry with her for actually having done so that I just say, "That's where she said she was going." I open my drawer and try to find some matching socks. "I can't believe she lied to me."

My mother bites her lip. "Oh, God, Adie. What are we going to do?"

"It's okay," I say. "She'll be back soon."

"How do you know?"

"Because she will." Outside, a cloud passes over the sun, suddenly dimming the room. I think about how this is just like the conversation Miriam and I had when our mother left last week, when Miriam told me not to worry. "*You* came back, right?"

"Yes. Yes, I did." My mother looks relieved at this. "You're right, Adie, as always. Of course you're right." She grabs my hand excitedly. "She'll probably be back today." Her fingers squeeze mine in a warm, sweaty grip. "Or tomorrow."

"Definitely," I say, trying to ignore the tight pain in my chest. "Tomorrow at the latest."

My mother starts pacing the room, planning out what we're going to do when Miriam returns. She doesn't want to make too big deal of it, because it isn't that big a deal in the first place— since obviously my sister isn't really going to run away—but maybe we should do something special, just to show my sister that there are *no hard feelings*. "Sometimes people just have these little misunderstandings," my mother says. "Especially mothers and daughters." She hurries out the door, telling me that she's going to head to Safeway, to see what's *on special*—

maybe we can dig the grill out of the garage and clean it off and have barbecue chicken. "Or ribs," she says. "Your sister loves those."

"Okay." My mother has left Miriam's good-bye note on my bed. I fold it up and stick it between the pages of an issue of *Seventeen* magazine.

When I come home from school that afternoon there are bags and bags of groceries, and the whole house is filled with a heavy, almost suffocating warmth: my mother has baked a chocolate layer cake with white frosting. "From a mix," she says modestly, but that still counts, after all, *baking is baking.* I help my mother unpack and put away my school things and sit down with her in the living room to do my history homework. We are on the French Revolution, and I try to distract myself by looking at the pictures of the guillotine and its scary blade for cutting off heads. My mother nervously pets the dog and pretends to read a copy of a magazine with Brooke Shields on the cover, but she keeps flipping back to the beginning, and every few minutes she gets up to peek out the front window to see if my sister is there.

I mark my place in the history book and get up to stand by the window with her. Everything is very still outside and there is nothing to see but the same old road stretching out in front of us. "I'm sure she'll show up any second," I tell my mother.

"You think so?" she says to me, her eyes still hopeful.

"Of course," I say, and a small, tucked-away part of me believes it. But that night we end up sitting at the table all by ourselves, with a giant platter of barbecue ribs between us. My stomach is twisted into a stiff little knot, and my mother just looks at the food, not eating anything. "I guess I'm not feeling very hungry, after all," she says, giving a little of the meat to the dog and putting the rest in the freezer. My mother and I stay up a little later than usual, pretending to keep busy with tooth brushing and face washing, and then say good night.

The next morning my mother gets up early and puts on her silk robe, the one with the gold and purple flowers and the fake pearl buttons. She pours herself some coffee and a bowl of cereal. I sit across from her, trying to swallow my toast and peanut butter, scanning the comics page.

"Don't worry," I tell her. "She'll be back tonight."

My mother looks at me. "Of course she will." We go back to our breakfasts, pretending that nothing has changed.

But something has changed in me. From this point on, I will understand that there are stories behind people, sort of like shadows. My mother's story is not yet clear to me, though its shadow is beginning to take shape.

20

〜

The next few weeks feel different from usual: quiet, dream-like. Miriam doesn't come back, for one thing. Right after she left I put a couple of chocolate bars and a vase filled with daisies on her nightstand, so she'd have something nice waiting for her when she came back. After a few days I threw out the flowers and ate the candy myself.

A regular person would call to say hi, but not Miriam. Instead she sends us a postcard every few days. She likes the ones with pictures of wildlife scenes. A beaver hard at work, building a dam. A family of deer, mottled and soft, standing in a meadow with the sun setting behind them. The cards, written in all capitals, are filled with descriptions of the beauty of the drive, the fresh fruit at the roadside stands, but not much else. *Today I saw the most beautiful sunset.* Or, *You would not be-lieve how big the watermelons are here!* We put them all on the refrigerator, one after the other, in the order they arrive.

My mother calls the police, and they take down Miriam's de-scription, but there's nothing they can really do about it. There's a difference between being missing or kidnapped, and just run-ning away. They do not have the resources for that sort of thing, they apologize, especially for someone who is almost eighteen and keeps sending postcards saying what a nice time she's hav-ing. There are just too many real crimes to worry about.

At first, my mother jumps for the phone every time it rings, thinking it might be Miriam. She answers with a breathless "Hello?" and I can see in her face how relieved she'd be if it was Miriam on the line. But it never is. It's as if Miriam is playing a joke on my mother, a long, drawn-out joke that is not funny at all, and that doesn't really have a punch line.

At the end of one postcard (a couple of bear cubs, splashing in a river), Miriam writes that she's staying someplace without a phone, but she'll call us as soon as she gets one. *Hope you're doing well!*

My mother is infuriated. "She could call us collect from a pay phone."

With Miriam gone, my mother becomes more reclusive than ever. She turns down an invitation to a neighborhood barbecue, pleading a headache. One of the men from the Jewish Community Center wants to ask her out, has had his eye on her for a long time. According to Lainey's mother, he's *very eligible,* a patents lawyer and a professional-level tennis player. "How often do you find a combination like that?" she tells my mother, her voice a suggestive purr. "You should at least let him take you to dinner."

But my mother isn't interested in dating or seeing anybody. Once she realizes that Miriam's not going to call, she doesn't even bother picking up the phone. When it rings, I say, "I'm sorry, my mother's not here right now. Can I take a message?" I dutifully write the names on a small notepad set aside for this very purpose, but my mother rarely calls anyone back.

After a few weeks, my sister finally calls. My mother is at the hair salon, getting her roots touched up, and I can tell Miriam is relieved she won't have to speak to her.

My sister's voice sounds smooth, mature, and very far away. "How's Maxwell?" she asks.

I try to think of what's new with Maxwell, who is sitting on the living room rug, scratching himself. "He had to get a flea dip."

Miriam laughs. "He'd hate it here then." She and Julien are

crashing at a friend's place near Ashland, sleeping on the living room floor. There are bugs everywhere, the biggest mosquitoes Miriam's ever seen, and she has to sleep with all the windows closed. "You should see my face," she says. "It's covered with bites."

I tell Miriam, without trying to make her feel bad, that our mother is worried about her. That she wishes she'd come home, or at least give us a way to reach her.

Miriam's voice dips to a snarl. "She should talk." There's an awkward moment in which we are both silent, and then she says, "Adie, are you all right?"

"I guess so." More than anything, I don't want Miriam to hang up, and I'm scared of giving the wrong answer. So I just say, "Can I come visit you?"

"Not now." Miriam clears her throat. Is she crying? "Later, when Julien and I get settled. I can take you swimming in the lake." There are noises in the background, some shouting, and I hear Miriam talking to another person.

Then she comes back on. "I've gotta go. I'll write you soon, okay?" She says good-bye, and the line goes dead before I can respond. I realize that she hasn't given me a phone number.

My whole body is shaking. I pour myself a glass of milk, which I drink all at once. I feel angry, but it's not the same sort of anger I used to feel when Miriam and I fought over clothes and candy and who got to choose which tape to play in the car. This is a different, more serious anger, more solid, somehow. Maxwell whines softly, scratching at the door to be let out. "C'mon, boy, let's get outside," I say. I take him on a long walk, circling the block five or six times, until my head stops pulsing and my breathing feels steady and sure.

When I tell my mother about the phone call she starts to cry. I replay the whole conversation for her, but change some of the details. I tell her that Miriam has found a really good job and is living in a nice apartment with two other girls. My mother is happy to hear that; it's difficult to find a good place to live, especially with people you like.

She begins making us dinner—a salad that uses all the leftovers from the fridge and anything she can find in a can: corn, button mushrooms, the peas that say *very small*. "What kind of job did she get?" she asks, studying a head of lettuce that's gone brown at the edges.

"She's working at a shoe store." I'm not sure where I get this: why shoes? "She said they might promote her if she puts in some extra hours."

My mother thinks about it. "I bet she's a good saleswoman. Your sister's always been very persuasive." She asks me more questions, and I tell her all about Miriam's apartment, the beautiful garden it has, with its dahlias and roses, and her roommates, Jenna and Susan, who are college freshmen at Oregon State. One of them, Susan, I think, is even Jewish. My mother nods appreciatively, especially when I mention the apartment's alarm system, and the police station right down the street. If I have to lie (which is, all things considered, usually a bad thing to do), I might as well tell a lie that makes my mother feel better (a good thing to do). After all, it's not going to help matters for my mother, who is always so worried about everything, to have to worry about Miriam too. If I can make things a little better by lying, why not?

At first, it's hard to move around with such a large lie always by my side. It pulls my hair, makes me stumble. Sometimes it itches. After a while, I don't even notice it any more, the way you don't notice the freckles on your arm.

My mother has started neglecting Maxwell. She's not mean to him. She pets him on the head, says "pretty boy" and all the usual things people say when they love their pets. She's not like one of those people you read about, who leave their dogs in the basement to starve to death or beat them because they have no one else to beat. She still tells him he's the *very best little dog in the whole world* and gives him treats off her plate.

The problem is that she keeps forgetting to walk him. Now that Miriam's gone my mother is supposed to take him out at night. But she keeps forgetting the evening walks. Instead she stays in bed, crawling under the covers right after we've finished dinner.

"What about Maxwell?" I ask.

"I'll do him later."

"I could take him."

"Absolutely not. You know it's not safe for you to be out there by yourself at night."

Sometimes, if I know my mother is fast asleep, I put Maxwell on his leash, and take him out on the sidewalk right in front of the house, but he doesn't want to go there, no matter how much I coax him, he just whines and sulks and pulls in the direction of the little park next to the gas station. "I'm sorry, Maxwell," I whisper to him. "But this is it."

Every once in a while, if we stay out long enough, Maxwell will give in and go on the sidewalk (always with a terrible, humiliated look on his face), but usually he just holds it. Instead he's started going in the house. Not upstairs in the main part of the house, but downstairs, in the den. There are small piles of dog shit everywhere, sometimes three or four at a time. The smell is terrible, a pungent mix of the downstairs' usual dampness, washing machine detergent, and dog shit. Sometimes I see Maxwell duck down the stairs, tail between legs, just like a dog in a cartoon.

Maxwell seems different now. For one thing, he barks more, a high-pitched bark that sounds like a doggy cry for help. He has become nervous, and he walks around with that shamed look dogs have when they've chewed something. Sometimes, when I try to pet him, he snaps at me, a half-hearted snap that doesn't really mean anything. And the dog shit, even when it's dried, really stinks.

I feel horrible. Poor Maxwell. So cute, and he's never done anything to hurt anybody. I decide to dedicate myself to making Maxwell's life as good as possible. "You will never suffer again," I tell him. He wags his tail and whines.

I get the dog brush from the closet and comb his lush brown coat, which is full of tangles. He yelps when I get to a knot but is passive enough to give in to the grooming. I even take a little bit of baby powder—something I read in a magazine—and comb it through his fur, to take away some of the smell. When I spray some of Miriam's old Jean Nate on him he sneezes, getting snot all over me.

Next I get the scissors out of my arts and crafts box and trim off the parts of his fur, under his tail and on his back legs, that still have some dried shit on them. While I'm at it I trim some of the long hair that grows around his neck. Maxwell looks a little patchy when I'm done but seems pleased, as if he knows what I'm doing. I remember the time Miriam trimmed my bangs, how calmly she did it, and how nice it felt to have her paying such close attention to me, the tiny details of my hair.

I consider cutting his nails, which are long enough to make a soft *click click* when he crosses the kitchen, but I don't trust myself to do it right. My own nails are a ragged mess. There isn't much I can do about his breath, except give him some extra dog biscuits and hope for the best.

"Look at you," I mouth quietly, holding a mirror to his nose. "You're a real beauty." I kneel down beside him on the shag carpet and stroke his head as gently as I can, hoping he can feel the words through my hands.

My sister has left behind one of her little sketchbooks, filled with pictures and poems. I've hidden it in my room and I search through it again and again, not sure what I'm looking for. There is a picture of Maxwell, curled up on the rug, and also a picture of my glasses, just sitting on a table along with a glass and a bowl: she must have drawn it sometime when we were sitting at breakfast. There is also a picture of our mother, except in the picture she is not really our mother but an angel, with her hair flowing in enormous waves all the way to the ground. On one page is a charcoal sketch of me. I examine the outline of my face carefully, wondering if that's what I really look like.

"Adie, we need to talk."

My mother announces this one night while we are unpacking a takeout dinner from the Golden Dragon restaurant. My mother pours out some grape soda while I open the Styrofoam boxes. I like the Golden Dragon because they always give you beautiful plastic chopsticks with red ink letters, instead of the plain wooden ones. I save them in a desk drawer with my pencils and pens, thinking that someday I will be the kind of person who cooks Chinese food at home.

We need to talk. Of course, by now, when my mother says something like this, I search it for meaning. My senses all go on high alert: my breathing quickens, my muscles tense. In science class we learned about how animals *react under conditions of stress*—how their bodies light up when they are being stalked by a predator.

"I'm worried about your sister." Here it comes. "She hasn't written in a while."

I take a bite of chicken but quickly spit it back out; it's still too hot. My mother is right; we haven't heard from Miriam in a few weeks. No more postcards, no more phone calls, nothing.

"I think we should try to find her," my mother says. "She's very young still."

"No, Mom." I say this as calmly as possible, barely looking up from my plate. "She's doing fine. She has a *job.*"

"So why haven't we heard from her?" My mother pours herself more soda, and I can see that her hand is shaking. Some of it spills on the tablecloth.

I'm not sure how to respond to this. I'm worried too: why hasn't Miriam written to us? "Maybe she ran out of stamps," I say, reaching for a napkin to wipe up the spill.

"That's not funny." My mother's voice breaks, and she gets up from the table.

"I'm sorry." I feel terrible; my mother is crying. "Really, I'm sure she's fine." I think of Lainey and her family, sitting around the dinner table, her brothers bickering over the last piece of cake.

My mother stares out the window as if she might find Miriam right there, staring back at her from the other side. Maybe she's hoping the same thing I am: that Miriam will show up any minute, loaded down with bags and gifts, saying, *Hey! You got*

Chinese food. Is there any left? She'll hog the fried rice, trade fortunes with me if she likes mine better, insisting that mine was the one she was supposed to get in the first place.

But I know this won't happen. Miriam is gone. Gone for good. I wonder what *gone for good* means. Does it mean leaving for somewhere else—a good place, a better place than the one you're in now? Or does it mean that the act of leaving makes you into a good person?

"C'mon, Mom. She'll be okay." My mother wipes her tears on her sleeve and comes back to the table.

We crack open our fortune cookies.

My mother's: *A person of great insight and wisdom, people turn to you in times of trouble.*

Mine: *You will soon go on a remarkable journey.*

21

The girls' locker room at school is a strange place, with a strange smell all its own, a combination of shampoo and dirty sweat socks and girls throwing up their lunches. There are mirrors everywhere, metal lockers, no windows. I imagine that this is what jail is like.

Lainey and I are getting ready for gym class. We are surrounded by girls of all shapes and sizes. Some of them walk around casually in their bras and underwear, but those are only the girls who know their bodies look good, who have *filled out nicely*, as my mother would say. Most of us try to cover up while we dress, hiding behind towels or locker doors.

Lainey stands with her butt facing the mirror, twisting around to get a look at it. "Do you think I look fat?"

There is only one right answer to this. "Of course not."

Lainey groans. "I've got to go on a diet."

Our gym uniforms are green and gold, the school colors. This is the first year we've had to wear them. Our parents were sent a note that said, "This measure will promote team spirit and will ensure that your child is modestly dressed." You'd think it would make us all look the same, but now, with the uniforms, it's even easier to see how different we all really are. The girls who are completely flat-chested look even worse next to the ones who are lucky enough to need sports bras. I feel shorter than ever when I wear my uniform, though at least my breasts are starting to grow, and this balances things out a bit.

I sit down on the bench and wait for Lainey to finish getting ready. "I think you look really skinny," I offer, but she's still staring at herself in the mirror, not paying attention to me.

I steal a look at Jenny Tucker, who last year had no breasts at all and came back from summer vacation with a whole new body; tanned and curvy, but still slim in her tight-fitting designer jeans. She is now one of the most popular girls in our class. We used to be friendly, even worked on a history project about the Salem witch trials together, but after the summer she stopped talking to me.

I watch as one of the other girls asks to borrow her hair spray. "Let me think about it," she says coolly, studying her nails.

Our gym teacher, Ms. Crenshaw, walks into the locker room. She blows her whistle three times, shrill and sharp, and the sound echoes crazily in the small room. "Hurry it up, people!" she says. There's a mad rush of bodies as girls struggle in and out of clothes, tug on their shoelaces, put on an extra bit of eyeshadow in case the boys' soccer team is using the field for practice. Lainey takes off her favorite sweatshirt, the one that says JCC SUMMER CAMP—STAFF on it, and stuffs her sandals into the double locker she shares with me.

Ms. Crenshaw comes over to us. "Adie, I just got a message that you're supposed to go up to the principal's office."

"Why?"

"I'm not sure. They just said for you to go right up."

I know she feels a little sorry for me. Other gym teachers have been mean to me, or have just ignored me, since I'm so terrible at sports, but for some reason she seems to understand that it's not my fault. She's one of the teachers I actually like. "Right now?"

"Yeah." She gives me a concerned look. "Don't worry, Adie, I won't forget to mark you excused."

"Lucky you," Lainey says. She hates gym as much as I do.

"Go on out there, Lainey," Ms. Crenshaw says. Lainey rolls her eyes and makes a face behind Ms. Crenshaw's back as she leaves the room.

I look at the pile of clothes in my locker. "What about my stuff?"

"Maybe you'd better take it." Ms. Crenshaw looks around the room, sees a girl still sitting on a bench. "Let's go, Sheila!" she says, back to her usual gym-teacher self.

She leaves, and I change back into my regular shirt and jeans, putting each piece on as slowly as possible. Someone has left a small makeup bag out on the bench. It is Jenny Tucker's. I open it, curious. Two lipsticks, a tampon, mascara, and a ten-dollar bill, folded neatly in a tiny square. I put the lipsticks and money in my pocket. I would just take the whole bag, but then she might just think she lost it. I want her to wonder who stole her things.

When I'm done getting dressed I linger for a few more moments, staring at myself in the mirror. My hair is finally at the length I want, just below my shoulders, feathered in two even waves. Someone has stuck a radio station bumper sticker to the glass, and I pick at the edges absently, trying to see if I can get the whole thing off in one piece. It is strange to be in the locker room alone. Unlike most rooms, it seems a lot smaller when it's empty.

When I get upstairs my mother is standing outside the principal's office, right next to the display case filled with school trophies. "Hi, sweetie." I can tell she's trying to sound cheery, but her smile is forced, and she's holding her purse tight against her body. She looks out of place here, unfamiliar, as if someone took a photograph of her and hung it on the wall.

"What's going on?" A slow wave of dizziness passes over my body. I lean heavily against the wall, my eyes taking in a blurred image of the pennants and trophies, secure in their little glass case. *Go Tigers.*

"I'm taking you home."

"But what about my report?" Next period I'm supposed to give an oral report on *Fahrenheit 451*. I stayed up until midnight preparing it, decorating the report cover with Magic Marker flames in orange and red, and then using a match to singe the edges. My idea was to make the cover look like it had been set on fire. My mother had even helped me, blowing out the flame before it could get too big.

But now she is grabbing my arm, pulling me toward the door. "Don't worry—I've taken care of it."

I hang back. "I have to at least turn it in." Maybe if I give her a few minutes she'll change her mind, tell me she just stopped by to say hello and wish me luck on my report (she knows I get nervous speaking in front of the class, and always tells me to just *pretend that the audience is naked*) and that I should have a nice day at school and remember to get some fruit at lunch, and she'll see me later. Maybe we can get pizza for dinner or see a movie. . . .

"Adie," my mother hisses, "we don't have time for this."

"Just one sec." I duck into the main office, where all the teachers have mailboxes, and leave the report in Mr. Arnold's box. I don't bother to write a note. My name is already there on the cover, in thin angry orange letters, just like the flames.

Once in the car, my mother starts up the engine quickly, screeching out of the parking lot like a bank robber in the movies. We race down the street.

"Mom, slow down."

My mother eases up a bit. I watch the school, gray and squat, get smaller in the distance. It's strange to see it from this perspective, in the middle of the day. I feel like I should be going to a doctor's appointment or on a field trip. Definitely not home.

At the stoplight my mother turns to me, her face drawn and worried, but also strangely excited. "Things are really starting to heat up," she says, glancing nervously at the rearview mirror.

The strange men in the white car have started following her again. She's seen them at the gas station a few blocks from our house, just hanging out and smoking, even though, as everyone knows, you're not supposed to smoke too close to the pumps. You could blow up your car—the entire gas station, possibly. That alone shows how dangerous they are—how *reckless*. "People like that are not to be messed with," my mother says, drumming her fingers on the steering wheel.

I'm not sure what to say to this, so I pretend to look through the papers in my math folder. My mother has not mentioned the men in the white car for a long time. Most of her worries seem to be focused on Miriam: at least once a day she'll ask me if I think my sister has *fallen in with a bad crowd*. She worries that my sister has become a drug addict, something that often happens to *teenage runaways,* at least according to the special reports she makes me watch on the ten o'clock news. I'd thought—hoped—that she'd forgotten all about the men in the white car, and that if I never asked her about them, they'd sort of disappear, and everything would go back to normal, at least our version of normal, which is not really normal by most people's standards, but normal enough for us.

But now my mother tells me that for a few weeks she's felt unsafe, as if someone was secretly watching her, tracking her every little move. Today was the last straw. She was on her way to the dry cleaners, to pick up the wool jacket with the real mother-of-pearl buttons, when she saw them, right in the lane next to her—pretending not to see her, but she knew it was them! In that moment she felt frozen, as if the car was driving on its own, but then she *gathered her wits about her.* She went to the bank and withdrew all her money, *in cash,* and then came right to the school.

"You and I are just going to go away for a little bit, 'til things calm down." My mother speeds up. "Like a vacation."

We pass a convenience store lit up with signs for beer and soda. My mouth feels dry. "Can I get something to drink?"

"Just wait 'til we get home," my mother says, keeping her eyes fixed on the road.

I am silent the rest of the way. When we pull into the driveway I race into the kitchen. I drink three tall glasses of water, one right after the other, so fast that some of the water drips down my shirt.

It's only then that I notice the pile of things sitting on the kitchen table. My mother's checkbook, in its special green leather case, her jewelry box, a hairbrush, makeup. The little notebook with the black-and-white photograph of the Grand Canyon, which we use for addresses and phone numbers. I watch as my mother stuffs it all into her favorite tote bag, the one that says ALOHA, HAWAII! in pink cursive script and has a picture of a sunset and palm trees.

She opens the jewelry box and sighs. "I really should sort through all this stuff. Most of it's junk." She starts to untangle a couple of silver chains. Then she gives up and just grabs everything, the plastic bangles and the freshwater pearls, the clip-on fake earrings and the silver school ring with the giant garnet. The jewelry, along with everything else, disappears into the Aloha bag.

"C'mon, Adie, let's start doing your stuff." My mother heads for my room.

I follow her reluctantly. "What about Maxwell?"

"We'll take him with us." My mother has already put some of my clothes in the yellow and white embroidered suitcase, but she's picked all the things I like least: the jeans that aren't quite the right color, the turtlenecks that leave me feeling sweaty and trapped. She fidgets impatiently while I look through my closet, trying to figure out what to take.

I hold up the sweater Miriam gave me for my last birthday. "Will I need a wool sweater?" I like this sweater, but it's getting a little small, and I don't know what the weather is going to be like.

My mother grabs the sweater out of my hands and shoves it in the suitcase. "Just take it." Usually my mother does not treat clothes roughly. My head hurts and I can feel the sharp pang of tears. I turn away from her and pretend to concentrate on packing my socks and underwear.

"Hurry up. I want to be out of here in half an hour."

I hold up two socks in different shades of blue, trying to get them to match. "How long are we going for?"

"Just pack some stuff, Adie, okay? I'll tell you about it in the car."

She leaves me alone and I look around my room: there are so

many choices. It's hard to pack when you don't know where you're going. "Will I need a bathing suit?" I shout.

My mother doesn't reply. I take the bathing suit, just in case, and some tapes for the car—The Police and Duran Duran. My brand-new pair of Nike sneakers, navy blue and white, just like the ones Lainey has. The sandals I never wear, thinking maybe this is a good time to start wearing them. Miriam's sketchbook. I shove everything else into a duffel bag and my school back-pack, which has a broken strap but is the only backpack I have.

I take a last peek under the bed to see if there's anything there that I need, and my hand touches something small and cold. It's a flea market ring that belongs to Miriam: a thin silver band with a small, green malachite stone. I borrowed it from her ages ago, without telling her, and she hadn't spoken to me for two days when I finally confessed to losing it. Now I slip the ring onto my finger, grateful that it still fits.

I join my mother in the kitchen, where she is hurriedly filling a paper bag with pretzels and potato chips and other snacks. "Help me take these things out to the car," she says, filling a water bottle with lemonade. "I don't want us to have to stop for a while." She hands me a bag of food.

Outside, Maxwell is bounding about, excited to be going on a trip. He lifts his leg to a tree and then abandons it, too worked up to even wait for the pee to come out. "You better go now, Maxie," I say, giving him a little shove. "Who knows when we're going to stop." He goes back to the tree a second time, as if he understands me, and lets loose a steady stream of urine.

"You all set?" My mother throws some things in the back: a hair dryer, a windbreaker, a cosmetic bag too full to zip shut.

I look around. The eucalyptus leaves have fallen all over our small lawn, covering its lush green with a dusty blanket of pink and gray. An unopened newspaper lies on the front step. "I guess so."

My mother locks the front door quickly and grabs the news-paper, muttering something about having to remember to sus-pend delivery. Maxwell is already in the car, panting excitedly with his head out the window, as if the car is already in motion.

"Did you remember the dog food?"

"Oh, shit." My mother opens the trunk and hands me the house keys. "You get it. I'm going to try to make these things fit."

In the kitchen, I find a full box of biscuits, shaped like cartoon bones. I put them in the yellow canvas bag we use for shopping, along with some of Maxwell's chew toys. Then I grab the watering can and make a quick round of the houseplants. The large cactus in the living room, which isn't really prickly at all. A fern by my mother's bed, which has done surprisingly well. The daisies on the kitchen counter will just have to die, but for now they look bright and cheery. I know it would be impractical to take the plants, that they can't really come in the car with us, but I'm still disappointed, since my mother loves them so much.

I take one last look at my room and straighten out the pillows on my bed. My bed is made: usually I don't bother, but this time I can't bear to leave it a mess. I try to picture a body there, sleeping soundly, a girl whose tiredness comes from everyday things like soccer practice or a newspaper route. But the room already seems empty, as if I'd left long ago. "Good-bye, room," I say, breathing in its quiet air.

Near the front door we have a small statue of a horse, a solid ceramic red and white figure my mother says is from somewhere in China. When I was younger, I would play with that horse for hours, giving my dolls rides on it. I would fantasize about it turning real and carrying me back to China, which I pictured as looking like a Chinese restaurant. Now, knowing that my mother can't see me, I give the horse a quick kiss for luck. Then I shut the door behind me, and we are gone.

PART II

22

After we've been driving for a while my mother pulls over at a gas station to fill up the tank. The attendant wipes off our windshield, which is coated with dust, and peers in the window. "Where are you ladies headed today?"

"Oh, nowhere special." My mother fiddles with the twisted seat belt and hands him some cash. "We're just going on a little trip."

"A little trip," he says, winking at me. "Well, bon voyage."

Bon voyage. *Good voyage.* I wish we were traveling by boat—one of those giant cruise ships, with a real pool and a restaurant, like on *The Love Boat.*

It is already the middle of the afternoon by the time we stop for lunch, at a roadside diner with a giant billboard that says ELVIS LIVES DINER. It has white lace curtains and a black-and-white checkered floor—more like a big kitchen than a restaurant. We slide into a booth near the front. In the corner there's an old-fashioned jukebox, and two life-size photos of Elvis: one fat and one thin. Above the cash register there's a wooden clock with pictures of birds—the same one Sidney's father had, I suddenly realize. It's like a cuckoo clock, but with a different bird for each hour. I always liked noon the best, the shallow hoot of an owl, twelve times in a row.

The waitress comes to take our order, and my mother doesn't

say anything when I order "The King" (a cheeseburger and onion rings) plus a chocolate milk shake all at once, even though usually she would caution me that *Our eyes are sometimes bigger than our stomachs* and *Why don't you see how full you are after the burger and onion rings and then see if you still want a milk shake.* My mother asks for some fries and an iced tea and falls into silence.

Outside you can hear the rumble of trucks, the steady drone of traffic on a weekday afternoon. "What does bon voyage really mean?"

"Have a good trip." My mother doesn't look up.

"So in France when they say that they really mean it?"

My mother frowns. "What do you mean?"

"They really mean, have a good trip." The waitress brings our food, and I pick apart my onion rings, which are too hot to eat. "It's not just a joke."

My mother thinks about it for a moment. "Yes," she says, a look of triumph suddenly creasing her face. "They really mean it."

"But do they have a lot of boats there?" I picture a large cruise ship filled with sophisticated people smoking cigarettes and speaking French. *Bonjour,* a tall French man dressed in a tuxedo says to a slim woman in a shimmering silver gown. *Voulez-vous coucher avec moi? Ah oui, merci beaucoup,* she replies, her slim pale fingers curling seductively. . . .

"Stop talking nonsense, Adie." My mother pushes her plate away. A tiny bit of ketchup clings to her lip.

The waitress shuffles over and refills my mother's iced tea without saying anything. My mother takes a few slow sips and studies the pattern on the curtains. I remember the Halloween costumes she made one year for me and my sister: Miriam was a country shepherd, with a creamy white dress and a bonnet trimmed with lace. I was her sheep.

"Mom . . ."

"What?"

"When are we going back?"

"Jesus, Adie, I don't know." She lowers her voice. "Anyway, you're very lucky to get pulled out of school for a trip. Most kids would kill for the chance."

Kill for the chance. I let the words rush over me, and suddenly it feels as if we're doing something dangerous and forbidden—not just eating hamburgers and milk shakes at a roadside diner. We are bandits, criminals on the run. I think of the movie Miriam and I watched on TV: *Bonnie and Clyde.* I want to say all of this out loud to my mother, want to let her know that *I'm in,* that we're blood sisters, *all for one and one for all,* but now she's digging for the loose change in the bottom of her purse.

"Do you think it's okay if I leave the tip in change?" My mother lines some nickels and dimes up on the table. "All of these coins are weighing down my purse."

I look up from my plate. "Sure. It still counts as money." I say this calmly, but I want to cry, that's how happy I am that she's asked my advice about something, however small. At the front of the restaurant the waitress stands by the screen door, staring at the parking lot outside. From the kitchen comes the sound of running water, the dull clash of dishes and pans.

My mother toys with the top button on her shirt, which is coming loose. "You know that Elvis Presley was a drug addict, right?"

"No."

"Prescription pills. He died from an overdose." She leans closer to me, as if Elvis might be sitting in the next booth and overhear our conversation. "He died on the toilet."

I listen to the song breaking through a tiny speaker just over our heads: *We can't go on together with suspicious minds.* My mother sips quietly at her iced tea, waiting for me to say something. I look at the second picture of Elvis, his body bursting out of the white satin jumpsuit, wondering what the connection is between going to the bathroom and dying. "Do drugs make you fat?"

My mother stares at me. "Sometimes I really don't understand what you're talking about, Adie." The bird clock in the corner quacks suddenly, almost ferociously. Three o'clock. Back home, Mrs. Demarco is walking her German shepherds—Jo, the puppy, and Minnie, who has trouble with her back legs. The vacant lot down the street from the high school is filling up with teenagers, smoking and muttering swear words at each other. Lainey is counting the minutes until dinner, having starved herself all day.

Suddenly my mother grabs my arm. "Adie," she hisses. "Get up and let's go."

"But we haven't paid yet."

"Just listen to me. Don't look across the room, whatever you do." My mother puts on her sunglasses and quickly walks out the door, head bowed. I follow her, trying to keep my eyes on the glowing EXIT sign, but it's as if a magnet is pulling me, and I can't help looking around. The restaurant is empty, except for an old man with a thin, lined face, reading a newspaper and eating an ice-cream sundae, a paper napkin tucked neatly under his chin. He's put the maraschino cherries on the side of his plate, and I remember something Miriam told me: that maraschino cherries never dissolve in your stomach, they just sit there forever, shiny and red, waiting for you to die. . . . My mother hurries us across the parking lot, her breath coming out in little huffs.

In the car, driving fast with the windows down, my mother explains: she didn't notice anything strange at first, but then she realized that the man with the ice-cream sundae was watching us, very carefully. And did you notice that he picked that small cramped table in the corner, even though the restaurant was practically empty—it wasn't a good table at all, right near the kitchen and no window—just so he could have a clear view of us? And did you see what he was wearing?

"Mom, slow down." My voice sounds strange, high-pitched—someone else's voice. "We're going ninety." My mother steps on the brake, too fast, too sudden, and for a moment the car veers into the next lane, dangerously—thrillingly.

"Thanks, sweetie. The last thing we need now is a ticket."

She looks calmer, serene almost. "Especially after skipping out on the bill." Soon our car is lost among all the other cars, just another speck on the freeway. I think about the old man, who must be gone by now, and wonder if the restaurant is now empty. The last thing I saw, walking out, was the waitress's face, her quick look of surprise, then anger. We really are criminals on the run.

23

My mother lets me pick the motel. We've driven for hours, and I'm exhausted and stiff from sitting in the car, but we're not stopping until I find a motel where we can swim. My mother's only requirements are that it doesn't cost too much and is reasonably clean. And, of course, it has to be a place that accepts dogs.

"We can always sneak Maxwell in if they don't allow pets," I say. I look in the backseat, where Maxwell is sitting. At first he refused to settle down, panting out of one window and then the other, jumping around like a puppy even when the car was in motion. He peed a little—just a drop from excitement, not enough to make a mess. But now he's fallen asleep, his tiny dog snores just audible over the sounds of the freeway. Every once in a while he twitches and snorts. I wonder if he's dreaming.

My mother shakes her head. "I don't think that's a good idea." A truck loaded with vegetables pulls into the lane in front of her, and she swears under her breath. "Maxwell's pretty big."

As we drive past endless strip malls and fast-food chains, my mother suggests that we think about coming up with a new name for me. Not legally, of course. Just for when we speak to each other in public, to throw the guys who are after us off the scent.

I turn back to my magazine, which is sticky with soda and

potato chips. "Lose 10 Pounds Fast! Perfect Date Ideas!" Never mind that I've read the entire thing at least three times since we left Las Palmas. By now I know the advice columns by heart. *Dear Marilyn: My boyfriend keeps pressuring me to "go all the way" but I'm not ready yet;* and the answer, in reassuring black-and-white: *No one should feel pressured to have sex.* I have always wanted to see the world, to get in the car and watch the dizzying images of new places pass by. But now that I've finally got the chance, I can't seem to stop reading the magazine.

"Is that okay?" my mother asks. We are passing an open field that looks like a stage set. A barn, a cow, a calf. We could be in the movies.

"Like I care." I'm trying out an attitude I've seen on TV. Actually, I find the thought of taking on a new name deeply appealing. Something sexy, but tough. *Amber. Marci.* I picture my new name on a T-shirt, a skintight, light blue T-shirt with iron-on purple lettering. I think about the girls at school who wear shirts like that, the letters of their names stretched out by their breasts.

A big wooden sign by the road promises HOMEMADE FUDGE AND CANDIES: NEXT EXIT, and I consider asking if we can stop. But I decide not to push it. My mother is in a tricky mood. I don't know how much longer we'll be driving, how many days we'll be away from home. I don't want to start things off on the wrong foot.

Finally I see a place that I like. *Motel del Mar.* I know from Spanish class that it means Motel by the Sea, even though we are nowhere near the ocean. But it does have a pool. I point this out and my mother begins to laugh hysterically; even she can see the humor in it. My mother, who has not smiled in hours, is now barely able to get out of the car, that's how hard she's laughing. "You are the silliest," she says, trying to choke back her laughter.

I unlock the door, get out, stretch a little. My muscles are tense from sitting for so long. The sky is bright blue, cloudless, and the smell of fried chicken clings to the air.

Maxwell is excited to be out of the car. I put a leash on him before he can run across the parking lot. He is already straining at a pigeon.

A kid zooms past on his bicycle. Wherever we are, it doesn't look that different from anything back home—just a regular four-lane road, a drugstore, a gas station. Some fast-food places down the street. We've been driving forever, but we might as well have stood still.

My mother fusses with something in her purse, serious again. "I'm going to check things out. Don't talk to anyone."

"Like who?"

"Just anyone. I don't want you telling people where we're from. Don't even say how old you are." My mother checks her reflection in the side mirror, smoothing down her eyebrows with a finger and spit. Maxwell laps eagerly at a small puddle of water that's collected near a patch of grass.

"I'm not going to talk to anybody. There's no one here anyway." I say this to be annoying, but it's true. There are only two other cars in the parking lot, and a beat-up van with the name of the motel printed in block lettering. I watch as my mother puts her hair back with one of Miriam's multicolored headbands, wishing my hair looked good like that. "How long are we going to stay here?"

"I'm not sure. Let's just hope it's clean." She grabs her handbag and gets out of the car, double checking, as she always does, to make sure it's locked. I follow her, pulling at Maxwell, who is determined to sniff everything. They say dogs can smell emotions, can pick up the scent of anger and fear, and I wonder what he's sensing from the motel: loneliness maybe? But then he just pees against another car. "Stop it, Maxie," I say, pulling him away.

My mother looks around and takes a deep breath and heads into a little room with a sign that says OFFICE: PLEASE RING BUZZER IF I'M NOT HERE. I stay in the lobby with Maxwell, who lies down in the middle of the floor, tail thumping. There are some dying plants—a cactus and a ficus, which I recognize from Mrs. Demarco's garden—and a torn print of a tiger above a fake stone mantelpiece. The tiger has a faint smile on his face, slightly mocking. On the other side of the room hangs an old, faded map of California that looks like something you'd see in a museum. Someone has written the words "You Are Here" in ballpoint pen, and there's even a gold star, just like the ones Mrs. Pallari gives out when you get an A on a test. I study it closely, trying to figure out how far we've gone, but I've never been very good at reading maps.

For a moment I pretend that my mother has planned this all as a surprise trip. We're going to visit Miriam, who has secretly called my mother to tell her where she is and that she really, really misses home, and wants to come back. We'll stay for a few days on the farm, picking apples, and then we'll all drive back together, stopping at all the places we've been meaning to see, like Lake Tahoe and Yosemite National Park. I think about the pictures of Half Dome in my geography book, the mountain climbers scaling its smooth face. Maybe we can visit a dude ranch, or an Indian reservation. . . .

"Honey, where are you?"

I follow my mother's voice into the office, dragging Maxwell behind me. The guy behind the counter stares at the trail of slobber Maxwell has left on the carpet. "That's your dog?" For a moment I think he's going to say that pets aren't allowed, or that Maxwell is too messy-looking to stay, but then he just pats him on the head. "Cute."

My mother takes her wallet out of her handbag and plays with the tiny clasp. "Do you take cash?"

The guy smiles at her. "Of course we take cash. Everyone likes cash." He looks at me. "You want your own key?" I nod, and he hands one to me, on a key chain with a blue plastic dolphin. "Enjoy your stay."

"Thank you very much," my mother says, her voice sounding extra polite and careful. The guy just smiles and turns back to his desk, but I notice him stealing a glance at my mother's legs. Maxwell pulls at the leash and turns in small circles of excitement.

"How long are we going to stay here?" I ask, as we climb the outside stairs to the second floor.

"Adie, shhhh. Keep your voice down." My mother struggles with the door to our room. When she finally gets it open I'm struck by the cloudy smell of cigarettes and air freshener. Maxwell trots in as if he's been here a million times, and immediately begins sniffing in the corners and behind the heavy gray curtains. The room is dark and damp, and the carpet has a funny tear in the middle, like a gash.

I sink down on the bed closest to the window. If Miriam were here she would talk my mother into turning around and driving back home. My sister has always been the kind of person people listen to. She would stand against the wall with her arms folded like a teacher and say, "This is just silly," and my mother would get a little angry (as she always does) and then sad (as she always does), and then she'd say, "You're right, this is silly." And then we'd get back in the car and drive right home. But Miriam is not here.

My mother shuts the door and closes the curtains. She starts looking through the bureau, running her hands along the very back of the drawers. "These kinds of places always have so much dust," she says, sneezing—an extra loud, energetic sneeze, as if to clear the air.

I start to kick off my sandals, then stop and carefully undo the straps. They're brand new; orange leather Dr. Scholl's, with a cork bottom and a brass buckle strap, and I don't want to ruin them. The bedside clock says five o'clock, its numbers glowing a clean, digital green. If we were back home, I'd be curled up on the couch with Maxwell as a pillow, watching *Happy Days* reruns. My mother would come in and say something like, *You should get outside; it's such a beautiful afternoon,* and then she'd sit down with me to watch the show, the ice-cream parlors and poodle skirts freezing a perfect moment in time.

Now I realize what's wrong with the room, what's missing. "There's no TV."

My mother doesn't look up from the drawers. "Of course there's a TV." She's crouched over now, butt in the air. I'm embarrassed by the sight of it, even though we are all alone and I am the only witness.

But there's no TV, even though the flashing neon sign outside promises a *color TV in every room.* "I'm going to see if I can get them to bring one in here," I say, putting my shoes back on.

My mother, relaxed now, lies down on the bed and stares up at the ceiling. "You know what would be fun? If we got our colors done." She has read about this in one of my fashion magazines.

"I guess."

"I'm feeling a little crampy, sweetie." She makes a face. "Can you get me some tampons from the drugstore across the street? And maybe some candy?" She rolls over, muffling her voice in the pillow. "Just take the money from my purse."

I don't answer, just nod, even though she can't see me. The money is wadded up in a large manila envelope at the bottom of her bag. As I leave the room, I catch myself sniffing the air, like an animal trying to get its bearings. The smell is somehow familiar. It takes me a minute, and then I figure it out: it's like my bedroom closet: closed and airless.

I head back down to the motel lobby, this time taking the stairs that are farther away from our door, so I can see more of the motel. The landing is covered with a ragged, stained brown carpet—more like a strip of felt than an actual carpet. With a slight shiver I realize that probably thousands of people have stayed at this motel, and the only trace left of them are the stains.

I want to look in the other rooms, but all of the curtains are drawn. A maid's cart, loaded with folded towels and sheets, is parked outside an open door. Inside the room I can hear the sounds of two people fighting on a Spanish soap opera, their voices ringing with anger.

I make my way down the stairs and out to the pool, which looks cold and still and only goes up to six feet, not nearly as deep as the one at the Jewish Community Center. No one is swimming, but an old man and woman, bundled up despite the heat, are seated at a small plastic table, playing a game of checkers. They look at me curiously and the woman gives me a small frown, as if I am in the wrong place. I suddenly remember that I am supposed to have swimming lessons at the JCC tomorrow: we're going to learn how to dive. Even though we're only using the low diving board, I've been nervous about it all week. I hate the thought of putting my face into the water first, before the rest of my body gets wet—it seems wrong, somehow. But now I wish I was going to be there.

The guy behind the desk stubs out his cigarette when I come in to the office. I tell him about the television, and he promises to bring us one from another room, as soon as the housekeeping staff is done with their afternoon shift. "A couple of our TVs have blown out," he says, looking a little embarrassed. "But don't worry, we'll have you taken care of in no time."

"Thanks." I'm not sure what else to say, so I start fingering through a pile of coupons and flyers for local restaurants: *Baxter's Beef Ribs. The Wurst House—the Best Franks You've Ever Eaten!*

"How's your mom?"

"She's okay." My throat feels frozen, and for some reason I want to apologize and tell him that I didn't even have time to really pack my best things, that my mother pulled me out of school early, that we've been driving all day. That usually I'm a friendly person, and I'd be in a better mood to talk if the day itself hadn't been so strange. I'd like to ask him: do a lot of women just show up at your motel, out of the blue in the middle of the week, with their thirteen-year-old daughter and a wagging-tail dog and no real plans to go anywhere next? But I just say, "She's taking a nap."

The guy yawns and says, "I wish I could take a nap about now." He starts sorting the mail, stacking the envelopes in neat little piles, and as I watch him I think about how it's been weeks since we've heard anything from Miriam. Her last postcard was of a kitten lying in a hammock, with the words TAKE IT EASY written across the bottom in bright pink lettering.

"My name's Dennis, by the way." He holds out his hand for me to shake, something adults never do with me. I see that his fingernails have been chewed short, down to the quick.

"I'm Amber." It's the first time I've said my new name aloud, and as I make my way out the door I already feel taller, prettier, and also a little older. I wonder what Miriam would think of my new name and decide that she would be proud of it.

Other than a little traffic there's not much to look at: an empty gas station with a plastic banner flapping hopefully in the wind (LADIES' DAY THURSDAY!—COMPLIMENTARY FULL SERVICE); a used-car dealership, the drugstore. Down the road I can see a McDonald's, with a giant statue of a smiling Ronald McDonald and an American flag. I feel a wave of tiredness coat my body. This morning I got up and brushed my teeth, packed my lunch (the banana, I now realize, going rotten in my locker), and went to school as usual. Now I am standing in the blazing sun on the side of a road I don't even know the name of. I look around, but there are no street signs; it is one of those places where you're supposed to know where you are. I lean against a telephone pole for a moment before I notice that it's covered with bird shit. The entire top of the pole is covered in pigeons, their little gray bodies battling for space.

An elderly woman shuffles down the street toward me, dragging a small metal cart overflowing with groceries. Long stalks of celery threaten to fall out of one of the bags. "Excuse me," I say, as politely as possible. "What street are we on?"

She hovers close to her cart, as if I might want to steal her vegetables. "Rialto Drive," she mutters without looking up.

"Thanks," I say automatically, but she is already past me.

The traffic pauses for a moment and I cross the street. Some boys are clustered outside the drugstore, smoking and drinking soda. They remind me of the kids who hang out behind the parking lot at school, cutting class and getting in trouble for stupid things, like graffiti and beer. One of them looks just like the eighth-grader who was suspended for spray-painting the words "Led Zeppelin Rules" outside the cafeteria and setting off the fire alarms on purpose. They go quiet, and I turn away when I realize that they're looking at me. One of them says, "What a dog," and the others laugh—that dumb, empty laugh teenage boys sometimes have. They start making barking noises, but for once I do not feel intimidated. *My name is Amber. My mother and I have run away.* Nothing they say can hurt me today.

Inside the air-conditioned store everything's bright and cool, fluorescent lights buzzing overhead. I find the tampons for my mother and then wander over to the cosmetics section. Before me is a row of compacts, filled with pressed powder in different shades of beige. Each compact has its own little mirror, its own tiny powder puff, and shuts tight with a satisfying click. In their miniature practicality, they seem to me perfect, like Swiss army knives for girls.

The powder is the same brand my sister uses, to keep her face from looking shiny, and I remember her letting me play with it once, showing me how to dust the sweet-smelling, chalky powder over my face. "Not too much," she had warned, "or you'll look like a clown." Now I slip one of the compacts into my pocket, my fingers running over the smooth, cool circle of plastic. It's about time I had my own. I take a deep breath and push my glasses back on my nose and make my way slowly down the brightly lit aisle, stopping to look at a mascara display. If I don't get back to the motel soon, my mother will start to get worried. And she wants her chocolate. She's probably lying on the bed right now, thinking about how nice it will be, after such a long drive, to have something sweet and delicious, a small reward for a day of hurry and confusion. She must be tired too. I suddenly feel very sorry for her, and wish I could get her something better than just a chocolate bar: a bouquet of tulips (she likes the yellow ones best), or the fancy jasmine soap she sometimes buys herself as a treat, the one that promises to *reduce stress and ease muscles.* . . .

There's a quiet tap on my shoulder. "Excuse me, miss." A tall woman stands over me, her eyes large and staring. Everything grows very still, and I am aware of my breath drawing in and out, the sweat collecting beneath my breasts. I can feel the outlines of my heart.

The woman leans in even closer. "Miss?" The compact is enormous in my pocket, a dead weight. All I can think about is making it to the front door.

"Does this base match my skin?" The woman smiles apologetically. "It's so hard to tell in this light." She holds out her hand to show me, glittering bracelets hanging loosely on her tanned and wrinkled arm.

I take a look. "Actually, you're supposed to test it on the back of your hand, not your wrist." I learned this from one of my magazines, just today in fact, in the car.

She raises an eyebrow. "I never knew that."

I smile. "A lot of people make that mistake." I go to the front counter and pay for the tampons and a couple of chocolate bars, making sure to get the one with almonds, the kind my mother likes best.

Later that evening, on our way back from getting dinner, my mother and I walk past a man in a wheelchair. He has long hair, and the back of the wheelchair is decorated with bumper stickers. I recognize one of them from a locker at school: PEACE NOW, in rainbow letters, with a peace symbol for the letter O. An old canvas bag with a picture of tropical birds hangs over the side of the chair, holding a newspaper and some books.

At first I think the man in the wheelchair is stuck, since he's just sitting there on the curb by the crosswalk, not moving at all. But then I see that he is sleeping. Sitting in his chair, fast asleep by the side of the road, looking as snug as a person dozing in an armchair.

Back in Las Palmas my mother would hurry me past homeless people, whispering, *You never know, they could be violent, and most of them are addicts anyway.* But this time she takes a dollar bill out of her pocket and tucks it inside one of the books. We walk back to the motel room without saying anything. I think about the wheelchair, how strange it must be to be able to sit and move at the same time.

When we get back to the room, my mother points out that we are in number eighteen, which according to Jewish tradition is a lucky number. "There's a reason you picked this place," my mother says. "Something special. I can feel it." My mother opens the door. "And look. They even brought us a TV."

"Great." I'm not sure what else to say.

That night, as I fall asleep to the sound of the traffic outside, I count my blessings. I am healthy. Except for my bad vision, which has been fixed by glasses, I am in pretty good shape. Even if I get picked last for teams at school, I can still run and walk. All of my fingers work. I have enough to eat, and I know how to read. And my mother loves me. That is worth something. Before I know it, I'm asleep.

24

When I wake up the next morning my mother is standing in front of the bathroom mirror, scissors in hand. "It's time for a new look." She holds her hair back from her face, examining her reflection from both sides. "I need you to cut my hair."

I stare at my mother's glossy black hair. Except for the trims I've given Maxwell, I've never cut real hair before, just doll hair, the thin plastic kind. My mother's hair is thick and wavy.

"I think I should change the color too," she says, studying her hair in the mirror.

"Can I do mine?"

My mother looks at me. "I'll think about it." This is too good to be true; unlike most mothers, when mine says, "I'll think about it," she's halfway there. "Remember all those pictures of me with red hair, when you were a baby?"

It's true; in one of our albums there is a series of photographs of my mother with all different kinds of hair, even blond. In one of the blond pictures she's holding me and wearing a cowboy hat, looking kind of like a country-western singer. I am wearing nothing but a diaper. I suddenly wish I had that picture with me, wanting to remember what I looked like as a baby. But the album is still back at our house, buried in a box in the basement.

My mother goes into the bathroom and turns on the faucet,

bending over to dampen her hair in the sink. "It's easier to cut if it's wet," she tells me. When she's done she takes a small plastic comb, the kind men keep in their back pocket, and parts her hair carefully down the middle. Maxwell watches curiously, wondering what we're up to. I wonder if my mother will want to dye his fur as well, if it's illegal to change your dog's hair color.

My mother wraps a small towel around her neck and sits down on the toilet, so that her back is to the mirror. "There, it's just like at the hairdresser," she says, handing me the scissors.

I stand next to her, not sure where to begin. My mother's hair is so beautiful, and there is so much of it. "Are you sure you want me to do this?"

"Yeah, go ahead." My mother closes her eyes hard, as if she's about to get a shot at the doctor's office.

I try to remember what hairdressers do when they cut hair. First I comb her hair into sections. Then I take a little bit— maybe an inch in length—between my fingers and cut. The hair comes right off in my hand, dark and shiny against my skin.

It occurs to me that I am holding a small piece of my mother in my hand. I show it to her. "How's that?"

My mother opens her eyes. "You'll have to do more than that," she says. "I want it short."

My mouth feels dry. I take a deep breath and keep cutting. I move from one side of my mother's head to the other, navigating around the toilet, trying to keep everything as straight as possible.

It looks good while I'm doing it, but by the time I'm done with one side it's clear that the first part is much shorter than the rest. So I keep cutting, working my way back and forth across my mother's head.

The hair gets shorter and shorter.

Maxwell lets out a low whine. If dogs could frown, he'd be frowning.

"Do you think Maxwell will recognize me?" My mother wipes a stray bit of hair off her face.

"Of course. You'll still smell the same."

My mother nods. "You're right. That's one thing we can't

change, right, Maxie?" Maxwell comes over and licks her hand, his tail wagging with what seems like relief. "Let's go downstairs after this, and see what they have for breakfast," my mother says.

"Sounds good." The truth is, I'm feeling a little sick to my stomach. I still have more hair to get through: every time I think I'm done I realize that it's still uneven. I can tell my mother's becoming impatient; she's even squirming a bit, like a little girl getting her hair cut.

Finally she puts her hand out for the scissors. "Maybe you better stop cutting." I hand them over, scared of what she'll think when she looks in the mirror.

For a minute she doesn't say anything, just touches the back of her head. Then she smiles. "Not bad. We'll go somewhere tomorrow and get it cleaned up." Somehow, the short hair makes her look younger, even though you'd think it would be the other way around. She hugs me. "Thanks, sweetie." I am so relieved that I almost start crying. I rinse off the scissors in the sink, trying not to let any of the extra hair go down the drain.

My mother takes off her shirt and shakes out the hair that's collected on the collar. Her breasts, covered by a white lace bra, look out of place with the short hair. It reminds me of the pictures in one of Miriam's favorite books, *An Illustrated Guide to Egyptian Mythology*—the gods with a cat or crocodile's head and a human's body.

"Between this, and dying my hair, I really think they won't be able to recognize me." My mother sighs. "I'd like to go blond again, but then I'd really stand out."

I don't say anything, just pick at a little bit of hair that's scattered on the floor. I want to know more about the people she thinks are after her, the drug dealers with the white Continental. How old are they, and are they all men? How many are there? Two or two hundred? And most of all, are they even real? The questions are spinning in my head, in small mad circles, but I can't get my mouth to put the words together. Every time I try, my mouth feels solid, wooden, like a puppet's mouth. So I just put on my clothes, dusting my face with a little bit of the shop-lifted pressed powder before we go out.

The motel room is its own little world. Everything in it is scaled down, a smaller version of its usual self. Petite soaps, tiny shampoos, a bathtub too small to stretch out in. Even the refrigerator is a miniature version of a real refrigerator, with a tiny, half-sized ice cube tray and a shelf that only holds six eggs. It is like playing house.

Still, everything fits just right. A half-sized ironing board drops down from inside the closet, which is only big enough to hang a few outfits. The tiny hair dryer, permanently attached to the wall, has its own little shelf. A basic set of four spoons, forks, knives, cups, glasses, plates, and bowls somehow fits in the wood cabinet over the sink, which itself is too small to hold more than a couple of dirty dishes.

The plates and bowls are decorated with a blue and green geometric pattern, and match the cups, which are made of green plastic. "Thank God there are four of everything," my mother laughs. "We'll only have to wash the dishes *every other* time we use them."

But the set bothers me. Every time I get a bowl or a cup I think about how the ideal number is four, not two. My mother and I, the plates seem to say, are not a complete unit on our own. We are an incomplete set.

We stock up on things that don't need to be kept in a refrigerator: peanut butter and jelly, bread, cereal, potato chips, nuts. The refrigerator is just big enough to squeeze in a half gallon of milk and some containers of yogurt. The motel has doughnuts and coffee in the morning, and I get used to eating the same lunch every day: peanut butter on whole wheat, with a banana snatched from the motel lobby. But for dinner we go out. "We can't just eat junk all day long," my mother says.

Every night for a week we eat at the diner down the street. Weekday dinners, if you order by five thirty, are only $6.99, and that includes a drink and dessert: a hot fudge sundae or apple pie with ice cream.

My mother and I stand out at the restaurant. All the other diners seem to be single men, half hidden behind their newspapers, or retirees, so the waitresses begin to recognize us. "And a Tab for you," my favorite waitress, Carla, always says to me. "With lots of ice and a lemon."

I know she's curious about us, wonders why we're there so much. "Your kitchen being redone?" she asks.

My mother laughs and says no. "No kitchen to redo."

Carla puts a bottle of ketchup down on the table. "Most of the women in here night after night are having stuff done. Or they just got divorced." Then she coughs. "Excuse me," she says, as if she's realized that she just said something rude.

"That's okay," says my mother. "We're on vacation."

"Here?" Carla looks puzzled. There's nothing around this area for a tourist to see, not even one of those big malls that people visit from other places.

I take over. "Visiting relatives."

"Oh." Carla nods.

"My uncle," I continue, "is a doctor." My mother is staring at me. "He's just discovered a cure for a very rare disease. We're here to see him get awarded the Nobel Prize."

Now my mother looks fierce; I read the warning in her eyes. "Actually it's not a Nobel," I finish lamely. "Something else big."

"That's very impressive," Carla says, not really listening. She takes a notepad out of her pocket and starts to flip through it. My mother sips her coffee, and I see that her eyes are filled with tears.

Nighttime is the best.

Every evening, after the stores are quiet and still, my mother and I go for a walk. We make our way through the hushed streets, hands in pockets, not really speaking. In the brightly lit windows we can see families at dinner, gathered around a table, eating in unthinking unison. Sometimes we are startled by a cat, or even a raccoon.

It's almost romantic.

Almost too quickly, the motel becomes our home. The bathroom floor is littered with our dirty underwear and socks. Soda cans collect on the table beside the room's one comfortable chair, where I spend most of my time, looking at old magazines borrowed from the motel's front office.

They've been left behind by other guests: old copies of *Consumer Reports, Biker's World, Reader's Digest.* My favorite is *Horse and Rider,* with its photos of saddles and riding gear, its odd descriptions of the differences between mares and stallions. *Note the male's proud bearing, the female's softer, more gentle features.* I study the pictures carefully, but they all look the same to me.

"Ta-dah!" My mother opens the bathroom door, wrapped in one of the motel's large yellow towels. She's dyed her hair. "What do you think?" She spins around slowly, so I can see her from all angles. Earlier this morning we went to the drugstore and spent a long time looking at the hair dye, trying to pick just the right color. There were dozens of small boxes lined up on the shelf, with names like "Country Blonde" and "Raven Lady." It took my mother a while to choose; she didn't want to buy just any old brand. "You really have to be careful with this stuff," she said. "It can completely ruin your hair." Finally she settled on a box that promised the sort of everyday color that's a little in between everything and you might just call light brown. It had seemed like an easy enough color, neither here nor there, but different enough from my mother's own rich dark brown hair, especially short. But now my mother's hair is a bright red, nothing like the box at all.

"What about me?" I thought my mother and I were going to dye our hair later, right before bed, so that when I woke up in the morning I'd have a whole new head.

"I don't think so, sweetie." She picks up a razor and runs it over a little bit of leg that she missed in the shower. "Anyway, I used the whole box."

I turn up the sound on the TV. A commercial for a new kind of high fiber cereal blares its way into the room. We've been at the motel for a week. Whenever I ask my mother how long we're going to stay here, she gets upset and tells me *she's not sure yet* and that I should go take a swim in the pool while it's still light out.

My mother wipes off her leg with the edge of the towel. "So, really, what do you think?"

I watch the kid on the screen fill a huge bowl with cereal. "It's kind of fake."

My mother's face falls. "Are you sure?" She moves to the mirror over the dresser and stares at her reflection. Her dark eyebrows and lashes look especially stark.

"You look like Penny Fitzgerald." Penny Fitzgerald is the secretary who answers the phone in the principal's office at school. Her hair is a beautiful, copper penny red, just like her name, and the color looks good on her. But on my mother it looks strange, as if she's hiding her real head under a wig. "I think you should rinse it out."

My mother wraps the towel tighter around her body. I can tell she's annoyed with me. "You know, Adie, the least you could do is try to have a positive attitude about this."

When we're outside walking the dog later that afternoon, Dennis, the manager, stops us. "Hey," he says to my mother. "You did something to your hair."

She pats it gently. "Nothing too drastic."

"It looks good." He gives her that funny smile men always seem to save up just for my mother. It's not the creepy smile that some women get when they walk down the street wearing miniskirts or tank tops. It's more respectful. Like she might suddenly surprise them, and turn out to be their mother too.

My mother works out a special rate on the room with Dennis, a weekly rate instead of the nightly one. At first he hesitates, not wanting us to pay so little, but the motel is only half full. He finally gives in, on the condition that we don't have maid service and that we'll leave immediately if someone else needs the room.

My mother is pleased with the arrangement. "No one needs

to change their sheets *every* day," she says. "It's ridiculous. And I don't want people looking through our stuff anyway." I think about how she used to search through my sister's belongings for drugs, and wonder what she is worried about someone finding.

Dennis has what Miriam would call *a thing* for my mother. I catch him looking at her when she's stretched out by the pool, her long, lean body browning in the sun. "Just a little crush," my mother sighs. Dennis isn't married, and as far as I can tell, he doesn't have a girlfriend. It seems like he spends most nights inside the little room behind the office, drinking beer and watching cop shows like *Hill Street Blues* and *Magnum, P.I.* "I kind of wanted to be an actor," he tells me, "but it didn't work out." The empty beer cans are crushed in a big plastic bag outside, waiting to go to the city dump and recycling center, where they give him five cents a can. "At the rate I drink," he says, "I'll be able to pay for my retirement."

I wonder what it would be like if my mother married Dennis, if I could just stay at Motel del Mar my whole life, passing my days in lucky room number eighteen.

25

After we've been at the motel for a couple of weeks I ask my mother if I can call Lainey. "I'd rather you didn't," she says, as if I'd just asked if I could turn on the radio.

"But she's going to wonder why I left without saying goodbye." I pick at the dry skin around my feet; no matter how much vitamin E lotion I use at night, it still comes back the next day, scaly and rough. "She might be scared something's happened to me," I say, thinking that the word *scared* might trigger something for my mother. Maybe Mrs. Aronowitz can drive Lainey here, or put her on a bus, and she can stay the night, the way she used to back in Las Palmas, when we'd stay up until three in the morning, eating potato chips and candy bars shoplifted from the Joe-La corner store. Or maybe Mrs. Aronowitz could convince my mother that it's time to come back home, could mention the nice, handsome man she just met at the Temple bake sale, *divorced, such a mensch, perfect for you. . . .*

My mother runs a comb through her hair, which is now fading to a rusty brown. "We just need to stay away a little bit longer, 'til things die down."

"How long?"

"Amber, we're talking about drug dealers here." My mother's

voice shifts to a higher pitch. "Remember the guy we saw on *60 Minutes?* They cut off people's ears."

I remember. Miriam and I had been forced to watch it. It was an interview with an ex-gang member, a heroin addict, talking about how he had *found Jesus Christ* and *realized the errors of his ways.* One of which was cutting people in fits of anger. They showed a picture of the man with the cut ear; it was sliced down the middle but had somehow healed, even though he couldn't hear very well anymore.

"He didn't really cut *off* the ear."

My mother looks disgusted. "Amber, my god. You're not taking this seriously." She grabs her wallet and leaves, shutting the door behind her. I know she would like to slam it, but she also doesn't want to call attention to us—she's told me to be careful about making too much noise, about doing anything sudden or strange that *might make people notice us.* I hear the sound of our car starting up, its familiar hum and groan.

Now, with my mother gone, I take off all my clothes and look at my body in the bathroom mirror. It's a three-way mirror, so I can see myself from all angles, and I am fascinated, having never been able to do this before. It is strange to see yourself from behind or from the side; it is like looking at a stranger who looks like you, but is not really you, perhaps a distant relative.

Maxwell stares at me in that funny way dogs sometimes do when you're naked. "You're a perv," I say to him, putting my jeans back on. He just wags his tail. I put my clothes back on, thinking about the gang member and the ear. He really did sound sorry. Maybe there really is something special about *finding Jesus,* something that Jews don't get to know about. I suddenly remember that tucked away in the nightstand, along with an old 1978 phone book and a menu for Chinese delivery and a couple of dried-out ballpoint pens, is a Bible, and now I open the drawer and take it out carefully. I cradle it in both hands; it seems like something you should hold gently. It's covered in faded blue leather, the words PLACED BY THE GIDEONS stamped at the bottom in gold type. There is a little business card bookmarking a page, with an address and a toll-free number from the Samaritans, the people who put up signs next to bridges, reminding you not to jump, and I wonder what they would do if I called them. *Hello*, I would say. *I am not interested in killing myself, but my mother and I are staying at Motel del Mar, in room 18, which in Judaism is a lucky number, and my mother is scared that people are after her. You will recognize the motel by the faded neon sign outside with a picture of a dolphin and the Ford pickup that is always parked in the handicapped space. I would appreciate it if you could come as soon as possible, because I have already missed two weeks' worth of swimming lessons and I really need to get home.* I open the Bible to a random page, skipping around in hope of finding the good parts, the sections with sacrifice and bloodshed. Maybe I can find some baby killings, or death by stoning. But mostly it is boring, the writing tense and stilted. I read:

> *We glory in tribulations also: knowing that tribulation worketh patience; and patience, experience; and experience, hope.*

The word *Romans* is printed in the top right corner in blood-red ink—the only spot of color on the whole page. *Patience. Experience. Hope.* It takes me a moment or two to puzzle out the sentence. I wonder if you can skip a couple of steps and just go right to hope. I stretch out on my mother's bed, being careful not to snag my foot in the part of the bedspread with the torn lining. If Miriam were here, she'd tease me for even picking up a Bible, would tell me I was becoming a religious freak. I turn to another page and find:

> *There be four things which are little upon the earth, but they are exceeding wise. The ants are a people not strong, yet they prepare their meat in the summer. The conies are but a feeble folk, yet they make their houses in the rocks. The locusts have no king, yet go they forth all of them by bands. The spider taketh hold with her hands, and is in kings' palaces.*

I have no idea what a coney is, and I've never seen a real locust. I look at the page again. *In kings' palaces.* I picture a spider with a tiny gold crown on its head, roaming the halls of a marble-lined palace.

Just then I hear the sound of my mother coming up the outside stairs; the jangle of her car keys and her quick step. I shove the Bible back into the drawer. By the time she opens the door I am lying on the bed, reading a copy of *TV Guide* from three weeks ago with a picture of Tom Selleck on the cover.

"Hi, honey." My mother has brought home fried chicken, and the smell of fat and grease quickly fills the little room. I take the bucket from her hands and set the table with takeout plastic forks and the gray-white, already dirty-looking napkins they always throw in. My mother unbuttons her light pink cardigan sweater, the one that says LORD & TAYLOR EXCLUSIVE on the tag, and hangs it over the folding chair by the door, being careful not to snag it on the chair's metal edge. "I'm sorry I snapped at you before, sweetie. I didn't mean to."

I swallow hard, wishing Miriam were here. "I know."

She perches upright on the edge of the bed, crossing her legs under her, very ladylike. "The thing about these people is that they're really sneaky. When I was at the chicken place I saw one of them, pulling out of the parking lot." She peels off a shoe. "He sort of ducked down, so I couldn't see his face, but I'm pretty sure it was him.

"I know this is difficult for you, but it's just for a short time, and you're so smart that missing some school won't hurt you." Something in her expression seems different from usual, as if she feels sorry for me. "Is there anything you want to ask me?"

I fold the napkins carefully and place them next to the plastic plates, thinking about all the questions I've stored up over the last couple of weeks: How long are we going to stay here? Will it always be like this? Will I be like you—beautiful and scared—when I grow up? But I know I can't ask any of these questions. So I just say, "What's a coney?"

"A coney? You mean like Coney Island?"

"I guess."

My mother looks puzzled. "I have no idea. My sister and I used to go to Coney Island all the time when we were girls." She sighs. "You could get a huge scoop of ice cream for a nickel."

We sit down at the foldout table to eat our chicken. The table is small, but there's just enough room for everything we need. We can even look out the window. It's a hazy day, and there's only one person hanging out by the pool, an old lady in a bathrobe and slippers staring emptily at the water.

My mother reaches for my shiny pink can of Tab and makes a face. "I don't know how you can drink this stuff."

I shrug. "You get used to it," I say, hoping she can't tell that I'm crying. My mother goes to the bathroom sink and pours herself a glass of water, using the little plastic glass meant for a toothbrush. I play with the soda can's pull-top ring, bending it back and forth until the little metal tab finally breaks off. The ring part fits right over my finger.

I think about something I once read in a magazine: that you should never just throw the pull tops on the ground because birds, attracted to their gleaming surface, can choke on them and die. Not just magpies, famous in fairy tales for stealing rings and other bright objects, but ordinary birds like seagulls and robins. It had seemed so unfair, that the thing the bird wanted most could hurt it.

My mother comes back, and we eat our dinner quietly, just like a mother and daughter on vacation, and act like nothing has happened.

26

One afternoon I watch as Dennis fishes the leaves out of the pool. He uses a long metal pole with a plastic net on the end. "You missed a couple over there," I tell him. I don't want to be rude, but really if he's going to clean the pool he should get all the leaves.

"You want to try it?" Dennis hands me the pole, which is heavier than it looks. Getting the leaves out of the water is kind of like sweeping, but in slow motion. When I'm done I lean the pole up against the wooden shed, just where I've seen him leave it.

"Maybe you can get a job here," Dennis says.

"Really?" I've never had any kind of job at all, not even a paper route. The closest I ever got was last spring, when Lainey and I were supposed to sell chocolate nut bars to raise money for the school's band trip. The chocolate was waxy and old, wrapped in red and white paper that said SUPPORT YOUR LOCAL SCHOOLS, with a picture of a bear holding a pile of books. We were only able to sell two bars, to the deaf lady down the street, and ended up eating the rest of the candy ourselves. I had to sneak money from my mother's purse to cover it.

"I'd hire you in a sec, but you're not old enough." Dennis lights up a cigarette and looks at me. "What's your mom do, anyway?"

"You mean for work?"

Dennis nods.

"She's a secretary." I try to sound casual, though inside I'm panicking. What did my mother tell me to say? "But she's not working now."

"I guessed that." He stubs out the cigarette; he never takes more than a few puffs. Apparently he's trying to quit. "She's a good-looking lady, your mother."

I never know what to say when people tell me this: am I supposed to say thank you? A slight breeze pushes at the telephone wires overhead. I pull my sweater closer around my body.

"Are you happy here?" Dennis narrows his eyes at me.

"Sure." I don't want to insult him, don't want to say that we could use a bigger room. Or that it would be nice if they got some new towels, because the ones we have are scratchy and old and don't even match. Or that in general the whole place is what my mother calls *a little on the dumpy side.* "If it were my motel I'd put out some fresh flowers and get some new plants that aren't dying," I say. "Just to brighten things up."

Dennis cracks his knuckles, loudly, the way Miriam does when she's bored. "Those are interesting suggestions," he says, staring at me. "I'll have to think about them."

I can tell he's just humoring me, but from then on he lets me help him out around the motel. In the afternoons I make a slow circle around the pool, straightening out the sun chairs so they're lined up perfectly, gathering up the empty water glasses and soda cans that have been left behind. If I see any gum wrappers lying around I make sure to throw them away. Old magazines and newspapers get piled up on the wooden bench outside the front office.

Sometimes I even empty the ashtrays, sneaking the leftover cigarette butts into my pocket. The musty, harsh smell reminds me of Miriam. I try smoking them a couple of times, but they just make me cough.

It's a rainy night. My mother is sprawled out on the bed, reading one of my fashion magazines. Her feet are bare, her nails colored a rosy, girlish pink. Without looking up, she reaches for a can of grape soda on the bedside table.

As for me, I'm deep into *Marjorie Morningstar,* a book I had never heard of until my mother and I watched the movie on TV, with Natalie Wood, who my mother said isn't really Jewish. The movie made us both cry, but it was the good kind of crying, the kind that makes you feel better. Now I'm reading the book, lost in Marjorie's world of dances and dates.

We've been inside almost all day; at first the rain was just a gentle drizzle, but now it's coming down hard and fast. I steal a peek at my mother. She is reading an article called "Making Your Dreams Come True: Six Easy Steps to Success!" Usually she shakes her head at the articles in these magazines, says that they're just trying to sell something. But this one seems to have struck a nerve. She has even folded over the page to mark her place.

"Listen to this, Adie." My mother clears her throat and begins reading. "*Most people live their lives in a state of fear and denial. They believe that their world is circumscribed by limitations—whether emotional, financial, or physical. But what they don't realize is that our dreams are within our grasp—we just need to be willing to reach for them.*" She turns to me and sighs. "Isn't that the truth?"

"What does *circumscribed* mean?" I ask, thinking of circumcision.

My mother puts the magazine down with a pleased look on her face. "What do you think it means? *Circum* and *scribed.*" She tries to make her voice patient and teacher-like.

I think about it for a second. "Um. A circle. And *scribe*—an inscription. Writing." I picture a tiny man drawing a giant circle, his face tight with concentration. "A circle drawn around something?"

"Exactly," my mother says with satisfaction. "Like a boundary, keeping things in or out." She turns back to the magazine. "In this case, it refers to the barriers we put in our way." Outside, the rain continues its steady drone.

"I think we should make a list." My mother flips on the overhead light, bathing the room in a dull yellow glow. "Of our goals and aspirations."

"Like what?" Maxwell barks at something. He's never liked the rain.

"What we want to accomplish. Even the small things." My mother fishes around in her purse for a couple of pens. "And then we can see if we have any in common." She tears a page from the blue spiral notebook she uses to keep track of our expenses and hands it to me.

I'm not sure where to start. "How long should it be?"

My mother thinks for a moment. "Just four or five things. Whatever comes to mind right away." She smiles. "Otherwise you'll think too hard about it."

I stare at the blank page. Usually I don't think about my goals at all. I'm the kind of person who concentrates on the *here and now*, as my mother likes to say. But I plunge right in. I write:

> *Go to college*
> *Learn to back float*
> *Find Miriam soon*
> *Lose weight!!! (10 pounds)*
> *Read all of Herman Wouk*

I write it all down as quickly as possible, so I can't cross anything out or change my mind. When I'm done I realize the losing weight part should be closer to the top of the list, but it's too late now. I wonder what my mother will think about it. "Show me yours first," I say.

She hands me her list. It reads:

> *Get a job!*
> *Start drawing again*
> *Visit my beautiful daughter Miriam*
> *Clean the venetian blinds*

She laughs when she sees my face. "The venetian blinds are for when we get home," she says. "It's a funny list, don't you think?"

Really, I am not sure what to think. My mother keeps talking about how we have to watch our spending and keep "to a budget," which means that we split meals when possible and try not to buy anything we don't really need. She hasn't worked for almost two months: how is she going to get a job when we're not even at home?

I look at the list again. "I didn't know you could draw."

"I used to be quite good." Then she reads my list. "Oh, my God." Tears form in her eyes. "We both put down Miriam."

She starts to sob. I've never seen my mother cry like this: real heavy violent crying, the kind that makes it hard to breathe. She is actually wheezing and gasping. After a few minutes she gets up and goes to the bathroom, shutting the door behind her.

I get up and steal a sip from my mother's grape soda. Outside, the rain lets up slightly. I think about Miriam's sketchbook, buried deep in the bottom of my duffel bag, the pictures she drew of our mother with the long hair. I wish I could show them to her without upsetting her—without her also seeing the sad, angry things Miriam had written in the margins—and that we could hang them on the wall, just so she could have something of Miriam's with her now, something to warm up our little motel room with the torn wallpaper and ragged carpet. But looking around the tiny room, where all of our things are jumbled on top of one another in a crazy mess, I realize I want something of my own, a secret something she doesn't know about, that belongs only to me. Maxwell whines suddenly from across the room, as if he knows what I'm thinking.

I hear my mother blow her nose several times, and the splash of water as she washes her face. When she comes out she smiles at me. "I feel a lot better now."

I pretend to read my book. "That's good, Mom."

My mother gets into bed. "I sure am tired, sweetie." She shuts off her reading lamp and pulls the covers close around her, so close that I can barely see her face.

"Oh, and Amber?"

"Yeah?"

"You really don't need to lose any weight." She rolls over and almost immediately begins snoring: gentle, sweet snores that hardly sound like snoring at all. I tuck myself into bed, and pretend that I'm Marjorie Morningstar, with nothing more to worry about than what dress to wear to the next party, but it still takes me a long time to fall asleep.

The next night, after we've taken Maxwell on his evening walk, my mother and I come back to the motel room to find a little box of chocolates on the bed.

I dive at them. "Where'd these come from?"

"Let me see." My mother snatches the box out of my hand, her voice sharp and hard. "You should never just eat strange things, Amber, they could be spiked with drugs, for God's sake. Remember that report we saw on *Nightline,* about people spiking candy with LSD?" My mother made Miriam and me watch a news story about drug dealers giving kids little candy with acid in them—pretty little colored strips that look like button candy, but are really laced with secret dangerous things. My mother was worried because I have such a sweet tooth, but Miriam said the whole thing was just a myth.

My mother looks at the box suspiciously for a moment and then sighs with relief. "They're from Dennis." She shows me a small piece of paper, torn from a notepad: *To the Lady of Room 18, From Dennis, Hope you feel better.* She sits down on the bed and hands me the box, which is wrapped with plastic and says RUSSELL STOVER CHOCOLATE TURTLES in green cursive script.

I struggle with the plastic wrapping. "I didn't know you were sick."

"I'm not. I think he's just trying to be nice." My mother smiles to herself, a small smile I remember from when we were spending time with Sidney and her father. Even here, living in this tiny motel room, putting on weight and barely brushing her hair and wearing the same clothes almost every day, my mother is still able to get men to look at her. It is a mystery.

At any rate, the candy is delicious: caramel and pecans and chocolate. I look at the box. "Why are they called turtles?"

My mother puts one in her mouth and starts chewing slowly. "I don't know."

"They don't look like turtles."

My mother stares at the box for a moment. "I guess they don't." I wonder what she's thinking. Being given a whole box of chocolate: it's the sort of thing that happens to women in the movies or in books, like *Marjorie Morningstar*. Of course, usually in books the women are given the chocolate on Valentine's Day or on a date. It's not just left on top of the bed in the dirty motel room where they're hiding out with their daughter, with the torn carpet and the peeling wallpaper and the faucet that always drips. But as my mother likes to say, *It's all the same in the end*. By the time the evening news comes on we've eaten the whole box.

27

Back home, my mother would take forever at the grocery store, studying the food labels for things like pesticides and artificial flavorings. "Everything these days causes brain damage or cancer," she would say, whenever Miriam and I begged her to buy some sugar cereal. At Lainey's house I would eat bowl after bowl of Cap'n Crunch and Froot Loops, wondering if they really would do something funny to the inside of my head. But now that we are staying at the motel, we eat whatever's convenient. Buckets of greasy chicken, cheeseburgers and milk shakes. Candy bars and potato chips. Soda, lots of it, especially since the water from the sink has a strange taste. My mother likes to joke that maybe something has died in the pipes, which I don't think is funny at all.

"My diet has really gone out the window," my mother says one evening, patting her bloated stomach in front of the mirror.

"You look really good." I mean it; she actually looks prettier now that she's gained a little weight.

"It's probably for the best. They'll never recognize me if I get really fat." She smiles at me. "I'll just keep eating all those doughnuts."

Every morning the motel serves doughnuts and coffee. The doughnuts stay on the platter day after day until they get picked, so the rejects—the oddball flavors, the ones without chocolate—

show up each morning until someone finally takes a bite and throws it in the trash. I feel a little sorry for them, actually. They remind me of being chosen last for teams in gym class.

One morning the doughnut selection is especially bad. Dennis sips coffee from the chipped mug that says CALIFORNIA: STATE OF POSSIBILITY and watches as I try to make up my mind. "Why don't you eat that one?" he says, pointing to an oddly shaped beige doughnut with yellow sprinkles. "I bet it's really good."

I know the doughnut has been there for at least two days, maybe even three. I stick my tongue out and make a retching noise the way Lainey used to whenever the school cafeteria served sloppy joes. I wouldn't have done that if my mother was around—she'd have shaken her head and said it was *crude, and not what young ladies do*—but she's still back in our room, taking a shower.

Dennis raises an eyebrow at me. "Okay, then," he says. "You want something real to eat?"

"Sure." Truly, I am sick of doughnuts.

Dennis takes me through a narrow hallway and into a kitchen at the back of the motel, with peeling wallpaper and an old-fashioned table, the kind that looks like it belongs in the fifties. I remember hearing the word for it somewhere: *Formica*. A voice on the radio, charged with static, announces the weather: *seventy and sunny, with a chance of showers in the afternoon*. The window is propped open with a large canister of Morton Salt.

Dennis catches me looking at it. "That window doesn't stay open on its own," he says apologetically.

I sit down on the one chair that's not covered with newspapers and look around. There are some scrambled eggs still warming on the stove. A pot of coffee. I haven't been inside a kitchen in a while. The table is covered with clutter, old magazines and a pile of bills: credit cards, electric, phone. The electric bill has a big red line on the envelope. I pick up the newspaper, to see what my horoscope says, but it's already two weeks old.

Dennis pulls a few strips of bacon out of their package and throws them into a pan. "A gas stove," he says, proudly. "Not one of those shitty electric ones."

I'm not sure what to say, so I just watch Dennis as he stands hunched over at the stove, wondering if all four strips of bacon are for me, or if we're going to share them. The smell of the bacon is overwhelming; I can actually feel my mouth watering. It feels like a long time since I've eaten anything that wasn't from the diner down the street, or out of a vending machine.

He puts a giant pile of eggs and bacon down before me. "Dig in," he says. The eggs have onions and tomatoes mixed in, along with some other flavor, paprika maybe.

"You sure can eat."

I put my fork down, embarrassed. Dennis laughs. "Go ahead. It's nice to see a girl eat." He gets a cigarette and his lighter and sits back in the chair opposite me. "So what's the story with your mom?"

"What do you mean?" I try to smile through a mouthful of food.

"What are you guys doing here?"

I chew slowly, to give myself time to come up with an answer. "Nothing much."

Dennis scratches the back of his neck. "I can see that." He hands me a cloth napkin that already has a stain on it. "You must be bored."

"Not really."

"You sure about that?"

I look at the pile of bills on the chair next to me. "Actually, no offense, but we're not going to stay here much longer." I swallow a piece of egg. "We're going to visit my big sister Miriam. She lives in Oregon." It feels so good to say Miriam's name that for a moment I forget my mother's rules about *staying anonymous,* like the girl in the *Go Ask Alice* book. *Don't tell anyone anything about us,* she's said to me a million times. There is a noise all of a sudden, a weird buzz, like a mosquito dying in one of those electric zappers. Dennis gets up. "That's the front desk. I'll be back in a sec."

He leaves the room, taking his coffee with him. I add more salt to my eggs, but I'm not hungry anymore. I scrape the rest of the eggs into the trash under the sink. The sink is already filled with dirty dishes and pans and glasses. I wash all of them, lining them up neatly on the drying rack.

When I'm finished I close the door quietly and go out to the pool. My mother is already there, sitting on a lounge chair with a cup of coffee and a newspaper. The ugly doughnut is on her plate. "Where were you?"

"In the bathroom," I say, taking the comics section from the paper. "I really had to go." For some reason, I don't want to tell her that Dennis made me breakfast. It feels as if it would be an insult to her, like: Why don't you feed me a real breakfast? Why do we have to eat stale doughnuts every morning, when you used to lecture me and Miriam about how *breakfast is the most important meal of the day?*

"I think it might rain later." My mother takes a bite of the doughnut and looks surprised. "This one's not so bad. Try it."

She hands me the doughnut and I nibble a tiny piece off the edge. She's right; it's actually kind of good, in a sticky sweet way. A hummingbird buzzes around a nearby bush, holding still and moving all at once.

A voice calls out to us from across the pool. "Hi, ladies!" It's Dennis. "How are you doing today?"

My mother looks up from under the hat that she's bought to keep the sun off her face. "Fine, thanks."

I'm worried that Dennis is going to say something about the breakfast, or ask more questions about my sister, but he just smiles. "Everything okay with your room?"

"It's great." My mother pats the towel next to her. "We could probably use an extra set of towels."

"No problem." Dennis winks at me. "See you later."

"He really is a nice guy," my mother says. I stretch out on a lounge chair next to her, sinking back into its soft padded cushion. The plastic cover is already warm from the morning sun. A flock of seagulls, far from the ocean, swoops and dives overhead, and I trace their uneven path with my finger, trying to predict where they'll go next.

28

We've been at the motel for almost three weeks. Our days unravel slowly and quietly. We end up going to the drugstore across the street almost every day. Usually we don't really need anything: we just pick up some Q-tips or a new razor. But I think the fact that we're shopping, out in public, makes my mother feel like our lives aren't that unusual. After all, in a store, everyone looks normal.

The drugstore always has new magazines, there are even a couple of chairs near the pharmacy counter where you can sit, not too comfortably, and read them. Sometimes I buy a soda and just hang out there for an hour or more, flipping through *Cosmo* and *People,* listening to people talk to the pharmacist about their heartburn and arthritis. The clerks don't seem to mind, even though there is a sign that says NO LOITERING. I guess I don't look like a loiterer.

There is a high school nearby, and the teenage girls who come to the store in the afternoons remind me of Miriam. From my chair by the pharmacy counter, I watch them giggle over the celebrity magazines and swear at each other and open the lipsticks to try them—even though you're not supposed to do that—and wonder with a small ache in the small of my back how my sister is doing. That ache is starting to be like a little tune that gets stuck in your head, always there, even if you're not really thinking about it, the kind of song that's stuck in your head even when you don't know all the words.

Sometimes I try to picture what the kids at school back in Las Palmas are doing. At eight thirty, when I'm still *lolling,* as my mother puts it, in bed, they're lining up for morning assembly, picking at each other and shoving, so they can get inside and recite the Pledge of Allegiance. At nine forty-five, when I'm up and hanging around the motel office, helping Dennis sort the mail and eating doughnuts, they're already watching the clock, waiting for first period to end. Ten o'clock is gym. I think about Liza Binel, the class track star, and how Lainey and I always lag behind the other kids, moving at a half trot, half walk, speeding it up only when Ms. Crenshaw looks over. Then comes science. I imagine the labs, dim and hushed, with that strange smell science classes always have, insects and formaldehyde and the general smell of dead things.

When we're in the motel room the television is almost always on. I end up watching a lot of Westerns, because they're on during the day, even though the only thing I really like about them are the horses. My mother keeps close tabs on the local news, making me stay quiet when there's a story about a drug bust or a gang-related murder. "You see?" she says. "It's going on all around us."

Other than that, we spend most of our time by the pool. But one afternoon, when we're just sitting around, my mother sighs. "Enough of this. We need to plan some lessons for you. I don't want you to get *too* behind in class." Her voice has that strange edge it gets when she's excited about a new project. She grabs a paper and pen and starts to jot some things down.

We drive to the B. Dalton bookstore at the mall. My mother crouches on the floor, surrounded by a pile of books. "What were you going to study in history this year?"

"Ancient Greece," I lie. "And Egypt."

My mother shakes her head. "You did that last year." I shrug, knowing I've been caught. "It's about time you learned some more European history." My mother was a history major in college, and she has always told me that we learn about the future by studying the past, especially the Holocaust. I am doomed. I look at a book that says *An Introduction to Art*, thinking about how much my sister would like it, and show it to my mother, but my mother turns away. "That's for college kids," she says.

There is a whole display of math workbooks. They are listed by grade and subject, color coded for different levels. Blue for easy, green for intermediate, and a dull brick red for advanced. "Does this look about right?" my mother asks, picking up a green book.

"That's too hard."

She fixes me with a look.

"I mean it." I'm really not lying this time.

My mother checks the sticker on the history book. "I can't believe this is thirty-nine dollars."

I want to see what mysteries they have, but my mother gets close to me and hands me the history book. "Take this into the bathroom and put it in your backpack," she whispers.

"Mom . . ." There are people all around us, but nobody seems to be looking in our direction.

"Just go." She gives me a little push.

"What about the math book?"

"It's only ten dollars."

The bathroom is in the back of the store, next to a display of maps and travel guides, with a handwritten sign that says PLEASE DO NOT BRING BOOKS INTO THE RESTROOM. SHOPLIFTERS WILL BE PROSECUTED TO THE FULLEST EXTENT OF THE LAW. I close and lock the door behind me.

The book is heavy in my hands. I look at the table of contents. *Imperialism. The Transatlantic Slave Trade. Tobacco and Spices.* My mind is already wandering. I consider just leaving the book in the bathroom. Maybe if I don't take it my mother will decide it's not worth the money, and then I won't have to read it at all. But somehow I know that's not going to work. I balance the book carefully on the edge of the sink, trying not to get it wet, and pull down my pants. While I'm in here I might as well pee.

When I come out of the bathroom, I feel a little sick. But then I see my mother standing by the cash register, beaming at me.

"There you are," she says. She hands the clerk some money for the math workbook. I try to look casual. Next to the register is a display of metallic markers, the kind that write in two colors at the same time. On a small pad of paper, meant for testing out the pens, someone has written the words "You Suck" in big shiny letters. "Can I get one of these?"

"Absolutely not." My mother gets her change from the clerk. "You don't need it."

I tap my backpack and look at my mother. "Please?" She stares at me for a split second. Then she shakes her head in disbelief.

"Oh, all right. I guess so."

The clerk looks sympathetic. "My kids always want them too," she says, putting the pen in a tiny paper bag.

When we get out to the parking lot, my mother stops and turns to me. "Don't you dare pull that one again." She sounds annoyed and a little proud all at the same time. "Anyway, you could have just slipped the pen in your pocket."

My mother decides to set up a formal schedule for my homework. Mornings, after breakfast, are "first period." We start with math, to get it out of the way. Fortunately, the answers are at the back of the book, printed upside down—as if having them upside down will stop someone from cheating. When there's a problem neither of us understands at all my mother just lets me skip it. "Sometimes the important thing is to try your best," she says.

We've given up on biology, though my mother thinks we should at least read some books on animals and nature. I pick a guide to different breeds of cats, which doesn't really count, but the pictures are cute. It turns out that there are some cats with six toes, others with no tails. My mother makes me read a book called *Underneath the Sea,* with photos of coral reefs and schools of fish, sea sponges, and anemones, colorful and fluid. We are surprised to learn that anemones are animals, not plants.

After studying, the rest of the day feels like a vacation. When we're not at the pool we go for a walk, or to the bowling alley, which has afternoon rates of two dollars a game. I love the solid black balls and the clean white pins. Usually my mother just sits and watches. When I get a strike or a spare she claps automatically, though I can tell she's not really paying attention.

I wonder what it would be like to be one of the old men who hangs out at the bowling alley, chain smoking and reading the sports pages. Are they married? It's impossible to tell anything from the way they just stand there, listlessly watching the ball roll down the alley over and over again.

One day we even go to the racetrack. The horses are beautiful, long-legged and eager. My mother places the bets for me and buys me a Coke. I'm cautious, betting just a few dollars to show on a reliable horse with 3–2 odds. My mother likes the horses with the fancy names, like Speedaway or Daddy's Girl or Plum Bun.

Sometimes when my mother has left me alone in our motel room, I sneak Miriam's sketchbook out of my duffel bag and flip through the now familiar pictures: the hand clutching a key, my glasses, and, of course, the picture of me. On the final page she has written the words "Someday everything will be different" in fancy calligraphy-style lettering, and I turn to that page over and over, trying to puzzle out what it means. Of course, I think to myself, someday everything will be different, but which *everything* does she mean, and when does *someday* come? Does she mean *someday,* next week, or *someday* next year? Or a *someday* much more distant than that, the kind of thing you can't really see, like when you look far over the ocean and can just make out the clouds dancing above the horizon? These are the questions I really want to know the answers to—not the ones in the school textbooks my mother halfheartedly makes me read each morning. But they're not questions I can ask my mother, and I can tell they're not questions I'm going to get the answers to anytime soon. So I just hide the sketchbook away, being careful not to crease the edges, and every night as I fall asleep I repeat the words *Someday everything will be different* over and over to myself, hoping its meaning will be revealed in the hazy tumult of my dreams.

29

We've been at Motel del Mar, with its fading neon sign and chipped painted roof, for almost a whole month. Other people come and go: mostly single men wearing business suits, looking tired and gray at breakfast. Every once in a while a family shows up with little kids. I watch them, curious, wondering why anyone would come to a motel like this, in the middle of nowhere, with nothing around. Most of them only stay for a night or two—on their way to someplace better, I imagine. My mother and I are the only people who have been at the motel for more than a few days. It feels as if the motel belongs to us, that the other people are just visitors.

Dennis is starting to ask more questions—how long we're planning to stay and where we're going next. "I'm sorry to ask," he says, trying not to meet my mother's eye, "but I really need to know so I don't overbook the rooms." It sounds reasonable, but really it's just an excuse, as the motel never has more than a few people at a time. Also I think he's upset that my mother is not interested in him.

"It's really none of his business," my mother says to me privately. She has never liked nosy people.

"Maybe it is." I can understand why Dennis would want to know more about us: the mother and daughter who have chosen his motel as a home. "He must think we're really weird."

"If he doesn't stop putting his nose where it doesn't belong we're going to have to leave." She sounds genuinely sad about this, as if the motel, with its stained carpets and broken screens, is one of the nicest places she's ever been.

As for me, I am getting tired of our perpetual vacation. Even the pool is starting to annoy me a little. The chlorine smells bad, a sharp metallic smell that I can't get out of my hair. I spend a lot of time in the shower, trying to rub out the smell with other smells: perfumed soaps, body washes scented with lilac or jasmine. My skin becomes dry, and I lather it with lotions and creams. Still more smells.

The days begin melting into one another, each one just like the next. I take Maxwell for a lot of walks, up and down the street in front of the motel, but there isn't much to see. I suppose that to a dog it doesn't really make much of a difference where you are, a walk is a walk. For me they're a way to get away from my mother, if only for a little while. Even though I'm out on the street, it feels private.

Sometimes I run into other people walking their dogs, and they always stop so the dogs can sniff each other. The dog walkers like Maxwell. "I haven't seen you around before," they say, patting Maxwell on the head. "Aren't you the sweetest thing?" They don't really talk to me. People never ask you anything about yourself when you have a dog.

I have trouble sleeping at night. My mother falls asleep right when she wants to, but I lie awake for hours, watching the shadows and lights of the traffic play against the curtains. In the mornings I feel groggy, my head muddled with bits and pieces of half-remembered dreams.

My restlessness starts to seep out of my body and fill our room. I find myself tapping on the wall, braiding and unbraiding my hair, trying to find ways to get rid of the tension in my body. Mostly I swim, trying to get in as many laps in the little pool as possible; lying around all day eating doughnuts is making my pants tight. The fashion magazines all say that swimming is *the ideal exercise for women;* it tones your arms and legs and *works your heart*. So I swim as much as I can, giving my little heart as much work as it can handle.

One afternoon we go to a yard sale at the church down the street. My mother and I hunch over the cardboard boxes, which are filled with other people's castaway things. We have so little of our own things, everything has been left behind in Las Palmas, and these people's things have already been broken in. They've already lived a life with someone else: moldy stuffed animals once loved and played with, now heaped together in a sad pile. Clothes stretched out by a body, tossed together in a heap of colors.

"What do you think of this?" my mother says, holding a plaid shirt against her body.

"I'm not sure."

"I could really use a few new things," she says, biting her lip.

I watch as she fishes through a pile of faded cotton sweatshirts. "Can't we just go to a real store?" There's a store we pass by all the time on our way to the diner, with discount clothes and a sign that promises EVERYTHING $9.99 AND UNDER.

My mother shakes her head. "Amber, we've been over this a million times." She tries on a pair of leather sandals and puts them back. Too big. "We really need to start watching our spending."

The woman running the sale smiles at me. "Amber. What a pretty name."

"Thanks." I want to say, *My mother usually shops at Macy's, we don't usually buy our clothes at yard sales.* I look through the boxes to see if there is anything that will fit me. There is a brand-new bikini with blue piping and thin straps that looks like something Miriam would wear, but in my size. I think about my purple and green striped one-piece bathing suit, which I've had for as long as I can remember, and which Lainey always says looked so babyish. Every day I have to rinse out the chlorine from the pool, and the colors have started to fade.

My mother sees me holding the bikini and says, "Absolutely not. You could catch a disease."

"But it still has the tags on it."

My mother takes the bikini from me and looks at it for a minute, examining the crotch area carefully, which somehow makes me feel embarrassed and naked, as if she is looking between my own legs. "I guess it's okay," she says slowly, peering at the tags. "As long as you wash it with bleach. Three times." She turns to the woman running the sale, who is tall and thin and wearing bright red toenail polish that matches her fingernails. "How much for the bathing suit?"

"Two dollars."

"I'll give you one," my mother says, handing her a bill.

The woman frowns at her and takes it. "It's for a good cause," she says, sounding annoyed. "It's for the church." I want to say, *But we're Jewish, we don't go to church,* but somehow I know that's not the right thing to say, and my mother has warned me again and again not to tell people anything personal about us. *They might be trying to gather information,* she always says. I run my fingers over the spine of an old hardcover Nancy Drew book, thinking about how they used to be my favorites—how much I used to love reading them under the covers at night, losing myself in Nancy's world of haunted houses and missing necklaces. Now my mother and I are the mystery, but there is nothing exciting about our life at all. I turn away, hoping that the woman with the red nail polish won't see that I'm crying. I am tired of wearing the same clothes all the time, tired of diner food, tired of camping out at Motel del Mar. Most of all, I am tired of not understanding what is going on. . . .

Suddenly my mother grabs my arm. "Let's go."

I look around but don't see anything, just a couple of guys kneeling in the grass, examining the chain on a rusty lawn mower. "What is it?"

"Just come on," she hisses, steering me away from the boxes and tables and almost pushing me onto the sidewalk. Without saying another word, my mother starts walking very quickly in the direction of the motel, staring straight ahead, and I have to do a little half jog to keep up with her.

"Mom, wait." She doesn't say anything, just keeps walking,

faster and faster. I look around, but everything seems the same as always.

When we get back to the motel she pushes the dog aside and rushes me into our room and says, "Amber, *they were there.*" She's having trouble locking the door, and when I look at her I realize that her hands are shaking. "Did you see them?"

"Who?" I realize that I'm still clutching the white bathing suit. I lay it down on the bed and then pull the curtain aside and peek out the window; the sky is starting to turn a dull gray.

"Get away from there. Someone might see you," my mother hisses.

"Mom, there's no one there." The pool and courtyard are completely empty, except for a few pigeons pecking at something, an old doughnut probably, under a broken folding chair. My body aches with something familiar.

Suddenly there's a knock on the door: sharp, insistent.

"Oh, my God, oh, my God." My mother grabs my arm and pushes me into the closet and pulls the coats and jackets around us. "They're here, they're here," she whimpers, crouching down on the floor. She pulls me down on the floor and tries to cover me with one of the coats. On the other side of the closet door I can hear Maxwell whining, a small, anxious sound.

Another knock. My mother clutches me, her nails digging into my bare arm. "Amber," she whispers hoarsely. "Whatever happens, I love you." She lets out a low whimper.

"Hey, ladies, how you doing in there?" It's Dennis.

The spell is broken. My mother stands up and opens the closet door and brushes the lint from her clothes. Then she opens the door to the motel room.

Dennis looks over at me. "Hey, what are you doing in there?"

"Just playing a game." I try not to meet his eye; I feel stupid sitting on the floor like a little kid, so I get up and come over as if everything's normal, rubbing the spot on my arm, now red and painful, where my mother grabbed it.

"Sorry to bug you," Dennis says to my mother, "but I think you dropped this running up the stairs." It's my mother's wallet, which folds open to a crumpled school photo of Miriam from junior year. "Is this your other daughter?" he asks. "She's so pretty."

"Oh, yes." My mother looks confused and nervous. Her wallet is falling apart and she's been holding it together with a rubber band. "I really need to replace that thing," she says.

"What's her name again?"

"Meredith," says my mother.

"Oh, right." He seems puzzled for a second and looks at me. "For some reason, I thought you said her name was Miriam."

My mother gives a small laugh that sounds like a lamb's bleat. "Miriam, Meredith," she says running her hands nervously through her hair, the way she does when she's not sure exactly what to say. "They're easy to mix up." A fly buzzes into the room and lands on my arm, attracted by the sweet smell of suntan oil.

"She likes to be called Miriam," I say. "But that's not her real name. It's just her Hebrew school name." My mother gives me a look to shut up. Dennis seems confused, but he's too polite to ask what I'm talking about.

Dennis squints at the picture, his large thumbs covering my sister's face. "How come she's not with you guys?"

My mother looks lost for a moment, as if she has just been discovered slipping something into a pocket, and the expression *caught in the act* goes through my mind. "She's in boarding school," I say. "A fancy boarding school with stables and horses. She has her own horse; he's all black with one white leg and his name is Midnight." My mother's look is a blade slicing through me, and I wonder why she has not thought of all of this ahead of time. "Her vacation isn't 'til summer," I continue, trying to remember a book I read long ago about a girl who went to a private school in the country, where she lived with other girls and played tennis and rode horses. Did they go home over the summer? Did they go home at all? I can't remember. Dennis's face is a funny blur of confusion, that sideways look grown-ups get when they can't figure you out and are not sure if you are lying. If Miriam were here, I think to myself for the thousandth time—many of my thoughts these days begin with *If*

Miriam were here—we wouldn't have to come up with this lie so quickly. We wouldn't have to lie at all because Miriam would have convinced our mother to take us back to Las Palmas. . . .

My mother starts snapping the rubber band on her wrist over and over. "I'm really not feeling very well," she says. When I look at her I realize that her face is round and puffy: a girl about to cry.

"I'm sorry," Dennis says quickly. "I'll see you guys later."

When he's gone my mother turns to me, her eyes cloudy with confusion and fear.

"What did you tell him about Miriam?" she whispers, even though we are all alone and there is no one to hear.

"Nothing."

"Jesus, Amber, how many times do I have to tell you? We have to keep ourselves as secret as possible. We have to be anonymous." Her voice is stretched thin with fear, and her wrist is covered with bright red marks from the rubber band, little temporary scars of pain. "Give me that," I say to her, as gently as possible. She rolls the rubber band off her wrist and hands it to me as if it is something very valuable. I remember Lainey telling me once that a too-tight rubber band around your wrist can *cut off the circulation to your arm* and that she heard a boy at school had died that way, years ago, and how I am older now and know right away that things like that are not true at all, but are just stories people make up to scare each other.

"There's nothing to worry about," I tell my mother. "Really." I think I would feel better if she would just stop whispering.

Later that afternoon my mother sends me downstairs with a bunch of quarters to put our laundry in the dryer. Dennis stops me outside the laundry room. "Hey," he says, playing with an empty bottle of detergent that's lost its cap. "I hope I didn't upset your mom before." He coughs the hard scratchy cough he has from all those cigarettes. "Bringing up your sister like that."

"That's okay," I say, picking a sock up from the floor. I try to focus on the sweet smell of bleach and fabric softener. "The thing is, she's not really in boarding school."

Dennis stares at me. "She's not?"

"She's in a school for kids who have problems. Like juvenile detention. My mother doesn't like to talk about it." The words are out of my mouth before I can catch them. I am not sure where I get this—if I had run into Dennis ten minutes earlier I might have said something completely different—but somehow I know it's something he won't touch, that the words *juvenile detention* will make him never mention Miriam to my mother again. The dryer softly tosses our towels in an endless circle.

"Oh." Something crosses his face, a pale gleam of concern. "That makes sense," he says, though he still looks confused. He hands me a pile of old magazines. "Well, anyway, will you give these to your mother? I know she likes them." I think he is waiting for me to say something else, but I just say thank you and take the magazines back upstairs to my mother.

"That was very thoughtful of him," she says when she sees the magazines. "I can always use something else to read." She sighs. "Though they really are sort of trashy."

I look at Maxwell, who is nose to tail in a small circle on the floor. "Mom?"

"What?" She is already looking at an article called "Fall's Newest Looks: Flatter Your Figure!" I feel something inside me slipping away: it is the middle of March, and the magazine is already six months old. Something about the days passing is making our little motel room feel smaller and smaller, as if the furniture and pictures and even the walls themselves might be shrinking, turning in on themselves. My mother curls a strand of hair around her finger.

"I want to go home." My mother doesn't say anything, just pages through the magazine, so I try again. "I'm going to miss the seventh-grade dance." It would be my first real dance, and I remember all the times I watched Miriam get ready for her school dances: the fall formal, the junior prom, and the trouble she took to make sure her shoes and dress were just the right combination, even dying the shoes one time to match the dress. Watching her, I always felt especially small and left out of the bigger world of grown-up things, things that are female. Now it's supposed to be my turn.

"A school dance isn't really that important," my mother says, peering closely at an ad for skin cream. "Kids place too much importance on those things."

"It's important to me." I think about how at the beginning of the school year, Lainey and I promised we'd be each other's date if nobody asked us. (*Girls do that all the time*, she told me, *and it doesn't mean they're lesbians*.) I wonder if any of the boys at school have asked her yet, what shade of purple dress she'll wear, if she'll have a matching purple corsage. "Everyone's going. You don't even have to have a real date," I say, and I can feel my voice shake.

My mother finally looks up. "My God, Amber, don't you realize how unimportant that is compared to what's happening to us?"

My gaze travels the quiet motel room, taking in the television set, tuned to a *Star Trek* rerun, the empty ginger ale bottles, the wet beach towels sprawled in a hump on the floor. "*Nothing* is happening to us," I shout. "Nothing is happening at all!"

"Amber, stop it!" My mother gets up, her face flushed with anger and something else: an accusation of betrayal. "You know how much danger we're in. We're not leaving here until it's safe; there is no way I'm going to risk my life, or yours. *You are my daughter,* and it is my duty to protect you! And look at how dangerous it is out there. Every day we hear about horrible things, terrible deaths—addicts overdosing, gang members shooting people, innocent people, over a drug deal. Don't we see stuff like that on the news almost every single night?"

I don't say anything, just get up to close the window so the neighbors won't hear our fighting. I can tell she is begging me to say yes, to agree with her—to make what she is saying true, so that all this time we've spent at Motel del Mar won't have been a waste, a joke, a mistake. She grabs me by the arm. "Didn't we just see that last night on *Nightline?*"

I just look at Maxwell, nervously chewing something on this leg.

"Answer me!"

"I guess so." The TV program was about a girl who became

part of a Los Angeles drug gang and got shot by her boyfriend, an older man with a tattoo on his forehead. "But not everything's like that."

My mother doesn't say anything.

"And another thing. I don't want you to call me Amber anymore."

"But that's the name you picked." She frowns at me. "That was your choice."

"Well, I don't like it anymore."

"You can't just change it. People can't just go around changing their names willy-nilly."

"Why not? I already changed it once."

That night when we run into Dennis I catch my mother looking at me closely, studying my movements, as if she is afraid I am suddenly going to betray her and tell him everything. But I won't do that. It would hurt my mother's feelings, and no matter how hard things are, how confusing and muddled they seem— like the muddled tea leaves at the bottom of a my mother's mug—that is the last thing I want to do. That night we go to bed, the tension between us still thick and weighted like a blanket of silence. As strange as our life here at the Motel del Mar has become, we never fight, and the air is charged with something new and different, something that reminds me of Miriam. I put my pillow over my head and squeeze my eyes shut, trying to block it out, but it's not the kind of thing you can just block out. It's there for good.

30

The next morning I wake up especially early. It's Saturday. Not that it really matters, since our weekends and weekdays at the motel are all the same. The only difference is which shows are on television, and the weekday super specials at the diner down the road. Time is starting to fold into itself: I mark our days here on the motel calendar, checking them off carefully with a big, solid X before I go to bed.

A dense morning light settles on the grass. Everything is quiet, the streets hushed with expectation. This morning I woke up restless, as if my body needed to move immediately or it might begin disintegrating, so I leashed up Maxwell and took him for a walk. Back at the motel, my mother is still sleeping. She won't wake up for another couple of hours, at least; she's been sleeping later and later. "I just feel so *tired* all the time," she tells me, even though we barely do anything that could make a person tired at all, and my mother too sounds confused by this, as if her exhaustion has just snuck up on her like a child playing boo.

I walk Maxwell down the silent street, past a couple of parking lots to the lawn in front of the church where we went to the yard sale. The church is very small and looks just like a house—almost like a house pretending to be a church. The only thing that really lets you know it's a church at all is a small wooden cross that's been painted white and a sign advertising the week's services: RISING UP TO MEET CHRIST. LAYING YOUR SOUL BEFORE THE LORD. EMBRACING THE SPIRIT. Maxwell lunges to pee on the grass. I look at the sign, wondering if you have to do something special to a house, like say a prayer or bless it, to change it into a church.

Across the street, a sprinkler wets the grass in controlled spurts. Maxwell sniffles around, taking his time, and watching him, I realize that I have to pee too—really pee. "C'mon, Maxie, hurry it up," I say. "You're not the only one who has to go." Then I notice that the side door of the church is open.

"You be a good boy and stay here," I tell Maxwell. "I'm just going to go inside and find a bathroom since I don't get to just pee outside like *some people*." I wind his leash around the stair railing, and for a second he gives me that look dogs always give you when you tie them up, as if you are going to abandon them forever, but then begins snuffling at a patch of dirt.

I go inside. I've never actually been inside a church and had always pictured stained glass windows, angel statues, paintings of Jesus. But this looks just like any other building. There are postings for events and meetings, just like at the Jewish Community Center, and a larger room with desks in a row, that looks a bit like a classroom. I find the bathroom down the hall and it is just the same as a bathroom anywhere else.

My whole body still feels stiff with anger and frustration from the argument with my mother last night. *I am so sick of being here,* I think to myself. I don't live at the Motel del Mar. My name is not Amber. I live in a regular place, with a normal family, where we eat at home. I start to cry. I think about Maxwell, waiting for me outside, and I wash my face and dry it with a scratchy brown-gray paper towel, but then I start crying again. "Okay," I say to myself, looking in the mirror. "It's time to go." I think about one of my mother's expressions—*let's pull it together*—and I blow my nose one last time.

I thought I was alone in the building, but when I open the bathroom door there's a guy standing there holding a bunch of paper bags. "Oh, hey," he says, looking startled. "You must be here for the meeting."

I am not sure what to say. "I just had to pee," I tell him, trying to blink back my tears.

"No problem," he says. "The meeting doesn't start for a few minutes." He studies my face and sees that I've been crying. "Hey, it's okay," he says, something focused and gentle in his voice, as if we've already been friends for a very long time. "You're safe here. Really." Something about the way he says it—so kind and caring without really even knowing me—makes me start sobbing even harder. I start to wipe the snot off my face with my sweatshirt and he opens one of the bags and pulls out a box of tissues. "Here," he says. "Use this. We have plenty." From somewhere in the building I can hear voices.

"Listen," the guy says. "I could use some help carrying some of this stuff. Do you mind taking this?" He hands me a bag filled with paper plates and cups, and I am not sure else what else to do, so I follow him. The guy leads me up a short staircase to a smaller room in the back of the building—a forgotten room with all sorts of things stacked against the walls: some costumes for a play, a table missing a leg, a framed poster from a circus. There are already a group of kids there, sitting in folding chairs arranged in a half circle, next to a table covered with books and papers. A couple of them are around my age, but most of them seem more like Miriam's age. They are chattering and laughing, the way kids do anywhere. A familiar scent washes over me; someone is wearing Lainey's perfume: a sweet orange scent that always reminds me of furniture polish. The room goes silent when I walk in, and I have a sudden flashback to my first day of school in Las Palmas; I wonder if they can tell I'm Jewish. The guy takes the bag from me and begins setting up the food and books on a table, arranging the paper cups in neat rows. "Here, have some juice," he says. "You'll feel better."

I manage to choke out a thank-you. I look at the table and see that someone else has brought cookies. In the corner there's one of those chalkboards that you can push around on wheels, with the words "Alateen Meeting Saturday 9 a.m. New Members Welcome" written in purple chalk. The girl next to me is holding a book called *Understanding Drug and Alcohol Addiction: A Guide for Teenagers,* and I remember how we learned about these groups last semester in health class. Mrs. Pallari, looking a little nervous, gave us a handout with a list of phone numbers, telling us that the meetings were free and that the *Anon* in the name meant "anonymous." *They're completely confidential, and everyone's really nice,* she had said, her voice suddenly a whisper, and I knew, without being sure how I knew it, that she had been to some of those meetings herself.

The boy puts his arm around me. "It was really brave of you to show up today," he says. He squeezes my hand, and I see that he's a little teary too. "I'm the speaker today, and I really need all the support I can get." I am not sure what to do. The door has been shut and everyone is sitting down, and it feels wrong to just walk out. The boy motions for me to sit down next to him. An older girl, maybe sixteen or seventeen with blond, feathered hair, takes a seat at the front of the room and starts reading from a piece of paper. She announces that there is another meeting tomorrow morning, and that she hopes to see some of us there as well. Everyone shifts around impatiently; it feels a lot like school. Finally she looks up and says, "Today's speaker will be Peter," and nods at the boy sitting next to me.

He clears his throat—a nervous, edgy sound. "My name is Peter and my father is an alcoholic."

"Hello, Peter!" everyone says in unison. I almost jump in my seat.

The boy starts to talk, on and on, with no one interrupting him. He tells us his father blacks out every night from too much drinking. "Sometimes he hits my sister." He stops for a minute, and when he speaks again, it's barely a whisper. "The only one he doesn't beat up is me, because I'm the boy." At first I think, *Lucky him,* but then I realize that makes him feel even worse. He begins to cry. A girl next to me starts crying along with him, and then a couple of other people are crying too, a chorus of crying, and the blond girl hands around one of the boxes of tissue. Peter blows his noise and keeps talking. Last night his father went out and didn't come back until five in the morning. When he returned he crashed the car into a tree. Someone called the police.

"Thank you, Peter," says the blond girl, sounding a little bored. "That was very courageous of you." She looks around the room. A short-haired girl with round John Lennon glasses raises her hand and begins to speak. The girl with the glasses has an uncle who is a drug addict. But he is the only person who really understands her; he's the only one who knows that she wants to go to art school instead of regular college. "There's no one else I can talk to," she says. A beeper goes off and the girl with the glasses stops speaking for a second, looks guilty. Then she continues. Her uncle has a friend that has a thing for her, and she thinks he's kind of hot, even though he's at least forty. But she can't tell the uncle that.

"Lisa," the blond girl says, with a slightly punishing look. "We're limiting our shares to three minutes." I realize that she is clutching a small timer between her neatly manicured hands. The girl with the glasses nods and falls silent. A bunch of people raise their hands the second she's done, and the blond girl calls on a black guy with longish hair. The hour goes by quickly. Everyone's story sounds like something my mother and I have watched on *The Phil Donahue Show.*

Finally, the blond girl turns and fixes me with that bright blue stare of hers. "We always save time at the end of our meetings for newcomers to speak. Is there anyone here who is a newcomer and would like to share their story?"

Everyone pretends not to know where she's looking, but obviously she is speaking to me. I raise my hand. "Yes?" she says, leaning toward me, eager as a teacher.

I clear my throat. "My name is Amber."

"Hi, Amber," they all shout.

I hold my head high. "My father is a heroin addict."

That afternoon, lying by the pool in my yard sale bikini, I think about what happened at the meeting, wishing I could tell

Miriam about it. For some reason, the kids there really seemed to like me. It was like having a whole new set of instant friends, with no one saying anything about what you look like or caring what you wear, and they seemed happy when I said I'd come back tomorrow.

No one else has a father who does heroin, and they are impressed. I told them that my father was a concert pianist with the Los Angeles symphony. For almost a year, he toured with them. He loved the traveling, loved the excitement of seeing new places. But one night a couple of his fellow performers invited him to a party up in Hollywood. That's where he first shoots up. He still manages to make it to his performances, even though he misses a note every once in a while. But soon the drug use starts to take its toll. His hands are constantly shaking. He can no longer play. He loses his job and spends his days around the apartment, doing nothing but getting high with his friends. When I sense they are losing interest, I start to add more details. He beats me. Not seriously at first. Just a slap here and there. But it gets worse. There's a thick leather belt with silver studs. Then a fist. I'm not sure why I told that story, exactly, except that I knew it would make the kids there like me.

I adjust my bikini top and stretch out on the towel, which has a small hole in the corner. My back is starting to burn. Across the pool from me there is a little boy wearing nothing but a diaper. His mother has a whole bag of toys for him: a plastic bucket and a ball, plus a little tube with a duck's head that he can float in. The mother stands in the shallow end and dips the baby in the water. "Up and down! Up and down!" she cries, in that dumb singsong voice people use with babies, as if the only reason they don't talk is that they're stupid. The only other person at the pool is an older man, treading water. He's been in there for at least fifteen minutes and has been looking at me the whole time. I squirm in my bathing suit—can feel him taking me in, running his eyes over my body. *Get the fuck out of my motel,* I think to myself, and I am surprised by how adult and mean I sound, even though I've only said the words in my head.

"Amber!" My mother is calling me from our room. She doesn't

even bother to open the door; instead she just sticks her head out the window, which is missing its screen. No one cares; everyone here shouts. "Time for dinner!"

The man gets out of the pool, dripping, and towels himself off. "Where you guys going to eat?" he asks. His legs are covered with dark, curly hair.

"I'm not sure," I say, trying not to look at him. He's standing right in front of me, and I think he wants me to notice how the wet bathing suit outlines his body. I gather my things: the small portable radio, which I always have set to KRKN—the Rock On station, the DJs always insist—and a paperback copy of *Animal Farm* that's lost a few pages, which someone left behind at the motel. "Wherever my mom wants to go, I guess."

The guy gestures at my book. "That's not just about animals."

"I know."

"It's about commies."

I don't say anything. My bottle of suntan lotion has fallen under the lawn chair, but I feel funny bending over to get it in front of him, so I try to kick it out with my foot.

He squints at me. "You know Ronald Reagan is the best thing that ever happened to this country." He crouches down with a grunt and reaches under the chair for the suntan lotion. "A real man," he says, handing me the bottle. "Not like that faggot Carter."

"Amber!" My mother's voice echoes across the courtyard. "What are you doing down there?"

I put the bottle and magazine in my little canvas bag. "I've gotta go." The man gives me a funny look. I run up the stairs to our room, not bothering to put on my sandals, my feet little targets of pain for the hot cement.

My mother shuts the door tight and looks at me. "What was that man talking to you about?" she asks, her voice nervous and unsure.

"Politics." I throw my wet towel on the floor. "He's just some dumb, old guy."

My mother's face relaxes. "He's not that old. He's probably

my age." She sits back down on the bed and tucks her legs under her. "Pick that towel up," she says, watching me get undressed. I don't want her to see me naked, so I go into the bathroom. I look ill in the glare of the fluorescent light. My hair is still wet from the pool, so I start blow-drying it, not bothering to rinse out the chlorine first. It takes a while: first the blow-dryer, then the metal curling iron, which threatens to scald my skin. With the hot iron held tight against my scalp, I look almost as if I'm holding a gun to my head. "Pow," I say to myself quietly. "Pow, you're dead."

My mother's knock on the door startles me. "Amber, let's go." She's started calling me Amber all the time, even when we're by ourselves. "We've got to hurry if we want to make the early bird special."

The thought of sitting in the same cramped booth at the diner, with its tinny piped-in music and the paper place mat advertising the all you can eat chicken and fries meal, makes me sick. I think about our kitchen back home. Even with the way things have been the last few months—the dishes piled in the sink, the "jumble sale" meals, the rotting food in the refrigerator—it was still *our* kitchen. *Our* home. My throat burns with anger. "Can't we go somewhere else?"

My mother is annoyed. "You don't even appreciate how lucky you are. Most kids only get to eat out on special occasions."

A rush of tears fills my eyes, tight and painful. By the time I've put on my clothes and brushed my hair my mother is already in the parking lot, waiting by the car. She is staring at some point far off in the distance, the lines on her face made luminous and fine by the late afternoon light. At dinner, we play with our food instead of eating it, not saying a word.

31

The next day I wake up to the sound of rain beating fast against the window. The electric clock by my bed says eight thirty, but the rain and the dark sky make it seem like the middle of the night. I turn on my side and shake out my arm; I've slept on it funny again, and it's all pins and needles. Maxwell looks up and thumps his tail at me, but other than that he's still.

My mother stirs. She's almost awake, could go either way. When I pour a glass of water from the sink she rolls over smoothly, not even disturbing the blankets. My mother sleeps so soundly that she barely has to make the bed in the morning— she just pulls the covers up a little bit and fluffs the pillow. I've never understood how she does this. In the mornings I always find myself tangled up in sheets and covers, as if my body has been trying to escape from the bed.

The meeting at the church starts at nine. I still have time to get there, but I need to do it without waking my mother. So I take each step carefully, the way a blind person might. Except for the rain there's no sound from outside; even the traffic is quiet. It looks like I'm going to make it. But then I drop my keys and my mother jars awake.

"Morning, sweetie." Maxwell jumps up at her voice and nuzzles her face, the doggy version of saying good morning, and then lies down again at the side of her bed.

"Hi, Mom," I say quietly, thinking maybe she'll drift off again. She struggles to speak through a yawn. "Where are you going?"

"Just to walk Maxie." I pull on the old blue and gold UCLA sweatshirt that used to be Miriam's. My mother gave it to her for her sixteenth birthday, when she was getting 4.0s on her report card and talking about colleges and scholarships. I stare at my reflection. In the mirror, the *C* and *L* in UCLA are backward, looking more like symbols than letters. The sweatshirt still smells like Miriam, a combination of baby powder and hair spray, and just a trace of cigarettes.

"You can't go out in that rain," my mother mumbles, her face turned to the pillow. Her hair is perfect, even though she's still in bed. I've finally gotten used to the color.

"It'll just be for a little while." I try to sound as casual as possible, as if it's perfectly normal to go out in rain like this, or any rain, for that matter. But, of course, it's weird; even Maxwell doesn't seem to want to go outside.

I duck into the bathroom before my mother can say anything else. My hair is flat and dull, and I run my fingers through it, fluffing it out, trying to get some of the wave to come back. I'd like to feather it, but I don't want my mother to think I'm going anyplace special. So I just put it back in a ponytail and smooth a little moisturizer over my face. My skin seems clear, brighter. I wonder if having a secret changes the way you look.

Maybe my mother won't think it's so strange that I'm going out if I'm wearing a raincoat, I think to myself, and I put it on, even though I hate its sticky, clammy feel. As I close the door she says, "Amber, stay here," but I pretend not to hear. "C'mon, Maxie," I say. He is reluctant and doesn't want to come, and I have to pull him out the door. Outside, the rain has made everything blurry and indistinct, and it's really coming down, cold and determined. I push Maxwell along as fast as possible.

By the time I get to the church the meeting has already started, and I'm sweating under the raincoat. The smell of air freshener is everywhere, the same peach-scented kind Dennis uses in the motel office. After a few minutes I make my way into the meeting hall with Maxwell and everyone looks up and smiles. I take a seat near the back of the room. "Sit down now, Maxie," I whisper. One of the kids is talking about how his father caught him masturbating, and then told his mother and older sisters about it. I look around at the other kids. A few of them nod at me, and Peter, the guy who spoke yesterday, comes and sits next to me. "Hey, it's so great that you came back," he says. The girl sitting right in front of me is wearing a shirt with the price tags still on it; maybe she's going to return it to the store after wearing it, the way Miriam and her friends used to do.

When the boy is finished speaking everyone says thank you as if he's given them a present and falls into a heavy silence. The room seems especially dark and still; everything has been hushed by the rain.

I've had a chance to catch my breath, and now I think about my mother, back at the motel room. After I left, did she make herself some tea with one of the Earl Grey tea bags stolen from the breakfast room and go back to sleep? Or is she sitting at the little table, looking out the window, waiting for me to come back, cold and dripping from the rain? The image makes me feel sorry for her, and also for myself.

Before I know it, I am crying, not quietly the way I usually do, but low and loud. I can hear the sound outside myself, as if someone else is crying. Maxwell looks up from the floor and starts to whine along with me, he always whines when people cry.

The boy sitting next to me moves his chair closer to mine, and then puts his arm around me and rubs my shoulder. Normally it would mean something special if a boy did that, it would be flirting, but here it seems as if everyone touches each other all the time. The boy nudges me. "It's okay," he whispers, taking my hand. "You can tell us."

I swallow hard. All last night I had planned for this moment, rehearsing the story I'd made up about my father, trying to figure out a way to keep all the details straight. But now, when I open my mouth, it's the truth that spills out. How my mother thinks she's being followed by drug dealers in a white car. How she checks my arms every morning for track marks and looks through my drawers. How we've been living in a cramped motel for over a month. "Amber isn't even my real name," I say.

"What about your dad?" This is from the masturbation boy. You're not supposed to ask questions; it's against the rules, and everyone shushes him at once. But I answer anyway.

"I've never met him," I say, sniffing loudly.

"He doesn't play piano?" the masturbation boy asks, his voice high-pitched and excited.

"I don't know. I don't know anything about him."

They are all staring now. It reminds me of being onstage at school holiday pageants—when the performance is over but the audience isn't sure yet, and doesn't know whether to clap. Everyone is quiet, and the boy next to me scoots his chair a little away from me. Finally the blond girl speaks, slowly and carefully. "Maybe it makes you feel better to pretend your father doesn't exist, but you don't have to do that," she says, her eyes cloudy with concern, as if she might start crying too.

A guy wearing a red and gold 49ers jacket nods. "You're safe here. He can't hurt you."

I start giggling. I know I'm not supposed to, but I can't help myself; the giggles just come out. Everything has shifted: I'm not really in the room. I'm somewhere else. I stand up so quickly that my chair topples over and Maxwell gives a little bark. "I'm sorry," I sputter, struggling to right it. "I'm really sorry. I've gotta go." Everyone is staring at me. The blond girl just looks at me sadly, as if I've broken her favorite toy. Somehow I stumble my way to the door with Maxwell, where I put on my raincoat hurriedly, not bothering to struggle with the buttons. As I leave, a wooden sign posted in the hallway catches my eye: TODAY IS THE FIRST DAY OF THE REST OF YOUR LIFE!

Just a few minutes ago the rain was pouring down, but now it's starting to ease up. Above me is an enormous, shining rainbow, dividing the sky in two. It's so clear and perfect that it almost looks fake. Last year, in science class, we learned that rainbows aren't really anything at all. They're just the sun's normal rays, bent by the rain. It's funny, the way a little rain can change things.

When I get back to the motel room with Maxwell my mother is still in bed, but awake, reading a magazine. She looks at me and sees that I've been crying.

She sits up and pulls me to her. "What's wrong, honey? What is it?" She isn't angry at all, isn't going to yell at me for going out in the rain. I remember the time I twisted my ankle and had to wear a brace—that same look in her eyes. I kick off my wet shoes and raincoat and get under the covers with her.

Curled up in the bed, with her stroking my hair, I feel like a little kid again. It's as if we're in our own little world, a cocoon, secret and warm.

"It's okay, baby." My mother sighs. "Are you lonely here?"

She wraps the blanket tightly around me and gets a glass of orange juice from the refrigerator. "Tell me what happened," she says, setting the glass down.

I wipe my nose with the back of my hand. "I saw them."

"What?" My mother stares at me. "Who?"

I hadn't planned this, but I can't stop myself. "The guys with the white car."

My mother draws her breath in quickly. Her eyes are enormous. I watch her mouth move, but nothing comes out. I think about the kids back at the church, wondering if they're still there, what they're saying about me.

Finally my mother speaks, and her voice is stern. "Are you making some kind of joke, Amber?" It's her absolute no-nonsense voice, the voice that means you are in trouble or have gone too far.

"No." I'm scared now. "I swear."

"Where'd you see them?"

I have to think for a second. "Outside. In the parking lot."

"Oh, my God." My mother opens the curtains just a crack and peers out. "I don't see anyone." Her voice is hoarse. "Are you sure?"

"They took off when they saw me."

Maxwell whines, his tail wagging fiercely. I give him half a dog biscuit, to shut him up, but he won't touch it, just nuzzles it and then leaves it on the floor. Dogs really do know when something's wrong.

"Jesus Christ." My mother's gaze sweeps over the room: the pile of laundry sitting in the corner, the stolen books and my homework, which I haven't even looked at for a couple of days. A couple of empty pizza boxes are sitting under the folding chair; there's even a piece of crust in the corner. We haven't emptied the tiny plastic trash can in a week.

"We've got to get out of here," my mother says, opening the bureau drawer and pulling clothes out, not bothering to keep them folded.

"Today?"

"Right now."

"Can we go home?"

My mother looks angry, as if I shouldn't have even asked. "Jesus, Amber. Let's just pack up."

She grabs the yellow and white embroidered suitcase and her duffel bag out of the closet and throws them on the bed. I look at the motel calendar hanging over the TV, the one I've been using to keep track of our days here. Thirty-two days. Almost five weeks. Each month has a different nature scene from around the world, faraway mountains and rivers, deserts and plains. "Can I take the calendar?"

My mother sweeps everything off the table—her special wooden comb and brush, a lipstick, a new can of extra-hold hair spray—and shoves it all into the yellow and white embroidered suitcase. "Just leave it." She pulls on her drawstring pants and goes into the bathroom. "Let's get everything into the car and then I can settle up with Dennis."

I take my clothes from the drawer and start putting them into the suitcase. The men in the white car were outside. They were hanging out—*idling*—in the parking lot, smoking cigarettes, just like when my mother saw them. One of them looked right at me—almost as if he knew me. As I pack my things I notice that my mother's thrown in her lipstick without the cap; it's going to get all over everything. I wrap it in a piece of tissue and tuck it in a side pocket for safekeeping; my mother always says that she never feels really dressed without her lipstick.

She pokes her head out of the bathroom. "C'mon, Amber. Let's get moving." She's thrown on one of Miriam's old tank tops, hasn't even bothered with a bra. You can see her nipples poking through, the way mine sometimes get when it's cold. I wonder if they hurt.

I look down. Something is stuck to the bottom of my shoe. It's a napkin, smudged with pizza grease and tomato sauce from last night's takeout. "Shouldn't we clean up first?"

"There's no time for that," my mother says, shaking her head. "Anyway, they haven't had to clean the place for weeks." She takes a twenty-dollar bill out of her wallet, hesitates for a moment, and adds another ten. "For a tip," she says, putting the money in a neat pile on the dresser. "Meet me down by the car." She shuffles out the door in her flip-flops, laden down with bags and clothes, Maxell's leash wrapped around her arm.

My stomach hurts, feels like its tumbling over itself in small circles. I open the refrigerator. There's nothing in there but a moldy, half-empty container of fat-free cottage cheese and orange juice. I throw away the container and empty the juice in the sink. It doesn't seem right to leave it behind for someone else to clean up, not after we've been staying here for so long. Outside, I can hear my mother down in the courtyard, talking to Dennis, her voice high-pitched and nervous. "It's just time for us to go," I hear her say. "Sorry for the short notice."

I check both closets to make sure she's taken everything, but all I find is an unmatched sock. It's almost spooky, how quickly we were able to pack up all our things. Except for the dirty dishes and the trash, which could be anybody's, there's no sign that we were there at all. My books and notepads are gone, so are Maxwell's chew toys. It just looks like an empty motel room that someone else has stayed in. At the last moment I take the thirty dollars my mother left on top of the dresser and tuck it in my pocket.

When I get down to the car I'm not even sure how to fit myself in. The floor is piled up with things—books and shampoo and clothes—so I have to sit folded over, with my knees to my chest. I won't be able to use the seat belt. Maxwell's lying in the backseat, curled up right next to his big bag of dog food, as if he packed it himself.

Everything's moving so fast.

"Mom." She's not looking at me; she's wiping some bird shit off the windshield with a paper towel. "I really have to use the bathroom."

My mother gets in the car and adjusts the rearview mirror. "We can stop on the way," she says, starting the ignition. "We have to get going now. There's no time to waste."

"But I really, really have to go."

"Jesus, just be quick about it," she says, looking around for something in the glove compartment.

"I will." But instead of going back up to our room I sneak around to the office. Dennis is sitting behind the counter, smoking, just like he was on the day we arrived. He doesn't look up when I come in.

I'm not sure what to say, now that it's time for good-bye. I want to thank him for letting me help out around the motel. But I'm afraid it'll sound stupid, and anyway, shouldn't he be thanking me? So I just say, "I guess we're leaving now."

Dennis finally looks at me. "Where are you guys heading?"

"I don't know." As I say it, I realize that if I knew where we were going, he'd be a person I'd want to tell.

"Well, so long then." He turns back to the pile of papers on his desk. I can tell he's hurt. "Make sure you recommend us to your friends."

That's it; that's the whole good-bye. When we left Las Palmas, I thought that if only we'd had a chance to slow things down a bit, to say good-bye to a few more people, everything would have made more sense. That if I'd told Lainey where I was going, or even my teachers, it would have seemed more like a vacation, a short trip. After all, if you take the time to say good-bye, doesn't it mean that you expect to come back? That you're not just disappearing, like someone who wasn't really there in the first place?

But this is a different kind of good-bye. I'm never coming back to this motel. I shut the office door behind me and go out to the pool, which is as still and silent as the first day we got here. The sky is a flat, noncommittal gray.

My mother honks. "Amber! Hurry up."

"One sec," I yell. I crouch down by the side of the pool, trying not to get my shoes wet. At the bottom are a few pennies someone's thrown in for luck, or maybe just to play a game with their kids.

I dip my hand in the pool, testing the temperature. In the water, my hand looks cool and foreign, like something under glass. It's freezing out. No one in their right mind will want to go swimming on a day like this, and the wind's going to blow leaves and all kinds of junk into the water. For a minute I think about telling Dennis to get the pool cover out, to keep the water clean and warm, but then I decide not to. Let him figure it out himself.

32

We head north, following the highway for over two hours, before my mother finally agrees to stop at a gas station. At first she didn't want to stop at all. "I think we should just keep going," she said. "Put some distance between us and the motel." But now the gauge is hovering near empty, and I point out that things will be really bad if we run out of gas and get stuck by the side of the freeway, *God knows where.*

My mother sighs. "You're right, Amber. As always." Secretly I think she's happy to stop driving for a while. Miriam once told me that it's hard to drive when you're not heading anywhere in particular. The car wants a destination. It will be good for us to take a breather, consult our foldout AAA map, figure out where we should go next. My mother will be able to rest her foot, which gets tense and painful if she drives for too long.

I steal a glance at her. She's steering with one hand, squinting into the sky, which is brilliant and clear from the morning's rain. She can't find her sunglasses, probably left them back at the motel. I picture the next guest who stays in our room finding them—tucked far under the bed, or on the bathroom counter—trying them on, wondering, just for a brief second or two, about the person who left them behind.

The lie I've told my mother feels enormous, exciting, a diffuse electrical current just under my skin.

"Did you get a good look at them?" my mother asks.

"Who?" I roll the window down, but the wind's blowing hard, and I roll it right up again. An ambulance comes tearing past us, siren blaring.

"The guys in the car."

In the past, my mother described the men in the white car as dark-haired, with mustaches—Italian maybe, or Middle Eastern. For some reason, whenever I imagine these men, I picture the Ayatollah Khomeini, turbaned and stoic, with eyes that are surprisingly gentle and soft.

"They had black hair." I squeeze some lotion out of the tube my mother keeps in the front seat and rub it on the back of my legs, which are sunburned and itchy. "And beards."

My mother starts to drum her fingers nervously on the steering wheel. I keep my eyes on the gas gauge, with its little arrow pointing sternly at the *E.*

If we run out of gas and get stuck by the side of the rode, here in the middle of nowhere, we'll have no choice but to hitch a ride. Maybe, if we're really lucky, we'll get picked up by someone who just happens to be going south—who is heading all the way to Las Palmas, in fact. *What a coincidence,* my mother will say, *that's where we're from. Is it okay that we have a dog?* It's still early enough in the day that we can be home by midnight—two a.m. at the very latest. We'll wake up in our own beds. I could call Lainey first thing in the morning, she prides herself on being an *early riser,* and see if she wants to go to the JCC, maybe take an aerobics class or do a Jane Fonda video or swim a little. My backstroke has improved from all the laps I've done at the motel, and maybe the guy she likes, the one who dropped out of tenth grade because of *behavioral problems,* is still working at the JCC as a lifeguard. . . .

"Jesus," my mother says. "I can't believe they actually managed to find us." But she looks secretly pleased, as if now she has an ally.

Finally we pass a sign for GAS and LODGING, a blue sign with an icon of a tank and a bed, both the same size, even though, of course, a gas tank is smaller than a bed. My mother doesn't slow down. She's gone quiet, but it's not the quiet of calmness. It's the quiet of intense concentration.

"Isn't it weird," I say, hoping to get her attention, "that the only time you see the word *lodging* is on a freeway sign?" It *is* weird, and I'm pleased with myself for noticing it, but my mother doesn't reply. She does, however, pull off at the next exit, where there's a gas station with a sign that says SODA & SNACKS. "I guess it'll be good for us to stretch our legs," she says.

It's a relief to be out of the car. My mother puts Maxwell on his leash, and I find the bathroom, which is behind the station. The floor is covered in muddy footprints, and there's no mirror. I look at my elongated reflection in the metal paper towel dispenser, trying to fix my hair, but it's hard to see anything clearly. My face is a blur, not really my face at all. Now I wish I hadn't lied to my mother and had just left things the way they were. Somehow I thought when I made up the story about seeing the men in the white car she'd want to drive back home, to Las Palmas—that after all this time, she'd realize that was the right thing to do. It didn't occur to me that she would want to keep driving still farther away, to a new place altogether. . . .

By the time I get out, my mother is sitting alone, on a small wooden bench by the side of the gas station. Maxwell sniffs around her feet, chewing at an empty box from Burger King. Just the sight of it makes me swallow hard; we haven't eaten anything at all today.

My mother looks up. "Hey," she says, like she's surprised to see me. "How are you feeling, sweetie?"

"I'm hungry." The wind starts up again, a haunting, lonely sound. My mother looks at the car, and then back at me. Usually she's the sort of person who knows exactly what she wants to do. But now she seems resigned, confused, like she'd be happy for someone else to take over for a change. "Let's just see what they have here," I say, tying Maxwell's leash to the bench. My mother waits for a second and then follows me inside.

The guy behind the counter looks up when we come in. "Afternoon," he says. He can't be much older than me—sixteen at the most, pale and thin, with a face completely scarred by acne. I wonder if he picks at it. All the magazines say not to; it can leave a mark, and for the rest of your life, people will say, *He picked his face; that's why it looks so bad.* But I bet he gets to go home after work and have dinner with his parents, in a real home, not a motel, and they all sit down together in front of the TV to watch a game show and talk about what happened that day.

I look around the store. In the corner there's a spinning rack with postcards—not of the town, but general California postcards, with pictures of the beach: dolphins leaping into the sun; the Golden Gate Bridge; the words WISH YOU WERE HERE printed across the butt of a woman in a bikini. My mother's scanning the newspaper headlines, which are in the thick black lettering that lets you know something important is happening; something about Reagan and the Contras and Nicaragua. I'm not even sure where Nicaragua is. How strange to think that the world is going on all around us, that wars are being fought in places I know nothing about, and my mother and I are still running away. . . .

My mother puts a strawberry yogurt and an orange juice on the counter, and I add a couple of chocolate bars to the pile. She scoots one away. "Put that back."

"But I'm starving."

"You can have some raisins if you're really that hungry."

"Raisins are gross."

My mother doesn't reply, just keeps her eyes on the newspaper.

"They look like rabbit turds," I say, loud enough for the guy behind the counter to hear. I know I'm acting like a baby, but I don't care.

"Get some peanuts then." My mother fumbles in her purse for her wallet, but can't find it. "God damn it," she says, biting her lip. My mother never swears like that, and I stare at her as she throws everything on the counter and takes off her jacket. Underneath she's just wearing the thin tank top, and the outline of her nipples pokes through the shirt, hard and pointy, as if she's wearing nothing at all. The guy behind the counter fumbles with a bag of potato chips, pretending not to look at her chest.

"Mom," I whisper. "You really should put on a bra."

My mother is still riffling through her purse, looking for the wallet. "Oh, God," she says, her voice pitched tense and low. "I think I left it at the motel."

My heart jumps at that. We'll have to drive back, and Dennis will smile and shake his head when he sees us. *I knew you'd be back,* he'll say, and I'll help him clean the dead leaves out of the pool, maybe even dive under and get the ones trapped in the gutter. When it gets dark, my mother and I can get our favorite Chinese takeout—pot stickers and chicken chow mein with broccoli—and watch TV. After dinner I'll get under the covers and finish the last few chapters of *Watership Down.* My mother will say, *It was all for the best, when you leave something behind it means you're destined to go back, and who would have thought I'd forget my wallet, of all things?* And then, after a good night's rest, we'll wake up early and drive back to Las Palmas, singing along to the oldies stations my mother likes (I'll hum along when I don't know the words, just to keep her company), maybe stopping at a roadside stand to get some fresh-picked strawberries, two pints for a dollar. . . .

But then my mother finds the wallet in the side pocket of her purse, right where it was supposed to be all along. She smooths out a ten-dollar bill and hands it to the clerk. "I must have been looking at it this whole time," she says, glancing at the glass case over his shoulder, where the cigarettes and *Playboys* are kept. My mother stares at the rows and rows of cigarettes, all lined up in their neat little boxes. "I kind of want to smoke," she says to me. "Isn't that weird?" I think about Miriam, taking such care to hide her Marlboro Lights, always asking me if her hair and hands smelled like smoke, and wonder what she would say if she saw my mother like this: her hair messy, braless, smoking. I just shake my head and shove another pack of gum into my pocket.

"Give me one of those," she says to the guy, pointing to a box with an Indian head on it. "And a box of matches." After she pays we go back outside and my mother lights a cigarette in the bright blazing sun, as casually as if she smokes every day. She looks so strange doing this, so unlike her usual cautious self, that for a moment I forget to eat the candy bar.

"Stop staring at me," she says. "You're making me feel self-conscious." I try not to look at her, this woman who seems only a little like my mother. I feel as if I am carrying a stone inside my throat.

The guy comes over to where we're sitting. His acne is even worse in the sunlight, and he looks nervous talking to my mother. "You're not allowed to light up over here," he says. "Too close to the gas tanks."

My mother toys with the cigarette for a minute. I picture her throwing it at the red convertible, the whole place going up in sudden, spectacular flame. Then she stubs it out. "I shouldn't be smoking anyway," she says, tossing the rest of the box in the trash. A cloud of pigeons circles overhead.

"Let's go, Mom." I untie Maxwell's leash from the bench. "I don't want to stay here anymore."

"In a second. I just need a minute to think." My mother buries her head in her hands and I realize she's crying.

Just then another car pulls into the parking lot. It's a normal white car, two doors, with a few scratches and dents where it's been hit on the passenger's side. Nothing about it looks scary at all. But before I know what's happening my mother grabs my arm, roughly, and shoves me and Maxwell into the car. I barely have time to shut the door.

As we pull away, tires screeching, I catch a glimpse of the person driving the white car. It's not a man with a beard. It's not a man at all. It's only a middle-aged woman, filling her tank, just like anyone who's run out of gas.

33

For the next week we move around, staying at a different place every night: Motel 6, which doesn't really cost six dollars, the way it once did, my mother tells me; and Best Western, where there is always a piece of chocolate on the pillow. "Well, isn't that sweet," my mother always says. "You eat both pieces; I need to watch my figure." I gulp down the chocolate quickly; it is the only part of the day I look forward to.

No one pays much attention to us, except sometimes to pet Maxwell or say something about the weather, which, we are told over and over again, is *unusually humid for this time of year.* Every morning after breakfast we get in the car and drive for a couple of hours, looking for a new place to stay. We're heading north, steadily getting farther and farther away from home.

"If we just keep changing our location," my mother says, "it'll be harder for them to find us." I think of the Boy Scout motto—*be prepared*—and repeat it over and over in my head like a mantra. It dawns on me that all this moving is just another, sped-up version of our life in Las Palmas—when my mother kept moving us from one apartment to the next, trying to find someplace safe. I know that eventually we will have to come to a stop and settle somewhere, sort of like when a top keeps spinning and spinning and then suddenly stops. You can't keep driving forever, no matter how many roads there are. But for now we are *on the move,* as my mother says.

My mother prefers motels just off the highway, with parking in the back, so that our car will be hidden from view. When she checks in she always leaves me and Maxwell in the car. "I don't want anyone getting too close a look at you," she says. For meals we get takeout (drive-through if possible, so we don't have to go into the restaurant), which we bring back to the motel room to eat, curtains drawn. My mother gets startled every time we see a white car, even though, of course, they can't all be *the car.*

"I still can't believe you saw them," my mother says, her voice full of wonder.

None of the motels are as nice as Motel del Mar—they don't have as much personality, for one thing. They always smell strange, from the scent of lemon furniture polish and disinfectant, and if you look closely you can see dust, sometimes a dull ring in the tub, the leftover traces of all the people who have stayed there before. In the past, my mother might have complained about the room, might have insisted that *we weren't paying good money to stay someplace filthy and could we please be treated with a little respect.* But now she doesn't even seem to notice the dirt or the strange smells—she just puts her purse down on the dusty bureau or the ratty armchair and goes to sleep. I watch TV, the sound turned down to a quiet hum, for hours and hours, until my mother wakes up.

In spite of the ugly motel rooms, the moving around, the days spent driving nowhere, my mother seems to sleep as quietly, as peacefully, as ever. At rest, she's as calm and still as if we were back in her bedroom in Las Palmas, under the pink and white bedspread with the old-fashioned floral pattern. Sometimes at night I pull the curtains aside and study her face in the moonlight, wondering if she ever dreams of the men in the white car. Maybe she does, but in her dreams they are smaller, weaker, not that threatening. Maybe in her dreamworld she yells at them to leave her alone, maybe she fights back, scratching and biting, grabbing the guns out of their hands and defeating them once and for all, and they get in their car and drive far away, never to return, never even daring to look back.

The weather turns cooler as we head north. I have the long, wool, button-down sweater Miriam shoplifted from Macy's on a dare. On me it's more like a robe than a sweater, and I wear it constantly—to the point that my mother says, *Can't you put on something else for God's sake*—but even with the heat turned up high, I can't seem to get warm. Before bed I cover myself with as many blankets as possible, only to wake up in the middle of the night drenched in sweat, sticky and wet, as if I've peed in the bed.

There's a dull ache at the back of my throat that won't go away, no matter how many cups of organic throat soother herbal tea my mother heats up in the motel microwaves. "You probably picked something up along the road," she says, stirring an extra spoonful of honey into my mug. "That often happens when people travel." I picture the germs, green and sneaky, hitching a ride in my body, hovering right under my skin.

Back home, I sometimes pretended to be sick so I could stay out of school and read mysteries and play Atari. Miriam taught me the right way to do it: how to make my voice sound hoarse and scratchy, when to sniffle, how often to cough. ("Not too many times," she warned me, "or it'll sound fake.") But being sick now is a waste—there's nothing to stay home from. And it means being trapped in the small motel room with my mother.

"Want another glass of water?"

"Don't you think you need another blanket?"

She hovers over me, bringing me cups of instant chicken noodle soup, mixing my cough syrup with soda water so it tastes better. Sometimes I catch her looking at me, her face shadowed with quiet concern. I just want her to go away—to give me just a little tiny bit of space to myself. So I keep asking her to get me things: another carton of orange juice, or some special tissues, the kind with the built-in lotion. The cherry-flavored lozenges in the metal tin that taste almost like candy. *Seventeen* and *YM.* I thumb through the magazines, opening them up in the middle or end and starting over again, the pictures of prom dresses melting into one another like giant bouquets.

A dull wave of pain washes over me whenever I try to stand up. Every three or four minutes I have to blow my nose, and I can't stop coughing: a dry, horrible hacking. I stay inside all day, huddled shivering in bed, except for in the early mornings, when my mother quickly packs up our stuff in the yellow and white embroidered suitcase and drives us to the next motel. Sometimes I take out Miriam's sketchbook, which is starting to get bent from being shoved deep in the bottom of my bag, and stare at the pictures, wishing she was there to draw me something new.

At the end of the week I'm still sick. My mother, a big believer in tea and bed rest, is confused. "You've been drinking lots of liquids," she says. "And taking those vitamin C pills." She studies the bottle. "It says they help your immune system."

I curl up tight and shiver under the covers, my body stiff with cold. Maxwell cuddles close and licks some of the snot off my face. Even with his warm, heavy body curled against mine, I feel tense and shaky. "I might get better if we stayed in one place for a while," I say. "If we went home."

My mother doesn't say anything, just calls the motel office, even though it's late at night, and asks for more blankets and a heating pad. When the guy comes to our room he peeks in curiously. "I could hear her coughing all the way down the hall," he says to my mother. "What's she got?"

"I don't know," my mother says, stifling a yawn. "Something with a lot of sneezing."

"What color is her, uh, snot?" The guy hesitates over it, as if it's a dirty word.

"Light green," my mother says. I am embarrassed; it seems like the sort of thing you shouldn't tell a guy.

"Green?" He makes a face. "That means it's bacterial."

My mother and I just look at him. Neither of us knows what that means.

"You should take her to a doctor. She needs antibiotics."

Lying there, I feel like Beth in *Little Women*—when she's sick and everybody's talking around her. (She lives, but then later she gets sick again and dies for real, which never seemed fair; it was as if the book had played a trick on me.)

"Definitely." The guy looks at me. "Do you have a doctor?"

"Of course!" my mother says. "Everyone has a doctor." He says good night and leaves, and my mother locks the door. Then she comes over to take my temperature, even though she just took it a couple of hours ago. "Mom?"

"What?"

"Can we go home?"

My mother reads my temperature. "Why?"

"So I can go to the doctor." My throat is tight. It's an effort just to choke out the words.

Something passes over her face, something vague and shadowy, like a cloud. For a second I think she will say, *Yes, of course we can go home. That is the right thing to do. You are very sick. The men in the white car are not real, it's all in my head, and it's time for all of this to stop. Let's go first thing tomorrow. This whole thing has gone on long enough.*

"Amber, my God." She throws the thermometer down, so hard I'm afraid it's going to break. "We can't go home. Don't you understand that by now?" She goes into the bathroom and turns on the shower. I stare at the little glass thermometer, wondering how they get the mercury in there.

The next morning my mother finds us a health clinic. It's not anything like our doctor's office at home, the one Miriam and I have been going to since we were little kids, where the nurses pretend to remember your name and give you a small toy or piece of candy on the way out. This place is crowded with people. No magazines or toys, just a bunch of folding chairs. And there are not even enough chairs for everybody—some people are crouched on the floor, one woman is even sleeping.

About the only nice thing in the room is the coffee maker, with its bright orange light and vaguely comforting hum. My mother pours herself a cup of coffee and we sit down under a frayed "Just Say No" poster, the same one hanging in the locker room at school. Nancy Reagan's smile is proud, confident: the smile of a winner. I keep my head down, trying not to look at the girl sitting across from me, bent over and holding herself, sobbing quietly. It's not until she gets up to take a drink from the water faucet that I realize she's pregnant, her stomach hanging defiantly over the waistband of her jeans. I've never seen a girl my age who is pregnant. My mother nudges me not to stare, and clutches her purse tightly as if it might run away from her. Above the receptionist's desk, a black-and-white clock ticks the minutes slowly.

A man staggers in on crutches, and it takes me a moment to realize that one of his legs is only half a leg. It's hard not to look at that empty pants leg, just hanging there. I get up to offer him my chair, but my mother grabs me by the arm and hisses, "You stay right here." She leans over and whispers, "You never know how many of these people might be addicts."

The walls are covered with posters. STOP SMOKING! YOUR BABY DOESN'T LIKE IT. HOW TO PREVENT GENITAL HERPES. CRACK KILLS. All the posters at my doctor's office back home are of baby animals, reminding you to drink your milk, or underwater scenes: angelfish, goldfish, a dolphin. In tiny letters, on the seat next to me, someone has written the words "Help Me," the writing shaky and scared. I trace the letters with my finger, wanting to write "You'll be okay," but my mother is sitting right there. I look around, feeling embarrassed. No one else, I'm sure, is here with their mother.

When it's my turn my mother wants to come into the examination room with me, but the nurse tells her to stay in the waiting room and then leads me down a dark hallway, humming something to herself. She hands me a blue paper robe. "Take off your clothes and put this on."

"But I'm here for my throat."

"It's okay, just put it on," she says, shutting the door quietly behind her. The robe is folded into a perfect square. I take off my clothes and struggle into the robe, which ties in the back. Every time I move it makes a strange crackling noise. I feel like a birthday present, wrapped up and ready to go.

There's not much to look at, just the usual doctor office things: a jar of cotton balls, some tongue depressors, a Red Cross poster on the wall showing how to do CPR. The most interesting thing in the room is a large brown filing cabinet, with taped-on labels that say things like EMERGENCY PROCEDURES and SUICIDE PREVENTION. I've just about worked up the nerve to open it when the doctor comes in. She's tall and walks with a brisk, no-nonsense step, like a person in a rush, but when she sits down on the little stool and turns to me I see how gentle and serious her eyes are. She steals a quick glance at her clipboard.

"How are you feeling today?"

Just those five words, and I start crying. I can't help it, all of the tears have been stored inside me for so long.

The doctor opens a brand-new box of tissues and hands me one. "It's okay," she says, her voice low and sympathetic, as if she already knows me. "Why don't you tell me what's going on."

"I'm just really sick." I take a deep breath. It felt good to cry, a huge release, but now, more than anything, I want the tears to stop.

"Is there something you can't talk to your mom about?"

She probably means, are you pregnant, or on drugs. I shake my head no and wipe away the last of the tears, which have suddenly stopped. The doctor sighs as if she's had this exact same conversation many times. "Okay, then. Let me just check out a few things." She takes my blood pressure, checks my reflexes with the little hammer. I sit still, feeling embarrassed and naked in the paper robe. When the doctor is finished she writes out a prescription and tells me to get it filled right away. "You can go to the pharmacy next door," she says, putting the pen back in her pocket. Everything about her is neat and orderly. She shuffles the papers in her file and says, "Do you have anyone else you can talk to? A brother or sister?"

The question makes me feel dizzy again. I remember how angry and upset my mother was when I told Dennis about Miriam, so I just say, "No. I don't have any brothers or sisters." I play with the end of my little blue robe. The tissue is damp from my snot, and she holds out a little trash can so I can throw it away. I guess she's not allowed to touch it with her hands, being a doctor; there are probably all kinds of things she's not allowed to do. "I think the most important thing is for you to just sit still for a few days." She looks at me. "Don't run yourself ragged." I wonder what she would think if I told her my mother and I were switching motels every night.

When the appointment is over my mother drives us to a new motel, chatting excitedly about how the pills will make me feel all better. "Just a couple of days and you'll be all back to normal," she says, unlocking the door to our room. "No more chicken soup."

I don't say anything, just shuffle into bed without bothering to take off my clothes. My body is damp and heavy with sweat, and I can't help but think about the doctor in her clean white coat. Telling her I didn't have any siblings felt terrible—an especially bad lie. It felt like an insult to Miriam, pretending she does not even exist. Of course, my mother and I have been lying to everyone we meet for weeks now, telling them *we're just taking a little vacation* or *visiting relatives*. And I have lied to my mother about the men in the white car. You'd think by now I'd be used to it. But for some reason this particular lie has sunk deep in my stomach. I can feel it in there, weighing me down.

I squeeze my eyes shut and swallow hard. The lie is rolling around inside me, sharp edged and painful. I race into the bathroom and throw up.

After a few minutes my mother knocks on the door. "You okay, sweetie?" She sounds almost shy. "Sometimes antibiotics have that effect."

I run cool water over my face and brush my teeth so hard that my gums bleed. "I'm sorry, Miriam," I whisper into the sink, so quiet even I can barely hear it. "I'm so sorry." And right then, I make a pledge. Somehow, I will find my sister. I don't know how I'm going to do it, but I have to. She is the only person, really, who will understand.

34

My mother, it turns out, is right: after a day or two of taking the antibiotics I feel a little better. The back of my throat still burns, and a small cough keeps forcing itself from my throat. But I no longer feel as if I'm half asleep all the time, weighed down and numb like a stone lodged underwater. Just the opposite: I want to jump up and down, make noise, break things—I keep finding myself staring at the motel room's glass ashtray, fighting the urge to throw it against the wall, or stopping myself at the last moment from picking up the motel phone and screaming at the receptionist. Instead I lie on the floor's thin carpet, practicing sit-ups and leg lifts, counting out the seconds slowly, the way Lainey taught me—*one, two, three, four, five.*

"You're just like Jane Fonda," my mother says admiringly. "Very impressive."

Maxwell pants loudly by my side, as if he's doing sit-ups too. I wish I could take him for a long walk, somewhere grassy and open and green, but my mother tells me not to go any farther than the twenty-four-hour convenience store down the street, and to *be quick about it*—she's starting to get the sense that *something funny is going on, something she can't quite put her finger on.* I trot Maxwell in slow circles around the store's parking lot, trying to fool him into thinking we've gone a long distance, but he still pulls at the leash and hangs back, whining softly, wanting to sniff at the bushes and shrubs behind the Dumpster.

"I know how you feel," I tell him.

On warm days I'm allowed to lie outside by the pool, but I have to wear a hat and sunglasses, and if I notice anything suspicious, *anything at all,* I am to come back to the room and tell my mother about it immediately. The hat is very embarrassing, a fake straw hat with a floral print bandana, which my mother bought for a few dollars at a grocery store.

At night I lie awake on the motel's hard mattress, listening to my mother's quiet, steady snoring, trying to figure out how I can find my sister. And for the hundredth time I feel a deep ache in my stomach, something between pain and longing, a feeling I finally recognize as anger. Miriam never bothered to put a return address or a phone number on all those postcards with the adorable kittens and galloping ponies because she wanted to make sure we wouldn't find her. She wanted to fade away, like a child's doodle slowly disappearing from a steamed-up window. I know that feeling—wanting to just disappear, cleanly, quietly, without a word. It's a feeling I had at school, when the other kids were taunting me, making fun of my glasses, or my height, or when Christie McPherson called my mother names—wishing I could just melt into my chair, leaving behind a small puddle that would eventually evaporate and join the air. And I know this need to vanish—like a ghost, or a magic trick—is something my mother shares too, which is why we had to get in the car and leave everything behind.

But my sister hasn't really disappeared . . . has she? I tell myself that Miriam is just playing a game of hide-and-seek with us, the way we used to do when we were younger. My sister was faster and could easily catch me, but she was always annoyed that I was able to squeeze into the best hiding spots—the narrow space behind the living room couch or under the small round table in my mother's bedroom—while she was stuck with the predictable places anyone would choose, like the hall closet or the storage area, crowded with mops and brooms, under the stairs. Whenever I was "it" I'd open the closet door with a nervous chill coursing my body, already knowing that my sister would be crouched there, but also knowing that she'd jump out, screaming, to startle me. And then, after I jumped in fright (something I also knew would happen ahead of time), she'd grab me close to her and stroke my hair and say, *Don't be such a baby, Adie, it's only a game.* So maybe now if I try not to be too frightened and just look for my sister I'll be able to find her, and she'll say that she didn't really mean to run away and scare anyone. That she was just playing, just having fun with us, and that if we didn't find her soon she would have come home anyway. It was all just *fun and games.* These are the thoughts I tell myself as I fall asleep.

It's late in the afternoon, and we're trying to figure out what to have for dinner, when my mother suddenly yawns and says, "I just want to take a shower before we go. My hair feels terrible, so dry."

"I think they put more chlorine in the pool here," I say, stretching out on the bed. In the past, my mother used to always talk about how important it was not to waste water, how we all had to do our part to *conserve resources,* but now her showers have been getting longer and longer. I understand; it's easy to get lost in there. The warm water runs over you and it's like being in a different place. And it's the only place in a motel room where you can get away from the other person.

I try not to let my mother see my face; I've decided that when I get a few minutes alone I'm going to sneak downstairs and call 411 and see if there's any way I can figure out the phone number for Miriam's farm, even though it's what my mother would call *a long shot.* I don't dare use the phone in the room, of course, but the moment I hear my mother step into the shower I slip out the door and head downstairs to the pay phone, which is tucked away in a little corner next to the motel's office. I bring Maxwell with me, so that if my mother gets out of the shower before I get back I can tell her that he absolutely had to go out, that he was whining and turning around in the tiny, tight circles that mean he can't hold it much longer, even though she'll be upset that I left the room without telling her where I was going. . . . Of course, she would be much more upset if she knew I was trying to call my sister, and for a moment I picture her face, lined and red from crying. I try not to think about all this as I pick up the phone, which has a big piece of pink bubble gum stuck to the handle. I brace myself against the wall, trying to keep my body from shaking, as I dial 411 and ask to be connected to an operator in Oregon. A man on the other side of the room shuffles impatiently—he's waiting to use the phone—and he stares suspiciously at Maxwell, as if the dog might want to make a phone call as well.

After just a few rings the operator answers, but it takes me a moment to speak. "Hello? Ashland?" I try to make my voice sound calm and adult, but it comes out shaky, like a bird missing a wing. "I'm trying to find a listing for a farm."

"What's the name?"

The man on the other side of the room taps his watch and gives me a look. I turn away and shield my mouth with my hand so he can't hear me. "I don't know. It's an apple farm."

The operator makes a clucking sound. "Lots of farms around Ashland." I can almost see her shaking her head. "I need a name."

"It's organic."

The operator sighs like she's disappointed in me. "Sorry."

"Okay," I say stupidly. "Thanks anyway." I'm determined not to cry, not with that man watching me. I keep my eyes on the floor, and Maxwell, following my gaze, licks something off the rug. Of course there are a lot of apple farms in Ashland, why wouldn't there be?

I'm about to hang up when the operator says, "Why don't you try the local chamber of commerce?"

"What's that?"

She explains it to me and gives me a number, which I write down on the back of an empty Publishers Clearing House envelope someone's left on the floor. It's a toll-free number; I won't even need to worry about having enough coins. If Lainey were here she'd tell me that was a *good sign* and that *the stars must be aligned in my favor.* I think about her World of the Planets

Astrology calendar, the way she'd always read me my weekly horoscope on the school bus on Mondays. *You see,* she'd tell me, *this was all ordained. From the moment of your birth, the stars have fated you to make this phone call. You cannot escape your destiny. . . .*

The man clears his throat loudly. "Are you finished?" I nod and tug at Maxwell's leash, a little harder than usual, and he gives out a small whine.

At dinner, my throat feels dry and closed, like I might get sick if I swallow anything. I push my spaghetti around on my plate.

I catch my mother looking at me funny. "You okay, Amber?"

"I'm fine." The envelope with the phone number is folded tight in my pocket. I look at the windows and think to myself, this is one of the last times my mother and I will eat in a diner like this. For a moment, I wonder if I'll miss it.

She frowns at my plate. "You're not eating very much."

"I think I have a little bit of a stomachache." My mother orders a bowl of clear chicken broth for me and finishes the spaghetti herself.

That night I toss and turn, shifting my body into every possible position—flat on my back, curled up on my left side, then on my right, then on my stomach—but sleep is impossible. I keep rehearsing the phone call in my head. *Hello, Ashland Chamber of Commerce, what's the name of the local organic apple farm?* And it will be such a small, friendly town that the person on the other end will say, *Oh! You mean the farm where Miriam works! Let me connect you right away.* When Miriam answers the phone and hears my voice, she'll be so relieved to hear from me, that she'll forget all about picking apples and come get me. I'll tell her about the motel and Dennis and the Alateen meeting and the guys in the white car, and she'll hug me and say, *Adie, you've been so brave. It was so foolish of me to leave you alone with Mom.* And then she'll start to cry, and say, *But don't you worry, everything's going to be better from now on. . . .*

At some point I fall asleep, but it's that strange half sleep that just makes you feel worse, as if your body is made of lead.

The next morning, as soon as I wake up, I sneak downstairs

to the pay phone. By now I have the Chamber of Commerce phone number memorized, the way a song gets stuck in your head, and as my finger strums the dial it's as if I've made this very same phone call a thousand times before. Everything is quiet, and the rings seem especially slow and loud. Finally the number connects. I hold my breath, but all I hear is a recording: *You have reached the Ashland County Chamber of Commerce. Please leave a message, and someone will return your call as soon as possible. Have a great day!*

I hang up the phone and try again. Same thing. Maybe it's too early.

My mother is still lying in bed when I get back to our motel room. She turns over, then stretches and yawns. "Hey, sweetie," she says, her voice heavy and hushed with sleep. I look at her, so still and peaceful in the bed.

For the rest of the day, whenever I get a chance, I go downstairs to the pay phone. The older woman who works behind the office counter gives me a knowing smile, as if we're sharing a secret, probably thinking that I'm calling a boyfriend. Every time I dial the number, I think, *This is it. In just a few minutes, I'll be talking to my sister.* But nobody answers.

I hate the cheery, upbeat voice of whoever recorded the message. What kind of place is Ashland anyway? I picture the Chamber of Commerce office—a small, dark, windowless space, with a telephone sitting on a table in the very middle of the room, ringing and ringing and ringing.

No one picks up the phone: not that night, or the next day. Or the next. After a week of trying to contact the Chamber of Commerce, I give up. If I want to talk to Miriam, it's not going to be on the phone. I am going to somehow have to get to Ashland myself.

With a sinking feeling I realize that I have no idea how I'm going to do this. I've never been to Oregon, and except for Miriam's postcards, all I know of it is the little orange rectangle on the wall-sized map of the United States that hangs in Mrs. Breyer's social studies classroom. At the beginning of the school year everyone in class stuck a colored pushpin in the states they'd been to, and I felt sorry for the states in the middle of the map that no one had visited and were all alone: Alabama, Mississippi, North and South Dakota, Kansas. But Oregon's orange rectangle was covered in pins; lots of people had been there, so maybe I can go too, and when I get back to school I can stick an extra pin on the map and brag about how I visited my sister on a real farm, how there are cows everywhere, just wandering around, so friendly they'll eat grass right out of your hand. . . .

I wish I had someone besides Maxwell to talk to; or that I would get another sign, like a shooting star or a rainbow, that might help me figure out the right thing to do. For a few days, I make pacts with myself, like, *If three blue cars pass in a row, it means I should run away and try to find Miriam.* Or, *If the next commercial's for shampoo, it means I should just stay here.* But no matter how hard I look I don't see any secret messages or clues anywhere.

So one night, while my mother's absorbed in the ten o'clock news, I decide to flip a coin. I've never flipped a coin to make an important decision before—only to choose movies or ice-cream flavors. But never for something like this, that could be a matter of life and death. I lock myself in our tiny bathroom and toss a nickel into the air, letting it land on the smooth black-and-white tiled floor. The coin spins for a long time before stopping, as if it's in slow motion.

"What are you doing in there?" my mother calls.

"Nothing." The nickel has landed on tails, right in the middle of one of the black squares. My stomach turns over. It's the answer I wanted, but it's still scary. Sometimes, fate calls you. You just have to do as it says.

I've stolen a Greyhound bus schedule from one of the motel bulletin boards. At night, after my mother's gone to sleep, I lock myself in the bathroom and study it. There's a big Greyhound bus terminal in Sacramento. (I've never been there and have always been puzzled by the fact that it's California's state capital.

Why not Los Angeles or San Francisco, so much more famous?) From there you can catch a bus to Oregon—to a city called Medford. Then you connect with another bus to Ashland. My mother and I pass the Greyhound buses on the freeway all the time, with the picture of the long-legged dog on the side, just running and running. But I'd have to get to Sacramento first. . . .

Miriam and her friends used to hitchhike out to the dunes at the beach, and I remember her telling me how it works. How if you're a girl, you'll definitely get a ride, especially if you are wearing the kind of outfit my mother would describe as *a shade too provocative.* No one in their right mind is going to stop for a man; he could be crazy like the Son of Sam or the Zodiac Killer, just waiting for their next victim to pull over and offer them a ride. Of course, the person picking you up could be a maniac too. Hitchhiking is a little like gambling; it could go either way. You take your chances.

My mother and I drive past hitchhikers all the time, holding their cardboard signs with the name of the place they want to go. "It's such a tragedy," my mother always says, speeding past, "that people are so lonely, so lost." And it's true, some of the hitchhikers don't even seem to be heading anywhere in particular; the signs just say NORTH or I-80. Once we even saw a sign that said ANYWHERE. That seemed sad to me, but maybe the guy holding it really didn't care. Sometimes you just want to get moving.

When we left home everything was rushed, a hurry of panic and confusion and throwing things into the car and there was no time to really consider what we might need. And we'd forgotten some really basic things: socks, for instance, which we had to buy at the drugstore, and my One A Day vitamins, which really upset my mother, since it's important for me *to get the proper vitamins and minerals.* This time I decide I'm going to do it right. I lie flat on my back in bed, listening to my mother's gentle, measured breathing, thinking about all the things I'll need to take with me. My oldest jeans, which are still my favorite, even with the holes slicing the knees. Miriam's UCLA sweatshirt. The bathing suit my mother hates, since my sister said there's a lake. Something to read.

I feel a little sick when I realize that I will need to leave a note for my mother—letting her know that I'm all right, that I have not been abducted or killed or raped—and I decide to write it ahead of time, in case I mess it up the first time, I want to be able to have a do-over. I want to get it just right, and I don't want it to have any pictures of hearts and peace signs the way Miriam's note did. It seems so dramatic—the kind of thing you might see in a made-for-TV movie or an afternoon soap opera. But when my mother realizes I'm gone her first thought will be that the men in the white car have taken me, and I can't have her worrying about that. She will have enough to worry about— with first Miriam running away and then me. Two runaway daughters.

In the past, I would have felt sorry for my mother, thinking about this. I would have heard the words in my head: *she'll be so sad.* She'll cry and wonder what she did wrong, and think about all the things she could have said to keep me from leaving, and then she'll perch upright on the edge of the bed, the way she always does when she's trying to figure out what to do next, unable to call anyone, worrying about me. But something inside me has shifted, as if my blood and bones and organs have rearranged themselves: I am beginning to feel sorry for myself.

Next to the bed is a tiny pad of motel stationery, too small for anything but a shopping list or a jotted-down phone number. I am relieved by this; it means I can fill the whole page with only a few words. Looking at the blank page, I remember how when we first started staying in motels I thought all the different stationery was exciting, the free envelopes and crisp white paper and notepads. It seemed like a fun thing to collect, and in the future, I could write letters on it, impressing people with all the different places I'd been (places they'd never even heard of), all the trips my mother and I had been on, to waterfalls and theme parks and gold rush towns. . . .

Dear Mom, I write. *Don't worry about me.*

I feel like an idiot; obviously she is going to worry about me, all she does is worry. But I want to stay *positive and upbeat*. As my mother likes to say, *Attitude is everything*. So I choose my words carefully: *I'm going to visit Miriam up north. I know where she lives*. Somehow the word *visit* makes the whole thing seem not so bad, as if Miriam has called to invite me to stay with her for a weekend, wants me to tour the farm and meet her friends and sleep over. I try not to think about the fact that my sister doesn't even know I'm coming—doesn't even know that we're not still at home in Las Palmas. A thin line of fear traces itself around my heart.

I'll call you. I love you and DON'T WORRY! Love, Adie. I fold the piece of paper in half, so that the edges match perfectly, and put the words *To Mom* in my best cursive handwriting on the outside. Of course, she will know it's meant for her even without that. There's no one else it could be for.

35

When I woke up this morning the sky was like a postcard, bright and clear, making it seem as if today was exactly the right day to leave. But now everything is gray and drizzly, the kind of slow, steady rain that you know is going to stick around for a long time. I should have thought to take an umbrella, but there were too many other things to think about. Earlier this morning I quietly put my clothes and bathing suit and other things in a little secret pile, so I'd be ready to leave when I got a chance. I had planned to take my backpack but not everything fit, so at the last minute I grabbed my mother's yellow and white embroidered suitcase and shoved everything inside.

Now it's almost five o'clock. I look back in the direction of the motel, nervously. My mother, in bed since four, is drifting through her "afternoon nap"—one of the naps which now lasts for a couple of hours. These days she sleeps so soundly, her breath hushed and quiet, and I hope the sound of the rain, dashing hard against the motel window, hasn't woken her. Of course, there are times when the rain actually helps you sleep better. It's hard to say which kind of rain this is.

Just a few minutes ago I knelt down on the motel rug and gave Maxwell a careful kiss good-bye. "I'll see you soon," I mouthed, not daring to say the words aloud. He met my eyes with what I could swear was understanding, as if he knew exactly where I was going, and for a moment I thought he might bound onto the bed and bark my mother awake. But for once he kept quiet, curling back against the dresser with a dull thud. Now I'm standing at the side of the road, right near the freeway entrance, next to a big, green sign that says 101 North—a place, I hope, where it will be easy for a car to stop. Before this, I never realized how enormous freeway signs were—they look smaller when you're whizzing by, leaving them behind almost as quickly as you see them—and I feel even smaller than usual standing next to it.

I balance the yellow and white embroidered suitcase on the edge of the road. Overhead, seagulls duck in and out of the rain, gray and white blurs in the distance. I arrange my features in an expression I hope makes me look not like a serial killer and stick out my thumb. The whole thing feels unreal, staged, as if I'm posing for a picture of a girl hitchhiking.

The cars rush by, faster than I would have imagined, and the rain starts to beat down hard. My body tenses. I had no idea it would be so scary standing by the side of the road, with the cars zooming past, and the rain is cold on my neck and arms. I look through the rain and imagine myself getting to Oregon and stepping off the bus and finding my sister, who is so happy and excited to see me, and somehow, in my fantasy, magically right there at the bus stop—*Thank goodness you're here, Adie; I've missed you so much*—but then the rain gets harder and the picture in my head falls down and Miriam is not there at all, I am wandering around all by myself, dragging the yellow and white embroidered suitcase behind me, unable to find my sister, who has run away again, this time to Seattle or Vancouver, and now I am lost and alone in a whole other state, and the rain is still falling. . . .

A car pulls over and a guy leans over and opens the window. "Hey," he says.

"Hey." I am not sure what to say. With his long brown hair and scraggly beard, he looks just like one of the guys from *The Final Ride,* the anti-hitchhiking film we watched in health class last year. He's wearing ripped jeans and a DISCO SUCKS T-shirt—the same one Lainey's older brother has—and a tattoo of a coiled snake ropes his arm. Looking at the tattoo, I can't help but think of the fate of the girl in the film—rape, torture, and death—and all because she was stupid enough to hitchhike, even after everyone told her it wasn't safe.

"Need a lift?"

"Yeah." I hang back. Maybe I should wait for someone else to stop: a woman driving a nice, clean car, the backseat piled high with bags from the grocery store. Or an elderly couple, tired and laughing, slowly driving home from a visit with their grandkids. I look over my shoulder; from here, I can just make out the motel's neon, blinking no vacancy sign. It would be easy enough to turn around and go back to the room, get under the warm, soft covers and watch the rain from inside. I always like the sound the rain makes, hitting the window in little bursts. . . .

"Where you headed?"

I swallow hard. "I'm trying to get to Sacramento." My voice comes out tiny, an abbreviated squeak.

The guy raises an eyebrow. "I can take you," he says, patting the seat next to him. "Hop on in."

I peek inside the car. Even from here it smells a little funny—cigarettes and sweat and a cold dampness from the rain. The upholstery is torn and stained, and there are old newspapers and empty beer cans all over the floor. They could have filmed *The Final Ride* in this car. I look at my watch. My throat contracts as I suddenly realize that I have no idea how long it will take to get to Sacramento.

The guy looks at me, impatient now. "You comin' or not?"

The rain starts coming down even harder. I wish Miriam, the expert hitchhiker, was here to tell me what to do next. I squeeze my eyes shut and try to picture what she'd do. She would probably just flip her hair and say, *What the hell,* and climb right in, as if the car was her own chauffeur-driven limousine. I try to toss my hair the way my sister would and stutter the words, "What the hell." The guy smirks a little, but he brushes the garbage off the seat and opens the door. I clamber in, trying to keep my shoes away from the fast-food wrappers.

"Don't forget your suitcase," the guy says.

"Oh." The yellow and white embroidered suitcase is just sitting there in the rain, looking small and tired by the side of the road. As I get back out of the car I realize, with a sinking feeling, that he can tell I've never hitchhiked before, that usually my mother drives me everywhere, that truthfully, I'm not the sort of girl who runs away and gets in cars with strangers. I push the suitcase into the backseat, where it's propped up against an orange milk crate filled with old records and a guitar case covered with bumper stickers.

"All set?"

"Yes."

It's strange to be in such a small, cramped space with a stranger—it seems you should know a person better if you're going to sit so close to them. The guy doesn't say much, just keeps clearing his throat with a violent, retching sound, as if he has something caught in it, and I wonder for a moment if he has the same cold I had. We speed down winding roads, taking the curves faster, really, than we should, and for a second the car swerves.

"Sorry," he says. "Maybe you should put on your seat belt."

I think about how my mother drives, how she used to be cautious but lately has become faster and more reckless. In the past, my mother was the sort of person who stopped for every yellow light, even if it meant slamming on the brakes (*Safety first,* she'd say, while Miriam sighed heavily), and drove exactly at the speed limit, shaking her head in silent judgment at the other cars as they sped by us. But now she always seems to be one of the fastest drivers on the road, zipping past the other cars (often on the right, even though you're not supposed to do that), laughing at their slowness. Sometimes, the cars we pass are filled with parents and children going who knows where—maybe to church, or a soccer game, or just out shopping, to buy a new toaster or a sweater or school supplies. I can't see them clearly, of course, but I always imagine that the kids are bored, and that my mother, speeding past, must seem exciting and dangerous, and that they envy us, driving faster and faster to an exciting new place, far away from the boredom of school and home. My mother is speeding and speeding, though it's not clear where she wants to go. . . .

"Aren't you a little young to be hitchhiking?"

"Not really."

He snorts. "How old are you, anyway?"

"Fifteen," I lie, sitting up as straight as possible, flipping my hair over my shoulder, the way Miriam taught me.

"Right," he laughs. "Fifteen." He shakes his head. "You want the radio on?"

"Sure."

"Nothing but shit out here, but let's see what we can get." He fiddles with the controls, swearing at the static, finally settling on a station playing the new Journey song. He opens the window, even though the rain is still coming, and starts singing along, leaning over, exaggerating the words as if he's singing them to me: *Someday love will find you* . . .

"My sister has this tape," I say, shifting my legs so they are as far away from him as possible. For some reason I feel as if I should try to have a conversation with him—it's what my mother would call *the polite thing to do*. Somehow it makes me feel a little better that one of Miriam's favorite songs is playing right now, at the very beginning of our drive. It's almost as if Miriam is here, instead of the man with the snake tattoo, and she and I have planned this whole thing together—a vacation, really.

We pass farms and old barns, a group of black-and-white cows, skinnier than cows should be, heads bowed from the rain. They're all facing the same direction, as if they've been stopped on their way somewhere.

"So what's your name?"

"Amber."

He nods appreciatively. "That's hot."

The rain starts to come down faster, in sudden sheets, almost like a solid mass. The guy swears under his breath (*mother-fucker, motherfucker, goddamned motherfucker,* over and over) and grips the steering wheel, so tight I can see the tension in his hands. Finally, he pulls over, into a little ditch by the side of the road.

"We're going to have to stop for a while," he says, killing the engine.

I try to look out the window, but there's nothing to see. The rain, fast and thick, has covered everything, like a blanket.

"Your hair's so pretty."

I don't know how to respond to this. I know I should be scared, but for some reason I'm not. The truth is, people never tell me that I'm pretty. Prettiness is something that belongs to my mother and Miriam. So I just say, "Thanks." The windshield wipers count off their rhythmic beat. One of them is slightly bent and leaves a streak instead of wiping the windshield clean.

"Looks like we're stuck here for a while," the guy says, clearing his throat again.

I stare at the window. With the rain beating on the roof, it's like being inside a drum. I wish I had something to read.

He leans closer to me, and I realize that his eyes are a soft puppy brown, like Maxwell's. Before I realize what he's doing, he reaches down and unbuttons his jeans. He's not wearing any underwear.

It's the first penis I've ever seen. The guy's clutching it as if it might run away from him, as if it's not really part of him at all. I'm not sure what to do. Does he want me to say something nice about it, now that he's told me I have pretty hair? As if he understands what I'm thinking, he says, "Don't worry. I just want to look at you."

He starts touching it, keeping his eyes on me the whole time. It is one of those awkward moments where you don't know where to look. I try to concentrate on the rain hitting the window.

When he's done he gives a little grunt like he's hurt.

"Hey, look," he says, as if nothing out of the ordinary just happened. "The rain's letting up." He opens the glove compartment and takes out one of those tiny packs of tissues, the kind my mother always keeps in her purse, *just in case, you never know when you'll need a tissue, and bathrooms are so filthy these days.* Then he wipes himself off and pulls his pants back up.

The guy turns to me, calm now. "You okay?"

"Yeah, fine."

He turns on the ignition. "I should be able to get you to the bus station by eight."

The rest of the ride passes in silence. I really have to blow my nose, but there's no way I'm touching those tissues.

Night descends, the sky darkening with a slow shading of clouds and fog. A mash of gray buildings appears as we approach Sacramento. I watch everything carefully, trying to record the details written in neon and lights: a large billboard with a picture of a smiling man clutching a handful of bills proclaims CASH FOR YOUR CAR, another advertises GORGEOUS GIRLS AND PRIVATE BOOTHS. The road becomes thick with cars, even as the streets grow narrower, and we crawl past boarded-up buildings and small stores: One-Stop Check Cashing, The Wig Palace, Dollar Mania, which has dishwashing soap and detergent and shampoo all clustered in the window. I think of the ninety-nine-cent store back in Las Palmas—the lavender soap I bought there one day as a surprise for my mother. She had kissed me on top of the head, smoothing my hair with her hands, and declared it her favorite soap, and the next morning she was still talking about it. "So many scented soaps make my skin itch," she said, "but this is just wonderful." At the time I thought, *Such a small thing makes her so happy,* and promised myself that I would surprise her more like that in the future, but I never did. I always wanted to keep the cheap lotions and lip glosses and hair clips I bought with my allowance for myself, even if I never used them. Now the images out the window blur as I bite my tongue, trying not to cry, wishing I had been the kind of person who gives gifts to her mother.

Suddenly I realize that we have pulled up in front of the bus terminal. The entrance is swarmed with people dragging suitcases, parents pulling their kids by the hand. A swarm of pigeons peck madly at a pizza box. The guy pulls over clumsily and lets me out, a half smile softening his features. "See you around," he says, something catching in his voice, like he thinks we might keep in touch. For a moment I imagine what it would be like to become friends with this stranger, pen pals maybe. On *Big Blue Marble* you can send in your age and address and write away for a pen pal from another country. When I was younger I always wanted a pen pal, from Sweden maybe, or Denmark—places I pictured as cold and icy and Christmassy-looking—and I imagined us finally meeting one day, to stand in the snow and join hands and sing the show's theme song, just like the kids on TV (*The earth's a Big Blue Marble when you see it from out there.*). But my mother would never let me do it. (*It's never a good idea to just give out your personal information to strangers,* she said, shaking her head at the TV screen. *Anyway, they probably just want to put your name on all sorts of mailing lists.*) I heft the yellow and white embroidered suitcase from the backseat and hold its handle as tight as possible.

Inside, the station is buzzing with noise and voices, filled with the crush and press of bodies on their way somewhere, hurrying this way and that. It's been a long time since I've been around so many people, and I feel as if all of my senses are turned on high: the din of the loudspeaker seems especially loud, the yellow of a child's raincoat brighter than it should be. A dull odor of sweat and alcohol hangs over everything. Overhead, a voice on the loudspeaker announces, "Bus number four thirty-one to San Francisco, gate seven. Bus number four thirty-one to San Francisco, gate seven."

An older woman bumps into me, her cane grazing my leg. "Excuse me, dear," she says, her voice somehow scratching its way through all the noise. "I'm a little unsteady on my feet these days."

"That's okay." I want to ask her to help me—to tell me what to do next—but then she is already gone, lost in the mass of people pushing their way to the gates. The suitcase is getting heavy, and its plastic handle is starting to bite into my hand. I lower it to the floor, trying to avoid the shallow puddles that seem to be everywhere, and shift it between my legs so it will be safe. My mother, I try to tell myself, would be proud of me for thinking of that, for *keeping an eye on my things,* even though really I know she wouldn't be proud of me at all for any running away, for any of this.

A deep breath steadies me and I look around. No one else in the big gray building seems confused. There are signs posted everywhere—departure times and bus numbers, plus some that say NO SMOKING and ALCOHOLIC BEVERAGES PROHIBITED, though people seem to be ignoring those. A big schedule board in the center of the room shows all the places I could go: San Francisco, San Diego, Los Angeles, Martinez, San Jose, Bolinas. There are even buses to Tempe and Salt Lake City, where the Mormons live. (Miriam had to write a report on them last year in her U.S. history class, and she told me that in spite of their modest clothes, they were *the horniest people in the world.* "Why do you think the men need so many wives?" she said.) For a moment the cities and times on the board start to shift and change—the words flipping about like a deck of cards being shuffled—and then rearrange themselves again to make sense.

It takes me a while to figure out what I want, but then I finally see it: a bus that goes through Medford and continues to Ashland, leaving in about thirty minutes. I pick up the suitcase and push my way into line, feeling even smaller than usual among the large crowd. Standing in front of me is a woman with a baby carriage and another child, who keeps tugging at her hand, whining for candy, and I wonder if these are the Mormons—if the children are really hers, or if they belong to another one of her husband's wives. Maybe she only buys candy for her real children.

The line inches along. I finger the money in my pocket, trying to make out the sound of the piped in music overhead. It's the Carpenters, singing one of the songs we had to perform at last year's holiday pageant: "Bless the Beasts and the Children"—

which some of the boys changed to "Bless the breasts and the children." Fifteen minutes pass before I make it to the front of the line. The woman working at the counter peers out from behind a glass window crossed with metal bars. It's as if she's locked away in a small jail, kept prisoner until her shift is over. Then I realize that the bars are there to protect her from us.

I stand on tiptoe and lean as close as possible to the window. You have to speak into a little hole. "How much is the bus to Ashland?" I ask, afraid I'm speaking too loudly.

The woman yawns her answer. "You're over twelve, right?"

"Of course," I say defensively. But when I see how much the fares are I wish I hadn't. Twelve and over is considered adult.

"Twenty-five dollars."

"What about one-way?"

She looks at me through the bars, her face tired and stretched out like an old blanket. "That *is* one-way."

"Oh." I had no idea it would cost so much. All I have with me is the thirty dollars I took from the motel room, plus a few more stolen from my mother's purse. A quiet pain seizes my throat and I want to say to the woman, *I'm not ready for this.* But it is too late to back out now, and anyway, where would I go?

The woman takes my cash and starts to count it. "You know that the next bus doesn't leave 'til midnight."

I look up at the schedule board. "But that says there's one in a few minutes."

The woman shakes her head as if she's been through this same conversation a thousand times today. "That's only on weekdays."

I stare at her blankly.

"Today's Saturday."

My stomach turns over. "Oh, yeah, right. I forgot." My voiced sounds bright and penny-shiny, the way my mother's does when she's lying. I shove my mouth into a smile. "How silly of me," I say, but the woman behind the counter is already helping the next person in line. I clutch the yellow and white embroidered suitcase in both hands and stumble my way through the crowds to an empty space in the corner, under a large clock that is missing a hand. I put the suitcase down in the cleanest-looking spot I can find, which is really not that clean at all, and arrange myself on top of it; all of the benches are full. Across from me hunches an old man, picking at a hardened scab on his leg.

I look up at the clock. If I were back at the hotel with my mother, we'd be tucked under the covers in bed with all the lights off, watching the Saturday Movie of the Week. This is our favorite part of the week, a ritual that we've held on to from Las Palmas, and just knowing we're going to watch it has made me feel that there is some order to our lives, something that has not changed since we got in my mother's car and drove away. On most Saturdays it's science fiction—something in black-and-white and not too scary, with a title like *Creature from the Deep* or *Abduction in Space*—and my mother and I pretend-scream whenever an alien or a monster shows up. If it's a Western, we talk about what it would be like to live on the prairie, the cowboy outfits we'd wear, and the horses we'd ride—my mother always wants a creamy white horse (the kind of horse a princess might ride), but I like the black ones, dark and shiny and heroic looking. If it's a romance, we make fun of the woman's hair and try not to cry at the mushy parts. After, when the movie is over, my mother always says, "Well, that was fun," and rolls over and goes right to sleep, while I lie in bed thinking about the aliens or the horses or the kisses, wondering what a movie of my life would look like. . . .

"Where are you going?"

I look up, startled. A tall man with a gray uniform and a badge stands over me. The radio on his belt buzzes loudly, and he turns away for a moment to speak into it. "Yeah, it's cool. Everything's under control."

Oh, God, I think dizzily. It's a police officer. And he knows exactly who I am, because the moment my mother found the note I left for her on the bedside table, she picked up the phone and called the cops, and they've sent all the police in the entire state of California to find me. Like on TV. An all points bulletin.

I look up at him, wondering if he can read the fear in my face. He's going to make me stand up and put my hands behind my back, and then he'll handcuff me, tight, so it hurts, to teach me a lesson. . . . Then he'll put his hand on my shoulder and escort me out of the building, slowly, so the man sitting across from me with the itchy leg and the Mormon woman and her children and all the drunk people sleeping on the benches can laugh at me. My mother will be waiting outside in the cop car, tired and angry from driving around looking for me, and when she sees me she'll shake her head with frustration, and something else, a disappointment that I've let her down. . . .But then I take a closer look at the man's uniform and realize that it has a picture of a dog and the words GREYHOUND SERVICE LINES, and I know that he's a guard for the bus station, not a police officer at all. Still, he's looking at me in a strange way, as if there's something suspicious about a small girl sitting on top of a yellow and white embroidered suitcase in the middle of this station.

I swallow hard. "I'm getting on the midnight bus."

He cocks his head at me, the way dogs do when you make a funny sound.

"To Davis. My sister goes to school there." I try to look like the kind of person whose family lives in a big house and has weekend cookouts and sleepovers, and who's just visiting her sister at college for a couple of days, staying overnight in a dorm, maybe spending the night on the floor in a sleeping bag. I imagine myself wearing a U.C. Davis sweatshirt, cheering in the stands at a football game or hanging out at a fraternity party, and Miriam in a cheerleader's uniform, the most popular girl in school. . . .

The guard nods. "That's a good school. Your parents must be proud." Another call comes on his radio and he leaves, and I watch as he makes his way to the back of the station where the restrooms are. My whole body feels limp and heavy, as if it's carrying extra weight, even though all I've done today is sit still. I'd give anything to have someplace clean and warm to lie down, and I realize with a pang that I miss the motel room, the warm blanket and the glow of the TV.

It's getting late, and the station is emptying out. People are starting to look at me funny. I know what they're thinking, can practically hear the question: *What's a young girl like you doing here all alone, so late at night?* I wish there were more people around.

A guy wearing a green jacket squats down next to me. I can smell that he's been drinking. "How you doin' tonight, sweetie?"

"Okay." I pretend I have something in my eye so I don't have to look at him.

"Where you headin'?"

"Oregon."

"You know they call that the Beaver State," he says, interrupting his own laughter with a loud hiccup.

"Excuse me," I say, grabbing the suitcase. I find the women's bathroom. Above the sink is a sign that says STOP GERMS: WASH YOUR HANDS AFTER USING THE FACILITIES—someone has crossed out the word HANDS and written PUSSY in thick red marker. I drag my suitcase to the stall at the very end of the row, making sure that it's clean, and lock myself in. For some reason it's warmer in here than in the rest of the station.

I figure I can hang out in here until the bus leaves. It doesn't seem that bad, for a bathroom. I can put the toilet seat down and sit on the lid like a chair. And if I have to pee I'm right here. I pull out my copy of *Watership Down*. The cover's bent from being shoved into the suitcase, and some of the pages near the end are falling out. I wish I had a paper clip or a rubber band to keep them from getting lost. I think about the time my mother and I fixed up some of her old paperback mysteries with Scotch tape, lining up all the books so we could repair the creased spines one at a time. "The book hospital," my mother called it, reminding me *how important it is to take good care of your things*.

The hours pass slowly. All kinds of people come into the bathroom. Most of them are drunk. A woman sits in the stall next to me for a few minutes, crying softly. Then she washes her face and leaves. A few people throw up, and I have to block my ears, because hearing the sound of throwing up always makes me want to throw up too. Still, I'm relieved not to be alone. Having all these people come in and out reminds me that I'm not the only one here, that there are other people in this halfway place, on their way someplace else.

When my bus is finally announced I wash my hands and take one last look at myself in the bathroom mirror. Something in my eyes looks older, knowing. This is the first time in a while that I've been somewhere without my mother hovering near me, and the space around me feels empty, gaping. I try not to think about how she would feel if she knew I was in this dirty, dank bus station, with all the drunk people sleeping on benches and other people wandering around mumbling to themselves, maybe high. A deep ache settles in my stomach.

I leave the restroom and glance at the clock overhead. It's almost midnight, and I'm exhausted, and I'm not even halfway to finding my sister. I get in line behind the people getting on the bus, though it's not really a line, more like a group of bodies shoving to the front. "No rush, folks," the driver says tiredly. "Plenty of seats for everyone." There is a pay phone on the wall next to me, right under the graffitied words *Reagan Sucks*. I finger the coins in my pocket. I could call my mother and wake her up, and beg her to get in the car and come get me. *I'll do whatever you want,* I imagine myself saying. *I'll stay in these stupid motels for the rest of my life with you, if that's what will make you feel better. Just please come get me.* But then I steel myself and take a deep breath. My mother had her chance to run away. So did my sister. Now it is my turn. I pick up the yellow and white embroidered suitcase and mount the stairs to the bus.

36

It takes a long time just to get out of the city. The bus lurches forward, then back, as if it's not quite sure it really wants to leave. People shift around, trying to get comfortable. At each stoplight the bus lets out a loud noise, like a sigh of relief that it doesn't have to move anymore. My God, I think, it will take days to get there at this rate.

But once we're on the highway, the trip smooths out. Everyone calms down, settles into their seats to read or sleep or just stare out the window. The babies stop crying. The bus jumbles along, quiet except for a chorus of snores. I look around me; the woman across from me is knitting a sweater out of dark green wool; so far, it only has one arm.

I take the little gray ticket with the words "Greyhound Service Lines" out of my pocket and study it. Six hours and thirty-five minutes. Almost seven hours. Lots of time to think—probably too much time. Until now, I'd just been concentrating on getting away from the motel and to the bus station. Everything was held tight in my body. But now that I'm finally on the bus my mind is opening up again, and all the things I've been trying to ignore, thoughts I'd rather not think about, have crept up quietly and lodged themselves inside my head.

We pass an empty field that even in the clear moonlight looks sad and lonely and abandoned. For a moment I panic: what if my sister has run away again? Maybe she left the farm. Maybe Oregon is not to her liking. It's supposed to be damp and cold, maybe she told Julien to take her someplace else—someplace bright and dry, like Arizona or New Mexico. In my mother's copies of *National Geographic* those places always look sunny and crystal clear, as if they've never been touched by rain.

I steal a glance at the yellow and white embroidered suitcase. I wish I had a gift to bring Miriam. My mother always says that you're *never supposed to show up empty-handed.* It's rude. But what would I bring her? A pad of motel stationery or a mini soap and conditioner from the motel bathroom? And when you think about it, I suppose I am gift enough.

I stare at the back of the seat in front of me, gray and neutral. I can hear the man in front of me breathing deeply, his snores in perfect time with the low, deep groans of the bus. I think about a bus trip my mother, my sister, and I had planned to take once, to San Pallente Beach. Miriam had received an unexpected A on her life sciences school report on "The Breeding Habits of the California Sea Lion Population: Implications for Conservation," and my mother came home the next day with a brochure that said "See Lions—Sea Lions!" declaring that this was *cause for a celebration* and Miriam had earned a special day out. Usually Miriam would have scoffed at such an idea, would have hated the thought of a day trip anywhere, even the beach, with the two of us, but this time she was eager to show off her hard-won knowledge, and kept walking around the house saying things like, *Did you know that an adult male sea lion can weigh up to one hundred and fifty pounds?* The next weekend we woke up early and packed up all of our things for the beach— the oversized plastic sunglasses Miriam had bought at the drug-store, my new purple plastic flip-flops—and my mother even made a picnic, with chicken salad sandwiches with lots of may-onnaise and celery, just the way Miriam likes. We were at the very front of the line to get on the bus, and I had just won a coin toss with Miriam to see who would get the window seat, when my mother grabbed my arm and scurried us away without say-ing anything. Later she told us that the man behind us in line was giving her a strange look—*you know, a look*—not a glance of appreciation, or flirtation, but something more treacherous than that, something deep and dark, threatening. There was something about him that *just didn't seem right,* my mother had said. When we got home Miriam tore up her report and threw it in the trash, and she did it right in front of our mother, trying to make her feel terrible, which it did. We never made it to San Pallente Beach, never even mentioned the sea lions and their mating habits again, and my sister ended up getting a C for the class.

I sink back in my seat. The bus chugs slowly along, the world outside blanketed by a sharp darkness. Cars appear out of the night and speed past us, their lights disappearing like a sudden ghost, but the bus just moves along, staying in the same one lane, as if it's afraid to try something new. The driver crouches low, possessively, over the wheel, as if someone might try to wrestle it out of her hands, staring straight ahead, seeming, in her stillness, more like part of the machinery of the bus than an actual person. All of a sudden she breaks the silence with a flurry of high-pitched sneezing, a sneezing very much like my mother's own delicate, feminine sneezing, and I find myself wondering if she is a mother, if she has kids, maybe a daughter like me? The bus passes a sign with a picture of a man clutching a handful of money and the words WE BUY GOLD: HIGHEST PRICES PAID. I finger the money wedged tight in my pocket—only three or four dollars left. My heart sinks as I realize that I have no idea what I'll do when I get to Oregon. I take off my shoes and rest my feet on the yellow and white embroidered suitcase, which is tucked on the floor in front of me.

I can't help but stare at the woman across the aisle, whose tight red jacket neatly enfolds her lean, long arms. She's wearing a silver bracelet, a small circle of silver, gleaming and confident, against her skin, and the crisscross stockings my mother calls *fishnet*—a word I've never understood, since they're supposed to go over your legs, not around a fish at all. Her hair is like Miriam's, and I feel a sudden urge to touch it. I wonder how she would react if I did so, if she would scream or yell, or if she would just sit there quietly, letting me touch her hair. Her shiny black shoes look like a grown-up version of the patent leather Mary Janes that were my favorite shoes when I was younger. (I finally had to stop wearing them when Maxwell, who before had shown no interest in chewing shoes at all, bit off the strap and ate the whole shoe, metal buckle and all.) The woman keeps crossing and uncrossing her legs, and without realizing it, I find myself doing the same thing, until she turns to me with a scowl and says, "What's your problem?"

"Nothing."

She's still looking at me like a small ant to be crushed with her shoe, so I sputter, "I like your legs. I mean, I like your stockings."

The woman's face relaxes into an easy smile. "Thanks, sweetie."

Then word *sweetie* shoots through me like a reproach—because that's what my mother has always called me, for as long as I can remember, it's been, *Sweetie, make sure you remember to take your vitamins,* or *Sweetie, come take a look at this magazine article about marijuana,* and usually the word bothered me, as if I were a piece of candy or a grape or something. But now I realize that my mother was using that one short word as a quick way to say "I love you"—even when she was just reminding me to vacuum my room or finish my milk or take out the trash. There was nothing to be annoyed about at all.

I stare at my reflection in the misted window, my head cloudy with the dull hum of regret. My head swims with a picture of my mother in the dusty motel room, waking up quietly, stretching, putting on her slippers and padding her way into the windowless bathroom, and suddenly understanding that I'm not there—that I've disappeared, just as Miriam did when she ran away, just as she herself did, when she left me and Miriam alone by ourselves. For some reason, when I try to imagine what happens when my mother finds my good-bye note, I never make it past this point. With strange clarity, I'm able to see her circling the small motel room, shifting open the window, calling my name, yanking open the closet door, bending down to look under the bed and seeing that the yellow and white embroidered suitcase is gone—but after that, everything stops and I replay the scene over again, everything the same exact way. It seems strange that I can't go any further than that even in my own head, where you would think there would be no limits and I'd be able to imagine anything I wanted. I realize that I've never defied her before, have always gone along with what she's said. Maybe I half believed it myself, because not to believe it would mean acknowledging that she was wrong, crazy, *delicate*—a mother who for all her kindness and beauty would never be like Mrs. Aronowitz or Mrs. Hauser or any of the other grown-up women I knew. And what would that mean about *me*? If I had a mother who was different from everyone else, who really did belong in *the loony bin,* as Christie McPherson used to say . . . I press my forehead against the cool glass of the window. From the back of the bus I can hear a man singing, very softly, "Swing Low, Sweet Chariot," and the low rumble of someone else snoring, almost in time with the singing.

The lights dim overhead so that the bus is almost completely dark, as if the driver has said good night and tucked everyone into one big rumbling bed. The woman across from me keeps crossing and uncrossing her legs, the same steady movement over and over again, until finally she stops and folds the leather jacket into a little red pillow and falls asleep. I try to do the same thing with Miriam's old UCLA sweatshirt, tucking it carefully behind my head, but my neck still aches with a small crick of pain. I force my eyes shut and try to play every trick I can think of to fall asleep—slowly counting from one hundred backward, picturing my bedroom back home in Las Palmas, imagining myself petting Maxwell's soft fur—but somehow I manage to outsmart myself and none of them work. I'm almost crying from tiredness, but at the same time I'm what my mother would call *too wound up* to sleep, an expression that always makes me think of a toy metal top about to spin off the edge of a table. I stare out into the clear black cool of the night, keeping my gaze fixed on the familiar shape of the Big Dipper, as if its dipping curve might somehow scoop me up in a warm, star-lit embrace and keep me safe. "Good night, Mom," I whisper softly against the window, my breath misting the glass.

I'm still awake when we cross the state border into Oregon. There's a giant sign like an advertisement on the median strip: WELCOME TO OREGON! After we pass, I look back, and the other side says WELCOME TO CALIFORNIA, with a picture of a man kneeling by a creek, panning for gold. I can't believe California didn't even bother to get its own sign. But I guess the road looks exactly the same on both sides.

When we finally get to Ashland early the next morning I am surprised by how small it is. Everyone is on a bicycle, as if cars are against the law. For some reason I thought it would be more like a real city, with busy streets and lots of traffic everywhere. But I guess this is how things are in Oregon.

The driver pulls over into the bus station lot and helps everybody with their luggage. My first thought is that the bus station, a gray little building you wouldn't even think was important, is the exact opposite of the one in Sacramento. It's just a tiny room with a few metal folding chairs and a soda machine with a handwritten sign that says OUT OF ORDER: WATER FAWCET ON OTHER SIDE OF ROOM in bright red marker. I stare at the sign for a long time, thinking about how upsetting it is when words like that aren't spelled right, on a sign that people have to look at every day. It's like having something in your eye or a rock in your shoe.

There's a poster on the wall for Crater Lake National Park, another for Mount Hood, and in the corner of the room a man is sitting on a little stool, reading a magazine with a big smiling Ronald Reagan on the cover. When he looks up I stumble back, startled: he looks just like Mr. Donovan, the shop teacher (*a little too attractive for his own good,* my mother used to say) who everybody loved until someone said he stood a little too close to the eighth-grade boys, and asked them a few too many times to stay after school to work on special projects. After spring break we came back to school and he just wasn't there anymore, he had been asked to leave, and I wonder if maybe he moved all the way to Oregon to find another job teaching kids how to make carving boards and birdhouses and ended up working at the Ashland bus station instead. For a moment I wonder if he'll say, *Adie, what in the world are you doing here? And by the way, I've been meaning to talk to you about your birdhouse project, the one you never turned in.* . . . But then I breathe deeply and shake my head and when I look at him again I see that he only looks a little bit like Mr. Donovan, that really he just has the same deep green eyes and bushy eyebrows, and I filled in everything else myself.

When I ask him about an organic apple farm, he folds his arms and says, "Hmm. Let me think about that one." He stares at the wall, as if the answer might be written there, runs his fingers through his hair. "I don't know much about organic stuff. I think most of it's bullshit, to tell the truth." He coughs. "Excuse my French." He opens up a black three-ringed binder, the kind I use for school, and starts flipping through it. "Hmm," he says again. "Hmm."

He closes the binder carefully and puts it back on the shelf, along with a bunch of others that look exactly the same. "Hmm," he says, scratching his head, dandruff falling gently over his dark sweater. I wonder if he knows about Head & Shoulders.

Finally he sighs and says, "There's a health food store down the street. They might know about things like that." He hands me a hand-drawn, mimeographed map and leans back in his chair as if our conversation has exhausted him.

I thank him and get out of the station as fast as I can. The town is quiet, kind of old-fashioned looking. There's even a drugstore with big glass windows and an ice-cream counter, like you see in the moves. *Maybe,* I think to myself, *Miriam will take me out for ice cream.* It's hot and I'm sweating through my clothes.

After another six blocks I wonder if maybe the fake Mr. Donovan made a mistake. Maybe he didn't know the answer to my question so he just made the whole thing up. He didn't seem too sure of himself. But then I see it: Darwin's Natural Foods. For a moment or two I stand out in the sun, looking at the display window filled with boxes of cereal stacked in an ambitious pyramid; it's the brand my mother used to get, when she was trying to cut out sugar. My heart starts to beat a fast *tip tip tip*— a dizzy combination of excitement and fear.

I take a deep breath and push open the door. The smell immediately reminds me of Miriam's bedroom back home—incense and candles, and something else, a kind of soapy smell. The walls are covered in old, frayed concert posters for Bob Dylan and the Grateful Dead, and two women stand behind the counter, talking quietly. In the corner, on a dusty velvet cushion, lies an enormous black cat, curled in the tightest of circles.

Now that I'm finally here, a strange shyness coats my body— I want to wait a minute, take my time. So I make my way along the edge of the room, past the food section, to a display of small, dark bottles of perfume and a sign that says ESSENTIAL OILS.

"I'm *loving* this book," one of the girls says, holding out a worn paperback with a picture of a rainbow on the cover. "It's all about how there really are no coincidences." She pulls herself up straight and pauses dramatically. "How our bodies make things happen when we *need* them to happen."

The other girl nods. "That is so true," she says, not really paying attention. She runs her fingers over her long braids, looking at me, and I feel a little self-conscious and out of place, wandering around the store without buying anything, so I point to the perfume bottles, lined up in a neat row like toy soldiers. "What's essential about them?"

She looks at me, puzzled. Then she gets it. "Essential, like essence. Not essential like necessary."

I pick up one of the little bottles, no bigger than my thumb, and dab a tiny bit on my wrists and behind my ears, remembering, from a magazine my mother and I looked at together, that those are your *pulse points*. The sticker on the bottle says SANDALWOOD; it has a deep, soft sweetness that's nothing like the sugar-sweetness of candy.

Small lines wiggle in front of my eyes. The room gets dark around the edges—a frame of blackness closing in on my vision—and I can tell I'm about to faint, even though I've never fainted before. I grab the table to steady myself, but before I know what's happened I'm on the floor, sprawled out like a doll that's been knocked off a shelf.

"Oh, my God." The taller girl kneels on the floor beside me, holding my wrist. She turns to the other girl, who's just standing there, gaping. "Get her some water."

I prop myself up against the bookshelf. There's a small cut on my arm—I hit the edge of the shelf on the way down—but other than that I feel the same as always. It's as if my body just wanted to faint, just needed to stop for a minute. I try to stand up, but the girl puts her hand on my shoulder. "You stay right there and drink this," she says, handing me a handmade pottery coffee cup that is missing its handle.

I am not sure what to say, so I just nod and look around. Both of them are watching me carefully like a broken thing, confusion lining their faces. From down here, I can see that the carpet is dirty and stained, its edges frayed and browned with time. I stare at the books loosely piled against one another on the shelf: *Miracles of the Soul: Yin and Yang in Perspective*; *Harnessing Your Body's Energy*; *The Lure of the Planets*. The cat lifts his head slowly and stares at me with golden eyes.

"Is there an apple farm near here?"

The short girl rolls her eyes. "Like a million." Looking at her, with her long blond hair and pretty skin, you can tell she used to be a regular girl, maybe a cheerleader or student council president. The T-shirt and baggy pants she's wearing don't really fit her right; they look like a costume.

"An organic one." I move to get up, but a wave of nausea passes through my body. "Where people live."

"She means Barker's Farm," one of the girls says. "Where Paul lives." The two of them start talking about Paul. He's really fine, but a *total asshole,* and he never wants to pay for anything. And he's slept with everybody, so you have to watch out. For a moment I think they've forgotten about me, but then the tall one says, "I guess I could drive you there. It's on my way home." She takes a pack of cookies off the shelf and hands them to me. They're the healthy kind, the wrapper says "Sweetened with natural fruit juices," but I'm so hungry I don't care. The girls watch me shove the cookies into my mouth like a crazy person. "Slow it down, girl," the tall one says.

Later, in the car, the girl tells me that her name is Harmony, and shows me the sticker on the dashboard that says LIVE IN HARMONY. "My real name's Stacey," she says. "But I never felt comfortable with it; it's too bourgeois, you know?"

I don't know what she means, so I just say yes to be polite and keep quiet. I stare out the dusty window at the green and brown patchwork of fields and try to say as little as possible. I don't want her to know I've run away, and I especially don't want to tell her about my mother, and I'm worried that even though her name is Harmony she might be the kind of person who is secretly really nosy and asks a lot of personal questions. But when I tell her I've come to Ashland to live with my sister, she just nods. "This is the kind of place where people just show up," she says, coughing over a clove cigarette. "And they never leave."

I look at the trees that seem to be everywhere, even blocking the sky in some places. "Are those the ash trees?" I ask.

"I'm not sure," she says, turning up the music on the radio. I think that's weird, how can she not know which are the ash trees?

The car circles fast down a windy and narrow road—barely a road at all. I hold tight to the seat, trying to stare straight ahead, feeling a little carsick, especially after all those cookies. In my head, I plan out what to do if I have to throw up. I remember one time when Miriam got sick in the car, and she just opened the window and leaned out and threw up right on the sidewalk. I think my mother would like it here, and for a moment I feel ashamed for coming all this way without her, knowing how much she'd like the mountains and trees, how she's always told me that she's wanted to see more of the Pacific Northwest, and that we should go to Ashland for the Shakespeare festival, because Shakespeare makes you cultured.

The girl pulls over to the side of the road, and at first I think she can tell I'm feeling sick. "Well, here we are," she announces, as if we've just arrived some place spectacular, like Disneyland or the Grand Canyon. She guides the car carefully over a dirt road, gravelly and rough, swearing under her breath. "It's just down here."

I look out the window. There's no sign or anything. Nothing saying *Barker's Farm, This Way* or *Apples for Sale.* For a moment, I worry that maybe I'm in the wrong place altogether. These farms all look the same, just trees and dirt, they're probably pretty easy to mix up. I probably should have called ahead just to make sure. But I thought it would be nice to surprise Miriam with my visit. And something else, that I've been afraid to admit until just now. There's a tiny part of me that's afraid Miriam might tell me to turn around, go back. I never had this thought at all, until I got to Ashland. . . .

The car lurches and groans over the bumpy road, and the girl winces. "I don't think my car's going to make it over this road," she says, her voice an apology. She backs out slowly, keeping her eyes on the rearview mirror. "You're going to have to hoof it." *Hoof it,* I think. Like a horse. She gets out of the car to help me with the yellow and white embroidered suitcase, and I realize that I want her to come with me, even though at the same time, I know I can't ask her. So I just say, "Thanks for bringing me here."

"It's really only a mile or so," she says, getting back behind the wheel. The car spins around and she is gone in a quick cloud of dust.

I put the suitcase down and look around. I am surrounded by large, empty fields, filled with nothing but grass. It's a different color from the grass back home, a duller, darker green, and more lush. In the distance I can see a brown horse with a white flank loping in lazy circles. Except for the telephone wires it's just like *Little House on the Prairie.* My muscles are stiff from so much sitting still. I stare at the road in front of me, rubbing my leg. The road winds around and gets lost in trees—impossible to tell how long it really is. A crow calls loudly overhead, startling me, then dips down quickly into one of the fields.

Maybe Miriam will come down the road in a truck, or even on a bike.

Something rustles in the bushes near me—a rabbit. It stares at me from the side, with one eye, unblinking. It's not looking at my legs or anything else; it's staring right at my face, and I realize, suddenly, how strange it is that all animals recognize faces. Then it takes off, alerted by a sound or smell, some warning that I can't hear.

I struggle with the yellow and white embroidered suitcase, trying to figure out the best way to carry it. It's the sort of road where you can't see much ahead of you. With each turn, I think, *Now I'm there.* But the turns keep coming, another, then another, until I can no longer tell which direction I'm going. Sweat soaks my shirt. I wish I had something to drink.

The road goes up and up, just slightly, sort of fooling me into thinking I'm not really going uphill. It is only when I turn around and look back that I can see how far I've come. I keep thinking that I've reached the top, but then there's a little more. It's very tricky, the way a hill can do that.

Finally, though, I reach the real top. And from there everything shifts and changes.

I'm looking down into an enormous valley. The road stretches down into a beautiful green space of trees: the sort of dream place where anything seems possible. And at the very bottom of the road I can see a building. A large wooden building, surrounded by smaller ones. I start to run, the suitcase banging hard against my legs.

For a second I almost don't recognize her. Her hair is in dozens of little braids, with turquoise and yellow beads. It is like she is trying to be Bo Derek in that movie where she comes out of the water. But it is Miriam. I can't believe she's right there, just sitting around a picnic table with a couple of other girls.

She squints at me for a second, not quite sure. My sister has always been too vain to wear her glasses. "Oh, my God—Adie?" The braids move when she speaks. "What are you doing here?"

"I missed you." The words seem like not enough, but I am not sure what else to say. Is there anything else to say?

Everyone stares. Miriam gets up from the table and gives me a nervous clutch of a hug. "How in the world did you get here?" she asks, taking in my messy hair and dusty shoes, and our mother's yellow and white embroidered suitcase, which looks especially bright and garishly out of place here in the woods. Her body tenses. "Where's Mom?" She looks around nervously. "Is she with you?"

"No. I came by myself, all by myself," I say, and it's not until I choke over my words that I realize I'm crying. When my sister said my name aloud I realized how long it's been since I've heard anyone call me by my real name. I've become so used to my mother calling me Amber, so comfortable with it, that I almost believed it was my real name—that Adie was just someone I met back in Las Palmas, a girl I knew a long time ago. I feel stupid and sweaty and hot, crying like this in front of Miriam's new, grown-up friends, but I can't help it, the tears refuse to stop. A girl with long, straight hair and big-framed glasses trips over in her leather sandals and hands me a paper napkin for a tissue and a glass of water. "You want a cookie?" she asks, looking at Miriam helplessly.

"No, thanks," I sniff. I gulp down the water.

"It's so weird that you're here," Miriam says, her voice full of wonder and something else, something *I can't quite put my finger on,* as my mother would say.

"C'mon, follow me." She picks up the yellow and white embroidered suitcase and I can tell she's surprised by its weight. She gives me a look and then takes it in two hands and leads me down a dirt path shaded with trees. I stumble behind her, trying to look around, even though she is walking so fast I barely have time to really see anything. We follow the dirt path past some fenced-in goats and a couple of wood cabins lopsided with age. At the end of the road is a little clearing with a metal shed that looks like it should hold rakes and potting soil and things like that. But when Miriam opens the door, I see that it's been decorated—transformed into a tiny room, just big enough to sleep in. A thin cotton tapestry, purple-gray and full of holes, stretches across the ceiling, though it doesn't hide the slats of metal entirely. There are half burned candles everywhere, all different colors and sizes, and a single mattress with a navy blue sleeping bag and what looks like a hand-crocheted blanket. I wonder who made the blanket—not my sister?

"Sit down," Miriam says, clearing some pine needles and a bra and some inside-out socks off the sleeping bag. I huddle cross-legged and look around. The shed smells funny, the half sour smell of dampness and unwashed clothes. A stepladder spattered with drops of white paint has been set up as an end table, and balanced on top of it is a banana and three cups, half filled with what I think is coffee. In the corner, covered with dust, is the portable tape player our mother gave Miriam for her birthday.

A fly lands on my arm and I swat it away. Even though I've never been here before, something about the shed seems familiar, and with a flush of recognition I realize that the shed is decorated just the way Miriam and I decorated the hall closet when we were little kids and wanted to play Zahara the Amazing Fortune-Teller. We'd seen the real Zahara once at the Fourth of July county fair and had been impressed not only by her glittering green eyeshadow and dangling gold earrings, but by the calm way she looked out at the crowds of kids and cotton candy and fairground rides, her face a mask of stillness and apparent wisdom. My sister and I would carefully hang a sheet over the rod in the closet and cover the floor with as many pillows and cushions as we could find. Miriam, who always got to be Zahara, would put on my mother's plastic junk jewelry and then cover her head with a turban (really, one of my mother's formal cloth napkins, that we never actually used for dinner) and would tell my fortune, using a made-up accent: *Zis is vhat I zee for your future.* Now I want to make a joke, to say to Miriam, *It's just like our old fortune-teller tents—playing Zahara really came in handy!* But somehow I know she would not appreciate my saying this—that to her the metal shed with its torn tapestry and half burned candles is dead serious, not play-acting at all, and if for some reason it happens to look a little like our Zahara closet I should just, as my mother would say, *keep it to myself.*

I run my fingers over one of the candles that seems too nice to actually burn: it's in the shape of an egg, mottled with streaks of purple and white. "Is this where you live?"

Miriam nods and swats a mosquito out of the shed. "Just for now. It's not as bad as it looks," she says, but her voice sounds wistful and small, and the shed truthfully does not look comfortable at all.

I cup the egg in my hands, trying not to meet her eyes. "Where's Julien?"

My sister rolls her eyes. "He took off about a month ago. Whatever." For a moment she looks like the old Miriam again, the Miriam hanging out at the food court at the mall, surrounded by boys, and I wonder if she misses that version of herself.

I unpack the yellow and white embroidered suitcase and give Miriam her sketchbook. "I can't believe you have this thing," she says, thumbing through its pages.

It's too hot to stay in the metal shed, so I follow Miriam to a group of trees that have been planted in a half circle. There's an old wooden picnic table under the trees, its green paint dull and washed out by rain, but Miriam motions for me to sit down on the grass instead. Here the ground is cool and a little damp, not dusty at all. Everywhere you look there are apples and more apples—some small and defiantly rock hard, others already decaying, split open, their insides exposed and rotting.

"These trees are funny," Miriam says. "They're apple trees. But they're not really part of the orchard, so we don't pick them." She grabs one of the smaller apples and wipes it off on her jeans, even though her jeans are torn and frayed and don't look clean at all. "You can still eat them," she says, handing it to me. I stare at it, thinking about how once, back in Las Palmas, Miriam and I picked some wild blackberries off a bush that was just growing by the side of a busy road. Our hands got stained and scratched from the branches and thorns, so much that when we got home our mother thought someone had attacked us, or that we'd been in some kind of accident. But other than that, I don't think I've ever eaten fruit right off the tree. The apple is a dull sand-brown color, nothing like the shiny, red apples from the supermarket, the ones my mother says are covered in wax and pesticides. I take a small bite. The taste is sweet and clean.

When I offer it to Miriam she just shakes her head. "No, thanks. My whole fucking world is apples. I never want to eat another apple again." She picks at something on the ground. "I'd give anything for a cheeseburger."

I start to tell her about all the junk food we've been getting from the motel candy machines and diners and fast-food drive-throughs, but Miriam lies down on the grass and stares up at the sky. "Why don't you just rest a little, and tell me everything later."

So I put my head in her lap, trying to make sense of everything that has happened over the last day. Everything jumbles together, a confusing mixed-up patchwork of buses and hitch-hiking and fortune-teller tents. Softly, before I know what's happening, I feel my body grow heavy and still, sleep blanketing me. The last thing I remember before drifting off is an image of my mother, winged like a bird and sitting alone in the gnarled branches of an apple tree, calling my name.

37

When I wake up, Miriam is gone. I am still lying under the tree. Someone has draped a cotton blanket over me. It's strange to wake up outside; the smell is so different from bed. With my head on the ground, my eyes are at grass level, and I watch an ant—much larger than the ants we have back home—nervously pick its way through the blades.

This must be what the world looks like from a bug's perspective, an unending sea of soft green.

I'm not sure how long I've been sleeping, but the sun is setting. I pull the blanket closer around me and look around. The sky is streaked with orange and purple, the trees lit up and glowing as if on fire.

There's noise and music coming from the big building where I first saw Miriam, so I head over there. When I push open the heavy wooden door I see a room full of people. The place is filled with the smell of onions frying on the stove. "Hey, sleeping beauty finally woke up," a guy says, smiling at me. He has long hair and a beard, and at first I think he's older. But when he comes closer to me I realize that he's only a teenager, maybe even younger than Miriam—not anything like a grown-up at all.

Miriam is sitting by a stone fireplace with a couple of other girls. They're passing something back and forth, and when I come closer I see that it's a joint. My sister gets up and hugs me, looking a little guilty.

One of the girls points the joint in my direction. "Want a hit?"

I stare at the small white stub, thinking about what my mother would say, and also wondering if it is rude to say no. But Miriam waves her away. "For God's sake, Janice, she's only a kid." She looks at me. "You can have a *beer* later if you want."

The girl named Janice starts to giggle. "That doesn't make any sense."

"Yeah, it does." Miriam looks at me. "Why don't you just have some tea, to start." She takes me into the kitchen, which is crowded with people, and pours me a cup of tea. It has a sweet, minty smell—a little like the herbal peppermint tea my mother used to drink. Then she slowly takes me around the room and introduces me to everybody. The girl named Janice scoots over to make room for me on the sofa. "You look just like Miriam," she says, and I can tell she's trying to compliment me, even though the truth is, I don't really look like Miriam at all. I try not to let the girl's clothes touch mine; she is wearing overalls stained with every color of paint you can imagine. Normally you'd take those off after you were done painting, but I guess here it is okay to wear them around. Everyone is wearing clothes that are torn or have holes or a stain, and I'm secretly relieved that I've been wearing my clothes for a few days so they won't look quite so new and out of place.

I look around the room. On one side of the wall there is a mural that takes up the whole wall and says "Barker Farm Collective Living Project," with pictures of rainbows and cows and, of course, apples. You can tell immediately that some of the people who worked on the mural were real artists, like my sister, but that others weren't, and it gives the whole picture a strange, uneven feeling. My mother always says that when you go to someone's house for the first time, it's polite to say something nice about it, to compliment the furniture or the view. So I say to Janice, "It's really pretty here."

She smiles. "It gets pretty crowded here, with so many people."

"Where do you all sleep?"

She scratches at some dried paint on her arm. "Everyone just sort of crashes wherever."

"With Miriam, if they're lucky," the guy with the beard says.

"Fuck you," Miriam says, but I can tell from the look on her face that she doesn't really mean it. She nudges me to get up. "Come on, it's time to eat."

Everyone sits down around the large wooden table in the center of the room. I hesitate, not sure where to go. Maybe the seats are assigned, maybe there are rules. But then Miriam pulls out a seat for me right next to her. She hands me a cloth napkin that already looks a little dirty and leans close to me. "All the food here is vegetarian," she whispers, "but it's not so bad once you get used to it." The table is crowded with jam jars for glasses and mismatched dishes and plates. Some of them are made of plastic, and some are pottery, uneven and chipped. Truthfully, they don't look much better than the bowls we made in art class last year.

Across the room, the tall guy with the beard is spooning something from an enormous pot into little bowls. At first I think he's a teenager, but then Miriam tells me he's one of the *old-timers* and is really thirty-five. In a normal place the rules for who is an adult and who isn't are very clear, and it is very easy to tell the difference, but here everything is a little confusing, muddled.

The girl with the joint brings everyone their serving. When she gets to me she says, "Careful, it's hot," and pats me on the head, like I'm a little kid. Miriam rolls her eyes.

I look down at my bowl. It's a mess of noodles, cheese, and mushrooms, like a casserole, just not in a pan. I'm starving. I'm about to try a bite, but Miriam touches my arm. "Wait a sec," she says quietly. "We take a minute before eating." She winks at me. "To give thanks."

"Like saying grace?" I've never seen anyone do this for real, just in the movies. I know some Jews pray before meals, but I'm pretty sure Miriam is the only Jewish person here.

"A little bit," she whispers, taking my hand and giving it a little squeeze to be quiet. Everyone is holding hands around the table, like a bunch of kids about to start a game of ring-around-the-rosy. The woman sitting at the head of the table bows her head slightly and says, "Tonight, let's be thankful for all the good things we have—our health, our friendship, this beautiful place." Her voice is surprisingly deep, almost like a man's voice. I try to catch Miriam's eye, but she just looks away and shrugs. Under the table, a dog brushes my leg with his nose, already hoping for scraps.

The woman doesn't mention God, just goes on for a couple of minutes listing all sorts of things that anyone would be happy about, like being warm and having a place to live. At the end she looks at me and says, "Let's give a special welcome to Miriam's little sister, Adie, who we're so lucky to have with us tonight." Everyone says, "Welcome," even though I've already been introduced to them, already been welcomed. I look around the table, all of us joined together, hand to hand.

That night Miriam lets me sleep in her bed. She camps out on the grass outside the shed, lying on a makeshift bed of blankets and pillows. "Won't the bugs crawl on you out there?" I ask.

"It doesn't matter. They'll crawl on you inside too," she says.

I keep the door to the shed open, not wanting to be alone, and we talk for a little while, our heads facing each other. She tells me about the guys who work at the farm, which ones are cute, which ones to watch out for.

Miriam has had sex with one of them. "It was nothing special," she says. "Believe me."

Not wanting to be outdone, I tell her about the guy in the car, exaggerating a little to impress her. "How many times a week do you think he does that?" I ask, wondering if it is possible to do it more than once a day.

But Miriam has already fallen asleep. I shift around, trying to make myself comfortable in the sleeping bag and listen to the sound of her tiny, hesitant snores. I think my being here has exhausted her, all through dinner she's looked tired and confused. My sister certainly didn't wake up this morning expecting me, of all people, to show up, covered in sweat and dust and lugging our mother's yellow and white embroidered suitcase. Who knows what she had meant to do today? Maybe she had plans, and my being here has ruined them. Whenever I start talking about the motels, our mother, and the men in the white car she shushes me and says, "Can we talk about all that a little later?"

Outside, you can hear the high, sudden sound of crickets. The shadows from the candlelight play against the wall. A strange, haunting noise pierces the darkness, deep and restless— an owl. The sound is weirdly familiar, even though I'm sure I've never heard an owl before. It's just one of those sounds you already know, like the low of a cow.

When I wake up in the morning Miriam is already in the shed, getting dressed. "Hey," she says, pulling on the same jeans with the holes and patches. "How'd you sleep?"

"Okay." I look around. The shed is warming up from the sun. "It's nice in here."

"When it rains the sound could make you crazy." Miriam checks her reflection in a tiny mirror that's been attached to the wall with duct tape. I still think she looks funny with her hair in braids. I'm relieved to see a bottle of Jean Nate. At least that's normal.

I squirm awkwardly out of the sleeping bag, my body stiff and sore from sleeping in the same position all night. My skin feels chalky and dry, as if the dirt from the fields outside has somehow seeped into my body. When Miriam turns away, I quickly sniff under my arms. I don't smell so good. "I need to take a shower," I tell her.

"You can use one of my towels." My sister hands me a small plastic bucket, the kind kids use at the beach, filled with shampoo and soap. She still has the same hairbrush, with the black plastic bristles and the purple glitter stickers that spell out

MIRIAM on the handle. I pick up the brush and run it through my hair, wondering how she brushes her hair with all those braids. I watch as she stands in front of the mirror tightening them, adjusting the turquoise and black beads, trying to get the whole thing to sit neat. "I like your hair," I tell her even though I think it looks strange, in fact all I can think of is the Barbie doll head we used to play with that got lost in one of our many moves— not a whole doll with arms and legs, just a giant head with long blond hair that we used to braid and rebraid.

"The shower's on the other side of the building." She shoots me a wicked look, a little bit of the old Miriam. "Outside."

I stare at her. "No way."

"There's a little plastic curtain thing you can pull around you. No one's gonna peek." She buttons her shirt, an old white blouse with a lace collar that might have been fancy at one time. Now it's tie-dyed blue and green. "Really," she says to my worried look. "There used to be one inside, but it's broken." She sighs. "It takes a long time to get things fixed around here."

It's Miriam's turn to make breakfast, so I have to face the outdoor shower alone. The water is cold, and there is something strange about taking a shower outside, like swimming standing up. A crow perches on the side of the building. "Go away," I say, but it just sits there, watching me with black, beady eyes. Just from being here a short time I can see how dirty you get. The dust gets everywhere, in your hair, under your nails, and when I blow my nose it comes out black. When I'm finished I wrap the towel around me and dash back to the shed as quick as I can, the morning air running a cool chill over my body. There's a big lizard sitting on a rock outside the shed, as calm as can be. I dab on a little of Miriam's perfume, even though she warned me that it might attract mosquitoes.

Everything's quiet and still, so the noises you do hear really stand out. A small plane flying overhead sounds real close. Not too far away a couple of people are arguing, and I can hear their voices rising steadily. "It's your day to do the laundry," one of them says. A dog's high-pitched bark pierces the air, and I wonder with a pang how Maxwell is doing. I feel a little guilty for not taking him with me, but how could I?

I pull on my sneakers and head over to the main building to find Miriam. She's in the kitchen, cutting onions with her sunglasses on. She smiles when she sees the look on my face. "They keep my eyes from watering."

In the daylight the room doesn't look nearly as pretty as it did last night. There's some dried tomato sauce stuck to the floor that no one's bothered to clean up. The sink and counter are piled up with dishes and empty glasses—much like the dishes that used to pile up in the sink back home. There are newspapers and magazines and stuff everywhere—shoes and cassette tapes and books—and the whole place feels heavy with dust. I stifle a sneeze. "Get yourself something to drink," my sister says, sweeping the onion peels into a bucket full of scraps. She looks a little dirty too.

I open the refrigerator door, which is sticky with something brown, and take out a pitcher of orange juice, so heavy that I have to use both hands. As I pour myself a glass I almost knock over a small plastic bag filled with pot and a little metal pipe shaped like a mermaid, with long, flowing hair. The end of the tail is where you put your mouth, and the whole thing looks like one of those special toy wands for blowing soap bubbles. My stomach turns over when I think about what my mother would say about the little mermaid pipe. *After everything I taught you, everything I warned you about, this is what happens.* Miriam has come to no good, she is living with a bunch of *potheads, teenage drug addicts.* I try to brush the thought aside, the way you might brush aside a moth circling your head, but it is still there, hovering: my mother's fear.

"I'm getting stuff ready for omelets," Miriam says, gesturing to a giant crate of tomatoes. "Want to help?" She hands me a large knife and sits me down on a wooden stool.

I look around. "Where's the cutting board?"

She shakes her head, the braids swinging back and forth, and the beads making a quiet little *tap tap tap* noise; I wonder if it annoys her. "Everyone just uses the counter." The counter is scarred with cuts and scratches, and some people have even carved their initials and names into the wood the way you'd see on a tree. Like everything else, the counter is pretty dirty, so I wet a paper towel under the faucet and wipe it off as best I can. There has to be a sponge someplace, probably under all those dishes.

The tomatoes are still a little hard, not quite ripe, but Miriam tells me not to worry, in an omelet it won't be noticed. I slip into the easy rhythm of cutting vegetables. I like it here. I'd clean it up a little, of course. The light streaming through the window is pretty and so are the views—you look right out onto the orchard, trees and more trees—but the furniture is full of holes and should be replaced, and the walls, which are stained with a brown-gray mildew, could use some pictures and a coat of paint. Yellow maybe, or a pale, soothing green. Now that I've been staying in so many different places I've developed opinions about decoration. A caterpillar makes its way along the windowsill.

"Today's going to be really hot," Miriam sighs.

It's easy to imagine myself living here; I can picture the days, each one just the same, rolling out ahead of me like a big green valley. In the mornings I'll make myself get up at sunrise—earlier maybe. Before you know it, I'll be the kind of person who wakes up automatically just when the sun is starting to light the sky, lingering in bed for only a few minutes, listening to the birds sweep the air with song. I'll pick apples until my arms ache with the weight of them; I'll be the fastest apple picker the farm has ever seen. And everyone will look around at how clean and pretty everything is and say, *How in the world did we ever run this place properly before Adie came along?*

Miriam rummages around in the little pantry by the side of the kitchen, looking for some spices, and stumbles over a milk crate. "God damn it," she says, rubbing her foot. "This place is going to make me fucking insane."

Of course, I'll still have to go to school—that's the law. I'm sure there has to be a school near here somewhere. Maybe kids in Oregon are different, smarter than California kids, who only care about the football team's latest scores, and who's going to be voted Most Popular or Best Hair at the end of the year. I'll probably have all kinds of new friends. Miriam's going to be eighteen in just a few months; we could find out how to make her my *legal guardian*. I saw that in an after-school special once, when the parents died.

Miriam comes over to see how I'm doing. "That's great," she says, wiping a dead fly from the windowsill. "It's such a pain, making food for so many people." She picks up a tomato slice and pops it in her mouth. Then she looks at me. "Do you remember the name of the place you guys were in?"

"What place?"

"The motel you were at with Mom." She clears her throat. "The last one."

"It was a Best Western. Someplace called Lockeford." I think about the motel, with its squeaky overhead fan and flowered comforter, and the machine down the hall where you can get a bag of ice for fifty cents. I left the good-bye note for my mother on the dresser, next to her purse. It seems as if that was a long time ago: days, months maybe. I squeeze my eyes shut, trying to erase the image of the motel room from my mind, but it just sticks there, like a picture you've looked at a million times in a photo album.

Miriam empties a plastic bag of cucumbers into a bowl. "We'll give them a call after breakfast," she says, rinsing the cucumbers in the sink. "We can leave a message if Mom's not there."

"No!" I can feel something inside me slipping. I'm going to live here on the farm with my sister, in a little metal shed decorated with candles and tapestries. I will pick more apples than anyone ever has before. "I don't want to call her. I don't want her to know where I am."

"Adie, you've been gone for almost two *days*." Miriam's voice is polished and hard. "She must be totally freaking out."

The room dips and sways—I feel dizzy again, the way I did at the health food store. "I want to stay here, with you," I say, grabbing a wooden chair for support, thinking that if I can just get the floor to stop moving in circles everything will be okay.

My sister puts one of the beaded braids in her mouth and chews it, the way a little girl might, and shakes her head. "Adie, you have to go back."

"*You* didn't." I can feel my throat tightening, closing up. "You ran away and left me all alone." Outside, I can hear the sounds of people laughing, along with someone playing Queen: *We will, we will rock you.*

Miriam doesn't say anything. She turns back to the pile of cucumbers—slicing off the peels methodically, taking off each piece in one long careful swoop, as if her life depended on it. It's not fair; Miriam got to run away and come here, and I had to run away with my mother. I think about all the motels we stayed in—their tiny rooms all in a row, each one just the same. The little soaps and shampoos, which after a while do not seem so special at all. My mother, lying in a state of quiet worry in the bed next to me, thinking about where we will escape to next.

"*You* got to leave." I watch as Miriam puts the peels in an old coffee can marked COMPOST. "You didn't even give me a phone number."

She doesn't look up.

I grab the paring knife out of her hand. "You knew how crazy everything was getting, but you didn't care—you left me behind." She still won't look at me, just stares at her hands, as if she doesn't know where the knife went.

All of a sudden I understand—and it's like a sharp, hot wave coursing through my body. "You left me behind so you *could* run away."

Miriam leans against the counter, her body bent as if with an enormous weight. For the first time, I notice that her eyes, usually so alive, are puffy, deep red and swollen with tiredness and worry. She takes my hands in hers, and I can feel them shaking, in the same way that our mother's hands shake when she is upset.

"Adie, you can't stay here." Her face is tight with tears. "You're a *child*."

I look at the mermaid pipe with its secret smile, the pile of empty beer cans, not yet crushed for recycling. "But Janice's little sister lives here." Last night I saw her, curled up on a pile of woolen blankets on the floor, playing with the toy animals from a homemade Noah's ark. She's only about six, skinny but strong, her face freckled and peeling from a sunburn. When I crouched down next to her she ran away, leaving me alone to pair up the rough wooden elephants and tigers and giraffes, two by two.

"That's Janice's *daughter*," my sister says. "She had her when she was fourteen." Miriam purses her lips and shakes her head hard, as if trying to get the thought to fall out.

My sister sits down at the table and buries her face in her hands. The room doesn't seem so big anymore. On the radio, the weatherman recites his forecast: a hot day, until evening, when everything will explode into storm.

Miriam looks at the pile of dishes, the dried tomato sauce and dead bugs, and sighs. "I'm not even sure *I* can stay here."

"Then you have to come back with me."

She starts crying again, this time steady and hard, like a child who's been sent to her room. And as I run my hands through her hair, undoing the beads and the careful braids, I realize that all of the teenagers I've met on the apple farm are just kids, pretending to be grown-ups. They cook their own meals and decide when to go to bed, but they're not really adults. They're just playing house. What Miriam and her friends have here is a pretend world—a prettier, sweeter version of the pretend world my mother has chosen to live in. Hers is all fear; theirs is all comfort. But they're both fake. For some reason, I think about the fishpond and the fake waterfall at the Hausers'. If it's fake, but the fish are happy, does it matter?

I smooth out Miriam's hair, brushing it into a shining, wavy sea of black. "A lot's happened since you left," I say, lining up the beads on the table.

There, in the kitchen, I tell her everything. And this time, she doesn't try to stop me. We forget about making breakfast. The sun beams through the open window, illuminating the little specks of dust into pieces of light.

When you haven't talked to someone for a long time—really talked—you forget who they are. Just a little bit. But it is enough to make talking to them again feel like something new and different, and yet familiar at the same time.

I think that, for a little while, Miriam might have forgotten who I was. But now she is remembering.

38

I can't seem to dial the phone number correctly. I mess it up twice. My finger keeps choosing the wrong number. It's as if even my hand knows that this is the hardest phone call I will ever make.

Before making the call, Miriam and I cleaned up the kitchen. It was not Miriam's turn. But we wanted to be able to look around and see clear surfaces, the nice smooth tile of the counter. And we both needed something to do, something easy and obvious. We wiped down all the countertops and washed the dishes, and then Miriam went through the refrigerator and threw away the rotten food while I swept the floor. Now you can see what a nice kitchen it would be if someone just took proper care of it.

The phone rings about ten times and I wonder if I should just hang up. Maybe it is a sign that I'm not supposed to call. But Miriam is watching me, and her look, steady and serious, says, *don't hang up.*

When the clerk at the motel finally answers I have to sit down.

"Hello, Best Western," he says, his voice crisp and official. But when I give him my name his tone shifts. "Oh, my God," he says, sounding almost shrill. "Your mother's been *so* worried about you." I can hear him talking to someone else. *"It's that girl."*

I wonder what my mother has said to the motel staff, if she's told everyone there to be on the lookout for me. "I have a number where she can call me."

"No. Let me get her right now." He puts the phone down, and then I hear him pick it up again. "Don't you dare hang up."

I turn to my sister. "She's there *now*." Miriam's eyes open wide, wider than I've ever seen them, and she looks like she might throw up. On the other end of the line I can hear footsteps and shuffling, the murmur of muffled voices.

I'm scared. My mother will be furious with me, and her anger is still a thing I'm not sure how to handle.

I take a deep breath. I have to remember, she is all the way over there and I am here. I can hang up. Even if she traces the call, Miriam and I will have time to get in a car, drive away. By the time my mother gets here we can be far away—Seattle maybe. I have always wanted to see the Space Needle. Or Canada. But even as I think this, I know there's nowhere else for us to go. We can't just pack up our bags like it's no big deal, drive down the highway and enjoy the scenery.

Only a minute or so passes, but it feels like forever. And then my mother is on the line.

"Adie?" Her voice is careful, cautious, like saying my name aloud might be a jinx. I know that feeling, when you want something to be true but are afraid to hope.

"Yeah, it's me."

I've forgotten what to say, even though Miriam and I have rehearsed it.

"Where are you?"

Hearing her voice makes it harder to speak. She sounds relieved, but scared too, knowing I could just hang up. That is exactly what I want to do. I don't feel brave at all. And it probably won't work. I look over at Miriam. She nods, takes my hand in hers and squeezes it tight.

Have you ever stood at the edge of a high diving board, knees shaking, scared to jump off? The world seems enormous. All you want to do is climb back down the ladder, to the safety of the ground.

But then you realize that the water is just waiting to catch you.

In the moment between leaving the board and hitting the water is a place of pure light. You don't weigh anything. Your body is nothing. And you are flying.

"I'm in Oregon," I say slowly. "With Miriam." I tell her that I took the bus here, that it cost twenty-five dollars. I measure the words out carefully: my sister and I are both perfectly safe; nothing at all has happened to us. My mother has nothing to worry about. Of course, I don't say anything about the hitch-hiking, or the guy in the car, or how I spent the night in the bus terminal with nothing to eat. These are not things she needs to know; they are not things she will ever need to know.

I look out the window, which is smeared with dust. Outside, a squirrel plays in the large oak tree, running up the trunk, fast as anything, then back down.

"Mom?" I brace myself against the kitchen counter. "Those guys were here." My voice is scratchy and hoarse.

Nothing. Silence. Did she hear me?

Miriam walks over to the sink, pours me a glass of water, but I wave it away. I am afraid to stop talking; I might never speak again. "The guys in the white car," I continue. "They followed me here."

A sharp intake of breath. "They *followed* you?"

"I don't know how they did it, how they knew where I was going." My voice is someone else's. I am listening to a record-ing.

My mother's questions, fast and broken, run over me. I don't hear them all. Miriam keeps her eyes right on me. I think she's forgotten how to blink. But she's squeezing my hand so tight I have to pull away.

"It was insane. They were here. But someone called the po-lice, and they came and arrested them." I try to remember what happens on TV cop shows. "I heard them say that they were going to jail for a long, long time."

Miriam takes the phone from my hands before I can say any-thing else. "Mom? It's me." Her voice is breaking; it's the voice of a little girl. "I miss you too."

She starts talking and crying all at once. I sink down on the cushions near the stone fireplace. I am shivering, even though outside, the thermometer shaped like a flower reads 72 degrees. One of the cats brushes against my body and starts kneading my leg, his green eyes big with trust. I scoop him up and tuck him under my shirt, his warm body buzzing against mine with a gentle purr. I feel like his tight warmth is the only thing keeping my heart beating.

From across the room I hear Miriam say, "It was awful. I've never been so scared in my life." If I sit here on the floor long enough, let the time pass, it will all be over. The only thing I have to do is keep my breath steady, pet the cat with slow, even strokes. "But we're all safe now," Miriam continues, her voice calm now, tempered. "Those guys are gone for good."

I curl my body into the cushions and close my eyes, which feel heavy, wooden. I can hear Miriam telling my mother about the weather in Ashland, how it rains all the time and can get very cold, but it's still beautiful. How there are fields everywhere, and cows, black and white, and how every once in a while you see someone riding a horse to the store, as if it's a normal thing to do, like driving a car. "Some of the people here even have llamas," I hear her say. "For the wool." And then Miriam does something we hadn't talked about. She gives our mother directions to the farm.

I want to get up, stop her, but it's already too late. Miriam's given her the phone number and the address, and is telling her about the sharp left turn that's easy to miss, and how you have to be careful to go down Lake View Road, not Lake View Avenue. And when you get here, make sure to close the front gate tight behind you, or the goats will get out, and let me tell you, it's no fun trying to catch them, goats are fast. She chatters on, as if nothing unusual is happening at all, as if she is just inviting our mother to a party.

My head feels dull and heavy, weighted with the tears I've held back. Miriam hangs up the phone and sinks down on the floor, curling up next to me. "It's okay," she says, holding me tight, her body smelling of a salty-sweet mix of incense and sweat. "Really, it's okay. We're together now."

I look at her. "You won't leave me again?"

"I won't leave you."

"Will Mom believe us?"

"What do you mean?"

"About the men in the white car." I burrow into the cushions. "Will she believe that they're really gone?"

Miriam sighs. "I don't know. She probably won't think they're gone forever. But for now, everything's going to be all right. And we'll have each other. That's the important thing." My body relaxes and lets go.

Later, Miriam packs her things. It all fits in just a couple of bags. "I guess I don't have as much stuff as I thought," she says, carefully wrapping the egg-shaped candle in tissue paper. She folds up the purple tapestry blanket and tucks it in with her clothes.

The mattress looks funny without Miriam's sleeping bag and blankets. "Who's going to move in after you?" A fly buzzes around the shed in wide circles, looking for a place to land.

"I don't know." She looks around the tiny space and sighs. "I really thought I could live here." Then she smiles. "I'm glad I got rid of all those braids," she says, running the MIRIAM brush over her hair. "I feel so much lighter."

I think about all the times my mother and I have packed up, how many times we've shoved our things into suitcases and thrown them in the car. And how strange it is that people spend their lives in big houses, with so much furniture, and clothes and toys, when really you can fit everything you need to live into just a few bags.

When Miriam's done she shuts the door to the shed tight, to keep the bugs from getting in. The only thing she's left is the little mirror, taped to the side of the wall.

The rest of the day passes slowly. Miriam shows me around the farm. I can't believe how big the orchard is. Rows and rows of apple trees stretch off into the distance, hundreds of them. It could make you dizzy, to think about how many apples are out there.

Miriam picks a few of the ripe ones and puts them in a paper bag. "Mom will want some of these," she says. It's true; our mother loves apples. She always says that they're the best fruit, even though they're the most ordinary.

My sister takes me through the barn, where everything smells of hay and manure: a soft smell, warm and dusty. There are a couple of horses that people ride, and some goats. The horses are smaller than they look from far away. One of them nuzzles my hand, looking for food, his lips surprisingly soft and gentle.

A baby goat stumbles over to us, bleating. "You can pick him up if you want," Miriam says. I scoop him up, and he just sits there in my arms, like a puppy. "What are the goats for?" I ask, thinking about milk.

Miriam laughs. "Nothing. They just hang out."

We sit down on a bench outside the barn. Everything's quiet. There's an old metal sign propped up against one of the walls, hot and shining in the sun, with the words JOHNSON'S FEEDS across the top. The paint has chipped, and the sign is rusty, but you can still make out a faint picture of a horse, running in the grass. I trace the letters carefully, trying not to burn my fingers.

Miriam scoots closer to me. "I still can't believe how grown up you look," she says, sounding almost shy. "You're so much bigger."

"I am?" I'm not sure what she's talking about. My clothes still seem to fit the same. I don't feel any different.

"Yeah," she says. "Look at you."

I stare at my reflection in the metal sign. She's right. I have grown. Somehow, I hadn't noticed.

My mother's car appears over the crest of the hill. I clutch Miriam's hand. She squeezes my fingers tight, and we watch the car make its slow way down the road, a cloud of dust shadowing it like a ghost.

LIFE IN MINIATURE

Linda Schlossberg

About This Guide

The suggested questions are included to enhance
your group's reading of Linda Schlossberg's
Life in Miniature.

DISCUSSION QUESTIONS

1. Adie, her sister Miriam, and her mother all take turns "running away" at various points in the story. What do they hope to accomplish by running away? How are these moments of running away similar? How are they different?

2. The story is told from Adie's point of view. How might the story be different if it was told from her mother's point of view? Or Miriam's?

3. How does the title *Life in Miniature* reflect the themes and plot of the novel?

4. What does Adie get from her various relationships with the adults in the story? What do they see and understand about her mother that Adie doesn't? Conversely, what does Adie understand about her mother that other people don't?

5. What is Adie's relationship with her sister Miriam like? How does it change and develop as the story progresses?

6. In the first half of the novel, Adie lives in a series of different places with her mother and sister. In the second half, she and her mother hide away in motel rooms. How does she feel about these different living spaces? What is the significance of all this moving?

7. At various points in the story, Adie briefly imagines what it would be like to live with other adults in the novel, for instance, moving in with her friend Lainey's family; being adopted by her teacher, Mrs. Ramirez; or living permanently at the Motel del Mar with Dennis. Why are these fantasies appealing to her? What might these different situations represent to her?

8. In many ways this novel is about the difference between truth and fiction, reality and illusion. But are these concepts always strictly oppositional? In what sense can we say that people's lies, fantasies, delusions, and stories are "true" for them?

9. The mother's individual fears and paranoia about drug use are brought on in part by the larger cultural conversations about drug use in the United States in the 1980s, as reflected in policies at Adie's school, the news media, and popular culture. How does the mother's delusion feed off these broader concerns? What are some issues today that worry parents, and how do today's media and culture at large contribute to these worries?